Sanctum:

Forests of Avalon

C.S. Kading
Tony Fuentes

SandDancer Publications

ISBN (ebook) : 979-8-9852825-0-4
ISBN (paperback) : 979-8-9852825-1-1
ISBN (hardcover) : 979-8-9852825-2-8

To the Spouses, Whose tireless hours of support and love (as well as confusion from being asked a ton of non sequitur questions about what was being written at the time – sorry) allowed this second endeavor to be made possible.

Contents

Foreward

Storytellers know how to find each other.

I don't particularly care if you don't believe me; it's true. Whether the story takes its form prefaced by the spoken words "So no shit, there I was..." or flows from a pen or keyboard after the words "Once upon a time..." we know. People who know the way to conjure an ephemeral world, conceive fully-realized people who never existed, and set them forth to accomplish deeds that are impossible to us but life-and-death to their creations can sense their own. The words that become their tells flow out of them unbidden, even in everyday speech, or crop up in the most innocuous, mundane email, chat message, or social media post.

I first knew that C.S Kading and Tony Fuentes were storytellers without them speaking or writing a thing.

For Tony, it was at a LARP, some twenty years ago. The character he played was cool, collected, sitting upright like an invisible string had him by the back of the neck. Every hand gesture had deliberate grace, and each expression of emotion had its own placidity. "Tetsuo Mawman," he introduced himself. I sat in awe of him, even as I tried to get my bearings with this new hobby. When the game was over, that carefully crafted persona vanished into nothing, and I was left with a cheerful, hilarious dude who was just as geeky as I was, and I could hardly believe the change that literally happened right in front of me. In the years that followed, I would hear many stories from him as I sat with him at a Denny's, or in his living room, or at a hotel for a convention, or at a sunny restaurant aboard the Queen Mary after years of falling out of touch.

For Charmain, it was far more recent, but no less unforgettable. Again, it was at a LARP, and the character she played had an effortless style to her, a lightness of being anchored by (and actively in spite of) centuries of pain. Danielle Ponciliet was an absolute confection to her dearest friends, but even then, she didn't suffer foolishness from them. With my character becoming friends with hers, we had two women who could delight in the petty, cut each other to the quick (but almost never out of malice), and stand back-to-back against any shared threats. At the core, Charmain had that same down-to-earth mindset, but more often than not, we like to get to the point and take far less thrill in torrid gossip, but we'd both be honored to have the other in our corner when the chips are down. We talk mostly in chat messages, but when we did so in character, the exchange was, again, effortless; simply two individuals other than ourselves taking part in totally natural speech for them. Nothing about their conversations felt stilted or stuttered as the real people who created them had to remember the traits of a character so distinct from ourselves, and when we were in person, the banter came just as easily.

No one who knows either of them, separately or together, should be surprised that these two fall together so naturally to create the stories that are in this book and the first volume of this series (and hopefully many more to come). They slip easily between the realm of the real and the characters they create without blurring the lines between either space, and they treat the world that has inspired them so, created by Todd Filek, with grace and care. They are enthusiastic but considerate, breathing life into a place that we readers may not have ever known existed otherwise. Just re-reading the first chapter of the first book, the heat of the desert kills the damp Bay Area chill of my office, if only for a moment.

And that's how I know I'm in the presence of storytellers.

~Renee Ritchie

Notes

Map of Avalon

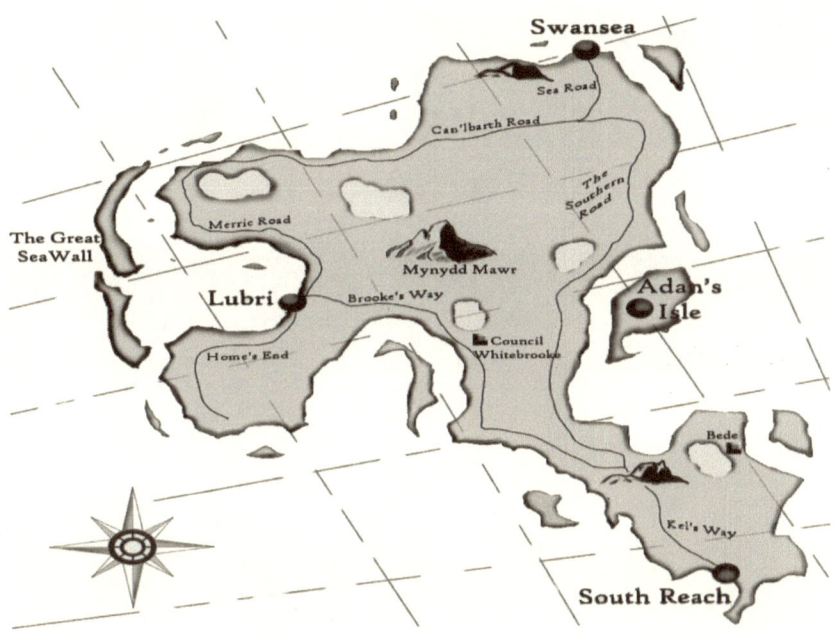

Introduction

Dawn was approaching on the horizon.

The sky changed from inky blackness to deep violet and then a deeper hue of blue. Soon the blue became lighter and lighter as the sun broke the line with a brilliant light. What clouds there were found themselves pushed back under the weight of the sun's light. Where there was darkness, there was light, and the sun slowly illuminated the forest below. Within the tree line stood a figure in dark brown robes. The fabric's color blended into the trees all around them, making them almost invisible.

The figure took a few steps forward into the patch of sunlight. Their gnarled toenails dug into the soil as they slowly stretched their gangly form skyward. Brown robes billowed softly in the breeze as the clouds drifted overhead. Like the figure, the massive oak trees had their branches extended skyward, leaves drinking in the precious sunlight. With the breaking of the sun in the clouds, the robed figure felt life stir within the forest as creatures began their waking routine. Pulling back their hood, the elf's greasy locks of dirty blonde hair fell onto their shoulders. They let their face bask in the sun for a few moments until a cloud bank drifted forward and obscured the sun's view. In the brief morning light, one could see an intricate tattoo interwoven along their features – but dirt and muck on their face obscured most of it.

"Today is the start of a new day," they said to no one.

Despite the brilliant green all around them, they focused on the gray clouds overhead as they dimmed the majesty of nature.

"Your sunlight is nice, good Lord, but I am more inclined toward the gray. Shades of gray, much like the rest of the world," they said with a bit of amusement.

Cries, bellows, and chirps that played their own song of life soon followed the brief appearance of the sun. Somewhere in that cacophony of nature, the elf swayed in time as if it were a song playing on the wind. Walking down the slope and deeper into the woods, the elf spread their arms outward while they swayed as if dancing with an unseen partner. Moving in tune with the song of nature all around them, the figure muttered to themselves as they ran their hands across the trunks of the trees.

"Compliments and pleasantries to see who was listening, you know?"

Though surrounded by life, the elf was alone here. Nothing would dare to approach them, and they would have no company on this errand.

The robed figure paused in step and held their breath to listen for... something. Closing their eyes, they slowly turned themselves around, trying to locate an item by sound alone. They walked forward as they filtered out everything else around. Inhaling deeply, the elf smelled the air. A smile crossed their face.

"There you are!"

Sharpened senses led them to the edge of the tree line that dropped off into a deep ravine. Had they taken another step, they would have gone right over. Staring down, they saw a river of fresh water making its way westward.

"Tried to hide now, eh? The nose always knows, hmm?" they said playfully to the river down below.

With an eerily graceful jump, they made their way down the hazardous slope of stone, roots, and mud. Anyone else without proper climbing gear would have surely lost their footing. At the very least, they would have tumbled to the bottom of the ravine and earned a broken limb. Had anyone been watching, they would have seen how the elf's bare feet landed on just the right stone or that a thick errant root had extended far enough for them to reach their next purchase. Such a dexterous display would have won both the applause and jealousy of even the most veteran of acrobats and thieves.

But there were no such eyes to watch this morning.

When they finally reached the bottom, their body gave a shiver as their bare feet touched the cold, wet stone ground.

"Refreshing... are you not?" the elf said to the river with a smile.

Dropping to their knees, they leaned forward and dunked their head into the water. Whipping their head back with a laugh, they let the chill of the water wake up their skin and scalp. With a cleaner face, the tattoos were more pronounced – the imagery of branches of a noble tree that spread from between their brows and across their forehead. They contemplated bathing here, as they could not recall the last time they truly had properly cleansed. Then they started giggling at the thought of a farmer drinking their bathwater.

"No, no – fun later, work now. We have a sacred duty to perform," they murmured to no one.

The elf turned right and found what they were looking for. Up ahead and hidden from above was a shallow cavern. Standing, they walked over and made their way inside. Within this hidden niche, they could see the water flowing out from the rocky wall, pooling itself in the center of the cavern before pushing itself outward to form the smallest of streams that would eventually become a river. This was one of many sources of fresh water on the island.

"Going to be quick about this," they said as they pulled out a small leather pouch. Opening it, they revealed a smaller cloth pouch within. The aroma that drifted off of the contents of the pouch was spicy and foreign.

"Time to give you some help, my little friend," the figure whispered. They gazed around at the rich, black earth all around them. Leaning down, they pulled a small stone aside and found what they were looking for. Pink and black night crawlers wiggled in a writhing mass. They had been quietly feeding on a mass of dead roots. Grasping the worms, roots, and all, they quickly added it to the leather bag.

Closing their eyes, they held the pouch in one hand and gestured over it with another. The shadows in the cavern darkened and their voice echoed as they spoke in an ancient tongue. Eldritch power soon emanated from them and swirled around the pouch. Opening their eyes, they walked across the surface of the pool as if it was solid earth, and walked towards the stone wall where the water flowed out. They paused and held the leather bag aloft with two fingers. With their other hand, they stuck out a sharp nail and quickly made several small punctures in the leather's skin. Tiny droplets of blackish blood seeped from the small pouch as it writhed. Then, just as quickly, they shoved the small leather object into the mouth of the wall and withdrew their hand.

For a moment, nothing seemed to have happened, and the elf frowned. "No, there were enough holes. This is easier than making..." they stopped mid-sentence as they noticed a single blackish line of ink within the clear water. Their eyes widened. They smiled. When the single line hit the pool below, it spread outward. Stepping back to the outside of the water, the elf watched as the black ink filled the pool and then bled out into the river.

"See, now that was a simple chore. Simple... anyone could have done it. Well... no, not anyone. Just me," they said as they looked down at the ground. "Did you hear that, my Lord? Me. No one else. Just me."

Turning away, the figure walked out of the shallow cavern and scaled up the side of the ravine. This time, there was no question about it as they commanded the roots and stones to aid their ascent.

When they reached the top, it surprised them to find a creature standing there. The elf was tall, but this creature was taller. The white monarch stag's rack was draped with fur, vines, and green moss. It stood tall and dangerous.

The elf smiled and slowly reached into their robes. "I have

something for you, my friend." Producing a large red apple, they rubbed it against their robes to give it a bit more sheen. "Freshly picked from yesterday." Holding the apple toward the stag, the elf slowly made their way forward. The massive creature bowed its head and took the apple from the elf's hand.

"Delicious no?"

The elf's other hand shot forward and tore into the beast's throat. It attempted to buck back, but the elf dug their hand further into the flesh of the beast. Red blood sprayed them both. With an unsettling crack, the beast's amber eyes went wide, and it collapsed to the forest floor.

"Well... that was rude," and they walked away, but paused in step. "No... that will not do."

The robed elf turned back and placed a foot on the shoulder of the beast. A shadow passed across the black eyes of the once majestic monarch. With bare hands and unnatural strength, the elf twisted, pulled, and removed the head from the body of the fallen creature.

A small flock of ravens took to wing, disturbed by the actions.

The figure looked toward the sky, "Tsk Tsk- no witnesses," they murmured and then looked back at the head.

"Time to go home and clean up. We will have a visitor soon."

Chapter 1

In the wastelands of the Seteshi desert, there were only three things that could be counted on:

The Radiant Lord's "Mercy" was never merciful.

The desert was no friend to the weak.

Sand would always find a way into your nethers.

Isolde stretched as sweat ran down her back. She shifted, uncomfortable with grit in creases that were never designed to be gritty. She braced to lift the next basket of sun-fired bricks onto the cart.

"Ready, Jamal!" she called out.

The driver steadied the beast at the front of the cart, clucking and cooing soothing tones. He waved his right hand.

She stooped and wrapped her arms around the basket, legs tensing as she shifted her weight once more to get underneath the balance point. Lifting with her legs she exhaled deeply and hefted the contents into the back of the cart. The boxboard bounced under the sudden load. The camel bellowed and grunted. Jamal held it in place.

"Ah! Thank you, Sister!" Menebhi smiled broadly and opened his arms wide to pull the Avalonian Knight into an embrace. He smelled of garlic, onions, and spices.

"Oof!" Isolde exclaimed, and forced an uncomfortable smile. She nodded and patted the burly merchant on the back. "Happy to help," she commented.

"I don't know what the Temple will do when you leave," the merchant replied as he released her and stepped back. "Your help has been immeasurable." He tapped the fingers of his right hand over his heart and inclined his head.

Isolde held her right hand over her heart and inclined her

head in reply. "I suppose we will just have to make certain that the loading crane is repaired before that happens," she grinned.

"Caravan!" a young girl's voice called out from the Temple walls. "Caravan!"

Isolde looked up at the walls of the Temple and shaded her eyes from the setting sun. Her heartbeat fast for a moment. Perhaps …

She hastened to the end of the loading ramp toward the animals' watering trough. Dipping her hands into the water, she scrubbed them as best as she could. Pulling out a clean-ish cloth from her waistband, she soaked it and quickly wiped her face free of the dirt and grime.

A merchant caravan of half a dozen camels and carts made its way through the tall gates of the Temple of Tarf-qua. The Knight took a place on the step to look out at the approaching group, searching for a familiar figure – someone easily a head or taller than any of the others. Less than a handful of travelers crossed the threshold of the temple. He wasn't among them. She released a hopeful breath and looked down, and nodded to herself.

Suddenly she felt a hand on her shoulder, turning her around, and an arm came up behind her legs, sweeping her off of her feet. She was raised up from the ground and twirled for a moment before being set back down, then bent backward as someone leaned over her. Golden brown eyes, the color of clover honey, smiled into hers.

"You are a sight that these eyes will never tire of seeing," Safar smiled down at her.

Isolde shook her head and chuckled as the Reysis held her in his arms. Travelers and members of the faith glanced up at the exchange and then went about their business, unconcerned.

"You only say that because you see me maybe twice a month," she countered.

"Ah … Island … you wound me! You know that is not true. When will you marry me?" The handsome Sun Guide smiled.

2

"And become one of your caravan wives?" she asked and forced herself into a standing position.

"Indeed!" Safar beamed broadly. "It would be a great honor!"

"For which one of us?" Isolde countered.

"Both, of course!" Safar smiled winningly at her.

"Mmm." Isolde pursed her lips. "And what will you do, Reysis, when my time in Tarf-qua is done, and I am free to explore the world once more?"

The man pondered her question. "You make an excellent point ..." he mused and scratched at his dark beard.

She moved to lean against the edge of a wall and crossed her arms over her chest as she watched him. "I suppose I could always come with you ..." she said with a slightly bemused look. "Your caravan would have my arm on every venture, and you could have me in your tent. Every ... Day ..." She smiled at him.

Safar's eyes widened as he realized the weight of her words in his world. He took a step back and held up his hands. "Now, now, Island ..."

"I am certain that ... what was her name ... that potter in Thyta ..."

"Tasneem," Safar said.

"Exactly!" Isolde smiled broadly. "I'm sure Tasneem would understand."

Safar pursed his lips and inclined his head. "I yield the field, Ser Knight." He held his hands up in surrender. "You are such a cruel woman! To strike at the very heart that beats faster for you so," he said with feigned hurt but with mirth in his eyes.

"Mmmm," Isolde nodded and kicked off of the wall. Walking over to Safar, she wrapped her arms around him tightly. "It IS good to see you, my friend."

Safar chuckled and returned her embrace, then inhaled deeply. "Augh! You smell like Menebhi!" Making a face, he broke away from her.

Isolde stopped and sniffed at herself and frowned. "I do. It is not a pleasant thing."

"You should be glad that His Radiance is not with me," Safar

3

tapped the side of his nose. "Sound sense of smell."

The smile faded from Isolde's eyes for a moment. "How is he, Safar?" she asked.

Safar's eyes softened. He reached out to place his arm around her shoulders. "Ahhhh, Island … you know how he is … he is … himself," He hugged her gently and then took her arm into his as he led her towards the main hall.

"Is he well? Can you tell me that at least?" she prodded as they walked toward the hallowed halls of the Temple. The sunset meal was just being prepared.

Safar shrugged noncommittally. "He is a busy man, Father Tulok," he said, looking over at Isolde. "More so since arriving in the capital," he added. "His Order … they have many questions about …" He gestured southward but said nothing.

Isolde nodded and clasped her hand firmly around the man at her side in a display of familiar camaraderie. Many of the villagers of Tarf-qua wondered at the relationship between the Wanderer and the Reysis. When he was present in town, the two were all but inseparable. They walked together, laughed together, took meals, drank, and told stories to one another late into the night and early morning. Some whispered that the Reysis had taken the Island woman as one of his many wives, but others disregarded such things as mere gossip from members of the village, seeking to add flavor to their otherwise humdrum lives.

"But you HAVE seen him?" she pressed.

Safar nodded, "Yes. I have laid eyes on our wayward friend, and been able to exchange a … *few* … words with him here and there." The Reysis stopped and turned to face her, taking her hands into his own. They were of equal stature, unusual for a woman; but Isolde was anything but typical. His honey-brown eyes searched the emerald green windows of her foreign soul for a moment. "You are truly concerned for him in this?" he asked her quietly.

The knight pursed her lips and nodded. "I am. I should have heard from him by now … or …" she frowned a little and blinked and looked askance, " ... or maybe I misjudged ..."

Safar continued to search Isolde's face. He dropped her left hand and tucked his fingers under her chin to lift her face and eyes back to him. "Isolde duAvalonne ..." he began, using her proper name instead of the nickname he always used, "If I thought that for one moment, you and I would have a very different conversation," He smiled gently at her, the former pretenses for public show fallen by the wayside.

Isolde nodded and leaned forward to place her forehead on his. "Thank you, Safar," she breathed.

Two women walked past the pair as they were caught up in their clandestine exchange. They covered their mouths and leaned into one another, whispering and giggling.

Isolde held Safar's gaze as the women walked by. "Rafika and Namira?" she asked him, neither moving nor looking at the women.

Safar pursed his lips and nodded. "Mmhmm,"

"Their clucking is going to have us espoused in the village eye ..."

Safar beamed brightly, his smile widened, and he pulled back, eyes gleaming.

"Is that a yes?"

~~~

Tulok took a deep, steadying breath and relaxed his hands. Then he carefully entwined his fingers together and rested his hands on the carved wooden table before him. His deep red eyes looked up at the figure standing before him. He began again.

"With respect Father, you have asked me that question five times now," the orc stated in a calm and even tone.

"And with respect, I will ask it once more," Father Kalal answered. Kalal was an older human, tall and lean, whose body bore the signs of one accustomed to fasting to demonstrate his commitment to the Tenets of The Radiant Lord. He stared back at Tulok with bright eyes surrounded by dark circles. His robes were pristine and without so much as a single stain from wear and tear.

Tulok sighed once more. "Then I shall answer the same for the sixth time, and the time after that, and again the time that follows." His eyes watched the gaunt figure of the man who was his superior. "We took nothing from the Temple of Silence, and the maps that led us there were taken by the Vidria merchant … Arman … and his accomplice, Nebiyre. Both assumed dead from the collapse of the Temple proper, the maps assumed lost in that same cave in."

"And neither yourself nor … the woman who was with you …?"

"Ser Isolde duAvalonne," Tulok inserted her name.

"Yes, yes …" Kalal waved the name off.

Tulok scowled at the display of disrespect.

"The foreigner. The Avalonian," Kalal continued. "Neither of you knows the exact location of the Ruins?"

Tulok shook his head. "No. I could guess, Father, based on how long it took myself and Brother Bengt to reach the location from Kas-qua, but the *precise* location?" He shook his head once more. "No."

"And Brother Bengt came to meet his end …?" Kalal led the question without finishing.

Tulok remembered exactly how Bengt Kalb met his end. On his knees, having asked for forgiveness and absolution for his involvement in the presumed death of the Knight Wanderer Isolde duAvalonne. Tulok had stepped away from his brother-in-arms to regain his composure at the unexpected confession. While caught up in wrestling with his own emotions, Arman and Nebiyre's people had ambushed their camp and murdered Bengt.

"At the hands of Nebiyre," Tulok replied calmly. "She cut his throat and gave his life to the sands."

"And you could not stop them?" Kalal asked.

Tulok closed his eyes and took another calming breath. This line of questioning was one he had answered multiple times since his arrival in Ophir. He had hoped that the Temple would be more interested in researching the existence of the Lost Temple of Silence and what ties Arman and Nebiyre might have had to it. Instead, they seemed more focused on who was still alive that knew about its existence.

"I may be an Orc, Father Kalal, but I am only one orc, and there were many of them. With barbed and poisoned nets, coupled with magic ..."

"So, you have said."

Tulok opened his eyes and looked directly at the gaunt priest across the table from him. "And so, I shall say again," he replied firmly.

Kalal met Tulok's gaze, unfazed. "And this woman ..."

Tulok stared at Kalal but did not reply.

"This ... *Avalonian* Knight," Kalal continued.

Tulok inclined his head ever so slightly.

"She was seeking the Temple of Silence for what reason?"

Once more, Tulok took a steadying breath, swallowing down the taste of the Gurkh that welled up within. It whispered angry thoughts to the priest of The Radiant Lord and attempted to coerce him into taking out his frustrations on the gangly, irritating man.

"She was fulfilling a Quest," Tulok answered simply.

Kalal opened his mouth to speak once more, and Tulok held up a hand, requesting that he pause. "With respect, Father Kalal. I gave all of this information to the Temple, and I was ... *assigned* ..." he emphasized the word, "the duty and responsibility of escorting the Wanderer's most Holy Witness in Her sworn duty. Ahsom Ibris signed the order himself," Tulok watched the priest's face as he offered the explanation. "The Champion could not ride on this occasion, and I was to undertake this charge. Does the Devout Champion Ibris deny he issued these orders?"

"He does not," another voice answered the question.

Father Kalal started ever-so-slightly at the interruption and turned to face the newcomer.

Ahsom Ibris was of Elven stock, blonde of hair, and bronze

7

of skin. Where Father Kalal's lean figure was because of his personal practices of devotion, the Devout Champion's frame was lean by the design of the Divine. Ibris moved with an almost unnatural grace. Tulok was uncertain if this was because of his connection to the Divine or because of his Elven heritage. He was clad in armor crafted from hardened leather scales sewn together and dyed the white and gold colors of the Temple. His almond-shaped eyes, carrying the color of the sea, were fixated on Father Kalal as he entered.

Kalal inclined his head in respect. "Most Devout."

"Father," Ibris spoke curtly. He looked over at Tulok. "You're done here, Father."

Tulok's eyebrows raised.

Ibris turned to look at Kalal even as the older man protested. "As are you," he ordered. "You have been questioning this *loyal member* ..." he emphasized, "of our faith for long enough. We have reviewed the testimony multiple times. It does not change. The truth sayers read it as accurate. You. Are. Done."

Father Kalal stared at the Radiant Champion, a cool fire in his dark eyes. He forced a polite smile and inclined his head.

"May His will be done," the priest intoned.

Ibris nodded once and then looked back to Tulok. "With me, Father," he said and turned without waiting for a reply.

Chapter 2

The sound of boots echoed on the polished marble floor as Ser Ahsom Ibris walked down the hall. Heads turned and bowed in both respect and reverence as the armored Champion of the Radiant Lord walked past them. Priests of the Faith carried the holy words of The Everwatchful Eye to all the corners of the world. They stood watch over the night to ensure that His eye was always present, always available to anyone seeking Him. For Devout Champions, their duty was something entirely different. Where a priest may offer words of encouragement and enlightenment, a Champion was the cleansing fire of His Mercy. If the Eye of the Radiant Lord uncovered darkness that warranted martial action, they called the Devout to mete out His Justice. They were swift, and they were uncompromising.

Father Tulok walked at the side of Ser Ibris, his enormous frame in stark contrast to the lithe Elven man. An uneducated assessment might have had their positions juxtaposed with the larger figure cast in the role of a warrior instead of a healer. Those of the faith, however, could watch the movements of the smaller man and recognize the training of a soldier in his every move.

A pair of temple laypeople clad in the white and gold robes of the faith turned and bowed their heads as the pair walked past them. Tulok inclined his head in response. Ibris barely noticed the duo and continued his pace with a determined stride.

"Are you well, Father?" the warrior asked as they walked.

Tulok blinked, not expecting the casual conversation from such a celebrated member of the Temple. "Ser?" he asked.

"Your health. Your wellbeing," Ibris continued. His sea-colored eyes watched the hallway as they walked. He always seemed to search for something. "Kalal has had you sequestered for ... how long now?"

"Three months, Ser," Tulok's deep voice replied.

Ibris pursed his lips and scowled. "Unmitigated ass ..." he swore.

Tulok blinked and balked. "Ser?!"

Ibris' eyes glanced up toward the tall Orc for a moment and then slid back down to continue watching their surroundings. "Kalal, not you, Father," he clarified. He reached up and scratched at his hairless upper lip with the back of his thumb. "Bengt Kalb's family are wealthy patrons of his. I'm sure they are looking for answers other than the ones they have been given."

Tulok nodded quietly, his eyes lowering as he searched the floor. "If I had better answers to give them, I promise you ... I would," he offered quietly.

Ibris looked up at the big priest and watched the language of the Orc's body for a moment. He nodded. "I believe you, Father."

"Thank you."

Ibris nodded curtly. He raised his right hand and gestured at a corridor on the left. "Down this way, please."

"Of course," the priest nodded and followed quietly.

"I apologize for leaving you in that situation for as long as you were," Ibris offered.

Tulok cocked an eyebrow and cast a curious glance down at the Sun God's warrior.

"I was in Agelia discussing security issues with the Order of Valor. I should have left better instructions in my absence. That is a fault on my end. I apologize."

The Order of Valor. Words Tulok had heard many times in his years coming up in Setesh; the fabled Order that stood for all the Realms of Sanctum. They were a standing army owing allegiance to no single faith and no single Realm. Sworn to a unifying principle, the safety and security of Sanctum; they were a neutral arm of both justice and security that any Realm could call upon. They filled their ranks with warriors and laypeople alike, merchants and craft workers, politicians and farmers. Many champions of the faith stood in the ranks of the Order of Valor, serving both the needs of Sanctum and the needs of the Divine. All faiths save one, The Radiant Lord.

The Radiant Lord of the Heavens was a jealous God, and He did not enjoy sharing the attention of his followers. When one took up the mantle of service to the Radiant Lord, one accepted that one's loyalties would forever be dedicated to one cause, one truth. The Devout of the Radiant Lord were called to co-ordinate information and security measures, but to date—no Devout Champion had ever accepted the invitation to join the ranks of the Order.

Tulok nodded and listened. "The needs of the Realm are many, Ser Ibris. I am but one humble priest. There was no guar-antee that I would even return from my assignment," he said as they walked.

"An accurate statement," Ibris replied. "Thank you for your understanding."

The pair approached a large door made of dark wood. Ornate sigils were carved into the dark polished wood; deep and an-cient. Brass hinges, lustrous in their bright polish, glimmered in the light that reflected off of them. Tulok's eyes danced on the sigils and carvings, the Librarian examining each one and interpreting their meaning. His eyebrows rose slightly. He looked down at the Elven champion.

"A Library?" Tulok asked.

Ibris nodded. The hint of a smile tugged at the right cor-ner of his mouth. "Where you SHOULD have been taken three months ago," he raised his right hand and rapped solidly on the wood with his middle knuckle.

There was silence for a few moments, then the sound of metal on metal as something was moved on the other side of the heavy door. One of the carved sections of the door pulled inward and slid to the side. A pair of sparkling blue eyes stared out of the slit in the door.

"Sister Leralyn?" Ibris asked the eyes.

"Maybe," a woman's voice answered, caution and suspicion in her tone. The eyes narrowed.

Ibris rolled his tongue across his teeth in obvious irritation. He continued. "This is Father Tulok of Tarf-qua ..."

The eyes on the other side of the door widened and darted to the orc. "Heaven's mercy, he's HUGE ... well ... no bother ..." her voice answered, tripping over itself in reply. "No, none. All that matters is he was there ... yes ... yes, yes ..." the section of the door slid closed. Once again, there were sounds of metal on metal on the other side of the door.

Ibris glanced over at Tulok. The priest returned the look, both curious and confused. Ibris smiled slightly.

The sound of a bolt being slid free was heard, and the door swung open. A gnomish woman stood in the doorway. She wore tan pants and a white tunic embroidered in gold. Her skin was mottled gray and her white hair stood out on her head like a strange stormy cloud formation. She was taller than Tulok expected a gnomish woman to be, then he realized why: she was on stilts! A pair of tall walking stilts elevated the tiny woman to an almost average human height. Her booted feet fit snugly into platforms with loops on them. Braces of some form appeared to lock around her lower legs. The silts bent backward, like the legs of a gazelle, and looked to be fashioned from a powerful band of metal that created a spring to her step.

"Come, Come ... I can't leave this open forever!" The tiny woman gestured them in.

Idris held his hand out for Tulok to enter. "After you, Father Tulok."

The eyes of the former Librarian of the Temple of Tarf-qua lit up with both curiosity and contained excitement. He nodded in thanks and respect to Ibris and took a step through the door, pushing it gently open.

The other side of the door was a room of enormous proportions. The ceiling stretched almost two stories high. A series of elegantly carved white pillars supported a second floor. Light emanated from sources both natural and magical. Long tables stretched the length of the room. Chairs of various heights and construction sat around the tables. Along each wall, from floor to ceiling, were expertly crafted shelves that contained written materials. Scrolls, books, leather-bound maps, tablets of clay, etched metal, crafted Vidria glass–a wealth of knowledge and information stretched before him.

At the far end of the room, two statues carved of polished dark stone stood, overseeing the whole of the library. The figures, each fashioned in the same style, depicted The Radiant Lord and His heavenly sibling, The Scribe. They stood side by side, visible to all within the confines of the Library.

They depicted the Radiant Lord as a tall and well-built man, his features clean and chiseled, though of an undetermined race. His upper body was bare save for an ornate collar that adorned his throat and shoulders. A narrow beard lined His perfect jawline. He wore a pleated warrior's kirtle, belted at the waist and clasped with a large round buckle, upon which was carved the Everwatchful Eye. His right hand was outstretched in silent benediction. Light from an unknown source framed His head like a disc of solar radiance.

The Scribe stood at their brother's side. Crafted of the same dark, polished stone, their features were similar but softer and without distinct gender. They were depicted in a scaled tunic that ended above the knees. In their hands were a tablet and stylus. At their feet and entwined around their lower legs were two delicate birds, their long necks wrapped around the calves of the Scribe.

Tulok's breath caught in his throat at the sight of the statues; the God of his calling and the God of his people. He felt a firm hand clap his right shoulder solidly. He blinked.

"They can be quite breathtaking when you see them the first time, I agree," Ibris commented at Tulok's side. "Perhaps doubly so for you, Father?"

Tulok nodded, still standing in awe.

"Close your mouth, or get a towel, boy! No drooling in the Library!" the gnomish Librarian scolded.

"I would never ..." Tulok protested, then looked over at the small woman on stilts. She was staring at him with curiosity and amusement. He harrumphed at her.

Leralyn looked over at Ibris. "Oh, I like this one," she said, smiling.

"That's so comforting to know ..." Ibris replied dryly. He glanced up at Tulok, "This is, of course, not the largest library here in Ophir."

"Just the most important," the Librarian quipped quickly. Stepping closer, she looked up at the big priest. "Nothing leaves these doors. NOTHING. No parchment, no scroll, no tablet, nothing. You want to take knowledge from here, you memorize it, or you make a hand copy for yourself ... AFTER I tell you, it is permissible." She placed her hands on her tiny hips and glared up at Tulok. If it were not for her formidable tenacity, she would almost be comical.

"I understand," Tulok agreed.

She continued to stare at him, unblinking.

Tulok cleared his throat and looked at Leralyn directly. "I understand fully that the contents of this Library are considered both sacred and controlled information, and that such information is not meant to leave the confines of the Library without the direct permission of the Chief Librarian," he articulated.

Leralyn continued to eye the big man, both unmoved and unbending. Finally, she nodded her head. "Good!" She turned and walked back to the door. "You can leave now, Ibris, we have work to do," dismissing the Elven warrior.

Tulok's eyes widened at the dismissive comment, but Ibris merely chuckled. It was a break in the hardened exterior of the Devout Champion. He nodded his head and joined Leralyn by the door. "As the Chief Librarian commands," he inclined his head in respect. He looked back over at Tulok. "This is where you were meant to come before Father Kalal interjected himself into this investigation." He looked between the two. "If you would excuse me, I need to attend to matters of policy regarding a certain Reysis and His Claim over the area in question."

"Reysis Safar?" Tulok asked carefully.

Ibris pursed his lips and nodded. He reached into his belt and recovered what appeared to be a folded letter bearing a small wax seal. "The same. His ... lineage ..." he paused, "affords him some small amount of leniency in this area, but not much. Should you speak with him, Father ... as the two of you appear to share a camaraderie ... you may do well to remind him of that," Ibris spoke plainly. He handed the missive to Sister Leralyn. "He left that for the Father when he was through last week. The Wanderer in Tarf-qua sent it. It was intercepted before Kalal could get his hands on it ... this time."

Leralyn nodded her head and looked down at the sigil on the letter. It appeared to be a strangely shaped metal flower of some foreign design embossed in deep blue ink. The seal was uncracked. She shook her head. "Stealing people's missives now. Has that man nothing better to do with his time?"

Tulok's brow furrowed. He stared at the missive in Leralyn's hand. "There ... have been ... other ... missives sent to me from Tarf-qua?" he asked slowly. A mixture of irritation and anxiousness wrestled inside the priest as a bitter taste filled his mouth. He took a breath and swallowed it down, silencing it.

Leralyn took a couple of steps toward Tulok, her blade-like spring stilts helping to close the distance quickly. She held out the missive to the big orc who took the letter carefully from the small woman's hands. "If it were a threat to security, I wouldn't be giving it to you, Father. Letters from home help us remember what we fight for," Ibris said.

Tulok nodded in humble thanks and stared at the letter in his hand, the sigil of the Wanderer embossed on the back. "My thanks," he said quietly.

Ibris inclined his head and looked once more to Tulok. "I will see if I can recover any others that were sent, pleasant studies," he intoned, and exited the library. The door closed and a series

15

of metal locks slid into place behind him, sealing the orc and the gnome inside.

Chapter 3

The Reysis and the Wandering Knight stared off into the darkened desert sky as the night played out. The watchtower near the southern outskirts of Tarf-qua was a remnant of the past when keepers spied the horizon for marauders. Now it was used as a beacon when a sandstorm was coming. The four lights in the sky above them were the only illumination in a blanket of space. Once upon a time ... or so the stories said ... the sky was awash with glittering lights in the heavens. Stars and Realms other than Sanctum. Homes for people now long lost, destroyed by the hunger of the mad god of Chaos and the Reaping. These were all that were left in the whole of existence. It was humbling.

Below the watchtower, the people of the village and temple continued their nightly pursuits. Animals were fed, stalls were cleaned, kitchens were stocked, meals were planned. The seasons had changed since her initial arrival here. This variation in the direct gaze of the Radiant Lord shifted patterns of behavior during the evenings, allowing more activity during the daylight hours. While they still conducted some daily activities after nightfall, the brutality of the heat had lessened. It was still dry in the desert, and the coolness of the weather shift did not bring any rain. Isolde had been advised that they might experience one or two days of rain this year.

One or two *days*.

At home, a day rarely went by without rain, mist, fog, or the morning dew. These concepts were unknown in the sea of sand that was Setesh. Tarf-qua was not without water; the village would not survive without it. Two large wells existed to support the village and provided the life-giving essence of existence here. There was no oasis, no open body of water here. It was the opposite of home.

Her heart ached a little for missing the shores of home.

"Wandering the Heavens, Island?" the dark-haired Sun Guide at her side asked quietly.

She blinked and shook her head, blushing a little. "Ah. No. Sorry," she apologized.

"For what?" Safar asked her. He pulled his long legs up and crossed them, resting his arms on his knees.

"Not being fully engaged in your company at this moment. It is rude," she shrugged and replied.

Safar shrugged a little and leaned in to bump her shoulder. "It is not to be concerned about. We are companions of some intensity and calling, yes?" he asked. His eyes drifted out to the sands. "To be wrapped up in one's own self occasionally is to be expected," He smiled a little. "I do not hold it against you, Island. You are a woman who answers to the call of the Heavens first. It is as it should be," he nodded.

"Thank you for understanding," the foreigner replied.

He pursed his lips and nodded. A light breeze picked up and danced across the rooftops, carrying bits of dust and sand in tiny whirlwinds. His dark curls ruffled lightly in the breeze. "When your duty is done here, where do you go?" he asked her.

Isolde shrugged. "I am uncertain." She leaned back on her elbows and stared at the dark sky. "There is an entire world to explore beyond the shores of Avalon. We have created less than half a dozen homely houses on this side of the sea. That leaves so much unknown ..." she mused.

"What is ... a homely house?" Safar asked.

"Ah," Isolde nodded. She sat up and turned to face the Reysis, "The Lord Wanderer does not have... *Temples* like The Radiant Lord does. We build homes ... places for travelers to rest at. A bed, a hearth, a warm bowl of food ... bandages and succor for the injured ... in exchange, we simply ask for the traveler to share their story."

Safar turned honey-gold eyes at Isolde with curious confusion. "No ceremony? No oblation or request for a donation?" he asked.

She shook her head. "The Landless Lord was never a supporter of high ceremony. He was a man of action and deed," came the reply.

Safar nodded appreciably. "I can see why He chose you. You are a woman of the same."

Isolde laughed out loud at the comment. "I thank you for saying so."

"It is only the truth, Island."

She nodded quietly and turned back to watch the sands. In the distance, lines of light extended in several directions from the gates of the village. Glowing markers left by caravans to mark safe passage across the darkened night.

"When do you leave?" She asked without looking at him.

"Two days. We travel from here to Obor-qua and Deneb-aal, and then back to Ophir," the Sun Guide replied, staring off in the distance at the lone stars.

She nodded and said nothing.

Safar's eyes slid over to Isolde and watched her in the platform's torchlight. By Seteshi standards, they would not consider her a beautiful woman. Her skin was pale, with tiny freckles across her nose and cheeks. Her nose was crooked from being broken in battle, despite having been healed and her hair was dark and curly, frequently pulled back and out of her face and eyes, and placed into a messy ponytail. She sported a scar that ran through her left eyebrow from some unknown injury. She was strong without being broad and tall, without being intimidating. It was her eyes that always caught his attention. Twin windows – brilliant green that almost matched the glory of Vidria glass, sparkling with honest curiosity and pure wonder that inspired hope.

"Come with me," Safar said.

Isolde blinked and looked over at him. "What?!" she exclaimed.

Safar sat up and turned to look at her directly. "Come with

me, Island. I will tell the Hemet that I need an extra pair of hands on this next leg and ask that he let you come with me as a part of your promise."

Isolde narrowed her eyes at Safar. "I thought we already had this discussion ..."

Safar waved his hand. "No. This has nothing to do with rumor and conjecture or me attempting to make any of it real," he countered. "You are dying here, Isolde. This is not your land. These are not your people," he began. She opened her mouth to protest. He held his hand still for a moment, asking for time to explain. "You cannot perform your duty to the Wandering Lord while trapped here loading caravan carts and carrying sacks of grain for a year! Come with me; at least for this leg of my travels. You will get to see Setesh from the eyes of one who loves her as a son to a mother," he offered, his eyes smiling at her.

Isolde shook her head. "I ... I don't know, Safar ..." she said hesitantly.

Safar reached out and placed his hands over Isolde's. They were warm and gentle. "You are my dear friend and I wish to do this for you. Obor-qua, then Deneb-aal, then Ophir ..." he trailed off on the last city, "where the grand Temple of the Radiant Lord stands."

And where Tulok is.

"If you come with me to Deneb-aal, you can also ask about the Vidria merchant that was involved in bringing you here. There must be someone there with information who can help, yes?"

I can pay respects to Reynard's grave.

Safar's offer sat in the scales of her mind. It would be good to get on the road again, certainly. It would be a chance to track down more information on Arman. Maybe she could determine if he left any information behind, and why he wanted the Magister in Deneb-aal. People were dead because of the merchant and the scarab amulet she and Reynard had agreed to bring here. The memory of the Temple of Silence still haunted her dreams. The strange priestess, Tulok bound in chains, and the hallowed niches with vases beneath it, almost like tree roots, and the map ...

Her heart ached for a moment at the loss of that information. That wonderful piece of artwork and all the stories it must have contained. All the villages, cities, and settlements from when the first people came to Sanctum. Buried again beneath the unforgiving sands of Ahsal. She had tried to recreate as much of it as she could, to preserve what could be preserved; but she had lost so much blood that day, the memories were faded and fuzzy. She needed to find a memory well and preserve them before they were gone forever.

Isolde's eyes met Safar's; she squeezed his hands with her own.

"If ... and only if ... the Hemet will transfer my service to you. I cannot leave before my term is ended. I cannot besmirch my leug."

Safar nodded in understanding. "Of course!"

"But if he will ..." she paused and smiled gently at the Reysis, "then I will happily join you, Reysis Safar."

Safar's smile reached almost ear to ear at the utterance of Isolde's words. The whole of his person came alive with exuberant joy. He titled his head back and yelled to the sky –

"She said yes!"

~ ~ ~

Tulok leaned back in the large chair, closing his eyes as he let his head fall back. A line of maps stretched out before him across several tables. Each of them depicted the mountains south of Nahral and west of the Oasis. On each, only two landmarks remained ever constant. The location of the River Lord's City, Nahral, and the location Kas-qua – the only source of water south and west of that same location before one reached the ocean coast. Nothing else was the same on any of the other maps. Some had notes showing watering holes and villages, others noted trails and feeding grounds. Three maps depicted fallen blocks with images that seemed to imply Ahsal. The location of the ruins on each of these was incorrect …

And none of them were the same.

Tulok raised his left hand and rubbed his head, feeling the fuzz of stubble coming in on his bare head once more. He would have to tend to that soon. There was no requirement for the priesthood to maintain a shaved appearance; Tulok simply preferred it. Orc hair was not like a human, Elven, or even dwarven hair. It was thick and coarse, like the hair of a camel or pack animal. It was heavy and inconvenient. The people of the sands – his people – often kept their hair braided or coiled in intricate designs. Some warriors had been known to weave weights into their braids and use them as weapons. There was an entire fighting style developed around this convention. Tulok had often found the practice distasteful and barbaric, though he also wondered if that were more because of his proximity to persons not of his people. He rubbed his face, checking the length of trim along his now bearded jawline. It had been almost a full season since he had ceased shaving his face clean, and instead adopted the style of facial hair worn by many within the Grand Temple. A line of dark hair traced along his powerful jaw and chin. It did not trail down his throat or neck, and it did not advance into a mustache; it was merely a well-kept, perfectly precise outline of his squared jawline.

He opened his eyes and stared at the plaster ceiling above him, gently tugging at his beard in thought.

"Well, are any of them right?" Sister Leralyn's voice prodded him from across the table.

He continued to stare at the ceiling and tug at his beard. He shook his head. "No. They are all wrong," he replied in his deep voice.

The gnomish librarian muttered many words under her breath, some of which Tulok was certain were curses in an ancient tongue. "Two dozen maps, spanning fifteen hundred years, and not a single one of them is correct?"

Tulok shrugged and sat back up. "The Devout were very

thorough in their initial purge of information," he offered. "One presumes we should be grateful for their dedication to the cause."

"And yet you found an accurate map with the approximate location of that damnable Temple in the Library of Tarf-qua!" Leralyn exclaimed.

"No doubt it made its way into the Temple archives from one of the many traders ... or raiders ... over the course of the village's history," the orc offered. His eyes slid across the varied objects once more. He reached out his long arm and pointed at one of them. "That one is probably the best for accuracy of the current geography of the area. And ..." he scowled and looked at the others. He pushed himself up out of the chair and walked down the length of the table. At the very end was an old parchment, carefully displayed on fine leather. Both were laid out on a thin wooden board for presentation. Tulok carefully slid his skilled hands under the board and walked the ancient item back over to where Leralyn sat.

"And this one is probably the closest for direct location, though ... the distances and scale are clearly off."

Leralyn made quick work of rolling up and setting aside the other documents, to clear enough space for both maps to be laid out side by side. The differences in scale were clearly noticeable.

Leralyn stared at both maps, her hands on her tiny hips. She pursed her lips and shook her head. "We'll need a cartographer to interpret these and determine the mathematical differences between them."

Tulok stepped back from the table and stared down at it, and nodded. He folded his arms across his broad chest. "Do we have one assigned here?" he asked.

Leralyn shook her head. "No, Milfin is in Port Kraken working with the Sea Port and Jalius is in Litharge cataloging the Grand Library."

Tulok pursed his lips and pinched them between the forefinger and thumb of his left hand in thought. "And ... the Reysis

..."

Leralyn barked out loud at the word. It was an unpleasant sound. "Reysis Safar al-Shifa has declared that no Sun Guide will aid in the recovery of information on the location of Ahsal ... and since they all bend a knee to him ..." she waved her hands at the ceiling.

Tulok furrowed his brow and then rubbed his forehead. *Dammit, Safar.* He rubbed the bridge of his nose in thought.

You know someone else who knows how to get there and could probably find it on the map; he thought to himself. *A woman with a broken compass that hangs around her neck.* His thoughts drifted to the Knight Wanderer, and their shared experience at Ahsal. The Temple of Silence had almost claimed both of their lives. The Holy Witness of The Lord Wanderer had walked that path alone, with no map, and only her faith to guide her. She could find it. The question was ... would she want to?

"Don't you have a letter from that Wandering Knight in Tarf-Qua?" Leralyn asked, as if reading the orc priest's mind.

"I do," Tulok nodded.

"She saw all of this, didn't she?" Leralyn asked.

"She did," Tulok replied quietly.

"Well, dammit man, send a hawk to Tarf-qua and tell her we need her here!" The gnome harrumphed at him. Her shock-white hair bounced wildly around her head in emphasis.

Tulok took a deep breath and let out a heavy sigh. "It's not that easy."

"Nonsense! Tarf-qua is a three-day ride from here. Send a message. She'll be here before week's end." Leralyn insisted.

"She's bound in service to Tarf-qua for another three seasons." Tulok offered.

And you swore her to secrecy. You carry a secret of hers as well in that pact.

"Bound in ... oh, for the love of our Lord ..." Leralyn threw her hands into the air and walked away, bouncing on her stilts. She turned back to face him. "It's an honor thing, isn't it? She gave her word and now has to fulfill it or suffer the consequences?" she asked. "Damned Avalonians and their fey magic blood ..." she swore and muttered and paced.

Tulok shrugged. "I cannot say for certain, other than to say her leug hangs in the balance."

"Leug!" Leralyn said in an angry tone. "Damned Avalonians and their secrets! Damned Avalonians and their mystical measure of worth over hard coin. Bah!" She paced back and forth on her stilts, hands on her hips in irritation.

Tulok watched the little woman in her irritation. "You ... seem to know a lot about the Island people, Sister Leralyn ..." Tulok began.

Leralyn stopped and looked at Tulok like he had suddenly lost the ability to reason. She gestured wildly around them both at the countless number of books and scrolls and the knowledge they no doubt contained.

Tulok's eyebrows raised in understanding. "Ah."

Leralyn continued to pace in her angry huff. She finally stopped and looked over at Tulok. "Send her a message, regardless. Let her reply, so we at least know the details of her service. She may point out an option for us to work with." Leralyn eyed the sealed letter on the table by Tulok's belongings. "She's writing to you, and apparently often enough that Kalal intercepted them. Something tells me she'd enjoy an excuse to visit."

Chapter 4

A gargoyle sat on the rooftop of the building across from the Harbor Master's office. Perched on the eves like a human-sized raven, it watched the comings and goings of the shipyard in measured silence. Untrained eyes would have never known it was anything other than a decorative statue. Rain fell from the skies above the city of Port Kraken and onto the gargoyle. It landed on the gargoyle's oilcloth cloak and fell off in rivulets to the street below. The figure remained in its position of observation, neither moving nor shifting as the rain fell upon its frozen form. Careful observation might have detected the occasional puff of breath that issued from the figure, as it exhaled slowly in the chilly night.

Travel by sea in the Realm of Sanctum was a risk. Ships followed established routes up and down the coast of the Mainland, never daring to venture out into the open seas. There were stories that spoke of a time when the Ocean Lord governed the seas, and both travel and trade were frequented by sail. Something had happened in the undetermined past to change that. Some claimed that the Ocean Lord was dead, and without His guidance over the seas of Sanctum – the great creatures beneath the waves roamed unchecked. Others spoke of a terrible curse that had befallen the seaways of Sanctum, felling the Ocean Lord and holding him in a state of ailing unconsciousness that begged healing, or at least the release of death. Whatever the truth of the matter – travel by sail between the Mainland and Avalon was a risky, but practiced venture full of caution. Only the deep magics of Avalonian Crafters, coupled with the skills of the strange aquatic beings known as the Incirrata, had secured a single route from the

Island Realm to the Mainland. This single route was the only avenue for trade across the open seas of Sanctum. Whatever bargains had made with the powers of The Deep were anyone's guess.

The door of the Harbor Master's Office opened and light spilled onto the cobblestone street from within. A lone traveler pulled their hood up against the storm, protecting themselves from Port Kraken's misery of cold and wet. The door slowly closed behind them.

The gargoyle's eyes darted toward the door. Its head tilted to the side, like a giant bird. It watched with interest as the light disappeared and the door closed against the storm. Trained eyes jumped from the doorway to the departing cloaked traveler. They walked with some confidence, as one familiar with the very cobblestones of the street. They continued down the street toward the gargoyle's chosen perch. Satisfied they were unobserved; the illusion of the gargoyle faded and became a humanoid figure. In a single, smooth maneuver, the figure pulled the very shadows around them like a cloak and leaped from one roof to the next.

The cloaked traveler turned from the lighted cobblestone street and entered the alleyway between two buildings. *Splash ... Splash ... Splash ...* the booted feet broke up the puddles of rainwater as they continued their unconcerned march. Unbeknownst to them, the shadows fell darker in the alleyway, stretching and obscuring the matters within from prying eyes.

The cloaked traveler stopped and leaned back against the stonewall of the building, unaware of the growing shadows behind them. Silent and with unearthly grace, the "gargoyle" stepped from the top of the building and landed in the alleyway before the cloaked traveler. Its oilcloth cloak flapped outward like two great wings as the figure landed solidly, knees bending to absorb the shock of the landing. Not even the sound of the rainwater disturbed its entrance. It slowly stood and looked down at the other figure. It said nothing.

"If I live another hundred years, I will never get used to you,"

Arman shuddered. The Vidria looked around the alleyway and noticed the darkness obscuring both ends, nodding in satisfaction.

The dark figure said nothing in return. It cocked its head to the side in bird-like fashion once more. Tiny red eyes seemed to glow from within the recesses of its hood. Watching.

"Were you able to find the information?" the smaller man asked.

Reaching into the shadows of itself, they withdrew a sealed leather tube. Their movements were fluid, though their limbs were long and angular. It held the tube in its right hand, gloved fingers wrapped tightly around it. It extended its left hand in silence. The figure's long bony fingers uncurled slowly, revealing an ungloved hand whose fingers ended in what appeared to be sharpened talons in a universal request for payment. Dark liquid covered its hand, mixing with the rain and dropping to the stones in the alleyway. It looked like blood.

"Of course," the Vidria nodded and withdrew a small pouch. The contents sounded like metal. He placed the payment in the bloodied palm, "As agreed."

The fingers of the dark figure closed slowly around the bag and squeezed it once. They nodded and handed over the sealed leather tube. Accepting the item quickly from the strange creature, Arman tucked it out of sight. The dark figure took a step back from the smaller man. Bright red eyes glowed in the darkness as it stared at him. It raised its gloved right hand to the shadowed area where a face should have been, right finger extended in a gesture of silence.

"Of course," the smaller man nodded.

The strange figure inclined its head then and stepped back once more. Shadows folded around it, taking it from vision. Only the small man and the rainwater remained in the alley, a rivulet of blood trailing toward the sewers.

~~~

He had been used to staying up all night to stand vigil. At the Temple of Tarf-qua, there had only been a handful of Faithful to tend to the needs of the village and the Temple. Someone always stood during the evening to serve as both Guardian and Guide while the Lord's eyes were turned elsewhere. That someone had always been him.

The Grand Temple in Ophir addressed the needs of the Faithful differently. There were more than enough priests and laypeople available to stand Night Vigil. Indeed, many times, they would work in squads of three. Two to three priests sometimes teamed with a Devout Champion. This group would be tasked with patrolling the grounds. Watchers stood in the towers at night, standing throughout the darkness of the evening sky. There was always someone in the main Temple providing guidance and offering hymns and prayers. Acolytes tended to the needs of the people. They worked in shifts and rotations, a well-oiled and fully functional machine.

And then there was Tulok. The orc priest had offered his services to the duty roster multiple times since his arrival in Ophir. Each time, they advised him that he was "already performing his assigned task" and that the Watch would contact him if they had need of him elsewhere. Until his assignment to the Library, Tulok had wondered if he could ever perform dutiful service to the Temple again or if they would sequester him for the rest of his days.

He stared out the window of his single room and into the lighted courtyard below. Dozens of people walked from place to place. Some were members of the Faith in their white and gold robes, while others were people from the surrounding Capital who had come for evening services. More still were visitors to the city, as many came to the Grand Temple for whatever reason their pilgrimage or calling had chosen for them. So many people in this single location at the same time. It was so very different from home.

He took a deep breath and turned away from the window and stepped over to the bed. It, too, differed from the bed he was accustomed to in Tarf-qua. The Radiant Lord ensured His Faithful were well taken care of, but the trappings of his personal quarters were more detailed than even those of Nahral. No one suffered from a lack of rest or discomfort from a lumpy bed here. He had initially wondered if he had been given this room because of his size, and perhaps the expense shown here was out of the ordinary. Then he had stopped by to deliver a missive to another member of the Faith and discovered that their appointments were likewise extravagant.

He sat down on the edge of the heavy, carved wooden bed. It groaned, but slightly under his weight. The bed was clearly designed to accommodate one of his people. It was an unusual experience.

A massive footlocker sat at the end of the bed. It was filled with both the gear he had been wearing when he arrived and the vestments he had been assigned. A washbasin, pitcher, and grooming tools were all placed neatly before a polished brass mirror in one corner. A writing desk, lamp, and chair sat next to that. In the opposite corner sat a large and comfortable-looking chair with a small table next to it, clearly designed for resting and reading.

The walls were pristine. The furnishings were polished and oiled. Everything looked as though it had never been used. When he departed in the mornings for his duties in the Library, he would return to find the room in perfect order once more. Whether it was magic or mortal hands that ensure this, he could not be certain.

Tulok's eyes landed on the writing desk across the way. A lone letter sat in the center of the desk, its blue wax seal staring upward at the room. Isolde's letter. Leralyn had instructed him to send word to Isolde in Tarf-Qua. He could not disobey the orders of the Chief Librarian under whom he now served. He had sent his winged messenger off at dawn's light. Tarf-Qua was a three-day journey on a camel from Ophir. The Temple's messenger Hawks could cover that distance in half a day. They should hopefully have a response from the village by tomorrow.

He stared at the letter on the desk. It had been with him

all day now, and he still had not cracked the seal. Why? What was it about the potential contents of it that made him wish to postpone opening it even longer?

You wanted to protect her from all of this; he thought to himself. He knew that if she had returned to Ophir with him, the reception she faced would have been less welcoming than the one he had received. Her position as a Champion – a Holy Witness for her Faith – might have bought her some leniency, but the Halsa would have demanded her Oathbound silence to all of it, or be slain. Tulok knew Isolde would rather die than swear another Oath of secrecy about Ahsal. It had been almost a full season since they parted ways at the docks of Kef-aal. He hoped that she had found a way of divesting herself of the memories in the means of her faith so they could be properly recorded.

Kef-aal.

He frowned at the memory.

They had shared *ZinHisal,* the soul balancing, in Kef-aal. Neither of them was held back by words ... or deed. They left nothing to weigh down their souls should The Grim Lord come for them. There had been words shared in silhouetted lamplight, and actions best not spoken of aloud for their taboo. They had parted ways afterward. Reysis Safar took her back to Tarf-qua to serve her pledge of service while he traveled to Ophir to advise them of their findings.

He continued to stare at the letter on the desk. If Ibris' words were correct, there had been other letters. Letters that Father Kalal had intercepted, and no doubt read, searching for evidence of wrong-doing. What had those letters contained? They had been meant for his eyes, no one else's.

The Radiant Lord had no restrictions on His people other than they serve Him first. That simple stricture often prevented servants of the Faith from creating relationships outside the Faithful. Choosing the bands of matrimony over the bonds of the Divine was not something any servant of the Divine ever hoped to have to be forced into. This was not the matter that concerned Tulok as he stared at the letter. He knew where his feet would always lead him, as he also knew where Isolde's would lead her. They were servants of the Divine, chosen by the Heavens for reasons only They could know. He would no sooner ask Isolde to set aside her compass than she would his vestments. A greater issue loomed that would have to be addressed.

He was not human.

The People of Sanctum had not always shared a home. The Divine of their homeland had saved each of their peoples and brought them here during the Reaping. Sanctum was a place of refuge for the last surviving mortals of the known worlds. The powers of the heavens had birthed from the clay of this world a scant few, but still more had been carried here from places now lost to history and legend. Their origins were not shared. Pairings between the races yielded no offspring. It was for this reason that society did not pursue unions between the races at large. When one is the sole surviving representative of one's people, one bore a duty to increase one's population and preserve them from extinction.

Cross-species relations were frowned upon, and at worst ... a cause for exile in some areas of Setesh.

ZinHisal would buy them both a blind eye for the actions of Kef-aal; but would it buy them enough?

The priest of the Radiant Lord took a deep breath and pushed himself to his feet. He took several determined steps across the room and reached for the letter on the desk. Hands skilled at addressing fragile documents lifted the letter ever so gently and carefully cracked the wax seal. He set his jaw and flipped the folded parchment open.

Letters written in the common Trade Tongue spilled across the page:

I am going to continue to send you letters until you either reply to me, or someone tells me you are dead ... though I truly hope the last thing is not the reason I have not heard from you. Are you well?

Tell me you are well. I worry for you, my friend; it has been too long.

Safar continues to carry my missives to you and says that he is happy to do so. Sometimes I think he does so to humor me. The village women here are gossips and irritating. You are far more patient than I am. I remember now what I hated most about Whitebrooke. Gossipy women. You must have been gifted with the patience of a stone.

The loading crane broke several days ago. I am helping to keep the caravans going by loading and unloading goods. Isik says we will work on fixing the crane soon. The knee and shoulder are holding up well enough, despite the overuse. Mother Ranpu keeps me in bandages and balms, but she is not the Healer that you are.

I see I am running out of parchment, but still have so much to tell you.

Write to me and tell me everything, or better yet, come home if you can, if only for a visit.

You are missed, Bookworm.

Yours always,

Isolde

He stared at the words and re-read them a second and third time. There was leeway; assumptions might not be made.

Who was he kidding? Ibris was going to have questions.

Dammit.

Chapter 5

"You lied," she stated flatly.

Safar shrugged a little. "Yes and no," he offered noncommittally.

Isolde clenched her teeth, setting her jaw as she stared out at the desert ahead from atop her camel.

Safar glanced over at the woman riding next to him. She rode with confidence, not present when last he watched her ride one of his animals. Sitting tall on the animal's saddle, she draped her right leg around the horn and reclined on the padded seat. Her left leg rested against the shoulder of the beast. Gloved hands held the loose rope and leather braided reins that looped lazily on the creature's neck. Safar smiled as he watched her.

"Stop smiling at me. I am mad at you," The Witness glowered.

"Yes, I am aware," The Reysis nodded. He sniffed once and looked back over his shoulder at the rest of the caravan train that trailed behind them. Half a dozen camels walked behind them; two carried riders, four carried trade goods bound for Obor-Qua. It was a small train; he would pick up different riders as they made their way to Deneb-aal. From there, the caravan might exceed thirty or more as they made their way to the capital.

"Your skills in the saddle have improved," Safar spoke gently.

"It seemed a reasonable skill to pick up while I am here," she replied curtly.

The Reysis nodded and reached to smooth his beard and mustache in thought. His golden-brown eyes searched the horizon for signs of conflict or potential storm. They came to rest on the woman at his side once more. He shook his head; there was plenty of both already here. "We should reach the gates of Obor-qua shortly past nightfall. We will rest there for the night. I will make arrangements with the merchants upon arriving to determine who will join with us to Deneb-aal or Ophir."

The dark-haired woman grunted in response.

Safar took a breath and looked over at her once more. "How long do your Island people hold grudges?"

Isolde turned to look at him. "Pardon me?"

"I would like to know how long I should expect this anger to last? I can plan the rest of this leg and determine if I can count on your help if we need it," he replied flatly.

Isolde's eyes went cold. "Noble Reysis Safar," she intoned, her voice flavored with the formality of the Avalonian Courts, "I offer you my word and bond … should trouble find its way to your doorstep or this caravan, my arm and valor will serve as a bulwark against the enemy," she stared directly into his eyes. "Despite the harm caused to my honor already at your hands – *my lord*," she spoke with emphasis, "… the duty to my *leug* would stand for nothing less."

Safar's eyes widened and then narrowed. He sucked on a tooth for a moment and then held up his hand to signal the train to stop. He pointed at Isolde, then toward an area in the shade of a dune. "Over there, outside of ears that need not hear our words. We are going to have this out now." He turned back to bark an order at the rest of the train, then turned to face Isolde.

"Of course," she inclined her head. Clucking at her mount, she squeezed it with her leg and tapped at it. The camel knelt. She slid off with expert grace, and without a glance backward, strode to the designated area. Safar watched her walk away in the sand, noting that she was tugging at her gloves to pull them from her hands.

She expected a fight.

Dismounting his animal, the tall Sun Guide tucked his chin

and followed the woman across the sands. His stride was a perfect slip-slide-slip-step that was born from the sands themselves. He approached the strong woman, jaw and shoulders set.

"Island I ..." he began.

Her hook was swift and directed at his perfect jawline. With preternatural reflexes, the Reysis dodged the blow meant for his face. She swung again. He held up a forearm and blocked her, twisting and grasping hold of her wrist. He held her tight.

"Isolde, enough!" he commanded.

Unbowed, the Knight glared at the handsome Sun Guide and stepped in, sliding her right leg between his. She hooked his knee and pulled, grunting as his grip twisted her arm in his hand. She felt the familiar sensation of pulling muscles in her right shoulder. An injury still healing. They fell to the ground in a tumble of limbs and a tangle of fabric.

Safar rolled expertly to the side to disengage from the angry warrior. Isolde lay on her back on the sand in the dune's shade, staring at the sky.

"Are we done?" Safar demanded.

Isolde lay there, thinking. "I haven't decided yet," she confessed, huffing.

Safar shot a glance toward the caravan and watched as the other two riders were carefully assessing the situation between their Reysis and the strange foreign woman. He could see them readying weapons. He waved at them to show the situation was under control. They relaxed.

"Gods be damned, woman, what was that for?" he asked as he looked over at his prone friend.

Isolde continued to lie where she was, silently contemplating her response. "You lied to the Hemet," she said quietly.

"So, I deserve to have my jaw broken?" Safar retorted.

Isolde's eyes rolled over to gaze up at Safar. "I have *nothing* to my name ... but my good name, Safar," she explained. "And your actions have robbed me of even that." She looked away from him and back at the sky.

The Sun Guide watched her, listening. His brows knit together in confusion for a moment and then rose in understanding. He nodded and shifted in the sand to sit next to her. He clapped the sand off of his pant legs. "I did not lie to the Hemet, Island," he replied gently. Isolde made a strangled sound of frustration and refused to look at Safar. "I told him exactly what we discussed. That I needed you for this journey that would take me to the Capital. That is not untrue. The journey will take us almost a fortnight, and I expect we will pick up a large train in Deneb-aal. I will need you."

The woman rolled her eyes in his direction, "And..."

Safar shrugged, "And ... perhaps ..." he began. "I did not ... *dissuade* ... the misperception that I would also be introducing you to my Caravan wife in Deneb-aal."

Isolde pursed her lips and shook her head.

"Island ..." Safar began, then his voice lowered. "Isolde ... please ..." he continued. "What they believe to be the truth has no bearing on what is or is not between us. Let them believe as they may ... if it grants you the freedom to return to your path ... and your God," he offered. He leaned over to look into her sparkling green eyes. "There is a world to see, Isolde duAvalonne, and a mystery that begs yet to be uncovered. Walk awhile with this sand dancer and let me help you find what you seek." He gazed down at her, his dark curls falling around his face. He smiled brightly at her.

She stared up into those honeyed eyes as he watched her. There were both value and truth in his words; with Safar and the traders, she might yet find the information on Arman and the scarab. It was an attractive offer.

Safar smiled then, "And who knows, perhaps one day you will let me change your mind ..." he grinned winningly at her.

She scoffed and shook her head, reaching up to place her hand over his face and shove him away from her, gently.

"Fine," she agreed reluctantly.

The Sun Guide chuckled and rolled to push himself up and then offered the prone woman his hand to aid her in standing.

She clasped his arm firmly and allowed him to leverage her up, wincing slightly as he did so. Safar eyed her suspiciously and poked at her shoulder. She slapped his hand away.

"We will get that tended to at Obor-qua." The Reysis stated with certainty.

"Mmmm," Isolde hrmmed in response and slid her arm around Safar's back. He draped his arm across her shoulders and they walked back to the caravan to resume their journey.

~~~

"She's not coming." The little woman harrumphed and tossed the missive onto the table. She placed her hands on her hips and scowled.

From across the library table, Tulok looked up from the map he had been reviewing. His back stretched and popped in several places as he sat up. "Excuse me?" he asked for clarification.

"The woman ... the Witness ... she's not coming." Leralyn gestured at the letter. "She left already with Reysis Safar," the Librarian almost spat the Sun Guide's name.

Tulok raised his right eyebrow in curiosity at both the comment and the emotion. "The Reysis convinced the Hemet to allow her into his service, perhaps?" he offered as he contemplated what it could all possibly mean.

Tulok and Safar had met on a couple of occasions since the orc's arrival in Ophir. Each time they had briefly discussed the current situation of research, and the need to protect Isolde from the hands of the Temple's information gatherers until she could do right by her own faith. Once she could secure whatever was necessary to her duties for the Lord Wanderer, there would be less need to divert attention and access. Tulok had balked at the idea initially, and struggled with the need to create a diversion to hinder the Temple's interrogation of the Wandering Knight. It was not until Safar pointed out to him that even the Scourge of Midnight would demand she tell no one about Ahsal, including her own people. The Scourge of Midnight was the Head of the Devout Champions, or as others called him – the HAND of the Radiant Lord. Given the level of conspiracy and heresy involved, Tulok knew they could not keep Isolde from the information gathers much less the Scourge, but he would do his best to buy her some time. Tulok hoped that was what Safar was doing now.

Leralyn scoffed. "Caravan wife," she replied disdainfully.

Tulok choked on nothing and coughed. "Pardon me?" he cleared his throat and blinked.

Leralyn gestured at the letter. "Read for yourself. He apparently convinced the Hemet to let him take her off of his hands so she could join his caravan," Leralyn raised her hands and walked away toward the stacks of books on the other end of the table, her spring-stilts bouncing her along the way. "And if the history of the Sun Guides of Setesh has anything to say about it, that means he intends to marry her and add her to his Hamula." She passed the books and moved to a separate table where the remains of lunch were scattered across a couple of plates. She reached for one bottle that sat there and drank from it, not bothering to pour herself a glass.

Well, THAT was not something they had discussed. Tulok mused.

Tulok pursed his lips and frowned in confusion, and reached across the table for the letter. "That seems ... hmmm ..." he paused, searching for the right words, "... out of character for Ser Isolde," he offered, and opened the missive. His eyes made quick work of its contents. Hemet Behdeti Kahr seemed to confirm Leralyn's interpretation of things, though he also noted that Safar showed the caravan would come to Ophir as part of its travels.

Leralyn continued to scowl. "That man has half a dozen wives, three husbands, and two dozen children scattered across the sands – that we have on record. Many of them Sun Guides ..."

Tulok's eyes looked over the edge of the parchment at the gnomish woman. "And so long as they are all willing participants of consenting age, Leralyn, and they are all capable of taking care of one another ..." the big orc began.

"Bah! Humans," she scowled.

Tulok's eyebrows raised. He nodded then in understanding. "The customs of the Sand Dancers are not the customs of all of Setesh, Sister. Neither are the customs of your people like unto mine," he reasoned. He looked over the letter once more. "If I know Ser Isolde, and I should like to believe that I do …" he began, "Safar is shortly to discover that he made a very poor assumption … if the said assumption was truly made." He folded the letter up and set it back on the table. He continued. "I am more likely to believe that Safar's reputation, as you have kindly pointed out, has gotten the better of things, and he has merely hired Ser Isolde for a season's travel. Hemet Kahr even stated that Ophir was on their travel plan. She will still come to us. Just … on another's schedule," he offered and gestured with his open hands. "Ahsal was buried for almost two millennia. It can stand to wait a little while longer before it is formally mapped once more. After all, it is not as if anyone else survived that collapse."

Leralyn continued to scowl from her place at the end of the table.

Tulok steepled his fingers and looked over at Leralyn. "You truly dislike him, don't you?" he asked her.

She huffed, "His arrogance is insufferable," she admitted.

Tulok shrugged a little. "He is very good at what he does … survive the unsurvivable … and ensure the people in his care do likewise," he offered. "His confidence is well earned."

She scoffed, "Your opinion, Father, is biased," she replied.

Tulok nodded and leaned back in his chair. "I freely admit that I owe my life to the Reysis, and that were it not for his actions, I – *and Ser Isolde* – would not have survived the encounter at Ahsal. I have worked with the man – *many times* – in my service at Tarf-Qua and always found him to be an honest and dependable soul." he gestured at the letter. "Ser Isolde still mourns the loss of her husband; Safar will not find success there. Let us just wait for their arrival and continue our research until that time."

Leralyn continued to scowl, but finally set her bottle down. "Very well," she agreed. "You mentioned there was a strange figure carved into the Temple wall there. Do you think you can draw it?"

Chapter 6

Lightning flashed in the sky, and the sound of thunder rumbled around her. She felt the sound echo across the area and through her body. Clouds swirled in a darkened tempest above her as a light flashed soundlessly in the heavens. With a delay in delivery, the shock wave of the sound exploded like a bomb. Instinctively, she knew she should fear the storm that threatened above, but she reached for the compass at her neck and wrapped her fingers around its metal shape. A wave of warmth and security washed over her.

Wind.

There was wind now, pushing at her body. It was strong and cold and smelled of ice and death. Darkness. There was nothing around her of familiarity. No fires in the distance burning for guidance. No lamps in the windows of buildings. The scant few stars that survived the Reaping were gone from the firmament. All that remained was the chill of the wind, the thunder, and the lightning.

There were sounds in the wind, something other than the rumble of the storm and its dance of lights. It was like voices whispering as one within the winds themselves. Or perhaps the wind was composed entirely of voices. She could not tell.

She shook her head and tried to focus.

Her feet were bare, and her toes were dug into the mud and loam of familiar shores.

Mud? Loam?

She had seen neither in several seasons – not since leaving home.

Water squished up from the ground and mixed with the mud and washed over her feet. It was the aching cold of the wet winter of the northlands. It dug through her skin and into her bones. Her feet burned from the chill of the cold.

She looked up once more, looking for a path, a landmark, anything.

Lightning flashed above her again, a rapid series of flashes, more common with summer storms. None of this made sense.

Focus.

Shadows and flashes of light back-lit an object in the distance. Looming and large, it dwarfed the landscape. She felt pulled toward it. She struggled with her feet, trying to pull them from the mud, only to discover the mud had risen to her knees and they held her fast. Ancient limbs of a strange tree spread out above her. Its gnarled fingers reached for the Heaven's as if trying to pull itself from the earth. More flashes of light. Other figures in the darkness now surrounded the ancient tree. She could almost make out their voices in the wind. The mud and soil around her stank of decay and death. She looked down and saw bodies writhing in the surrounding mud. Their forms were misshapen and deformed. Tangled roots of the great tree wrapped around them, pulling them apart even as it pulled them down. The image was familiar, somehow.

She should try to escape; she knew that if she did not, her end would come. She stared at the tree and the figures that surrounded it. She felt the gentle caress of a mud-covered hand on her cheek. Yes, this was how it was intended. The land could not survive without her. Yes.

Light flashed again. The silhouette of a compact figure stood next to the tree. A soft green light emanated from it. It held something in its hand that she could not make out. Light flashed again. The green light shifted into the hand of the figure. The figure placed its hand on the trunk of the great tree. The light shifted from soft to sickly green as it melded with the tree and bled into it. It began to form a familiar pattern, round and almost insect-like. A scarab. Voices in the wind wept.

Her eyes flew open, a strangled scream in her throat. As if seeping from the darkness, the shadows clung to her form. Their icy embrace held her tightly and constricted all around her body. Violently ripping her hand free, she clenched the compass icon of the Lord Wanderer around her throat. The darkness obscured everything – unfamiliar surroundings. She reached for the weapon under her pillow.

The door flung open. Light that spilled into the room hit the wall of liquid darkness. The silhouette of a tall, lean figure stood there. She could make out the shape of a curved blade in one hand. She blinked, trying to focus. Her head swam as the tendrils of the Morpheum clung to her mind and body, trying to drag her back into its depths. She closed her eyes and clenched her jaw.

"… I am the LIGHT IN THE DARKNESS AND I FEAR NO ONE!" she shouted in her native tongue through gritted teeth. An energy field born of the Landless Lord exploded from Isolde duAvalonne, banishing the threads of darkness and nightmare back to the dreamscape whence they came. The figure in the doorway staggered back slightly and then stepped forward, lowering its weapon.

"Island!" a familiar voice called.

She opened her emerald green eyes and shook her head once more as things came slowly back into focus. Her left hand clasped her icon, her right hand clasped the hilt of her dagger as she sat in her bed. A man's figure closed the distance from the doorway to the bedside and knelt by her quickly. Her eyes fluttered and rolled. She shook her head once more and dropped the dagger. Her right hand reached out, searching for something. She found purchase on the bare shoulder of the Reysis. Her fingers dug into his bronzed flesh, like an anchor seeking purchase in a gale.

Safar dropped his black curved khopesh to the floor and reached for her. Light from the doorway spilled across his figure, glistening in the desert air. Ebony tattoos and white scars decorated his bare flesh. Artistically designed giant black scorpions faced one another across his collarbones and reached back across his shoulders. Their tails disappeared behind and wrapped around his neck. His dark, curly hair, no longer confined to his headscarves, fell around his face and shoulders, tangling in his perfect beard. Golden brown eyes that seemed to carry an unearthly light searched Isolde's face, a look of earnest concern flavoring them.

"Isolde …" He reached for her, his caring, gentle hands seeking to grant comfort.

She closed her eyes and leaned forward and onto the man before her, allowing him to take her weight into his arms.

"Father?" a man's voice asked from the doorway.

"Everything is well, Casper," Safar replied to the voice, not moving from where he knelt at Isolde's bedside. "Our guest was … visited … but they are gone now."

"Shall I put the water on for the samovar?" Casper asked from the door.

Safar pushed Isolde back gently and looked into her brilliant green eyes. He gently brushed her dark hair from her face and searched for an answer in her countenance. She nodded silently.

"Yes, my son. Please," the Reysis replied with a nod.

"As you wish," the man nodded and left the pair alone.

Safar leaned in and placed his forehead against Isolde's in a gesture of warmth and compassion. "I am so sorry that you have come to harm under my roof, dear lady," he apologized.

Isolde leaned against him and shook her head. "No. This was … nothing you could have prevented," she spoke. She shifted then and slowly moved the covers from her feet, dragging her legs over the edge of the bed. They felt heavy and cold. Residual effects of the Morpheum.

"Light the lamp?" she asked.

Safar nodded and with a single gesture and a word that burned in Isolde's ears that disappeared as soon as it was uttered, a light came to the various lanterns in the room.

Isolde turned surprised eyes to Safar.

He shrugged. "The time for secrets has passed."

~~~

The home in Deneb-aal was very well appointed. A two-story open-air villa with a courtyard in the center it boasted several sleeping rooms, a kitchen, and two gathering areas to entertain guests. Upon their arrival that evening, they had been welcomed with open arms and bright smiles by a middle-aged man, his wife, their two children, and an older woman. Safar had greeted the older woman with warmth and affection Isolde had not seen from him in the past. The woman had given Isolde a cautious eye until Safar had mentioned something to her in a shared tongue that Isolde did not understand. Then the older woman's countenance had changed entirely and Isolde had been made to feel welcome as well. The older woman did not speak the Trader's Tongue, so neither woman could exchange words, but Isolde had made herself useful upon being welcomed. It was a simple gesture that bridged any gaps between them. Hospitality and respect were languages that crossed cultures. Rest within a proper home was more than welcome to the Avalonian Knight.

They had come to Deneb-aal more than a full week after leaving Tarf-qua. Their visit to Obor-qua had been brief; an exchange of riders, a sale of some goods, a trade for more, and a visit to a healer to mend Isolde's shoulder once more. Once done there, it had been several more days to Deneb-aal; the city where Isolde's Knight, Ser Reynard the Swift, had met his untimely end, and her journey had begun. She hoped to spend a few days speaking to people in the city about the Vidria merchant Arman, the man who had duped herself and Tulok and almost killed them both at Ahsal.

Isolde sat in a low chair, feet pulled up and tucked beneath her. She wore a simple caftan of soft, sand-colored cotton embroidered with colorful designs. Her dark hair was loose and flowed down past her shoulders. It wanted for a brush, but that was for later. She curled up around an earthenware cup of warm liquid.

On the table before her sat an elaborate item crafted of brass and glass. A container of oil sat beneath a glass carafe heating water, atop that sat another glass carafe with tea. A series of brass tubes connected both, forcing boiling water to the top where the tea steeped and then "fell" back to the bottom for serving. It was as beautiful as it was unique.

Across from her sat Reysis Safar al-Shifa, on a similar low chair. He wore loose pants and a robe the color of sunset that opened down the front. It was embroidered with golden scorpions. His head was uncovered. At his side stood their host, Casper.

Casper seemed to be a man in his late twenties with the same dark hair and golden eyes as Safar, though his eyes did not dance in the light as Safar's did. Casper eyed Isolde from across the table, assessing her as Safar once had. Safar looked up at him and clucked his tongue disapprovingly at the man.

"Enough of that. She is not for you," Safar chided in the Seteshi native tongue.

Casper inclined his head in respect. *"Apologies, I did not realize she was yours, Father."*

Safar clucked his tongue at him again and shook his head. *"She is her own woman."* He tapped his heart and gestured to the sky. *"Her heart belongs to the Heavens."*

Casper's eyebrows raised in both surprise and understanding. He placed his hand over his heart and inclined his head toward Isolde. "You honor my home with your presence. If you have a need, please but ask," he looked at Safar and nodded in respect, excusing himself.

Isolde watched the other man depart, her eyes searching as he walked away. Same gait. Same grace. She looked at Safar, an unspoken question in her eyes.

"My son," the Reysis answered.

Isolde's brow furrowed in confusion. Safar did not seem nearly old enough to have a child of that age.

Safar smiled if a little humbly. He traced the edges of the scorpion tattoo on his collarbone. "Servants of the Divine walk many paths and receive many gifts, Island," he said softly.

Isolde's eyes widened. "I … I did not know. I … oh … well … uh …" she stammered and blushed a little.

Safar chuckled and held up his hand. "It is no matter. Those who need to know, know. That is all that is important."

The Wandering Knight gazed over at her companion once more, examining him with newfound curiosity. She nodded at his exposed tattoos. Safar looked down at himself and back up to her. He nodded.

"Yes?"

"But … who …" she asked quietly.

"Ah," Safar answered, and nodded. "Yes, I forget. She is the Lady of the Beautiful Tent." He touched the scorpion tattoo on his left collarbone with gentle reverence. "She who gives breath and takes it away. The Healer."

Isolde frowned. "But … a scorpion?" she asked.

Safar chuckled a little. "Ah … Island … your people are so remarkably …" he paused and edited himself, instead shaking his head. "Who better to govern the arts of healing and medicine than one with the power to end life with a single strike?" he asked.

Isolde frowned and shifted her position. "I see. And so … when we were attacked …" she asked, referring to the time when Safar had been 'slain' by an Emperor of the Sands.

Safar pursed his lips and looked at the floor for a moment. He sniffed and looked back up at her. "A personal matter of some import. Between myself and my sibling," he offered.

"It tried to kill you!" Isolde exclaimed.

Safar threaded his fingers together and nodded. "… and failed …" he offered. "And will no doubt … try again …" He sat up and waved it off. "We are not on the best of terms at present. It is no matter."

She nodded and looked into her cup. "Witnessed," she whispered quietly.

Safar nodded appreciatively, then unfolded himself and placed his bare feet on the woven mat before him. He leaned forward, honey-gold eyes examining her. "Tell me. What did you see that has caused such turmoil in your soul?" he asked.

She sighed and frowned a little as she called the memory of the dream back up. She shook her head. "I … don't really know?" she began. "There was a storm … and an ancient tree …

48

like the ones from home."

"Your Island?" he asked.

Isolde nodded. "Yes ... and there were figures around it in the shadows ... and voices on the winds ... and ..." she paused, trying to call it all to the forefront once more. "Bodies ..."

Safar's dark eyebrows raised. "Bodies? Of the fallen?" he asked.

She shook her head. "No ... and yes ... I ... no ... they were bodies given to the land ... to nourish it ..."

Safar sat back and scowled.

Isolde watched his response. She waved her hand. "It's a ... land thing ... at home ... I can't really ... talk ... about it?" she said carefully.

"Ahhhh," Safar nodded and held up his hands. "Secrets of your people. I understand. Continue."

Isolde looked over at Safar quizzically.

"You are not the first Islander I have known in my years ..." he offered. Then he smiled winningly. "Just the only one I have liked."

She shook her head and sipped her tea, thinking. "There was another figure ... and a light. He was ... he was making the tree sick ..." Isolde's eyes widened suddenly. "No," she whispered. "No, no no no ..."

"Island?" Safar asked.

She shook her head. Leaning forward, she set her cup on the table and hid her face in her hands. "No, please. No."

"Isolde?" he asked softly, using her name.

Isolde looked up at the ageless figure of the Reysis and locked eyes with him. There was both determination and deep concern there. "Arman. He's alive. I don't know how, but he survived the sinkhole when Ahsal collapsed."

Safar watched her and listened carefully to her words. He paused and shook his head. "That cannot be. There has been no activity in that area since you and our mutual friend made your way out. My people ... ensured ... there were no others," he said, carefully choosing his words.

Isolde narrowed her eyes for a moment. "You mean they killed them."

Safar scowled. "You are always so brutal with your words, Island," he chided. His eyes met hers. He nodded. "Yes, fine," he agreed. "Ahsal's secrets are secret for a reason and must remain so."

Isolde shook her head. "No, you must have missed him," she began. "He's Vidria. Maybe he shaped the stone and walked under the sand ... I mean ... is that a thing?" She stumbled over her words. She stood up then and paced. "I don't know how ... but he is out there, Safar."

"Listen to yourself, Island. It was a dream. A ... a nightmare," he offered.

The Knight turned angry eyes on her friend. "No!" she snapped. "Don't do that. Don't talk to me like I am a child, Safar! The Landless Lord shields me from the realm of nightmare ... that is not what this was," she corrected him. "This was tied to the land and the Morpheum both." She gestured at him. "You felt it. You know my mind is sound ... this is real."

Safar nodded and stood, walking over to the foreigner. He reached out to place his hands on her shoulders and look into her face. "I apologize, you are right. Something has happened here tonight. Of this, we are both certain. If you believe in your heart of hearts that this is tied to the actions of a dead man, then ..." He stopped and contemplated his response. "Then I will go with you to Ophir and we will speak to the Temple of the Radiant Lord on this matter together."

Isolde looked deeply into Safar's honey-gold eyes and nodded. She smiled gently. "Thank you. Thank you for believing me."

Safar nodded and leaned in to press his forehead to hers. "There is too much to risk otherwise, my friend. I will have Casper take the caravan to Ophir. You and I will take the korsers, they will cover the distance in less time. But before we depart in the morning ..." he paused.

"Yes?" she asked.

"We will pay respects to the grave of your knight and the shrine you built to your Lord. Do what you must to appease your God before we enter Ophir, Island."

Isolde frowned and pulled away. "But … why?"

"Because the Scourge of Midnight is no friend to me, and a Holy Witness in all of this when he is trying to bury this information is going to make him … irritable."

Chapter 7

"Shut up, Owen!" Ygraine hissed at the boy next to her. She pulled the string back on the hunting bow and leveled it at her eye. Staring down the shaft, she lined it up with the antlered elk at the other end of the glade. She raised the level to account for distance and adjusted it to the right of the center to counter the cross breeze. The shaft loosed and flew toward the target.

The bull raised its head, alerting to something, shifting just enough that the spruce shaft missed the kill spot behind the front leg of the animal and embedded in the neck. It bellowed in pain and loped off, injured and bleeding.

A young boy snickered at the missed shot. "Told ya," he commented snidely.

Ygraine turned angry eyes at the younger figure and shoved the bow at him. "Well, I hope you are happy. It's wounded. Now we have to track it and put it down," she growled at him. Her unkempt mass of tangled curls danced in the breeze around her face as emerald green eyes glowered down at her younger sibling.

"Aww, come on, it's late, we could be out here for hours trying to find it …" the boy complained. He was a head shorter than Ygraine, and perhaps two years younger. His dishwater brown hair hung in greasy strands across his dark eyes.

"Should have thought about that before you decided to be an asshole," the girl quipped. She reached for a sharpened spear and started out after her quarry. "Come on," she told Owen. Her long legs made quick work of the distance between their place in the brush and where the elk had been shot. Owen trailed behind her, carrying the bow and an assortment of arrows and knives.

Ygraine knelt in the grass and searched the area, looking for signs of the injured animal. A pool of dark and wet colored the ground. She dipped her fingers in the warm liquid and raised it to examine it. It was bright red. She'd nicked an artery. This could be over quicker than she feared. She looked up from the hit site, eyes following the direction the bull had bolted off into. Thicket and hill.

Dammit.

Owen caught up to his sister, panting. He bent forward and rested his hands on his knees, then stood and stretched, trying to breathe. Ygraine looked up at him from her kneeling position, assessing his situation. He was never good at this.

That's why father sent him with you, Ygraine. He needs to learn. She scolded herself.

She held her fingers up to Owen. "What do you see?" she asked the younger boy.

Owen frowned and looked at Ygraine's blood and dirt-covered hand. "Uh … blood?" he replied, squinting at her fingers.

Ygraine sighed and shoved her hand at his face. "Color? Consistency?" she asked firmly.

Owen looked at it again. "Bright, uh … I dunno … thin? No bubbles … so … not lungs?" he asked.

She nodded and wiped her bloodied hand on her leather breeches and stood. She nodded toward the tree line. "He went that way. Arterial nick, could be over quick, could bleed out over the next couple of hours." She checked the weight on the spear and nodded. She looked down at her sibling. "Injured doesn't mean it's not dangerous …" she cautioned.

"I KNOW, Ygraine!" Owen huffed at her.

Ygraine pursed her lips and poked her finger into her brother's collar bone. "That animal is in pain, and wearing a rack of weapons that the gods granted it for its protection. It will not hesitate to take us with it before it dies. Remember that."

Owen scowled and nodded. "Fine."

Ygraine nodded and looked skyward. Dark clouds overhead obscured the sun. The smell of rain was in the air. They needed to find the bull before the weather shifted, or they would have to leave it for the other predators of the woods.

Unless it was already being hunted by one.

She frowned at the thought of losing her quarry to wolves or great bear, but either was always possible. She'd not seen signs of either in the area, so that was a small favor. However, if they could not find the animal before the storm let go, the whole of it would have to be relinquished to the land.

She looked around once more, noting the broken branches and scrub in the direction the bull had gone. Taking a breath, she gestured for Owen to stay behind her and keep his eyes and ears open for movement and sound. The younger boy nodded and followed as instructed. The pair slowly left the open glade and entered the shadows and close quarters of the thicket. Ygraine held the spear before her and at the ready. Her eyes searched the ground and the foliage for blood and the sign that the noble beast had broken through the area. Tufts of fur, blood, broken branches, pieces of bark pulled from trunks of trees – all signs of the passing of the injured creature. She followed them slowly, watching for the creature, both upright and fallen.

The sound of crashing branches ahead alerted her. She reached back and flagged Owen to drop to a knee. She lowered herself, to not draw as much attention to their location. Her bright eyes searched the area for movement. Something in the distance. Something large. It did not sound like the patter of hoofs on the ground. She frowned. Not looking at her brother, she gestured back to him with one hand, the sign for "caution" and "enemy". Owen watched her fingers, his brow furrowed. He nodded and rested his hand on his hunting blade.

They waited.

The strange crashing noise continued. It sounded like something struggling. Ygraine gestured for them to advance slowly. Low to the ground, crouched and slow, they crept forward toward the disturbance.

Shadows played in and around the trees. Dark pools of wet, like puddles of oil, seeped from the ground around trees that erupted from the soil. Branches reached toward the skies, arms and fingers grasping at the clouds above. Between the trees, the shape of an elk thrashed and pulled and gasped for air. Tendrils of wet shadow wrapped around the creature. It tried to bellow, but was silent.

Ygraine and Owen stopped their advance and stared in both disbelief and horror at the sight before them. The dark oil-like substance wrapped its shadowed tentacles around the bull and pulled it down. Ygraine had seen animals stuck in quicksand before and watched them pulled below the surface of an otherwise smooth pond. This was something very different.

A chill breeze blew through the trees, carrying with it the smell of carrion.

Owen's smaller hand found its way into Ygraine's. "Ygraine … I'm scared," the boy whispered.

The bull's antlered head turned then, dead eyes somehow searching the tree line for the sound of the voice. They seemed to fixate on the pair. A sickly glowing green light stared at them from the creature's dead orbs.

"Owen, run."

~ ~ ~

He hated Avalon. It was cold; it was wet, and its people eschewed the use of money for transactions. Accomplishing anything on the island Realm was next to impossible for someone who was not from their backward lands. Avalonians relied on the concept of honor and a good name to propel them forward in their society. A Lord who was responsible for the well-being of a dozen people who left them to the cold or to starve, while he and his family lived warm and healthy lives, would find his personal trade rights reduced in the local township until he corrected his ways. The local township would then take up the responsibility of caring for the Lord's mistreated people to ensure their well-being. Persons of faith enjoyed high levels of respect and honor in the society, for their calling served all persons of the Realm. Islanders seemed to eat, breathe, and sleep the ideals of altruism and service over personal gain. It was foreign and, to a merchant from the Mainland, almost painful.

For him to accomplish anything of true purpose here, he had to employ native people. Persons who would work for the currency of the Mainland and used their own goodwill and names to accomplish tasks for him. What these people did with the monies he funneled to them; he never knew. Perhaps they spent them on importing items from the Mainland to introduce to the trade here. Maybe they melted it down and decorated their armor for all he knew.

He sighed and glowered as his booted feet stepped off the gangplank and onto the dock of the port of Lubri. The single port city that made trade possible with the Mainland, Lubri, was the center of all commerce for the Island Realm of Avalon. Where Ophir was the Capital port of Setesh, and Port Kraken the grand port of the Mainland, Lubri dwarfed them both in size and scope. The grand city of Lubri spanned just shy of 25 leagues from gate to gate. Blue spires capped turrets of alabaster white on embattled walls that ran the length of the border of the city. Redbrick buildings mixed with smaller homes and businesses of limestone and thatch within those walls. Windows of colored and patterned glass looked out onto cobblestone streets. Tall posts crafted from worked iron stood on every corner, lamps hanging from hooks to provide light to travelers and residents alike. Soft blue light emanated from them, created by luminescent lichens that were grown and harvested for this sole purpose. He had made the mistake of asking about the possibility of acquiring the lichen for growth and cultivation on the Mainland. His trade contract for that season had been revoked.

Fecking fey-blooded freaks. He thought to himself.

As if on cue, a blue cloaked figure pushed themselves off of a pillar on the dock and stepped toward him.

"Master Arman?" the figure inquired.

Arman looked up at the figure who had addressed him. It was a young man … no … young elf; he corrected himself. The dark-haired youth stared at him from almond-shaped eyes the color of silver. Delicately pointed ear tips poked gently from his strands of spider-silk, fine hair. His clothes were clean and well pressed. Tan-colored pants, white shirt, and vest of cornflower blue. On the breast of his sea-blue cloak was embroidered the badge of the Trade Guild. The Vidria dwarf looked the boy up and down and then nodded.

"Aye."

The Elven boy nodded and smiled and extended his hand. "Lucan Paxton. Maitresse Lynet sent me to meet you and assist you in traveling to the Guild Hall." he looked past the dwarf at the ship. "You have a shipment that needs to be ferried to the Guild, sir?"

Arman took the boy's hand and shook it firmly. His eyes searched the boy's features and stance, assessing him for a moment. Smooth hands, skin free of wrinkles, smile lines or freckles, voice the timbre of youth just come to adulthood. This boy had only just earned his cloak and badge. What manner of honor could he carry here? Was Lynet slighting him?

Arman nodded. "Only a few things on this trip, Master Lucan," the merchant spoke. He nodded back to the ship. A handful of small crates and two chests were being unloaded. They all bore the same sigil stamped on their sides.

Lucan took a quick mental note of the items and nodded quickly. He smiled at the dwarf. "Of course, sir," he turned then and waved back down the dock and shouted a few words in his native tongue. Several other hands waved back at him and suddenly activity sprang up around them as people made their way up the docks to collect the marked crates and belongings and load them into a waiting cart.

These were activities that Arman would have expected to recompense with coin from his purse. Instinctively, he reached for his belt pouch. Lucan's silver eyes watched Arman's movement; the hint of a frown touched the boy's lips, but he said nothing. Arman's fingers stopped their habitual reach, and he looped his thumbs into his belt. He watched the actions of the group, nodding appreciatively.

"Excellent work, I knew the Guild could be counted on to handle this well!" Arman exclaimed, loud enough for several passersby to hear. They looked up, noted the workers and their task, and smiled warmly in recognition of their actions. Lucan's chest puffed up a little as he watched his team proudly.

Internally, Arman shook his head and scoffed at the Avalonians and their bizarre methods of trade and worth. How could praise and well wishes keep them warm at night?

The last of the goods was hefted into the cart. Workers waved at Lucan and dispersed to their next job. The Elven boy looked down at Arman and gestured to the cart.

"It's not much, but it will get us where we need to go. The Guild Hall is close to the docks after all," the boy offered. "Unless you would prefer to walk?" He smiled an open and honest smile.

Arman considered the offer and shook his head. "No, my boy, I'll take the offer of the ride, if that is all right? Still trying to get my land legs back," the dwarf nodded and walked toward the cart. Lucan fell into step beside him.

"Will you be with us long, Master Arman?" the boy asked.

"Oh well, that will all depend, my boy," Arman replied without answering.

"On?" Lucan inquired.

"Fate and the will of the Gods, Master Lucan."

Lucan's finely arched eyebrows raised in curiosity and surprise. "Indeed. Well, Master Arman, if we need to secure the services of an Oracle for you while you are here, please let us know."

They stopped at the side of the cart. Lucan pulled down a set of steps for the dwarf to step up to the buckboard seat next to the driver. Arman stepped up and sat firmly down on the padded seat next to another youth in the same blue-styled cloak.

"I will keep that in mind," Arman nodded in thanks and

Lucan departed to the rear of the cart to hop up onto the back with the gear. The driver looked over at Arman, smiled, nodded, and then turned their attention to the two draft horses hitched to the front of the cart. He clucked and snapped the reins. The cart lurched into motion.

God's teeth he hated Avalon.

Chapter 8

Temperatures in Setesh dropped quickly and sharply in the desert. Where it had been an almost blistering afternoon when they had headed out toward Ophir, the chill in the air was worthy of the Northern Reaches at home. The fire crackled, granting welcome warmth and light to the small encampment Safar had erected for them.

They were just two travelers on a speedy trip to the Capital from Deneb-aal. The trek would have typically taken three or four days by camel, but they bred korsers for speed and endurance in this environment. They had covered almost twice a camel's normal distance in a single day. There were larger waypoints for security and common rest areas along the route from Deneb-aal to Ophir. Places where caravans stopped for a break against the wind and sand, where small wells or pools of water offered sustenance from the bleakness of the desert. Safar knew these, even those often forgotten or used with rarity. He was a Reysis of the Sands, King and Commander of the Caravans. This was his home and his hearth.

The animals lowed and chuffed and chewed on their feed as they lay in the sand by the tent, legs and feet tucked beneath them to conserve body heat and moisture. Safar paced the outskirts of the encampment, pausing periodically to place a bare hand on the sand's surface. He closed his honey-gold eyes in thought and meditation, while Isolde watched him quietly. She prodded the fire absently while observing him with curiosity, trying to glean what he was trying to see.

The Reysis stood and brushed his hands off on pants and crossed to sit next to Isolde. He nodded to himself. He stared up at the sky for a moment and then off to the korsers, then took a breath and finally relaxed.

"Everything all right?" the woman beside him asked.

The dark-haired sand dancer nodded and pursed his lips. "Well enough," he commented.

"That is not reassuring, Safar," Isolde prodded.

He furrowed his brow in thought. "There are no immediate threats within the area," he offered.

"But …" she asked.

Safar shrugged. "It is the desert, Island. She is always unpredictable, always testing," he glanced over at the knight. "What is safe now may not be in two- or three-hours' time … it is the way of survival here," he replied in a matter-of-fact tone.

Isolde nodded. "Then you should get some rest now," she stated. Safar bristled at the comment; she held up a cautionary hand. "I know … Reysis," she said, using his honorific, "That I am your charge on this journey. However, we are only two people, and we will both need rest tonight." She met Safar's eyes with her own, those emerald green windows filled with equal parts strength and compassion. "I also know that we are both stubborn and neither of us is going to let this go easily."

Safar pursed his lips in displeasure at the observations. "I do not like it," he managed.

"I accept you do not care for the situation, but that does not change it, Safar," Isolde replied gently. She sighed and stabbed her fire poker into the sand and turned to face him. "You just assessed the area and determined there are no immediate threats, yes? Then now is the best time for you to rest and let me stand the watch," she reasoned. She reached over to place her hand on his forearm. "You have provided safety and security, my friend. Let me do this for you. You are not the only one with a duty to perform." she smiled gently at him. "I will wake you when Braag reaches his highest point," she looked into his eyes, "You have my word."

Safar glanced at her hand on his forearm and then up into her face. "Are you always so insufferably logical?" he asked with the hint of a smile on his lips.

Isolde thought about it for a moment, then squeezed his forearm. "If you asked Tulok ... only when I am not running headlong into trouble ... which is ... most of the time ... so ... I think that's a no," she smiled in reply.

The sand dancer chuckled at her response and nodded. He watched her for a moment and then placed his hand over hers on his arm. "Are you ready to see our friend tomorrow?" he asked her sincerely.

Isolde's brow furrowed, confused. "Should I not be?" she asked.

Safar maintained his contact with the Knight. "It has been some time, Island, and he has had ... many questions to answer ... and actions to account for," he added cautiously.

She frowned. "Is he unwell?" she inquired.

Safar shook his head. "Not that I am aware, no. But his people ... The Faithful of the Radiant Lord ... are demanding, Island ... and often ... unforgiving," he commented.

Isolde held Safar's gaze, assessing the man's comments and trying to find their meaning. She scowled a little and nodded. "I understand," concern danced behind her eyes for a moment, then its darkness was banished. She smiled warmly at Safar. "Then I shall simply have to assure them there is nothing of concern!" she beamed, once more filled with the almost endless sense of hope and optimism her Lord inspired.

Safar chuckled again and patted her hand. "If anyone can do so, it would be you," he squeezed her hand and released it, shifting to push himself to a standing position. He gazed skyward for a moment. "When Braag is at his zenith, yes?" he stated.

Isolde nodded. "Yes," she agreed and remained where she was, smiling up at the tall Sun Guide. "Rest well, my friend. I will guard your dreams."

Safar nodded and turned to walk to the small tent that had been erected as proof against the elements. He stopped and commented over his shoulder. "I still dislike this," he said firmly, and flung the tent flap open. He walked inside and pulled it closed behind him.

"I know," Isolde replied quietly, and snatched her fire poker from the sand. She pushed herself up from her position and shifted to place the fire behind her, so its light would not blind her in the darkness. It was too cold to wander too far from its light and warmth. Her eyes searched the dark horizon as she settled in to guard the sleep of the Reysis.

The Avalonian Knight lowered her chin to her chest for a moment and inhaled deeply through her nose and exhaled. Every true-born native of the Island Realm was inherently tied to the realm of Morpheum, the place of dreams. When the magics of the Founding Families saved Avalon from the Reaping of the Devourer, they carried not only the people but the lands as well. Legend told of ancient powers that bound the souls of the people to the land and the realms of dream. Others spoke of how Avalon was not a realm of the material world at all and was pulled out of the dreams of the many worlds and made manifest here. Whatever the truth of the matter, the connection to the realm of dreams was without dispute.

Bridges across the realms were not impossible this far from the Island, but they were harder to cross and harder to create. Regardless of these challenges, something had attempted to reach out to her earlier on the previous evening. Faithful of her Order were not given to nightmares. The Lord Wanderer granted protection to His followers from the creatures of that realm of dreams. The Landless Lord sought to inspire hope and courage in the world. Those creatures born of fear, doubt, and anxieties were all His enemies. Whether her dreams had been a misguided creature of nightmare, or a true vision of home, she was uncertain. Nonetheless, she would stand careful watch until better clarity was achieved.

She raised her chin and opened her eyes, searching the horizon with eyes trained to search for the beyond. The desert before her was empty. No strange paths or gateways stood in the sand that would lend access from the realm of dreams to the world of man. Nodding, Isolde stood and carefully scanned the surrounding area, waiting for anything out of the ordinary to alert her to its presence.

A familiar scent of wet leaves and moss wafted across the air. She shook her head to clear it. Despite the small wellspring they were camped next to, those scents should not be possible here. Her hand drifted to the hilt of her sword. She narrowed her eyes and slowly walked around the perimeter. Something was not right.

The korsers napped in the sand, leaning on one another for warmth. They did not alert. Whatever it was, it was not something they could sense.

Maybe it was nothing. She thought to herself, padding around the tent. She could hear Safar's rhythmic snoring. The Reysis had given himself to the realm of dreams already. For all of his resistance to her suggestion, he needed the rest. She smiled gently as she listened to his restful breathing. Isolde had been happy to give him the few hours of peace that he would need. She rounded the perimeter. There was nothing.

You are seeing things, Isolde. She chided herself as she took a breath and settled back down into her position of protection. She lay her sword across her lap, stretched her neck, and set her eyes on the horizon once more.

Her thoughts drifted to her dream of the previous night. An ancient tree. A group of bodies in deep mud. Rain. Lightning. The dwarven figure of the merchant, Arman, and the sacred scarab carved into the trunk of the tree. What did it mean? There had been light, a sickly green glow that seemed to bleed from the tree and into the ground.

The image felt familiar. Akin to another image that she and Tulok had seen once at the Temple of Ahsal. The Temple of Silence. The Faithful of the Everburning Lord had believed it was the cult of a rival deity, seeking to dethrone the patron of the skies. What they had found had been something very different. The image danced in Isolde's mind. A figure carved into the walls of someone bound in chains. Each chain led to a niche in the wall. Inside each niche had been ... something ... what was it? A jar? A vase? A container. There had been five such jars, one tucked into each niche. Five chains binding someone ... some ... thing.

What did the scarab have to do with it all?

Reynard the Swift – her knight, had died protecting Isolde from the power in the scarab. She remembered watching as the object seemed to desiccate his body before her very eyes. She had seen it do the same thing to the Folk Magistrate in Deneb-aal. It was like a spider, draining the blood from a fly.

Arman had captured Tulok and bound him in the depths of the Temple, stripping the orc priest of his reason, leaving him with nothing but rage and chaos to command. Neither Isolde nor Tulok had ever discovered the reasoning for this. They had figured out they wanted Tulok for some sort of sac-rifice that was to have taken place in that ancient space. Tulok had brought the Temple down upon itself before they could be successful, but questions remained. To whom was the Temple dedicated? And for what reason, why had they captured Tulok?

There had been more in that buried Temple. Stones that collected sound and could be triggered for explosives. Isolde had never seen their like before. They were beyond dangerous. Beyond this had been the single greatest heartache of the Wit-ness's life. The loss of an ancient map that depicted the settle-ments of the original founders of Sanctum. There had been cities, settlements, and geographical notations on that image that existed nowhere else. The destruction of that knowledge had almost broken Isolde. She had spent the last season re-creating every image that she could recall, hoping to preserve some of it. There was no way to reach a memory well on the Island to ensure the proper recording of the information, and there were no homely houses dedicated to her Lord here in Setesh. Safar had done the next best thing he could for her by ensuring she was able to visit the small shrine in Deneb-aal that she had dedicated when Raynard had died. It was not much, but it was something. Whispered words sent on the winds to her Lord's ears. Tales of glory and sacrifice, of lost history for Him to hear and know. It had also allowed her to wrap the drawings into a scroll case and ship them by courier to the Grand Temple in Port Kraken. They would be cared for there. It had taken the last of her coin to ensure their delivery.

What of this information was it that Tulok's people wished so desperately to keep silent? The figure? The stones? The map? Part of this? All of this? Whatever it was, both Safar and Tulok had worked together to ensure she had not been forced to vow silence once more on this matter. Her calling was to bear Witness to the World for her Wandering Lord. To force silence upon a Holy Witness would be the gravest of injuries she could endure. She carried a shared vow already with Tulok. She had vowed to not speak of the location of Ahsal to anyone but the Wandering Lord, but in exchange, Tulok had vowed not to reveal that the legends of the blood ties of the Avalonians to their land were real. A secret for a secret.

She paused in her thoughts and glanced back over her shoulder at the tent where Safar slept. The protection of the Reysis had not gone unnoticed by her. Safar was a man of great respect in the sands of Setesh. His words carried weight here, and his reach was far. He was a man whose god had also blessed him with an extended life span.

How long? How much of this information did you already have, Safar? How long have you been watching over Ahsal and what it contains? Isolde wondered.

And why permit me to record it with my Lord if you need to keep it secret?

A sense of warmth and security pressed against Isolde's back for a moment. The feeling that Her Lord was listening and standing with her on this cold and dark evening. She sat up a little taller, stretching her neck from side to side. Her hand grasped the hilt of her sword, and her eyes focused on the horizon once more.

You already know the answer to that question.

Chapter 9

The City of Ophir was the Capital of Setesh. Here all trade began and ended. Caravans by land arrived and departed daily. Here, too, was the only port for the entire northern section of the Realm. While no trade from Ophir traveled across the ocean to Avalon, ships skirted the coastline and traveled north to the trade capital of Port Kraken. With those ships came people, trade goods, and information.

Buildings pressed tightly against one another like sandstone-colored walls with decorative windows. Brightly colored fabrics hung from windows and eves, some serving as canopies stretched from rooftop to rooftop. Decorative lanterns of colored glass lit the city against the darkness of the night, giving the city a feeling of warmth and welcome. Unlike the river city of Nahral, travel on the hard-packed clay streets of Ophir was all by foot, carriage, or camel.

Tulok had volunteered for patrol every day since his arrival in Ophir. He felt it was a duty and obligation, regardless of position. Walking patrol for the Watch was more than simply pacing the courtyard of the Grand Temple. Patrol typically comprised two to three priests, or a Devout Champion acting as third. It was an exercise not only in maintaining order but in demonstrating a show of presence to the people of Ophir. Several teams were assigned at sunset and given specific parts of the city as their designated watch for the evening. They would return at mid-evening to change out with another team who would finish out the night watch in that same sector. When the young acolyte had knocked on Tulok's door shortly before sunset to advise him he was on rotation tonight, he had been filled with both excitement and regret. He was excited about finally being able to perform this sacred duty, and regretful not being able to spend his hours in the Library. Despite his burly and massive build, Father Tulok loathed combat and preferred the gentler duties of a scholar. The change of pace meant that perhaps he was finally being accepted here. He smiled to himself as he tugged at his weapon harness and checked the great mace that hung from his side. Armed and armored, Father Tulok was an impressive and often terrifying visage. He stood easily a head taller than most men, his shoulders and figure bore the powerful cut of the Orcish people. White and gold robes of the Temple draped over his full suit of armor. He looked like an image taken from ancient heroic tales told around the fire. Heads turned and eyes widened as onlookers passed by in the courtyard. Faithful and visitors alike were both shocked and surprised at such a sight.

"Well, you – are – an impressive visage, Father," the even tones of Ser Ahsom Ibris spoke from behind him. "I had heard the descriptions but, I confess, they do not do you justice."

Tulok cleared his throat uncomfortably at the observation. "Ahem. I ... thank you, Ser," he replied politely.

Ibris stepped around from behind the giant of a priest and looked him up and down with the trained eye of a military commander. He nodded. "Good." He reached out and tugged on one pauldron to straighten it ever so slightly. "Better."

Tulok stood rigid and still while the Champion inspected him.

"All right, we've got the Merchant Quarter and the Sun Guide Guild," he stated, and turned on his heel, headed for the gate.

Tulok blinked, confused, then took a couple of broad steps to catch up with him. "Ser?" he looked around. "Don't we have another member to wait on?" he asked.

Ibris shook his head. "No. You are more than enough of a visual statement to the populace, Father. We can make do."

Tulok frowned. "Of ... course ...," he offered cautiously.

Faithful turned and inclined their heads in respect as the Champion and his orc companion passed by. Tulok watched each of them, noting faces and placing names where he could. Ibris walked slightly ahead of him, head held high, shoulders back, a presence that commanded attention.

"Forgive the question, Ser …," Tulok began, "but … do you often walk the night patrol?" he asked.

A slight smile tugged at the right corner of Ibris' mouth. "No, Father. I do not," was the reply.

"I … see."

Ibris stopped at the top of the steps that led down from the Temple into the city streets below. He gazed out across the city as if taking everything in and either analyzing it or cataloging it for future use. His eyes landed on something only he could know in the distance. He nodded to himself and started down the steps at a quick clip.

Tulok followed the smaller Elven knight in his direction. It was easy enough for him to keep up with Ibris, as his stride was almost twice the knight. The press of persons on the street parted before them in silent amazement and awe. Eyes focused on both the beautiful Elven Champion of the Temple and the enormous priest at his side. Tulok continued to watch the actions and observations of the crowd as they passed through. Slowly, realization dawned upon him.

"We are making a statement?" he asked quietly of Ibris.

Ibris' countenance did not falter as he continued apace. "Mmm-hrmmm," he replied.

Tulok took a deep breath and stood up a little taller, his figure becoming a little more imposing as he walked. Ibris nodded almost imperceptibly at his side.

As the pair passed, whispered voices followed them. Prayers to the Lord of Light, quiet blessings, soft words of reverence spread throughout the crowd. Here and there, furtive characters with ill intent on their minds stepped deeper into the shadows, having no desire to draw the attention of the Champion and the Priest. Fingers that might have lifted a purse paused and reconsidered their actions, if only for a moment.

Tulok learned early in his youth that the best way to drive

off unwanted attention was to carry oneself as one who knew the streets as if born to them. Even when uncertain of direction or location, one took care not to display that information in public view. So he walked in relative silence at the Champion's elbow, allowing him to thread their way through the throngs of people in the populated streets and squares.

"Brother Kalb's family is pressing for justice for the death of their son," Ibris spoke gently.

A cloud of discontent colored Tulok's red eyes. He felt his Gurkh rise momentarily, a soft rumble in his chest, seeking to battle the challenge. He swallowed it down.

"Center, Father," Ibris cautioned quietly. "We walk the square tonight to demonstrate the Temple supports you."

Tulok pursed his lips and frowned. Ibris cleared his throat. Tulok's countenance returned to one of passive protector.

"They want the body of Bengt Kalb recovered from the deserts for interment."

Tulok sighed deeply. "And they do not understand ...,"

"If they understand ... they do not care," Ibris replied. His eyes watched the crowd for a moment and he turned – taking them down another street. The crowd parted once more for them. Ahead Tulok could see the main merchant square where all caravans signed in and out of the city. They set merchant stalls up around the square that spanned a hundred feet on the side. In the center of the square was a large fountain. Ten feet tall on a side, the square edifice was crafted from multicolored mosaic tiles that depicted various scenes of historic figures from the foundation of Setesh. Water flowed from the top of the square pillar and down the sides of the tiles, where it pooled in a raised trough wide enough for one to dip a cup or a water vessel. Along the trough, long, smooth figures of crocodiles adorned the water's edge. Standing atop the fountain was an elegantly crafted golden statue of a woman, her hands outstretched and her face turned upward toward the sky. Visitors to the market square stopped at the fountain, taking the gift of life from its bounty.

Ibris walked them both up to the fountain's edge, ensuring they were both visible to all people in the square. His sea-colored eyes scoured the people of the market, never stopping on any of them for too long. Tulok stood beside him, back to the fountain, arms folded across his wide chest.

A group of children gathered several paces away from the pair, each whispering and looking over at them. Finally, one of the older boys shoved a smaller girl toward Ibris and Tulok. She stumbled forward slightly. Instinctively, Tulok quickly knelt down – holding out his hand to catch the small child from falling face-first in the middle of the square. A shared gasp was heard from the crowd as the giant of a priest carefully helped her to her feet and, with delicate fingers, brushed off her tunic. Her rag doll had fallen from her grip when she stumbled. Tulok reached to pick up the helpless toy and offered it to the child. She stood there for a moment and then accepted her doll.

"Are you all right, child?" the orc inquired softly.

Wide eyes stared back at him. She nodded slowly. "Umm … Father …?" she asked.

"Yes, my dear?" Tulok replied.

The girl held out her doll to the big man. "Will you bless my dolly? She gets scared at night," the little girl stammered.

Tulok smiled gently, placing his hand right hand on the doll, and his left hand over the large ornate medallion hanging from his neck. The Everwatchful Eye of the Lord of the Heavens stared out at the world.

"Lord of the Sky, Keeper of Light, whose Everwatchful Presence brings life to this world – bless this creature of cloth and sand, that it may feel the warmth of your embrace and know the safety of thy merciful gaze," he intoned reverently. Then he lifted his hand from the doll and lightly touched the little girl's nose with his forefinger and winked at her.

The little girl's eyes widened even bigger than they had been. She pulled her doll back and clutched it fast against her chest. She smiled brightly up at the tall orc. "Thank you!" she beamed and backed away, turning back to the group of children and joining them. They swarmed her, each reaching to touch the doll and look back at Tulok.

Ibris maintained his position and did not move while all of this took place. "You are very good with them," he commented as he watched the crowd. The eyes of adults had slowly turned in their direction in greater numbers.

Tulok remained in his kneeling position, watching the children. "Tarf-qua is an orphanage, Ser Ibris," he replied. "I helped raise many children in my time of service there." He nodded at the children, who all turned and dashed off to parts unknown. Tulok slowly stood back up and brushed off his knees.

Ibris nodded in satisfaction. "So I recall reading," he commented.

Tulok glanced down at the Elven knight but said nothing.

Ibris nodded toward one building across the square. Three stories tall and painted alabaster white, lighted multicolor windows showed invitingly from each floor. The door stood open onto the market square. Many people clad in caravan robes and decorative headscarves stood under the eaves of the porch. A large wooden sign hung above the door; an ornate and embellished sun, upon which was painted a large black scorpion. It seemed to glitter in the fading light. Tulok's eyes followed Ibris'. He raised his right eyebrow in curiosity.

"We are expecting a message from Sister Leralyn's favorite person," Ibris replied.

A man in sand-colored robes, trimmed in blue and gold, sighted the pair by the fountain. He touched his forehead and bowed his head respectfully.

Tulok looked over at Ibris. "Safar?" he asked.

"The same," the knight replied and headed toward the building. Tulok followed suit, watching the crowd around them and the group by the door.

This was the Sun Guide's Guild and, if Leralyn's words had any truth to them, most of the Guides were Sand Dancers related to Reysis Safar in one fashion or another. Tulok had a good relationship with the handsome and enigmatic Sand Dancer. However, Safar's relationship with the Temple of the Everburning Sun left something to be desired.

"Is everything all right?" the big priest asked, concern flavoring his tone.

The pair approached the Guild Hall. Men and women dressed and adorned in the colorful markings of the Reysis and Sun Guides turned, trained eyes on them, sizing them up. Several of the women and two men leaned in to comment to one another and then smiled wide smiles as they approached. Tulok could see Safar's smile lines on their faces. Other men tugged at close-cropped beards in thought and assessment, gestures all too familiar to the big priest.

Ibris nodded to them all as he approached and headed for the open door.

"I suppose we should find out."

Chapter 10

The Guild Hall of the Sun Guides was more than a simple meeting place for organization; the building was an extension of the community. Tables in one corner were set up with men and women discussing and organizing caravans on both local and extended routes. They tacked contracts up in an orderly fashion labeling location, destinations, cargo, travelers, expected duration, and terms of payment. An older man and a younger woman stood behind the tables discussing, and occasionally arguing, with the various Guides who came to turn in their contracts for recompense and to sign on for additional work.

A long bar stretched the length of one side of the building. Two women and one man, all dressed in caravan gear, manned the taps and bottles. The smell of spiced meats wafted in the air from the kitchen. A plump older matriarch and a strong-looking man with a neatly trimmed dark mustache were visible through an open serving window. They talked loudly to one another, gesturing broadly and speaking in the language of the Sand Dancers.

Tall tables and chairs were scattered throughout the room, as well as low tables with cushions. Guides, Scouts, and other Reysis populated the room, each occupying places of rest and conversation. Some were engaged in games of chance or strategy. Children danced and played at a hearth while adults clucked at them and gave them gentle instruction or reprimand. Throughout the building, carved into the trim or adorning brass lanterns, were figures of small scorpions. Hanging over the hearth was an elegantly woven tapestry depicting a golden sun upon which was woven a large black scorpion.

Double doors in the back of the hall seemed to lead to a private meeting area. Stairs led to a second floor above the meeting hall. This was not merely a place of business. This was a gathering of family. As he stepped across the threshold and took in the ambiance of the Hall, Tulok smiled a little.

Conversations dropped notably as the Devout Champion and the Priest of the Radiant Lord stepped inside the Hall. Various people glanced up from their conversations and activities to note the newcomers. Some quickly nodded in acknowledgment and respect before returning to their activities, while others continued to stare and assess the pair for threat or welcome. Suddenly the plump matriarchal figure from the kitchen clapped her hands together loudly and directed the serving staff. Her male counterpart smiled widely at Ibris and Tulok and moved to exit the kitchen and step out onto the main floor.

"Welcome, Welcome!" he called out to them as he finished wiping his hands on a wide apron tied around his waist. He waved them both in. "I am Kefu, once Reysis of the Eastern Sands, now Keeper of this Hall and its occupants. The Radiant Lord honors this House with His presence on this night!" Kefu opened his arms wide to welcome them. Several of the occupants tapped the edges of their tables in acknowledgment of the proclamation.

Ahsom Ibris stood as tall as his lithe Elven frame permitted, his shoulders back and head high, as the honor was bestowed upon them. He inclined his head respectfully to Kefu and lifted his right hand to his chest. He tapped his heart twice. "The Radiant Lord thanks those pledged to the safety of the sands for their welcome and hospitality on this evening. All honor be due to the Lady of the Beautiful Tent," he spoke formally.

Once again, hands tapped edges of tables, and heads nodded in satisfaction and acceptance. Kefu's eyes brightened at the mention of the patron of the Guild. He nodded, and the smile on his face relaxed into something more earnest and less rehearsed. He gestured for the pair to join him.

The Lady of the Beautiful Tent was another name for

She who Opens and Closes the Throat. The keeper of poison and perfection. The Healer. The Lady was a patron of the sands. Where the Changebringer brought storms of sand, The Lady brought life-giving rain. Where the Radiant Lord's gaze brought testing and firm judgment, the Lady's embrace brought relief and release. To Her was given the weight of both bountiful life and painful death, each in equal measure. Without Her gentle compassion, caravans would lose themselves in the Seteshi Sands. Absent Her command of nature's poisons, the medicinals needed to provide the healing arts would have nothing to be tested and proved against. The Radiant Lord brought a challenge to the physical form and tested the will of the people. The Lady brought compassion and tested their hearts. Reysis of Setesh paid homage to The Lady, for, without Her, the ferocity of the Everburning Lord would destroy these lands and its people.

Kefu nodded to Ibris and welcomed the pair as they stepped across the room. The women behind the bar observed them. The tall man working with them leaned in and whispered something to the women. They turned, eyes filled with confusion and disbelief on him. He nodded and gestured with his chin in Ibris and Tulok's direction. They all turned their attention back to the pair once more, with additional interest. Whispered voices followed in their wake as onlookers continued to assess them from their tables. An older man, his dark skin creased with age, and once dark beard now feathered with silver-gray, dressed in the blues and golds of a Reysis, stroked his chin thoughtfully as his honey-gold eyes watched them with interest. Keeper Kefu turned and walked toward the back of the Hall to the double doors. Ibris and Tulok walked quietly behind him. The orc priest nodded respectfully as he passed them all. Many of those gathered in the Hall nodded back to him appreciatively.

The pair behind the contracting tables at the far end of the hall held up their hands to stop the conversation as the Keeper and his guests approached the double doors at the rear of the Guild Hall. Negotiations ceased. Kefu turned to them and spoke in the tongue of the Sand Dancers.

"See that we are not disturbed."

The woman nodded her head in acknowledgment. "Of course, Father," she intoned politely. The older man at her side folded his arms across his chest and scowled a little. "As you wish, Keeper."

Kefu frowned at the other man, noting his stance and position. "Do we have an issue, brother?" he asked.

The other man sucked on his teeth for a moment and then shook his head. "No issue. Lady's grace be with you."

Kefu nodded and reached for the doors. "Come. Reysis Safar sends word that is for your ears alone on this night," he spoke quietly and opened the doors. They slid open and recessed into the wall.

The room beyond was smaller than the hall, but elegantly attired. A large low table sat in the middle of the room, surrounded by cushions, low chairs, and a settee. Tulok and Ibris followed behind Kefu as the woman at the tables closed the doors behind them. Conversation levels returned to their previous sounds as she did so.

"Please, be comfortable," Kefu gestured to the table, then paused and looked over at both Ibris and Tulok, noting their armored attire. He pursed his lips in thought. "Perhaps we stand?" he offered with a slightly embarrassed smile.

Ibris held up a hand. "It is no worry, Keeper Kefu. Your hospitality is noted and welcome," he offered politely.

Tulok inclined his head from his great height. "The Radiant Lord thanks the Lady of the Beautiful Tent for Her offer of hospitality and accommodation," he intoned reverently, then added, "and Her understanding ..." He cleared his throat a little uncomfortably.

Kefu looked over and up at the orc priest and then chuckled and nodded. "Yes, yes, let us dispatch with the formalities," He gestured at the table. "The seating is designed for formal negotiations for those wearing city or caravan gear, not intended for those wearing battle gear. I have no desire to create discomfort for my guests. I can have taller chairs or stools provided?" he asked in warm earnest.

Ibris steepled his fingers and rested his arms against his torso in a position of practiced rest in armor, but said nothing.

"We still have patrol yet tonight, Keeper Kefu; but with your permission, I would enjoy returning on a later night to enjoy the hospitality of your Hall?" the big priest offered.

Kefu nodded then and smiled. "Yes, this is good! I accept!"

Tulok offered as much of a smile as his orcish mouth allowed and nodded.

Ibris sniffed simply, "What message does Reysis Safar have that needed to be delivered in this fashion and not simply sent to the Temple?" the Champion asked.

The smile on Kefu's face faded. "As you wish," he replied. He reached into the pocket of his apron and pulled out a small slip of paper. Tulok recognized it immediately. A hawk had delivered it. Kefu handed the paper to Tulok, his eyes on Ibris.

Tulok unrolled the small scrap of paper and read as Kefu continued to speak.

"Reysis Safar al-Shifa will arrive in Ophir tomorrow, ahead of his caravan."

Ibris' right eyebrow twitched slightly, "Ahead of his caravan?"

Kefu continued, "He brings with him the Holy Witness of the Lord Wanderer – Isolde duAvalonne," Kefu watched between the two. Tulok continued reading the small scrap of paper, his brow furrowed in concern and thought both. "Reysis Safar al-Shifa wishes the Radiant Lord to know that the Holy Witness is formally under the sponsorship and protection of The Lady of The Beautiful Tent, and she will not be remanded to the custody or care of the Temple of The Radiant Lord while she is in Ophir."

Ahsom Ibris pursed his perfect lips. His right eyebrow twitched slightly. A dozen unspoken thoughts danced behind his sea-colored eyes in a matter of seconds. He tapped his thumbs together in quiet thought as Tulok finished reading the missive and carefully rolled it back up. The orc glanced down at the elf and then slowly folded his hands in front of himself and lowered his eyes and chin. Staring at his booted feet, he chewed on his lip in silence, contemplating the meaning of the statement and its implications; to both Isolde and the relationship between the Temple and The Lady.

In the ranks of the Faithful of the Everburning Lord, the Champions were both the strong right arm and the diplomatic arm of the Temple. Priests were charged with overseeing both the devout and the intelligence of the Order. When a matter of high diplomacy was at hand, they were often paired together to ensure all avenues and situations were covered. Tulok's mind raced, playing out the various scenarios that Ibris would be suggesting. None of which would work on the Sand Dancer that was his friend.

"I ... see," the Elven Champion finally managed. He nodded his head and continued without looking up at Tulok. "You know the Reysis, Father, yes?" he asked.

Tulok nodded quietly. "I do."

"What do you think if we suggest ..."

"No." Tulok shook his head, cutting Ibris off.

Ibris nodded. "Hmm. What about offering ..."

"Absolutely not," Tulok countered, shaking his head again.

"I see. And then ..."

"Won't work on Safar," the orc countered once more.

Ibris scowled slightly, pondering his options. He opened his mouth, paused, and closed it once more. He continued in contemplation, then started again, "If we offered the Witness ..."

Tulok shook his head. "That would be worse. She has her own Oaths to maintain, and she's Avalonian."

Ibris pursed his lips again. "Mmm, yes, of course, " He looked up at Kefu then. He cleared his throat and inclined his head politely. "The Temple of the Radiant Lord understands and acknowledges the protections offered by The Lady of the Beautiful Tent, and will respect the wishes of Reysis Safar al-

Shifa in this matter." the tone was filled with neutral flavors of formality.

Kefu smiled once more and looked between the two members of the Temple, a small smile of satisfaction on his bronzed face. "Excellent! We have an understanding then!" he nodded at them both.

Ibris continued to hold Kefu's gaze as he spoke. "What else did the esteemed Reysis have to say in his missive, Father?" he asked.

Tulok chewed absently on his upper lip for a moment and then cleared his throat and raised his head. "The Witness has been visited by visions which the Reysis believes are of dire enough import to separate him from his caravan and bring her here with some immediacy," the big priest replied.

Ibris' stoic mask broke for the briefest of moments, as his eyes darted upwards toward Tulok. He blinked and then recovered his demeanor. "I ... hrmmm. Noted," he offered. Thoughts once more danced behind his almond-shaped eyes. He looked at Kefu and inclined his head. "The Temple thanks The Lady for Her due diligence in this matter. We will send someone to meet with the Reysis and the Witness tomorrow evening then?"

Kefu's smile was broad. "We will look forward to entertaining you!"

Chapter 11

It had been two hours since Arman had left his name with the Herald of the Guild Hall to announce to Maitresse Lynet that he had arrived as agreed. Two hours of staring at master-crafted woodwork, statuary, and paintings. Two hours of politely nodding and smiling to the dozens of other people who came and went from the Hall as he waited his turn. Not being of Avalon, Arman had no leug upon which to base his place in society. The courtly affairs of the Realm of Avalon matched and possibly surpassed the pomp and ceremony of the Grand Temple of the Radiant Lord in Ophir.

He was a master artisan in his own right of Vidria glass and cartography, but these were recognized in the Halls on the Mainland. There was polite respect for fellow artisans, but rankings and titles did not always travel across the dead sea that separated the Mainland from the Island Realm. While the general people of the Island Realm observed common courtesies in their day-to-day lives, formal proceedings often occupied the better part of one's personal day. Appointments were a necessity if one wished to be afforded dedicated time and attention. Arriving unannounced and expecting an audience with any ruling body of the Island was laughable.

It was a bittersweet situation that Arman found himself in. On the one hand, his rank and privilege, along with his personal fortune, had afforded him a place of comfort in Setesh. But with that comfort came name recognition, something he hoped to avoid at present. Word had reached his ears that both the orc priest Tulok and the Wandering Knight Isolde duAvalonne had survived the cave-in at Ahsal. Reysis Safar al-Shifa had not perished at the poisoned barbs of the giant emperor scorpion that had pulled him beneath the bloodied sands. It should not have surprised Arman to learn this, given the lineage of the Reysis. The man seemed practically unkillable.

Earning the ire of one of these persons would have been easy to navigate; but because of a series of truly unfortunate circumstances, all three still lived and would not be pleased to discover that he had survived the loss of the Temple of Silence. Safar was not known to wander far from his precious desert, so that was something that Arman counted in his favor. Father Tulok had been a Librarian and leader of the small Temple in Tarf-qua, a homebody of a priest if there ever was one. It would take a great deal of inspiration to motivate him to leave the Seteshi sands, even in pursuit of the man who had helped to take him captive. The Wandering Knight, however ... she was the one wild card in the whole of it that Arman could not pin down. She had survived an attack by a giant scorpion in the desert, a direct attack in the streets of Nahral, being knocked overboard and into the Iteru river at the mercy of The Confessor Crocodile, and been saved from the Crossroads by the will of the Radiant Lord Himself. Arman swore quietly. Was she fate blessed then?

Oh, how he hated the Danuae and the magic that danced in their blood.

Yet, despite his dislike for the people of the Island Realm, he still needed something from them. Trademaster Lynet was the only person in Lubri who could provide him with the travel permits and information that he needed as a foreigner. He had been happy to supply the Trademaster with her favorite spices and teas from the Mainland for years. He also sent word ahead of other shipments of items that would be rare commodities on the Island, to give Lynet a leg up on any of the other trades seeking access to the same. Coin of the Realm may not have value on the Island, but information was still valued.

A throat cleared itself behind him. Arman blinked and turned to face its owner.

A small man, roughly the same height as Arman, greeted

his gaze. He was Folk, a member of the race of people that The Mother Herself had crafted from the clay of Avalon after escaping The Reaping. Helpers and healers, they were birthed to be the hands of the Mother in the new world.

Vidria dwarfs were often confused for Folk. Both were of similar size and stature. Both tended toward crafts involving their hands, working with people, or mercantile trades. The Folk were born of the clay of Avalon; the Vidria, however, were born of the sands of Setesh. Other dwarven people of Sanctum often refused to claim these sand shapers as their kith and kin, despite any similarities in speech or culture. Unlike their other dwarven cousins, Vidria were beardless. This trait was not merely a cultural choice but by Divine design; Vidria dwarfs were incapable of growing facial hair. It was for this reason that many of their people were often confused with Folk. No one knew for certain what Divine claimed the creation of the beardless dwarven sandshapers of the Setesh. There were rumors and stories, of course, but nothing in any living memory that could be confirmed.

One fact that rang true was both were among the few races on Sanctum that could truly claim this world as their home.

Arman and the Herald stood, examining each other quietly for a few moments.

Arman Dah'ay was young looking for his age. His features were strong and well-defined. Broad-shouldered and narrow hipped, he cut a handsome and notable figure. Short-cropped reddish-brown hair topped his head. His eyebrows were curved upward ever so slightly. Whether they were naturally this way or the Vidria styled them so was unknown. A smattering of freckles danced across the bridge of his nose and cheeks. Clever and alert steel-blue eyes met and held the eyes of the other man. Arman stood a little straighter in his burgundy-colored, high collared velvet jacket and dark brown trousers. He tugged at the hem of his cream and gold brocade waistcoat.

The Herald was of undetermined age, clothed in the blues and tans of the Guild Hall. His dark brown hair was worn in a way that made tousled curls fashionable. His chestnut brown eyes were wide and warm, filled with welcome, set in skin the color of deep mahogany. The Herald's white shirt was crisp and clean, and it accented his cornflower blue jerkin with elegant embroidered flowers in indigo and gold. On the breast of this finely crafted vest was the sigil of the Herald of the Hall. He examined Arman with the trained eye for criticism and critique; assessing and weighing the worth of the foreigner silently.

"Master Arman?" the Herald asked politely.

Arman nodded and returned the smile. "Indeed, Master Herald," he replied formally.

The Herald inclined his head politely and gestured that Arman should follow him. "Maitresse Lynet has just concluded her daily obligations with the resident Guildmasters and has made time in her schedule for you. I have taken the liberty of clearing the rest of her meetings for the afternoon so that you may meet at your leisure." The right side of the Herald's mouth twitched upward ever so slightly.

Arman nodded in simple thanks, careful not to comment. The Herald of the Hall controlled all the activities of the Trademaster and the schedules for the Hall itself. They maintained the measure of leug for the attendees and ensuring everyone was accommodated according to their station. Without the permission and grace of the Herald of the Hall, no one entered the Hall's meeting areas or offices. Running afoul of the Herald would cause social chastisement and a degrading of leug in the public eye. He was gracious, precise, and deadly.

They approached the elegantly carved door to the Trademaster's private offices. It was a massive thing, hand-carved from what appeared to be solid oak, that had been stained to match the dark wood of the chairs in the waiting area. Into the wooden surface was carved the symbol of the TradesGuild; a wide, round wheel, in the center of which several tools crossed upon another to form a sort of eight-pointed star. The Herald stood at the door and stepped to the side. He reached out, rapped three times, and then opened the door by some unseen latching mechanism, pushing it in.

Arman inclined his head in thanks once more.

"Master Arman Dah'ay, of the Vidria, of the Realm Setesh, Master of the Arts Cartography and Sandshaper," the Herald announced Arman to the occupant of the other room.

"Hello Arman," a sultry voice greeted him.

Arman smiled, bowed deeply, and stepped through the doorway.

"Trademaster."

The door closed softly and silently behind him.

He hated Avalon.

~ ~ ~

"That arrogant ass!" Sister Leralyn swore.

Tulok's eyebrows rose into his non-existent hairline at the gnomish Librarian's response. Opposite him, Ahsom Ibris sat comfortably at one of the long tables in the Library. The Champion chuckled a little at the gnome's response and moved a random piece of parchment back and forth on the table.

Leralyn huffed at Ibris. "Fine, you laugh. It has been the tolerance of that man's actions that afford him the ability to behave as he does!"

Ibris' eyes slid over to Leralyn. "You know that is not true, Leralyn," the Elven knight cautioned.

The Librarian threw her arms into the air in exasperation, turned, and walked away – her backward bending stilts bouncing her along her way.

Tulok stood quietly at the end of the table, his arms folded across his wide chest. He chewed on his upper lip in absent thought. His dark eyes drifted over to Ibris. "If I may ask?" he began quietly. "What ... precisely ... has the Reysis done that bothers her so?"

Ibris looked up at the orc priest and then down the long hall of the Library. Leralyn had secluded herself in the stacks of scrolls on the left-hand side of the shelves. He tapped at the parchment before him, considering his words. He sniffed and pursed his lips in thought.

"The Reysis …," he began carefully, "takes his duties to The Lady of the Beautiful Tent … seriously," he replied, his eyes on his hand and the parchment.

Tulok shrugged. "He is a devout follower. The Healer is a needed and welcome balance in the desert. Where is the harm?" he asked.

Ibris shifted the parchment under his fingertips again. "The Lady is not merely a Healer, Father," Ibris offered carefully as he glanced up at the big priest from his seated position.

Tulok frowned slightly. The Lady of the Beautiful Tent held a place of hallowed esteem in the pantheon of Setesh. She was a Healer and Lifegiver. What could be the issue … he paused and looked at Ibris. "The Lifegiver?" he asked softly.

Ibris shrugged and continued to shift the paper back and forth. "The Reaping was not kind to many races, Father. The gnomish people were not a … prolific … people, to begin with."

Tulok took a deep breath and nodded. His gaze followed down to the end of the hall where Leralyn continued to shift and sort scrolls. Several clans of gnome had been saved from the Reaping and brought to Sanctum by a variety of Divine. The relocation of their people had not always proven fruitful, and their numbers had not flourished as greatly as many others.

"The Lady has not been kind to Leralyn's people in this," Tulok agreed.

"The Reysis flaunting the … benefits … of his lineage has not helped," Ibris replied.

Tulok scowled and looked down at Ahsom Ibris. "Forgive me, Ser, but … you have both referred to Reysis Safar's lineage several times now, as if his parentage has some bearing on how he needs to be treated. Is he descended from some Royal Family somewhere that I need to be aware of?" the orc priest asked plainly.

Ibris ceased moving the parchment on the table and looked up directly into Tulok's eyes. "You mean to tell me that, for as well as you know the man, he never once told you?"

Tulok shrugged and shook his head. "Told me what?"

"Reysis Safar al-Shifa is The Lady's only son."

Chapter 12

Isolde's first visit to Ophir had been almost two seasons earlier, upon her return from Ahsal. She had convalesced in the back of a sand sled along the route from Kef-aal in the company of Safar and his caravan as they made their way north. . The trip from the coastal city had taken almost three weeks' time. Her health had recovered appreciably, and she had visited a few of the locations in the Capital City before, once more, having to depart to Tarf-qua and her Oathbound duty there. The most important of these obligations had been the small shrine to The Landless Lord that lay in the less-traveled section of the City. The Lord Wanderer's Faithful had not made their presence known in a permanent fashion in Setesh; there was no formal place of gathering for those seeking solace or support. No Well of Memory existed here for Wanderers or the people to tell stories to, hoping The Wanderer would hear them and they would be recorded.

That same small shrine sat in a narrow section of an older mercantile area of the City that overlooked the harbor. A miniature building, crafted in the ornate style of Avalonian architecture, sat atop a three-foot-tall brick pedestal. It was painted in the blue and white scheme of the Island Realm's capital city. Someone had inset tiny windows into the miniature building, mimicking stained glass. It was in perfect scale and seemed suited for dolls. At the right time of day, the windows caught the sun's light and illuminated the shrine as if from the heavens themselves. No one remembered who commissioned or built the shrine but, as it was dedicated to a member of the Divine Host, members of this section of the City maintained it. While the Wanderer was a foreigner in the lands of Setesh,

He was still Divine, and the Divinity of Sanctum were very real and very capable of making their displeasure known if someone toppled even this small place of worship.

They had tied decorative scraps of fabric to sections of the shrine with words and symbols written on them. Each section of cloth contained snippets of stories that visitors had brought to share, prayers of goodwill to those off on exploration, or requests against the creatures of the nightmare realm. Isolde smiled to see the small shrine once more. She pulled her gloves off and quickly brushed the pedestal free of fallen palm fronds and sand. She chewed her bottom lip and stared at the small building, memories of the Island coming back to her. They were bittersweet.

"Hello, My Lord," she spoke in the language of her people. She stepped up and placed her hands on either side of the pedestal and stared out over the shrine at the ocean harbor beyond. "I have so much to tell you, and no well of memory to leave my stories in." She looked at the scraps of fabric that decorated the small house. "But these too are important for you to hear, and have been here far longer. Please take these tales and prayers to your ear and to your heart, that they may be known and not forgotten."

A faint light began to glow from within the shrine. Unlike the light that the sun's rays created from its position in the sky, this light was warm and welcoming, like the gentle glow of a hearth on a cool winter's evening. It spread from within the center of the small figurine until the whole pedestal glowed gently, like a soft beacon of hope in the world's darkness.

"Thank you," the Holy Witness intoned and gently dropped her hands back to her sides, smiling at the vision before her.

A warm hand touched her shoulder gently as her companion joined her. "You are truly blessed, Isolde duAvalonne," Safar whispered quietly by her side.

Isolde smiled and nodded simply. "Perhaps someday one of the Faithful will travel from home and build a homely house here." She looked up at the sky and the fading light of the Radiant Lord then looked back out at the harbor. "That would be nice."

They stood together in joined silence for a few moments, side by side, staring out over the shrine into the harbor. Dozens of ships floated lazily in the delta harbor, some awaiting unloading, others waited for passengers or gear meant for parts elsewhere. At the end of the docks were moored a handful of river barges, bearing the markings of Nahral, the River Lord's city. A few passersby noticed the pair attending the shrine in its reverence. They inclined their heads in respect or made signs of reverence to the Divine as they passed.

Finally, Isolde sniffed and wiped at her eyes, then reached for her gloves, which she had tucked into her belt. "Right then."

"You have done what needs doing?" Safar asked of her, his honey-gold eyes searching her face and her stance. "We can stay as long as you need," his deep voice spoke sincerely.

Isolde nodded once as she pulled her gloves on. The breeze from the harbor brushed past them both. Loose ends of her sun-bleached dark hair danced in the wind. "For now. I need time… and ability… to write things down so I can send them on." She looked up from her gloves and met Safar's gaze. She smiled. "You wanted to introduce me to your Guild?" she asked.

The handsome Sun Guide smiled brightly at her words. "I do!" he exclaimed happily.

They turned then and walked beside her down the passage and back toward the merchant square. Isolde tucked her thumbs into her belt as they walked, her green eyes searching and watching. As they had entered the market area, Safar had tasked a young man with taking their korsers to the Guild, to ensure their belongings were taken care of, while he took Isolde to pay her respects.

Isolde marveled at the city as they walked side by side. It differed from Nahral, and likewise from the harbor city of Lubri. All three cities were large and built on the water's edge. All were functional trade ports for their respective areas.

Nahral and Lubri seemed far less cosmopolitan than the grand city of Ophir. Isolde noted many races of people, along with colors and cuts of clothing she had not seen before. She attributed this to Ophir's being a gateway to the access of the Iteru and to both the city of Nahral and the great necropolis of Litharge at its furthest end. Isolde was certain that she could spend an entire lifetime witnessing nothing but the goings-on of the grand city of Ophir. She would not be the first Witness to choose to remain in a single area of the world and simply document everything that happened there. So many wonderful similarities and differences. So much history that The Wanderer had never seen. So many stories and memories to be shared. She took in a deep breath and refocused herself. This was not why they were here.

Heads turned and eyes followed the pair as they walked down the streets of the city. Slowly, Isolde broke out of her wonderment and made a note of this. She continued matching the stride of the Reysis. She leaned in slightly and whispered, "You have a following."

"Hmm?" Safar mused, and followed her gaze. Several persons ducked their heads and turned away, others met the Reysis gaze and nodded simply. "Ah," he commented. "It is nothing. We are close to the Guild Hall, familiar faces in a sea of people..."

Isolde glanced over at the bronze-skinned Sand Dancer and narrowed her eyes in an assessment of his words. Safar looked over at her and then looked away. He looked back at her again and then lifted his hand to place it between the two of them so she could no longer see him.

"Is it a trait of all Wanderers that they can look into the soul of someone so effectively?" he cleared his throat a little uncomfortable.

"Does it bother you?" Isolde grinned from behind his hand.

"A little, if I must confess." the Reysis replied.

"Good!" Isolde laughed, and shoved Safar with her shoulder. He chuckled in response and pushed his hand into her face playfully. She dodged and slapped it away ineffectively. They continued their feeble, if amusing, attempt at slap-fighting in the street until they gathered a small crowd of concerned persons. Many of those gathered wore the clothing of caravan masters. They exchanged concerned glances and words. It was Isolde that noticed first as she dodged Safar's left hand that was aimed at her ear.

"Stop," she said, and reached up to grasp Safar's wrist inches from her head. The Reysis tried to twist his arm away from her and then realized Isolde's eyes had lost their mirth. He turned to look over his shoulder at what had caught the gaze of the Knight Wanderer. The smile on his face dropped as he met the gaze of several of those gathered. He nodded to Isolde, who released him, and then rolled his eyes at the onlookers.

"Well?" he asked in the tongue of his people.

"Is this woman bothering you, Reysis?" one of the larger men asked.

"Is this woman ...," Safar repeated incredulously and then launched into a string of heated words and gestures that stung the ears and shocked the eyes of all those gathered. His reaction concluded with him shooing the gathered group away and down the street, planting a firm kick into the backside of the large man who had asked the initial question. He finished berating the group, smoothed his robes and ran his forefinger deftly over his eyebrows, then turned back to face Isolde.

The Knight stood with her arms folded across her chest, a look of amusement on her sun-tanned and freckled face.

"More family?" she asked with the hint of a smile.

Safar shrugged and grinned. And for the first time since meeting him, Isolde thought she detected the hint of a blush on his bronze skin. "The Sand Dancers are a ... Hmm ... fruitful ... people," he offered with explanation.

Isolde raised her eyebrows and stifled a laugh. She nodded in response. "I had noticed."

Safar pursed his lips in thought and then nodded. "Come. The Guild has no doubt tired of waiting on our whims. They will start sending people to fetch us if we delay further," he gestured down the street and across the square to the multi-storied building of the Guild. The front porch area of the Hall was occupied by at least a dozen or more people, all looking toward the Reysis and the Knight. The assortment of persons stared directly at the pair as they approached. Stern and unhappy faces stared out at Isolde and Safar. Some leaned against the alabaster wall of the Guild Hall, others leaned forward across the heavy railing outside the doors. Several simply stood, with arms folded, watching.

"I suppose it's a good thing that I am not easily intimidated," Isolde said with a smile, leaning in to whisper to Safar.

"I counted on it," came Safar's reply.

Isolde's eyebrows raised. She turned around then and walked backward for a few steps, looking at the face of the handsome Sun Guide. His eyes met hers. He smiled warmly.

"Safar?" she asked

"Yes, Island?"

"I am still not marrying you," she winked and turned back around.

Safar gaped at her and then clutched at his chest dramatically. "Wounded! See how I bleed, that you deny me so!"

Across from them, the Guild members watched and listened intently. At Safar's proclamation, faces that had been focused and severe burst into laughter and joy. Hands clapped onto backs, coins were passed from hand to hand and nods of resignation exchanged. Voices carried back into the Hall itself, and a roar of responses flooded out onto the streets.

Chapter 13

The raucous revelry of the Guild Hall reminded Isolde of the festivals of home. Laughter, joy, and merriment carried across those gathered within the multi-storied building. They greeted Safar with embraces, smiles, and the occasional chastising wag of a finger from some of the older members of the assembled. Words flowed in a tongue that Isolde did not comprehend, but the energy of the room was easy to read.

She found herself introduced to person after person as Safar guided them both through the press of Guides at the front of the main hall. Smiles, handshakes, and solid pats on the back were offered. She accepted them all in stride.

"Yes, yes. It is good to see you too," Safar smiled and nodded. "Yes, I will make time to speak to you about that before I leave," he commented to one of the other Reysis, who flagged him from across the room. The toll of the throng finally reached Safar's limits. Isolde watched him take a deep breath, sigh heavily, and then grab a nearby chair. Pulling it to him swiftly, he stepped up on top of the chair to get a better vantage of the room.

"Fellow and Family Guides, a moment please!" he called out. Several voices lowered; others seemed to fill in the vacuum. Isolde looked up at Safar and watched as he tried to control a room filled with excitement and high energy. She folded her arms across her chest and grinned in amusement. She nodded here and there to those who seemed to wish to seek her attention. After a few seconds of realizing that the gathered group would not give Safar the quiet audience he desired, she reached out and tapped the Reysis on the calf. He looked down at the knight.

"Island?"

"Allow me, Reysis," she smiled and winked. Taking a deep breath, the Avalonian sounded out in a loud clear voice that seemed to echo off of the rafters, "Oyez! Oyez!" the tones rang, rich and foreign. "Pray attend!" she called.

Voices dropped. Whether it was the call itself, the woman calling, or the strange words used to call attention; it did not matter. It achieved the desired effect.

Safar stared down at the Avalonian knight and shook his head, a brilliant smile on his lips. Isolde nodded at Safar. "Room's yours," she replied.

He nodded in acceptance and looked out at the gathered group. "Hello. Good evening. Thank you all for being here tonight. The sands are demanding, and time is fleeting, so I shall be brief."

Several men chuckled. Comments of "Not likely" could be heard. Safar turned keen eyes on the speakers; he pointed at them, as a father might when warning a child, and continued.

"The voice that has called your attention belongs to a very special woman."

Again, there were hushed comments and the occasional snicker. "Kabil, are you four years old?" Safar chided.

"No Reysis," the chastised man blushed and looked at the ground.

Safar rolled his eyes at the ceiling. "I see where this is going. Fine," he sighed and gestured to Isolde. "This is Ser," he emphasized the title, "Isolde duAvalonne of the Island Realm. She is the sworn right arm of the Landless Lord, and His Holy Witness!" he exclaimed.

Opinions shifted palpably in the room. Several heads nodded appreciatively. Guarded stances shifted for different reasons. Bodies that had been pressed closer to hers stepped away to grant the Champion her space.

"Ah. Good. NOW you listen," Safar replied, watching everyone. "This woman has a calling from Her Lord that we have benefited greatly from. For SHE sees the Dancers of the Sand

95

and the Divine shall forever remember us! For this, while she resides here in the Capital, she is under the protection of Our Lady of the Beautiful Tent. So let it be known; so, let it be done!"

Once more ripples of opinion shifted through the room and eyes fell on Isolde, assessing, measuring, wondering. Isolde, listening to Safar's words, suddenly balked at his declaration. A measure of both surprise and irritation flooded her emotions. She fought back the urge to challenge the Reysis before the assembled group, but the look on her face spoke volumes to Safar as he climbed back down from the chair.

He met her eyes and forced a smile. "You are going to hit me again, aren't you?"

"I am considering it," she replied quietly in response.

Safar nodded and reached up to smooth his dark beard with his right hand. "Perhaps you will give me time to explain?" he asked as the bustle of the crowded Hall resumed.

A burly man wearing an apron suddenly forced into their hands cups of spiced tea. He smiled at Safar and then turned to Isolde. "Welcome, Welcome! I have heard many things about the woman that tried to battle Swammerdami to save this worthless bag of korser bones." He nodded at Safar.

Safar scoffed at Kefu's comment. Isolde smiled and nodded at him, accepting the cup. "It was a very big scorpion," she commented. Her eyes fell on the various decorations throughout the Hall that bore the symbol of the scorpion. She cleared her throat, "I ... erm ... hope I did not offend?" she asked in a cautious tone.

Kefu chuckled and looked at Safar. They locked eyes for a moment. Safar's head twitched slightly from side to side. Kefu opened his hands and took a half step back. "Swammerdami killed several members of your caravan. You did what was necessary. You saved lives," Kefu jerked his head to Safar. "Probably even his."

Isolde frowned, trying to remember the details of that night when their caravan had been attacked by the gigantic figure of the Emperor of the Sands – the giant black scorpion. It had stabbed Safar and drug him back beneath the sands; she had tried to save him but could not pull him free. The Reysis had never fully explained how he had survived that encounter. She looked up at Kefu. "I have but one regret from that night," she offered.

"You have a regret for that, Island?" Safar asked, suddenly focused on her.

Isolde nodded. "I do." She swirled the tea in her cup. "That after you risked your life to wrest my sword out of that terrible beast, I lost you to the sands. I had just lost Reynard … and then you. I was supposed to be a knight, and it was the second time I lost someone. Reynard used to say that failure was the only true teacher," she looked him in the eyes, "I am sorry I could not save you."

The mirth in his eyes dimmed down at this revelation. "Isla … Isolde … From what the Radiant Father told me, he had to pull you out by your legs. You almost sacrificed yourself for a stranger. There is no nobler act that I know of. Not even your Landless Lord can deny that," He reached over and lightly gripped her arm, "No more regrets about that night. I will not have it. The only regret you should have is not saying 'yes' to my proposals," he added with a smile.

She looked up at him. An eye roll and a shake of her head soon replaced the release of regret.

Kefu cleared his throat and looked at Safar, and changed the subject. "Your rooms are prepared upstairs, Reysis. Oh, your niece Niya sends her love from the south. Your favor came this morning. Also, the representatives from the Radiant Lord will join us after their sunset ceremonies."

Safar nodded and drank deeply from his cup.

"The Radiant Lord is sending people here?" Isolde asked. Hope and anticipation colored her words.

Kefu nodded. "Yes. The Elven champion and the orc they sent earlier left with their tails tucked after hearing they would not be allowed to take you into their custody for questioning."

Safar continued to drink from his cup, avoiding Isolde's eyes as she turned to face him. "Take me into ..." she handed her cup back to Kefu. Her eyes narrowed. "Reysis Safar, I believe we need to have a discussion ... there is clearly information that I am missing ... my friend."

Safar nodded quietly and lowered the cup. He licked his lips and wiped his mustache with his thumb and forefinger. He looked at Kefu. "Upstairs you said?"

Kefu nodded. "Mmmm," he replied. "Third floor, both rooms."

"Thank you, Master Kefu, for your excellent hospitality. It is appreciated," Isolde replied in a polite, controlled tone.

"Of course!" Kefu smiled. His eyes slid over to Safar.

"Pray for me, cousin. She may be the death of me," Safar said in the tongue of his people.

"Third floor?" Isolde asked.

Kefu nodded once more. Isolde cast an irritated glance in Safar's direction and then turned and headed for the stairs.

"I will drink deeply at your funeral," Kefu replied to Safar with a smile.

~~~

"I am not a helpless child, Safar!" Isolde yelled.

Safar stood opposite Isolde in the uppermost rooms of the Guildhall that had been assigned to them. He held his hands up before him, to both ask for patience and deflect any incoming blows from the angered Avalonian knight.

"I am aware, Island ..." he began.

"Are you?" she demanded. She ran her tongue over her teeth and turned away from him to unbuckle her left vambrace. "You continue to treat me like some defenseless, wet-behind-the-ears foreigner who does not know thing one about this Realm. What do you think I have been doing this entire time in Tarf-qua?" She pulled the protective gear off her arm and tossed it onto a nearby table. It clattered and rolled away onto the floor.

"In my defense, Island ... you ... are ... still ... a foreigner,"

Safar offered. Isolde swung her head around to glare at him. "But, perhaps not as water-fat as you once were," he added, then winced at his choice of words.

Isolde shook her head and turned back away from him. She tugged on her right vambrace.

"Why does the Radiant Lord want to take me into custody?" she asked plainly.

Safar slowly lowered his hands and stepped to the other side of the room. They had designated the upper floors of the Guild Hall as his for some time. These were a personal sanctuary from the toils and challenges of leading the Sand Dancer Tribes of Setesh, and being the lead Reysis for the Guild. The members of the Guild and his extended family had spared no expense in providing for their protector. Rich tapestries, scarves, and paintings adorned the walls. Elegant lamps hung from the ceiling, and rugs woven of the finest materials covered the floor. A selection of eclectic furnishings occupied the room, granting a sense of luxuriousness and comfort.

He slowly reached for a pitcher of spiced tea that had been left for them and poured two cups.

"I ... imagine ..." he began, "that the Everwatchful eye of Sanctum would like very much if you were to document where Ahsal was ... and then forget you were ever there."

Isolde grunted. "I cannot do that," she pulled the other vambrace off and tossed it to lie with its mate. She shook out her arms. Sand flew off of her and onto everything.

Safar watched her from across the room and chuckled a little. "I am aware." He picked up the two cups and walked across the room to her. He offered her one of the cups. "Truce?" he asked, standing to her side.

Isolde glowered at Safar and took the proffered cup from him.

"They can be ... hmmm ... insistent." Safar offered and drank from his cup.

Isolde watched Safar and then looked at the dark liquid in her cup. She swirled it around for a moment. "Tulok warned me this might happen," she said.

Safar's eyebrows rose slightly. "Oh? I was not aware."

Isolde drank from the cup in thought. She nodded. "We were in Nahral. There was a … discussion. I cannot go into details." She drank down the rest of the tea and shoved the cup back at Safar. Her eyes met his. "I cannot talk about it," she said with finality.

While in Nahral, Tulok had explained to her that the Temple could try to impose their will upon her, forcefully, if necessary, to keep the secret of the Temple of Silence out of living memory. The orc priest knew this was not something that Isolde could do without violating the tenets of her Faith. Instead, they bound one another into a pact of silence, a secret-for-a-secret. She would speak to only the Landless Lord of what she discovered in Ahsal, and in return, Tulok would never speak of Isolde's bloodborne link to the lands and magic of Avalon. In this, the mysteries of their people would be preserved and neither would violate the requirements of their Faith.

Safar watched Isolde's eyes, searching her face. He opened his mouth to speak. She shook her head. "There is an Oath. I cannot," the Knight replied.

Safar's eyes widened. "You are already Oathbound on this matter?" he asked, and quickly set the cups aside. "Island …" the man's voice was flavored with honest compassion and concern. He reached out to place his hands on hers.

Isolde shook her head. "I am not prevented from my duties, and I have already discharged them. The Temple may attempt what they will, but the story has already been told," she replied quietly.

"They will not be pleased," Safar cautioned.

Isolde nodded. "I am aware," her thoughts drifted back to everything she had witnessed in the Temple of Silence. The ancient carvings of forgotten gods and frescos of ancient cities now buried beneath the sands. So many stories. So much history.

"Was this why you did all of this?" she asked him.

Safar nodded. "It is … I …" He paused. "We … could not allow the Temple to misuse a Witness. The risk was too great to too many." He looked deeply into her eyes.

Isolde's brow furrowed. "We?"

"Mmm, yes. The Radiant Father and I …" he admitted.

"Tulok knew about this?" she asked.

Safar shrugged slightly. "A little?" The irritation returned to Isolde's face. "He was going to let me know when it was safe for you to come to Ophir," he replied quickly. "But … here we are?" he offered her a winning smile.

Isolde pulled her hands from Safar's and reached up to rub her eyes and the bridge of her nose in frustration. "I hate politics," she sighed.

Safar laughed out loud at that. "Says the Avalonian Knight!" he exclaimed. "I thought your people were made of pomp and ceremony, Island. Or are the stories not true that one can stand in court for three days' time just to get their name on a list for the following Season's festivals?" The Reysis seized on the opportunity to change the subject.

Isolde waved Safar off, declining to answer, and walked away toward the balcony that overlooked the street below. She rested her elbows on the railing and looked down into the merchant square. Safar refilled their cups and joined her, standing next to her. She took her cup from him and sipped its contents.

"Do you believe there are troubles on you island then?" he asked her quietly, their former arguments left by the wayside.

She nodded, holding the cup in her hands and watching the skyline.

"You will return to your people then?" he asked softly, not watching her. There was a hint of pain behind the Reysis' eyes as he asked the words.

Isolde chewed on her top lip in thought and did not answer. Specific movement in the square below caught the trained eye of the Witness of the Landless Lord. A massive figure, clothed in the white and gold of the Temple of the Radiant Lord. The crowd parted before him like water before the bow of a boat.

Isolde's eyes lit up with unbridled joy at the sight of the orc priest making his way through the crowd toward the Guild Hall.

"Tulok!"

Chapter 14

Until coming to Ophir, Tulok had seen the Fallarubi – the Sunset oblation~ as more of an "intimate" affair. Less than 20 or 30 people took part in giving their thanks to the Radiant Lord in Tarf-qua. In the Grand Temple, intimate was a foreign word as hundreds both within and without paid homage to the sun as it drifted down the edge of the horizon. Every priest and acolyte within Ophir attended this oblation. While the orc was the head of his temple in Tarf-qua, he stood now with the acolytes, laypeople, and other lower priests. It did not bother him much, as each time he took part in these services, he felt his soul rise to the heavens and drift within his god's light. From prayers and blessings to allowing the timbre of his voice to resonate within the many voices of the priesthood's chorus – he truly enjoyed it all. He even smiled at the fact that he could easily hear the chorus of voices from anywhere in the city. The cacophony danced around the ears of all, clarifying that this was, in fact, the Radiant Lord's city.

This was not his first time in attendance; in fact, the large priest was often one of the first to arrive and the last to leave. This was not him seeking praise or accolade; rather, it was the closest that he ever felt to his god. The noontime service was hard for any newcomers to the faith as they were awash in the Sun God's full glory overhead. Evermore trying was the interior of the solarium that focused light on all corners of the temple so that they could find not a single shadow. While he did not revel in the weakness of others, Tulok lost himself in those moments of his faith. If it were not for the circumstances that brought him to Ophir in the first place, he would have been content here.

Tonight, was different.

Tonight, he had a weight of apprehension that kept him grounded to the earth rather than allow his spirit to fly within the ceremony. He wanted his obligation to be done so he could leave. The sooner this was done, the sooner he could ensure that the 'Avalonia Matter' could be put to rest.

That is what Ibris called the entire situation.

For Tulok, it meant something much more – it meant that ensuring that Isolde would be safe.

—

After they completed services, he headed to his room to change out of the ceremonial vestments and into something less formal. The Guild of the Sun Guides was the controlling force in all of this. Tulok was not too worried about them. His concern was more about how Ibris would act. He was a Champion and used to getting his way; for the Radiant Lord of course, but his way nonetheless. Tulok's mind wandered through various possibilities. Each time seemed to end up with a negative outcome. He shook his head and muttered to himself as he reached over for his medallion – but it was not there. He stared at the contents of the desk. Nothing seemed out of place. He cocked his head to the side to look underneath, but if it had fallen, he would have heard it do so. He took a step back to survey the whole of the area when he caught a glint from the corner of his eye. Turning his head to face the large reading chair, he saw a figure occupied it carefully, holding his medallion.

"I never thought you would be a mutterer, to be honest. It is not a bad thing, mind you. Though it is quite telling," the figure said very matter-of-factly.

Tulok took a step forward and raised up a finger in protest when the lights dimmed slightly in the room. Turning around, there were two other figures, fully robed and with hoods pulled down, obscuring their features. He turned back to the figure in his chair. They were a human or an elf. They were too short to be an Orc and too tall to be Vidria or Gnomish. Again, he raised his figure to say something when the seated figure put a finger to their lips and simply said,

"Shhhhh".

He could not move.

His limbs refused to move and no amount of strength or strain allowed them to budge. He could breathe and move his eyes, but all movement was halted. His mind raced back to the Temple of Silence and how Nebiyre had held both him and Isolde fast with her dark magics. The image of the life fading from Isolde's green eyes rolled to the surface of his memories. He felt the swell in his gut – the Gurhk wanted its chance to test these bonds. Instead, Tulok closed his eyes. This was not a problem for strength. If they wanted to kill him, they would have done so already. He opened his eyes again and looked at the seated figure. They were wearing robes that were common to the order – but not.

Standard robes of the priesthood were always white linen with a fabric of woven gold along the hems and cuffs. The greater the status one held in the priesthood, the more their robes bore iconography of the Radiant Lord in the designation of office. The robes of the seated figure were very simple – but with a subtle difference.

The golden border near the sleeves shared a dark blue trim.

A Priest of Dusk?!

"Observant too. Sharp mind ... brutal strength. While you are not ready yet, you definitely have potential. Now, I am sure you probably have dozens of questions but, unfortunately, there is no time for that, and you are not ready for the answers. However, my large friend, I have a message for you, so please pay attention,"

The figure stood up and walked over to Tulok while taking out a rolled-up sheet of parchment from their robes. Unfurling it before Tulok, he held it so the priest could see the images scrawled there. Tulok's eyes twitched a bit. There were several images – most of them repeated and with grand passion or ferocity.

A sun viper slithering along the grass and biting a fir tree.

Boots black as night stretching outward.

A black, sunless horizon.

"The seers have been tearing their hair for the last two weeks because of these images. For some of them, it has been repeating more and more. It was as if this was building toward ... something. I have sent our eyes and ears to the far north only to find nothing." The figure turned its head to one other behind Tulok.

"However, our brethren have been wise enough to think outside of the box. We are not the only continent with a north," they added, and rolled up the parchment and placed it in Tulok's bag at the desk.

Avalon.

Isolde.

"Now you get the picture, brother. I have calmed the seers down, but there is fear of far-sight madness among them. I cannot have that. We need them." the figure sighed a resigned sigh and waved dismissively in Tulok's direction.

"Make whatever deals are necessary for us to gain access to Ahsal. We will pay the cost that the Lady's Son desires. It is well known what he wishes. Ibris will definitely be against it. Simply tell our Champion that ... even honey ferments. That will settle the matter and he will go along with Son's price." The figure walked back over to the paralyzed priest and placed the medallion into his outstretched hand.

"As for your Wandering Knight ... she is your entrance to the island realm. This ... thing, whatever it is ... is a threat to all of us – including those people. We placed our faith in you when we told Ibris to send you to Ahsal. We are placing our faith in you again to investigate this. Do our Lord well."

The figure patted the orc on the shoulder. Tulok could see the bottom of their face, it bore a curious smile, but neither race nor gender could be determined.

There was a loud knock at the door. Instinctively, Tulok turned his head. Suddenly, the lights were all on in his room and he could move once more. The door opened, and Ibris poked his head in. "There you are! How long does it take you to get ready, man? Never mind – come along, we're going to be late."

Looking at the medallion in his hand, Tulok quickly put it on and grabbed his bag. Reaching inside, he could feel a roll of parchment inside. He swallowed and said nothing as he followed the Champion out the door.

—

"TULOK! UP HERE!" Isolde shouted again.

Looking up the side of the tall building, the orc spotted a bittersweet sight. The last time they had seen one another, they had simply waved goodbye at a distance. He wanted to shout and smile at her, but with Ibris there – the most he allowed himself to do was give a wave and head toward the building she was in.

Isolde and Safar watched as the enormous figure made his way forward through the crowd below, following an armor-clad individual. She looked over at Safar, a sense of disappointment on her otherwise cheerful countenance.

Safar simply motioned to the figures below, "He is not alone, Island. Otherwise, his greeting would probably have been a little more ... animated."

Accepting this, she nodded her head. "Who is he with?"

"That is Devout Ahsom Ibris – a Champion of the Radiant Lord ... much like yourself for your Wanderer. The Sun God has the priesthood to administer to the people, and he has his Champions to bring His Light of Justice where they go," the Reysis said.

The emphasis on justice was not lost on her. "I take it you do not care for them?"

Safar sucked his teeth and paused a moment, as if wording a proper response. "The Champions provide justice for the people ... the Sun God's people. I am not saying they are biased in their rulings ... but sometimes there is a sense of generosity given to those who follow the Radiant Lord. Whether this is a tenet of the order or a direct mandate from the sky above – I do not know. However, the followers of the Radiant Lord take care of their own – especially in Ophir."

Isolde looked down at her cup and took another drink, quietly wishing it was something stronger.

"You will probably want to put your armor back on. I'm not saying there is trouble but, knowing this Champion, they will … respect you more if you look the part of a Champion of your faith," he said.

Isolde frowned, "A Champi …," she paused, "I am a Holy Witness for my Lord. A Wandering Knight empowered by His will and I will be damned if I allow myself to be judged badly simply because I do not … look … the part!" Her voice raised slightly in anger.

Safar cringed slightly and raised his hands up. "Please Isolde. I am not being disrespectful; I would never do that. However, these Champions are … literally … the shining example of their god's diplomacy and judgment. Yes, you are under the protection of this Guild," he raised his hand to stop her from interrupting, "Which I know you do not need. But as you said earlier – this is politics. Tonight, it is a game that we are going to have to play. Our large friend is going to be playing a hard game himself. He will do everything he can to ensure that things do not go south, even at his own expense."

The Wandering Knight leaned her head back and bellowed at the ceiling in frustration. She closed her eyes, tilted her head forward, and took a deep breath. Opening her eyes, she walked over to where she had thrown off her protective guards. She scooped them up and rearmed herself. As she tightened the buckles and straps, she paused and let her hand brush the side of her hip. She spoke aloud with a slight cadence to her voice, "A knight needs their weapon secured and at their side at all times." She looked over to Safar, "May I request use of your blade for this?" The request was clearly painful to ask. It was not because of any sense of pride, but the reason for it.

When Tulok had been captured and Bengt killed, the orc had

been carrying her possessions that she had left on the boat during their crossing of the Iteru. Her armor, shield, and sword were lost to the sands near that damnable temple. She had only recovered pieces of her armor, never the sword. While they could replace the shield and armor, it was the loss of the blade that hurt most. Yes, it was made from Avalonian Iron, but it was also Reynard's sword. It was one of the few things she had left of him, and it was gone. Losing his sword hurt deeply. It was something she could not explain to Safar.

The Reysis' face suddenly lit up with a smile. "NO! Of course not!" and promptly walked out of the room.

She was stunned at the sudden turn of events. She just stood there with her mouth open and the unbuckled vambrace fell to the ground. Did she just break some unknown law or cross some martial taboo?

Without a word, Safar walked back in, carrying a roll of well-oiled leather. Quickly, he placed the bundle in her already outstretched hands.

Isolde stared at the bundle and then back at the Reysis.

"Well – open it Island! You cannot very well use it like that," he said.

Cautiously, Isolde unfurled the gifted item. Inside the leather, wrapped in finely woven linen, lay an Avalonian blade. Reynard's sword. It shined in the candlelight. Someone had taken the time to clean and polish the steel. The head of the Questing Beast stared up at her from the pommel. Her hand reached out and with her fingertips, she gently touched the sculpted face. Tears flowed from her eyes freely. She turned to face Safar. Marching over to him, she embraced him tightly and sobbed into his shoulder.

"Thank you …," was all that she could say.

"Island, it is just a …," he paused as he felt the weight that the gift lifted off her soul. Instead, he wrapped his arms around her, allowing her to let go of the pain of loss that the blade represented.

She sniffled. "I am still not marrying you," she said into his shoulder.

Safar simply laughed and gently patted her back.

Chapter 15

Blood dripped from her hands and covered her arms. She dragged the body of the young boy away from the glade where the battle continued to rage. He had stopped breathing moments ago. Shouts and yells surrounded her, drowning her in their cacophony. Pulling the body out of the fray, she crossed into the treeline and collapsed.

"Over there!"

"Where did it come from?!"

"To the right of you!"

The voices of her kith and kin called from the gruesome scene of carnage before her. Once verdant and green, the glade was awash red with the lifeblood of her tribesmen. The creatures had risen from the bog along the lakeside, leaving a trail of death and decay in the wake of their passing. Grass wilted and faded to the color of ash. Leaves crumbled and withered on branches, now black with rot. Animals fell to decay as quickly as plant matter. It had been the bleating and screaming of the forest dwellers which alerted them to the incursion.

Ygraine panted from her position, trying to catch her breath. She had forgotten that rabbits screamed and that their screams often sounded like terrified children. She rubbed her blood-soaked hands onto her pants legs, trying to wipe them clean. Beside her, the body of her kinsman grew cold. Galan had been four years her senior. He had passed his trials earlier that summer. His dark matted hair clung to his lifeless features. Intricate black and blue tattoos decorated his forehead and face, depicting the leaves and horns of The Huntress. His dark, empty eyes stared upward at the forest canopy. She reached over and closed them.

"I'm sorry, Galan," the young woman intoned.

In the glade before her, a dozen men and women stood toe to toe with a creature born of nightmare itself. The creature stood over fourteen feet tall. Two massive arms, covered in thick brown fur, swiped effortlessly at its attackers. Each arm ended in huge paws tipped with wicked-looking claws. The head and face of the creature were large and round. It bore a long snout that peeled back into a ferocious snarl. Razor-sharp teeth gnashed and snapped at the tribesmen. It stood upright on two legs. Its legs were covered in a patchwork of dark fur and blistered skin. They were solid, like the trunk of a tree. The creature roared and swung one of its deadly appendages at a woman who stood poised with a spear. The spear shattered in her hands at the impact. Her body flew from the glade and crashed into a formation of stones. She slumped to the ground, broken and bleeding.

Bile rose in Ygraine's throat. She swallowed it down. Forcing her exhausted form to stand, she darted across the glade to the body of the fallen woman. She skirted around the main battle to pass to the other side. The woman's body lay on the faded and blood-soaked grass bent into unnatural angles. Lifeless eyes stared at the battle.

Ygraine closed her eyes briefly to whisper a prayer for the departed. Keeping her attention partially focused on the combat behind her, she slid her arms under the woman's arms and dragged her body from the battle. They could not allow their fallen to become compromised by the Decay.

"Under the arm. The spear!" a deep voice yelled. It was Cinioch, the Chieftain's youngest son, his cornflower blue skin was decorated with red and brown designs depicting animals, geometric designs, and the sun. His dark wiry hair had slipped the tight knot he held it in and exploded around his face like a fearsome mane. His beard was coated in black ichor.

The hunters rallied at Cinioch's voice, trying to do as commanded. The creature roared once more and turned to face the voice that dared to challenge it. Its lips peeled back into a snarl of teeth that better belonged in a shark than any land-based mammal. Cinioch stood firm. He presented the beast with his round wooden shield and heavy axe. Taking a deep breath, he roared back at the creature. With deadly intent, the giant beast raised its massive paw and snarled at Cinioch. As it lifted its arm, the soft under-flesh in the joint became exposed. In unison, two members of the band shifted their positions to aim the sharpened tips of their spear points. Placing both hands on the heavy wooden shaft of their weapon, they drew back and, with an exclamation of brutal force, shoved the leaf-headed points into the horrid creature.

The creature roared in pain and staggered, off-balance suddenly. Dark, sticky ichor oozed out of the wound. In that moment of unbalance, Cinioch charged. With a roar of un-bridled rage, Cinioch Aerfyn rushed the creature. His own massive form colliding with the bloodied and mutated body of the beast. His shield shoved into its ribs as his mighty arm wrapped the haft of his ax around, elbow bending, wrist snapping back, pulling the heavy-bladed ax back and cleaving deeply into the monster's flesh. Almost as if on cue, the rest of Cinioch's warriors pushed in on the creature, toppling it to the ground.

The creature roared and howled in both pain and anger. Blades rose and fell. Screams echoed across the glade and into the forest. Three more bodies fell beneath the claws and teeth of the terrible beast before it finally ceased to move. Five souls to mourn tonight.

Ygraine pulled the last fallen body away from the carnage as the creature ceased to move. She was covered in blood – the blood of her people. Her heart pounded in her ears. Something inside her ached to do more than simply tend the dead. It did not matter the importance of the task; a gnawing, gnashing need burned within her that begged for both acknowledgment and release.

A heavy hand fell upon her shoulder. She jerked away and crouched into a ready position, knife in hand.

Cinioch's deep-throated laugh answered her challenge. "You have done well, Little Wolf!" he chuckled. "Your teeth will soon taste blood. There is no need for them now." he gestured at her knife.

A tall woman carrying a broken spear approached them. Her dark curly hair hung in wet ringlets on her bronzed skin. Green and blue tattoos adorned her face and hands. She looked at Ygraine. "How many?" she asked.

Ygraine bowed her head in respect. "Five, Urram."

The woman nodded in response and turned to look at Cinioch. "You took a significant risk with that challenge."

Cinioch sucked on a tooth and spat. "What of it?" he asked. He met the woman's eyes with his own. They were still filled with a desire for battle.

The woman stepped to Cinioch and met his gaze. "You will address me properly," she stated.

Cinioch sniffed and growled a little and met the woman's gaze with his own. He pressed his nose against hers and continued to stare. The other warriors in the band ceased their actions and turned to watch in silence. Ygraine tested the balance of her weapon in her hand and shifted her weight from foot to foot.

The pair continued to stare, unblinking, into the eyes of the other. Unmoving. Unflinching. Finally, Cinioch lowered his eyes and took a step back.

"Apologies, Urram Mael." Cinioch spoke.

The woman took a step back and looked at the gathered group. She took a breath and addressed them all.

"Do not assume that our victory here will be the outcome of every encounter," she began. "We do not know what the enemy is. And we do not know where it comes from," she looked at Cinioch. "We cannot assume that our battle tactics will succeed in all cases." She looked over at the creature. "There is a time and a place for the battle that is born in your blood."

"It was a bear, Urram," one warrior offered.

Urram Mael's brow furrowed. She turned to the speaker.

They were a young man with brown hair and hazel-green eyes. His first set of triskele tattoos were still healing on his shoulders.

"You are certain?" She asked.

The young man nodded. "There is still enough of its spirit intact that The Huntress could confirm it."

Urram Mael walked back over to the creature that lay in the center of the glade. Taken in the right light, the outline of a cave bear could be seen beneath the warped and twisted figure that had attacked them. Its snout had elongated and sprouted sharper teeth. Its legs had grown, extending its reach. The shaggy pelt that once covered its body had fallen away in large chunks, leaving blistered skin exposed. Its paws had grown and expanded to the size of a giant. The paws ended in sharpened claws, the size of a man's hand. Its prone body oozed black ichor, mixed with blood. Where the liquid coated the soil, the earth was already turning to the color of ash. She looked at her hands and then glanced at the bodies of those gathered.

The blood of the creature covered them all.

"Gather the dead. Build a pyre," she said quietly, but firmly.

Several warriors looked back and forth from one another. Ygraine frowned, as if she had not heard the woman's words properly.

"We ... will not be returning them to the land, Urram?" one woman asked.

Urram Mael shook her head and placed her hand over a colorful tattoo on her collarbone. A three-pointed knot, entwined with a golden circle. The symbol of The Mother. "They carry the taint of Decay. We cannot," she pointed at the earth around the body of the felled beast. The ashen rot had already spread.

"But ... the Cycle ...," one woman whispered.

Mael shook her head. "We will pray to the Keeper of the Crossroads to release them from their bonds that they may return." She looked up at each of them. Her voice was firm. "But we WILL NOT dedicate these bodies to the Land."

Cinioch cleared his throat and asked that was in all of their hearts.

"What about us?" the Chieftain's son asked.

Urram Mael looked at her hands, covered in blood and ichor. She turned around to face the group. "Line up. I need to see your hands."

Uneasily, the warriors slowly stepped up and stood next to one another. A couple of them took obvious steps away from others, who were clearly coated in the black substance from the malformed bear.

One by one, Urram Mael inspected those gathered in the glade. One by one, she found them to be contaminated in some form. All save one. The young tender of the dead, Ygraine.

Mael called the young woman over to her. "Open your mouth, let me see inside you," she instructed. Without hesitation, Ygraine opened her mouth for the Urram to look within her. Mael nodded. "Good. You know the berries of the Juniper, and the flowers of the Nettle, and where they can be found close by?"

Ygraine thought about it for a moment. She remembered passing both on the way here, not too far from the area. She nodded. "Yes, Urram."

"Good girl." Mael smiled. She turned slightly and presented her hip to Ygraine. Fastened there was a tooled leather scabbard. The simple wooden handle of a knife peeked out of the sheath.

"Take it," Mael instructed.

Ygraine's eyes grew wide. "I cannot. That is a silvered blade, meant for an Urram," she protested.

Mael looked into Ygraine's eyes, holding them for a moment. They communicated an unspoken moment of dire need in that silence. "You must take my blade and use it to bring me both juniper and nettle. You must use this blade to recover them, Ygraine … and it must be your hands that perform the task … for the rest of us are tainted."

Ygraine nodded and carefully removed the silver blade from the hip sheath of the Urram.

"Do not take the items with your own blade and do NOT wash in any of the water along the way. Do you understand me, child?" Mael asked.

Once more, Ygraine nodded as she carefully tucked the blade away into a secure place upon herself. "I do."

"Then run child. Run with the fleet feet of a deer and the strong heart of a lion … and do not look back."

Ygraine bowed her head. "Yes, Urram," she replied, then turned and bolted from the glade.

"…and if the Little Wolf is unsuccessful?" Cinioch asked from Mael's side.

"Then we join our brethren at the Crossroads."

Chapter 16

Kefu met them as before and led them into the same comfortable meeting space. A circular table had been added that sat low to the ground in the center of where the cushions had all been placed around. The table's smooth sandstone surface was unadorned, but its craftsmanship was apparent: Vidria hands had been here. Ibris raised his eyebrow in question and looked up at Tulok. The priest only nodded his head, answering the unspoken question. This was a negotiation, and Safar fired off the first volley. The big priest looked around the room and continued to quietly nod to himself. Something as simple as a table could set the scene and attitude for a meeting. Here, a circular table essentially told all; there was no head or authority. A square table would have established a sense of formality depending on who was involved and how they were sitting. While it was not a direct jab at the Radiant Lord's need for ceremony and formality, the message was simple. Tonight, everyone was equal, and the conversation was going to be ... candid.

The doors to the room opened, but it was not Safar or Isolde who stepped through. A small group of men and women, all bearing trays of food, entered the room. The scent of hot food and spices filled the air until there was nothing else. Evening meals were being prepared everywhere, and this room was across the way from the guild's kitchen. The fragrance in the air was enough to make one's mouth water at the very thought of what savory desert delights were being prepared. Whether it was the nervousness of the meeting, seeing Isolde, the mystery of a Dusk Priest, or simply the fact that they rushed here: the orc's stomach felt like it was twisted in knots with both anxiety and hunger. The low rumble in his chest was thankfully masked by all the activity inside and outside the room.

As quickly as they entered – the men and women nodded their heads and exited. They filled the once bare table with plates and bowls of various items. Olive, dates, and various sauces filled their containers along with various kinds of fowl and that sizzled with flavor. There were other items, but the most eye-catching was a crystal decanter of clear liquid with four rounded crystal cups set around it. The condensation along its body noted its cool temperature – another move by Safar. Refreshment was standard to have at any sort of negotiation, but a decanter of clear, cold water gave a pointed message – the Guild wanted for nothing. Whatever was going to be exchanged this evening would not come as wealth.

A low growl broke the silence of their observation in the air.

Ibris slowly turned his head to his companion, and they heard again the growl. Looking up at Tulok, his eyes widen as if to say "Really? Right now?"

Tulok felt his face run flush, but before he could answer, a voice cut in. "Food is not meant to be admired by your Radiances! Please sit Champion Ibris! We are all friends here, are we not Radiant Father?"

Turning around, the envoys of Radiant Lord watched as Reysis Safar entered the room, followed by the Wandering Knight. Safar bore his usual smile of confidence, while Isolde gave a neutral nod of greeting. Safar stepped back and motioned her toward a spot around the table.

"Please – I want to make sure we all have enough room to enjoy this."

Isolde said nothing, but made her way to the cushions without looking at either of the Radiant Lord's people. With little ceremony, she unbuckled the sheath carrying her sword and set it behind her. It was out of sight, but within reach. Tulok's eyes honed in on the pommel; its design was exactly like the one that they had lost back when the sands reclaimed Ahsal. His eyes moved over to Safar; he wanted to ask him how.

119

He could not.

"We thank you for the hospitality of your hall, Honored Reysis," Ibris began.

"Bah! The honor is mine to provide hospitality for the Sun Lord's Hand and Heart, but please gentlemen … sit. Everyone from thieves to holy men is sitting down to eat and we should follow their example!" With simple grace, the Reysis took his seat. Following suit, both Ibris and Tulok lowered themselves onto the cushions. With polite nods and silent acknowledgements, everyone reached forward and took a plate. Soon, trays and bowls were passed around in simple politeness, giving everyone a taste from all the offerings. Inwardly, Tulok let out a sigh of relief. There were other Champions whose reputations were as merciless as the sun's wrath, and such things as breaking bread would have been ignored. It was a relief to see that Ibris was prepared for it and, from the look of his plate, he was going to enjoy it.

"If this is a simple evening meal, Reysis, I would love and hate to see what a celebratory feast would look like," Ibris said, holding a two-pronged fork that skewered a piece of the bird. Tulok had heard that elves were particular in their eating habits. They never let their hands touch the food they intended to ingest. Ibris had either expected this meal to happen or had been carrying his own eating utensils.

"I hope all this was not just for us?"

"Nonsense your Devout Radiance! Honored guests deserve the best of a host's hospitality. All are treated with kindness and respect, as we honor them for their work. For example, Ser duAvalonne not only kept her word to help serve the people of Tarf-qua, but she also protected this realm in a way that some would say was beyond necessary. Especially for a land not her own. As a guest in my house such service should be rewarded, and a person of that quality should be cherished …"

Before he could continue, Ibris interjected: "Then I congratulate you on your impending nuptials, Reysis. I had heard word that she was taken as your bride."

Isolde's face went flush, and she slowly turned her head toward Safar. Internally, she was shaking Safar and yelling at him. How far had that tale gone?

Tulok looked down at the lone olive on his plate and refused to look up.

Safar's smile did not falter, and raised his finger. "You were always a being knowledgeable of rumors and connections, Champion Ibris – though congratulations are far from in order. My charm has not been enough to win over this Holy Witness to the Wandering Lord. Her mission does not allow her to be pinned down to a single man. Am I not right Ser duAvalonne?"

Isolde forced herself to relax her jaw. "The Reysis is too polite of a man to say that I declined his marriage proposal several times … including this evening. You will find he is a persistent man in everything he does."

"My apologies, Ser duAvalonne," Ibris added with a slight smile. "I had heard that your oath of service was given over to the Reysis as you accepted his marriage proposal. I assume you will head back to Tarf-qua to fulfill the rest of your promise?"

The question hung in the air for a moment.

"The Hemet …" Safar began, but was quickly cut off by Isolde.

"My oath-bound word was given to the village of Tarf-qua to serve a year and a day. The honored Reysis asked the Hemet if it would be a possibility for me to serve as Reysis' Hand while he performed his duties for Setesh as a Sun Guide. Any assumptions of that purpose were that, and only that: assumptions. I gave my oath to the village. It, in turn, was given freely to this man who asked for my help. He did it because he understands the oaths I hold to my Lord. My pledge of service was genuine and honest, and Reysis Safar gave me the opportunity to use that service in tandem with my devotion. As a peer I'm sure you would understand the need to fulfill the tenants of your lord." her eyes rested on Ibris," The Reysis has given me the opportunity to see the sun more than once a month if that makes better sense."

Ibris thoughtfully chewed on a piece of flatbread as she spoke. His eyes were trained on her, watching every detail of her face and movement of her hands. Isolde could feel the weight of his eyes and met them without flinching. The surreal quality of both holy warriors did not seek to overshadow the other. Rather, watching their spirits was akin to two serpents dancing around each other.

After a moment, Ibris simply nodded his head and said, "Fair."

Dabbing his mouth with a napkin, Ibris rolled his neck from side to side. "You will need to give my compliments to the team in your kitchen, Reysis. I have not eaten that well in some time. However, with casual dinner conversation out of the way, we need to discuss the matter at hand."

Tulok looked over to Isolde, and for the first time during the meal, he caught her eyes. The simple look told each other enough: it was about to get difficult.

"You wish for me to talk about what I saw in Ahsal and what I did there?" Isolde asked.

"Initially yes. We would also like to know how you made it out of the Iteru and ended up in Kas-qua," Ibris took a drink from his cup. "And finally, how did you find Ahsal without a map … and could you do it again?"

For the first time Tulok spoke aloud, "I recreated most of the journey that myself and the late Brother Bengt made initially. However, since the cult ambushed us – I've hit a wall. I have provided as much as I could, but the temple of His Radiance requires your help, Is… Ser duAvalonne." He cleared his throat and picked up the cup and drank. "My apologies – but to continue, the Temple would appreciate your help to scour the evil we were exposed to, and eventually leave it behind us."

Isolde could hear the sadness hidden in Tulok's words. He did not want her to do this, and his words were carefully chosen. She stared at her friend. She could see it in his eyes. He had to make his case … but there was something else. Her mind went back to the night in Nahral. The Radiant Lord's people would demand her silence. Her earlier trip to the small shrine where Reynard's remains lay, had ensured that the tale was told to her Lord, but she would not give that up.

Despite being a well-meaning ass ... she needed to let Safar make his play. If this was going to work, she had to give the Sand Dancer his due.

Chapter 17

"Then let us start with an act of goodwill, Ahsom," Safar started with a frank tone and using the Champion's given name. "My people have secured and respectfully taken possession of Acolyte Bengt Kalb's body. While it was exposed to the elements and Seteshi denizens, I have used a favor of mine with one of the Grim Lord's people to ensure that he will be more ... presentable ... to your people and, more importantly, his family."

Tulok's mouth fell open and Isolde turned to Safar, echoing the same shock in her face. Safar had mentioned he had an opening card to play to throw the envoys off their balance, but she was not expecting that. She found Brother Bengt a small and deplorable man, but his death was unwarranted. Safar's opening gesture was grand, but how grand was it?

Like a seasoned card player, Ibris rested his cup against his breastplate and raised an eyebrow. With a nod of his head, "That is indeed an act of goodwill. It will do enough to buy the Radiant Father his freedom from further questioning. The goodwill is appreciated, but it only benefits one party here who may have other issues on their hands. This entire ordeal tested the sanctity of vows and oaths that others might question, or should I say, *have* questioned. While admittedly it is a gracious gesture, it will not lessen our need for the Ser's aid," he motioned to Isolde, meeting her gaze, "as well as responsibilities tied to it."

Unblinking, Isolde met Ibris' gaze and simply leaned back into the cushion with her cup in hand. She turned to Safar and gave him a slight turn of her head. Safar nodded in response, but held up a finger as if to say wait. Inwardly, Isolde hated all of this. She hated this game, and she hated politics, but this was important. Important enough that he found her sword – Reynard's sword – and brought back Bengt's body. All of this was necessary, but afterward, she was going to want to hit something or drink the irritation away, whichever came first.

Tulok felt the weight of Ibris' question and request but kept his own stoic face hardened. Ibris had mentioned on the way there that he might have to strain some of the orc's ties to these people, but it was necessary for the Temple to ensure that Ahsal remained buried in the past. Yet, it made him wonder ... how many of Isolde's letters were intercepted? Did Ibris know of how close they were?

He watched Isolde and Safar in their silent conversation. She seemed different somehow, though he couldn't place a discerning finger on it.

Safar turned back to Ibris, shaking his head. "Why cannot an act of goodwill simply be that, my friend? Until this moment, I did not realize my actions would have provided any gain to someone here. Had I known it would have helped the Radiant Father, do you think I would have withheld doing so? Now ... had I the opportunity to actually speak with my friend before all of this and know his plight, I would have been able to retrieve your honored dead more quickly. Instead, no word is heard from him in over a season, a season of time that allowed the sands to pick and degrade the body of your man." he motioned to Tulok. "Did your people find any benefit or gain in keeping this one out of reach from those that call him friend?"

Isolde wanted to shift in her seat, but felt that any movement would be detrimental. Only a few minutes had passed since this conversation began and things were already bordering on accusatory.

This did not bode well.

"Fine Safar. It is an act of goodwill. I will not sit here squabble over the body of a dead man; that is for the Grim Lord's people to hash out. I will be blunt." he looked over at Isolde. "We NEED you to come with us and show us the way to Ahsal so that place can be picked apart and turned into sand perman-ently. While it may have collapsed, there is a chance that some of the sound crystals survived, and there were questions about the wall mural found. The only way to know for certain is for us to raise it and demolish it at its very core."

"And then afterward?" Isolde asked pointedly.

"Then afterward, the matter needs to be forgotten. Left in the desert … where it belongs," Ibris returned.

"What does that mean exactly for me? I am sure you know of my faith and our traditions … what will the Radiant Lord have me do?" she said, feeling a fire in her belly. While the tale was already told to her Lord, the act of silencing was abhorrent to her beliefs. She would not do it.

Tulok looked down at his hands. He wanted to say some-thing, anything, to break the tension in the air. This was the line in the sand … and someone was about to cross it.

Ibris' face became very serious and his eyes narrowed. Isolde knew what was coming, but before he spoke, Safar reached over and opened the crystal decanter of water.

The light from the candles in the room caught the decanter's faceted sides and sprayed the room in tiny rainbows of colors. He filled each of the cups and handed the first to Tulok. "Have a drink Father. You look thirsty with worry," and gave the orc a smile.

Turning his attention to Ibris and placing the water glass before the elf, "What if I propose an alternative, Ahsom? What if I provided a secured passage to where I found my two friends in the middle of the dunes and the exact location of the temple itself?"

Safar set another cup in front of Isolde. "As a bonus, I can provide you the bodies of those who tried to seek the temple afterward."

With a suspicious eye, Ibris asked, "What good would dead men be of use to me, Safar?"

Tulok spoke up with a bit of caution. "Assuming they were not given the proper burial rights, it would delay their souls for judgment. In theory, one could speak with a representative of the Grim Lord to allow for a ... conversation ... to be had before their souls have truly departed this realm," it was a shrewd move on Safar's part, but some members of the faith would have flat out dismissed such an idea because it meant going to the Soul Speakers for help. He did not know how Ibris would take it.

Ibris picked up the glass of water and looked at it as if trying to discern whatever trick was about it. He looked over at Tulok, who cautiously held the glass with two fingers and was already sipping it. He sighed and took a drink to clear his throat. "Does your generosity know no bounds?"

"It is what I keep telling her, but she continues in her denials of my earnest self!" Safar said as he shot a glance over to Isolde, who, at that moment, chose to ignore his existence.

"Alright, Safar, I am one to take a wager. What is the price of your generosity?" Ibris asked.

"Price sounds unclean Ahsom – I would much rather a favor or three. Some things that are well within the Temple's power, and in time they would find benefit from," he said with a smile in his golden eyes.

Silently, Ibris motioned to Safar with his hand to continue his pitch. Safar leaned back into the cushion and took a sip from the glass. "First, Ser Isolde duAvalonne is free from any responsibilities involving Ahsal. She is free to come and go in this land as any citizen of this realm and as required by her faith."

"With you providing the location to the temple and safe travel there ... we can agree to this," Ibris said. "Second?"

Safar's smile was wide. "Next season, every temple of the Radiant Lord will staff a member of my faith as their resident healer, as well as provide someone who will be schooled in Her Arts to ensure that it is not just their souls that gain succor, but their bodies as well."

Ibris swished the water around in his mouth. "I see. While I can appreciate the sentiment of this idea, do you really think it would be possible to supply that many knowledgeable healers at one time with a mentoring attitude for all of Setesh? Learning your arts takes years of study, so what kind of time frame are you looking at? Also, what of the current healers within the Temple? They may not be trained in your Lady's ways, but they do good work. Do we push them aside in the name of your Lady? It seems unreasonable my friend."

"Radiant Father," Safar said as he looked over at Tulok, "How old were you when you learned the art of healing?"

Tulok paused a moment, "I want to say I was not quite twenty years of age when Renka taught me," he looked over to Ibris, "She lived in Obor-qua when I started in the faith. Admittedly, it helped me with my studies as a novice."

"To add, my friend, based on what I know of your people, a being of your years at that age was akin to what? Older than a child, but not quite an adult, correct?"

Tulok saw where Safar was leading him and allowed it with a nod of his head, "I would say I was in-between fourteen and sixteen years of age when I learned. Unfortunately, it is not an exact number, but that is a decent guess. I was technically her youngest student."

Going back to Ibris, "Also to note, Renka is family. She was the granddaughter of my first son of my second wife. If a member of my faith and family could teach a young orc how to mend a body while he learned the mysteries of his faith and the soul, then the Radiant Father is a living testament to my Lady's work."

Both Tulok and Isolde just stared at Safar as they wrestled with the information that the Sun Guide just laid out. Tulok's conversation about Safar's lineage was now affirmed, while Isolde was lost in the map of his ancestry.

"That will require … some discussion with the Temple before I make any formal decisions. Agreeable?" Ibris said with a bit of reluctance. "And your third deman… I mean favor?"

Safar raised his finger in jovial warning, but his smile was sharp. "The last is simple. A member of the Radiant Lord's faith must accompany every caravan that rides in Setesh, no matter where it goes. Whether it is Champion, Priest, Acolyte, or Layman, their representation and presence assure travelers that the Lord of the Skies is watching over them all. Despite the attack of an Emperor, having the Radiant Father and Acolyte Kalb with us changed the attitude of many in the caravan. Travelers pushed themselves more and looked to each other not as strangers but as brothers and sisters on a journey where all rely upon each other. This is something that needs to continue to happen in order to promote a willingness for more travel."

This time it was Ibris that leaned back in his cushion and smiled. "No."

"What do you mean, no?" Safar asked.

"It is exactly what it means – no. The Clergy of the Radiant Lord are not tour guides! We provide leadership, justice, and diplomacy in order to assure civility among the peoples of Setesh. The priesthood adheres to their worries and earthly needs so they may find salvation in the Ever-Burning Lord's embrace!"

He set the glass on the table and placed his hands on top of his knees. Ibris' posture straightened. His tone was exasperated, as a parent would be with a child. "No Safar, that request is utterly ridiculous and yet this has been the fourth time, in as many years, you have brought this to the negotiating table. Do you purposely put this out just so I can tell you no? I know this game as well as you do. I was willing to remove the request for the Wandering Knight in exchange for Ahsal, but after that ridiculous motion ... maybe we should go back to that part of the discussion of what we need from her afterward. I believe her silence has just become necessary in this matter."

The vein in Isolde's forehead twitched as she set her jaw tight. Her fist slowly unfurled their fingers on the cushion.

Safar's demeanor shifted much, as if his features and eyes became sharper. He bore a simple stillness, like a serpent waiting for its moment to strike.

Tulok felt the whispers in his ear. The Gurkh felt the pull of tension all around, and it wanted to come into 'play'. Closing his eyes, he let his mind still itself. Reason was needed here, not emotions.

There had to be a way out of this.

Slowly, the words crept into his thoughts from afar, and there it was.

"Champion Ibris, please, let us take a moment to consider everything. A single favor should not spoil the progress both sides have been making. Even fermented honey has its uses," Tulok offered with raised hands.

Ibris twitched for a moment, and then turned to the orc, "Wha... what did you say?"

"Even honey ferments ..." Tulok said quietly, correcting the phrasing the Dusk Priest had told him.

Ibris looked down at the table and absently tugged at the bottom of his ear. He sat silent for a moment and then stood up. Looking toward Safar, "As Champion for the Radiant Lord, I accept all your requests. Ser Isolde duAvalonne is free from all responsibilities concerning Ahsal, but we ask for your polite discretion in the matter. Next season, we expect you to have your volunteers ready to begin instruction in our temples. Finally, we will require a daily, updated list of the caravan treks made across Setesh. This will take time to coordinate and will require much of your attention. In return, we accept the offer of dedicated transportation to the ruins, the bodies of the alleged cultists, and the body of Acolyte Bengt Kalb. Do we have an accord, Reysis?"

For once, the confident smile on Safar's face was shaken. He stood up and held out his hand. "We ... we have an accord."

"Excellent," Ibris said as he grasped the Reysis' hand. With a firm shake and a nod of the head, he made his way to the door. Stepping around Tulok, he held up his hand. "You are free to stay Father, I need to take care of some other pressing matters. As the Reysis noted – your friends miss you. We will talk again when you are ready."

With that, Ibris left the room.

It was silent for a moment before Isolde finally spoke up. "What just happened?"

"I think … we won?" said Safar, just as confused.

Tulok said nothing and just let out a sigh of relief.

Chapter 18

Tulok remained seated, staring at the closed door.

Isolde looked between her two companions, and then the door where the Radiant Lord's Champion exited. She waited for a few beats and then let out an exhausted bellow, falling back into the pillows she was seated on. Her arms outstretched, she stared at the ceiling.

"I. Hate. Politics," she said to the room.

Safar looked over at the big priest. "What was it you said to him to make him change his mind? I have known that man for more than a decade and he never gives in!"

Tulok shook his head and shrugged. "I just tried to reason with him. Everything seemed … intense. I had to say something." with that, Tulok reached over and pulled a leg off the dinner bird and chewed on the meat in quiet relief. He felt a little guilty at not sharing the whole truth of the matter, but all faiths had their secrets. It was only partly a lie. He did not know what the phrase meant, only that he had to say it when the time was right. At that moment in the negotiations … it was right.

Safar did not give Tulok a second look and accepted the fate that fortune had presented him. He glanced over at Isolde, who was staring at the ceiling. "Did you discover the truth of the Heavens on my ceiling, Island?" he asked. He leaned over to where the Knight lay sprawled across the pillows on the floor. He placed his head next to hers.

"Maybe?" Isolde replied. She squinted, trying to focus on something. "Unless … tell me, Reysis, do the children of the Guild play with darts?" She asked.

"Sometimes … why do you …," he asked as he turned to look

upwards. Suddenly, his pleasant smile faded, and he muttered in his native tongue. Isolde did not know what he was saying, but understood the tone of a displeased parent well enough. She chuckled and looked over at Safar. He shook his head and then smiled winningly at her.

Tulok cleared his throat uncomfortably from his position at the table. "Am I interrupting?"

"If I said yes …," Safar began.

"No," Isolde replied, and shoved her open hand into Safar's face, pushing him away. He laughed. It was rich and full of earnest mirth.

"No, my friend. I assure you," the Sun Guide shook his head. With practiced grace, he unfolded himself and stood. He offered his hand to Isolde. "As amusing as it will be to watch you try to get up while in your gear …"

Isolde scowled at Safar and accepted his hand, allowing him to give her the leverage she needed to pull herself to a standing position. "You insisted."

"'Tis true," Safar nodded. "I accept full responsibility for ensuring you were properly attired when meeting Ser Ahsom Ibris."

Isolde harrumphed at Safar and then turned her gaze to Tulok. She moved around the table, embraced the orc from behind, wrapping her arms around his neck and shoulders. "And you … you stupid bookworm," she said and squeezed him tightly.

Tulok's eyes widened a little at the strength of her embrace. He chuckled and patted her arm. He shifted from his seated position to turn toward her and opened his arms awkwardly. As he was about to return the embrace, Isolde reached out and looped her right index finger around his left tusk and pulled his face to hers. His eyebrows climbed into his non-existent hairline. Nose to nose, she stared into his red eyes. Her voice lowered, "Not. A. Damn. Word. In. A. Season! Nothing!" she chided. She released her grip on his tusk and shoved him back. Balling up her fist, she punched him solidly in the shoulder.

Tulok flinched. "They sequestered me in a single room for the first month. They only let me out to pray, eat, and nothing more save to answer question after question! I just found out all my correspondence was being intercepted, especially from you!" He rubbed his shoulder and looked over at Safar for help. The Reysis held his hands up and took a step back.

"She tried to break my jaw once already ...," He commented and rubbed his bearded chin for emphasis.

Tulok turned his eyes back to the woman warrior. "Isolde ..."

She slapped his shoulder. It was not hard. "Nothing," she slapped it again. "Nothing from you," she stepped in. Tulok's eyes widened. He reached out quickly. His massive hands closed over her wrists, stopping her onslaught. She tried to pull away for a moment and then stopped. The anger quickly faded away from her eyes and was replaced with tears. Letting go of her wrists, he gently pulled her in close. "I missed my favorite patient," he said and rested his chin on top of her head.

She laughed and sobbed into his shoulder. "Good ... you had better ..."

Safar groaned loudly as he rolled his eyes. "The both of you ...," He shook his head. "I am done with you both while I am sober. I am going to ask Kefu to bring us wine and we are going to properly celebrate. Until then, no more yelling ...," he pointed at Isolde, "or violence. This is a Guild Hall! Do that outside with the respectable people!" He smiled and chuckled, and the Sand Dancer walked out of the room.

Slowly releasing his embrace, Tulok looked down at her. "Sun-kissed – I finally got it!" Tulok said with realization.

Looking up at him, "What?"

The big orc smiled a little. "You were much paler when last I saw you. You have more color on your face now. And your hair is lighter. Sun-kissed ... lightly, but the mark of Setesh nevertheless," he said, partially amused.

She sat next to him and reached up to drag a loose strand of hair in front of her eyes to examine it. She shrugged. " I had to make myself useful, and working outside was part of my promise. What about you? What is this on your face?" She reached out and lightly slid her hand over the beard that traced the line of his jaw. "Very dignified sir."

Tulok rolled his eyes, but there was still a slight blush on his cheeks.

The door to the room pushed open once more. Safar walked in with bottles in hand. He stared at the priest and the warrior and just shook his head. "Lady, grant me the grace to deal with the both of you again!" Setting the bottles on the table, "Are we all good now? Through with the hitting and the tears? This should be a happy moment! Both of you are free from bondage and I ... I just became very, very busy."

The Reysis let out a deep sigh. "I still cannot believe it. I knew we could free Island of the obligation. That was the simple part. I figured the healer request would provide enough focus for us to debate upon. The last request, admittedly, was a gambit because he had always said no to it. I did not think he would react in such a fashion."

"There may have been more pressure involved than we first realized," Tulok carefully added. He knew there were other hands at play. He just did not realize how far it went until tonight.

Safar began pouring wine and passing the filled glasses to his companions. "The Temple of the Radiant Lord carries many secrets, my friend. Some I know, and some I fear knowing. Regardless, I would rather us benefit from this outward pressure than succumb to more secrecy."

"Yes ... about that ...," Tulok said as he looked at the floor.

Safar raised an eyebrow while Isolde sighed, "What now?"

—

Ahsom Ibris stood on a balcony that overlooked the western portion of the city. From this vantage point, coupled with his own vision, there was very little he could not see. From the movement of Ophir's citizens and to the patrols within the city, all went about their lives ignorant that they were being watched. Normally, this place brought him a sense of peace;

but tonight, it was far, few, and fleeting. He knew to expect company after the negotiations. His superior would have questions for him he would be hard-pressed to answer. The priesthood would have dozens more and probably would demand his badge of office.

"You worry too much, Ahsom," said a quiet voice.

The Champion did not bother to move; he knew who the voice belonged to.

"That is easy for you to say. You will not be the one accused of bending knee before the Sand Dancers. I will be lucky if they allow me to use a toilet by myself after this," he said with an irritated tone.

The hooded figure shook their head in a chuckle. "You can see like an eagle, yet you are as blind as a bat on the empty dunes. The location of Ahsal has been secured. That is a win for all of us. With the Avalonian released from her obligation to Tarf-qua, we can use her value elsewhere."

Ibris only adjusted his head, "Elsewhere?"

"Something outside of your concern ... for now," the figure said. "Also, you provided us with an unforeseen gift," they added.

Ibris raised an eyebrow. "I would ask how do you know ... but I do not care. Working in the shadows is distasteful. What unforeseen gift are you speaking of?"

"The mandate that requires a member of the temple to accompany all caravans. We can keep a quiet eye on them now. We will learn as much as they do about the mysteries of the desert. You did well Ahsom. In an hour, I expect you will receive a commendation from your superior. I also imagine that the Kalb family will not forget the great favor you have done by bringing their only son home for a proper funeral. Again, you have done more good for the Radiant Lord than you could fathom. You should be proud of yourself," they said as they leaned forward on the stone rails.

"What about Tulok?" Ibris asked. "Does he know about ..."

"No ... not a thing. That secret is safe with us. We only

instructed him to act when it was necessary. I believe he did well. He has the makings of becoming a fine priest for the order. It will take time ... but We are patient," they said, slightly amused.

"What about the Avalonian? They are ... close ...," Ibris added cautiously.

The figure shrugged. "People make choices all the time and learn from their mistakes. What friendships he cultivates and how is completely up to him. Far be it for you or me to tell him otherwise. He will learn. We all do."

"Yes, but that could be seen as ...," Ibris started, but his companion raised a hand, cutting him off.

"He will eventually have to make a choice – as will she. They are creatures of obligation and they will have to answer for them. He is a smart lad. He will do right by his Lord, his people, and by us," they said as Ibris felt a hand pat his shoulder.

"I hope so for his sake," Ibris said.

"He will Ahsom, as was said... *even honey ferments*," was the reply.

Ibris lightly tugged the bottom of his ear and turned to face his companion, but they were gone.

He loathed the Dusk Order, but there was no escape from them. His fate was sealed long ago with his own missteps in the past.

For a moment, he wondered if he could spare the orc his own fate by warning him in some fashion, but then he felt a cool breeze drift along the back of his neck in the warm night air.

He froze up and pushed the thought from his mind.

"Good boy ..."

Chapter 19

Arman pulled his coat closed against the chill and spray of the ocean. It was always cold here. He looked up at the skies, covered in dark clouds, hoping for a glimpse of the sun. There was none. He would never understand how people could live here.

Beside them and in the distance, the coastline of Avalon passed by. Miles of huge white cliffs served as a natural wall from the ocean's approach. At their highest peak, they were almost 500 feet from the sand below and stretched for nearly 15 miles. Legends of the area said the cliffs were littered with caves where the sea-dwelling denizens made their homes. From a distance, one could see flying creatures along the line of the cliffs. Some of these were birds. The Vidria stone shaper shuddered a little as he realized that some of those winged shapes were something altogether different.

The Mainland of Sanctum was crafted from the clay of this world. When the Reaping came to the outer worlds, those Divine powerful enough (or clever enough) spirited their people to this world for the sake of safety and preservation. They lived now on faraway shores; a gathered group of peoples, cultures, races, and religions. However, unlike the people of the Mainland, the Whole of Avalon was transported to this safe-haven by magics no one spoke of. With it came its people, its economy, and its ecology. Creatures of fantastical legend – both boon and bane, dwelt on these shores. There were stories in the beginning, of how Traders had tried to buy and sell creatures and plants from these shores, hoping to establish commerce with the Mainland. Many of the fauna and all the native flora failed to thrive on the Mainland. Some said this was because the Avalonians themselves were not wholly made from the realm material, but crafted from the stuff of dreams. Others claimed it was because the Divine force of The Mother refused to bless the Mainland when She arrived here; keeping Her blessings for Her people alone. It was said that in Her desire to create something that would bridge the divide between Avalon and the Mainland; The Mother had crafted the Folk from the clay of Avalon itself. Rather than see Her creation as a needed hand in a new world, The Divine Parliament rebuked Her; and this was why Avalon remained apart from the rest of the world.

Regardless of the truth, the Island Realm of Avalon hosted creatures and creations that could be found nowhere else on Sanctum. Many of them terrifying.

"All's well, Master Dah'ay?" a woman's voice asked.

Arman looked back over his shoulder at the source of the voice. A tall human woman stepped up to stand at his side. She was lean but athletic in build. Her skin was tanned and weathered from the sea and the wind. Her sun-bleached hair was short-cropped. The sides of her head were shaved, revealing decorative tattoos in blues and greens. She wore simple sailcloth pants, dyed brown, and rolled up at the knee and a shirt of flax linen.

Arman nodded. "Indeed, Captain. Just ... admiring the view," he gestured at the cliffs.

The woman nodded and folded her arms across her chest. "The White Cliffs are an inspiration, no matter how many times I see them," she acknowledged.

"They are made from chalk, is that correct?" the dwarf asked.

The woman pursed her lips and nodded. "Aye. They are." she looked over at Arman. "Something you can work with?" she asked.

Arman scratched at his bare chin and rubbed it in thought. "I've not worked in chalkstone before, but it would be a pleasant diversion," he looked up at the woman. "Are you looking for something in particular, Captain?"

The woman considered his words. "I had thought about asking you if you could replace some broken pieces to a game set I have ...," she mused.

Arman shrugged. "It might be easy enough to do. Depending on the intricacy of the pieces, they may be better replaced by carving than shaping ...," he took a breath, thinking, "Shaping is for ... hmmm ... larger works usually, though I ... have ... worked in smaller shapes as well," he replied. His thoughts drifted briefly to the wooden trunk in the ship's hold that carried his best work on a small scale. The five stone vessels from the Temple of Silence. Each of these had been crafted from stone that was unique to the specific Divine depicted on them: An owl-headed jar shaped from lapis lazuli for The Strategist – she whose spear pierced the heart of The Devourer himself and ended the Reaping. A black jar shaped from the deepest Onyx and topped with a wolf's head for the Runegiver. A green jar, shaped from Seteshi sands into Vidria glass, and topped with the head of a Phoenix for the Radiant Lord. A vessel of the purest emerald, decorated with the head of a doe for The Huntress of the Triskele.; Last, a simple vase, molded from the earthen clay of Avalon's shores and topped with the head of an elegant mare, for the Mother. One for each of the Divine who sat on the Parliament of Regency in the Heavens. One for each of the leaders of the surviving pantheons of the time before the Reaping.

It had taken him years to finish them. They were his life's crowning achievement. Yet, no one but a handful of people who walked this earth would ever see them, or know them for what they truly were. Vessels designed to contain the sacred spark of a descendant of the Founders of Sanctum.

"... waste your time ...," the Captain continued.

Arman frowned and blinked, and looked back up to the human sailor. "Apologies, Captain, the wind carried your words away before I could hear them," he offered.

The Captain nodded. "I was saying that I understand. The

hands of a master are best put to work on his chosen scale. I would hate to waste your time."

Arman waved her off. "It's no waste. As I said, it might even be a pleasant diversion," he smiled at her.

"Yes? Well, that is good to hear. I'll show you the set tonight at suppertime then and you can let me know what can be done."

Arman nodded. "Of course. It would be my pleasure to assist such a fine woman as yourself. The Guildmaster's recommendation could not have come higher," he complimented her, loud enough for others on deck to hear.

The Captain smiled at Arman's words. A positive impression of others influenced the leug she might carry going into port. The greater her leug, the more she and her crew would have access to. The more prestigious her contracts might be.

"Tell me, Captain Fiske, what are … those?" he gestured over at the cliffs and the activity going on.

Fiske narrowed her eyes and looked over at the winged creatures who were flying around the cliff side. She reached to her waist and withdrew a telescoping spyglass. Arman had seen such things used by the caravan Reysis in Setesh, but they were made from hardened leather, not metal. She placed the glass to her eye and stared off into the distance at the cliff.

"Gulls and Kingfishers, Master Dah'ay," she paused. "Ahh … wait. I see them now … you have a good eye, Master Dah'ay," Fiske commented. She lowered her glass and looked to the pilot of the ship. "Mister Oberson, give those cliffs a wide and respectable berth. The Teryton are hunting for lost souls. We'll need to let the harbormaster know when we make land."

"Aye, Captain," the man at the wheel replied and hefted the large wooden wheel one notch toward the open sea. He counted to ten and then pulled it back. The ship adjusted her course and continued on.

Arman continued to look out toward the cliffs at the strange winged creatures. "What are … Teryton, Captain? You must forgive my foreign curiosity."

Captain Fiske nodded and replaced her glass into its holster at her side. "Cursed wanderers, Master Dah'ay," came the reply. "Whatever they did, they died far from their homes and out of favor with the Divine. There aren't many of them left these days."

"And they are cursed?" Arman asked.

Fiske nodded once more. "Could be cursed by any of the Divine of the Isle; but typically that's the doing of the Keeper of the Crossroads."

"I … see," he replied. "You said they were hunting for lost souls?"

"Aye. It's the only way they can be forgiven for whatever crimes they committed. They have to take a life to exchange for their own," Fiske answered plainly. "But I would not worry too much, Master Dah'ay. They look to be those poor souls who threw themselves off the cliffs for whatever reason and have been denied the right to enter the Cycle anew." Fiske looked to Arman. His face was filled with confusion. She nodded to herself and explained. "They are patrolling the cliffs looking for those seeking to end their lives anyway. They hope that if they kill someone who is already looking to die, they will both be forgiven and get to move on."

"So … they are sentient?" Arman asked.

"As are many things here, Master Dah'ay," she chuckled. "We'll be to landfall in a couple of hours. Make yourself comfortable until we arrive," she patted the dwarf on the shoulder and turned to return to her post.

Arman Dah'ay stared out at the white cliffs and the creatures patrolling their steep faces. Those strange creatures had once been people! Now their souls were bound in these strange forms and cursed to remain so until they could claim another life for their own? He looked over at Fiske and the rest of the crew calmly going on about their business, seeming unconcerned about the existence of these things. He shuddered. At least firesnakes made sense.

He pulled his coat closed a little tighter and glanced once

more toward the heavens. Such a strangely different land than the Mainland Realms. The Mainland had areas of cold and wet as well; most of these were in the northern areas of the continent, where snow was frequent and the seas were frozen over. There were a handful of forested areas scattered across Sanctum that ranged from the Capital of Agelia to the ring surrounding the mountains and valley city of Sybaris. The Elven peoples had laid claim to many of said areas upon their arrival here and it was rarely wise to dispute territory with a people so keenly tied to the wilds. Trade in wood was often at a premium, though it was something the Avalonians held in abundance.

The northern lands of The Veldt were rumored to be mostly coastal prairie, mudflats, and scrubland. Few had ever ventured into that area and returned. It wasn't really considered a territory of its own, but more akin to empty lands devoid of proper civilization and governance. Some said the Trollkin, Ogroid, and other monstrous fellows of cast-off cultures and forgotten Divine dwelled there now. Arman often wondered what set the Orckind apart from the creatures of the Veldt; they seemed every bit as monstrous as the bog-dwelling Trolls or hillock denning Ogres. Yet they did not count the Orcs among the more nefarious denizens of the world. Indeed, they were welcomed and recognized as any other people. People, not monsters. Not *animals*, Arman corrected himself. People with a culture, a civilization, and their own customs. Remember that. You may have to trade with them while you are here.

Arman nodded to himself and secured the idea to the front of his thoughts, where he might remember it with greater ease. His thoughts dwelled briefly on the memory of a specific Orc. He was going to have to look for another to fill the vessel assigned to the Radiant Lord. They had secured the Orc priest, Tulok, while at the Temple of Silence. His lineage had been brilliantly preserved by the tale keepers of his Clan, who were happy to have it and the rest of their lineages recorded, transcribed, and sent to the Grand Library in Litharge for safekeeping. It had cost Arman a not-insignificant amount of coin to bring a historian to the village in the middle of nowhere, and have them record those stories. There had been a couple of promising candidates from that list, but Tulok had managed something none of the others had:

He had been accepted into the service of the Radiant Lord.

This creature, blessed with wisdom from the Hand of The Scribe, born of the lineage of a founding father of Sanctum, who had found his way into the sanctity of the Radiant Lord? Whose sacred spark shone brighter than many of those Arman had ever encountered? He had been too good a thing to pass up. The opportunity was lost now. It would be far too difficult and dangerous for him to attempt it a second time. He would have to find another once he was finished with his errand here.

It should not take too long, if Lynet's information was accurate, for him to find the old sage and be done with the exchange.

He only hoped that Phaendar was in a receiving mood.

Chapter 20

"I'm telling you, she tried to break my jaw!" Safar exclaimed.

Isolde rolled her eyes and tore at a section of the spiced meat. Cooked juices and grease dripped down her fingers as she shoved the meat into her mouth and ignored the comment. Beside her, Tulok sighed heavily and reached over to hand the Knight a cloth napkin before she could wipe her hand on her pant leg. She smiled with cheeks full and accepted it. "Dank coo".

Turning his attention to the Reysis, "I am uncertain which you are more concerned about, Safar. That she struck you, or that she may have been able to mar your signature profile," the orc commented as he picked at a handful of olives. He glanced over at Isolde. "I learned the hard way that she is more than capable of defending her honor, and will certainly do so ... if the need arises," he continued eating. "You expect me to believe she struck you for no reason?"

Safar ran his hand across his bearded chin. "I ... *may* ... have deserved it," he offered.

Isolde threw her soiled napkin across the table at Safar in response. It hit him in the face.

Tulok pursed his lips as his eyebrows rose. He looked between Safar and Isolde. He popped the last olive into his mouth and held up his hands, showing he was not getting involved in their squabble.

"I understand you left your caravan to ride ahead at a great pace?" the priest asked as he reached for his cup, trying to change the subject.

The comment sobered Safar's mood. "Yes," he replied. He glanced over at Isolde. She nodded. "Island was assaulted by

145

nightmares while we were in Deneb-aal."

"They were not nightmares!" Isolde insisted.

Safar muttered an unpleasant comment under his breath. "Fine. Visions then? Living darkness? Some ... *insight* into something happening back on the Island ..."

Tulok's brow furrowed. He turned to look at Isolde. "I thought the Lord Wanderer's Chosen were not given to fear?"

Isolde gestured to Tulok, while staring at Safar. "As I tried to say," she replied. Safar harrumphed at her. She turned back to Tulok, "I do not suffer from dreams born of fear, what you would call a nightmare," she affirmed. "For me, Nightmares are real. They are creatures, violent denizens of the Morpheum ... those are another matter. While not full Nightmares ... something was trying to grab my attention. Violently."

The knight and the priest exchanged a knowing glance. Isolde had shared with Tulok many things about her people and their land when they were in Nahral. They bound all those secrets under an oath of silence.

The orc simply nodded. "I see." He drank from his cup. "Two questions, if I might?"

Isolde nodded. "Of course."

"The first: Can you tell me what happened? And the second," he looked over at his friend. "Are you all right?" the healer asked sincerely.

Isolde's face softened with a smile. "I can answer both." She took a breath and reached for her glass, drinking deeply from the dark liquid. "The second first," she began. "Yes – I am fine. Safar, and his son's family in Deneb-aal, were excellent hosts and took excellent care of me before, during, and after the incident." She looked across the table at Safar and offered him an earnest smile.

The Reysis inclined his head and tapped two fingers above his heart. "Anything for you, my friend," he replied.

"The first ..." Isolde took a deep breath and rubbed the back of her neck in thought. "I ... how to explain?" she asked and continued. "A dream? There was a storm. Lightning. Bodies stuck in the mud at the base of a tree. The tree had ... a scarab carved into it?" she paused, trying to remember the details.

"... with roots black as night ...," Tulok whispered softly.

Isolde's eyes darted over to him. She nodded. "Yes! Exactly! Wait? You've seen it too?" she asked, her voice flavored with excitement. "Then you have also seen him?"

Tulok shook his head. "No. These were visions that some of our Seers have reported." He sucked on a tooth in thought for a moment, then looked back up at Isolde. "Saw who?"

Safar and Isolde exchanged glances. Safar shrugged and leaned back into his cushioned seat.

"Arman," Isolde said.

Tulok's face was a mask of confusion as he tried to decipher what had just been said. The Vidria merchant had been responsible for capturing Tulok, binding him, and almost successfully stripped him of his thinking mind – his Ghal, leaving behind only a rage-filled monster born of the Gurkh. It was perhaps one of the greatest offenses that could be committed upon Orckind. Tulok had killed at least one man in that state of mind and had almost killed Isolde. The merchant had been at Ahsal, but there was no trace of his body after the cave-in. Bile rose in Tulok's throat, along with an unbidden rumble deep in his chest. The Gurkh, the internal Rage, danced on the edge of his calm mind.

He closed his eyes and took a settling breath.

Lacing his fingers together, Tulok rested his arms on his thighs. The gesture was one of calm control, but his knuckles were white and his fingers dug into the flesh on his knees.

"Please. Tell me everything."

—

Safar made a face at the paper. "Are you sure he was not suffering from a disease?"

Tulok rolled his eyes. "For the third time, no. Seers are ... gifted. They are also troubled. Some force many of them to watch the beginning and end of people's lives. They see all things that come to pass. Imagine living constantly in the future of your mind's eye, but not really being able to live your life. Visions of people dying and being unable to stop it. What is worse, you do not know who they are. And moreover, you get these." he motioned to the scrawls on the parchment that Isolde was looking over. "Vision of things that make little sense to you and they cannot escape them until they do."

Safar raised his hands in surrender. "Fine, fine. I understand. All I am saying is ... how are you able to discern anything from ... that?" he simply motioned his hands to the images.

"It is really not that hard when you break it down," Isolde said, as she shifted the paper from different angles. "So, if we take what I saw and this ... Arman is the viper biting the tree, or rather poisoning the tree?"

Tulok nodded his head. "Possibly. Though I am not sure what the tree represents ...,"

"Did the seer who gave it to you have anything else to say?" she asked. "I mean there could be more meaning we are not seeing."

"It was not from the seer directly but one priest who works with interpretation. When the vision started appearing among the seers, they sought the possibilities to the north. When those came up dry, they threw another idea on the table. This is not the only continent with grand fir trees," he said cautiously.

Safar raised an eyebrow in question.

Isolde's head fell forward and softly shook from side to side.

The Reysis looked at her in concern. "What is it?"

"Avalon," she said aloud. "If Arman is the serpent, then whatever he is doing is not only happening on Avalon, but will spread from it. The danger will come from my home," she said with a sense of worry.

The mood hung in the room like smoke from a snuffed-out candle.

Isolde looked up at Tulok. "Is this happening now? Can we prevent it, whatever it is? I mean, there has to be something 1 can do. I owe him for what he did. What he did to you! We ..."

The big priest put up his hand. "They have asked me to investigate this possibility. However, given the difference between our cultures, I have been asked if you can aid me in this as this is something that affects your people, as well as bringing a Seteshi criminal to justice."

Safar's laugh broke in. "So that is why Ahsom will let her go. They KNEW this! Ahsom had another game going this entire time! The Island Nation does not like outsiders poking too far inland, and if one of ours is there … she is the perfect tool to open that door!"

Tulok shook his head. "Actually, no Safar. Champion Ibris did not know about this. I was only given this missive right before coming here. While I admire his reputation, the Champion is not known for his … *craftiness*," the orc said before quietly drinking from his cup.

Unsatisfied, Safar shook his head. "Yet, the results of the negotiation speak for themselves: whether it was him or someone else within the priesthood, they knew they needed a way to investigate this matter on the island."

"Safar, what if this is not some sort of conspiracy? What if it is just what it is? Visions do not usually carry an agenda with them," Isolde implored.

Still shaking his head, "It is easy for you to say Island. You have not dealt with the priesthood for as long as I have. Our friend here is, no offense intended, from the top of the well."

Isolde made a face. "Tulok's what?"

Tulok answered, "*Top of the well.* Safar is implying that I am fresh, transparent, and clean. He believes that the further you go into the priesthood, deeper down to the bottom of the well, the darker and cloudier you become. To which I say he is not completely wrong; the further you delve into mysteries of the priesthood … there are tendencies to be seen as more secretive," the priest replied.

Safar reached for his glass and took another drink. "It is neither here nor there. The point is: they may have let you go Island, but there was still a cost. I am sorry Father, but there will always be a cost." He paused and stopped himself. "My friends, I am sorry. You are both considered friends and like family. I just feel that there is always something more going on. Not so much an insidious conspiracy, but the convenience of the matter is something to consider. Nevertheless, this means we will need a Mazdan."

Both Tulok and Isolde looked at Safar. "Wait, what?" said the confused knight.

"Why would we need a spell crafter?" Tulok added. The Priesthood regarded with ... caution ... those who crafted magics from things other than the Divine.

"It will take weeks for you to get to Port Kraken," Safar said. "Neither boat nor land travel will get you there more quickly. You will need to have a Mazdan, who possesses the ability to open a gateway and get there sooner rather than later. There are few in Setesh. As chance would have it, I know one. We will just have to hope they are in a good mood."

Isolde narrowed her eyes at Safar. "What did you do?"

"It is nothing of import ..." Safar began, but was cut off by the orc.

"No Safar," Tulok cut in. "Those that delve in arts of teleportation are a wild lot. Spell crafting aside, those who study that type of magic are ... often unreliable and dangerously unstable. Why would one be upset at you?"

Safar shrugged and tugged a little at his beard, uncharacteristically sheepish. "Well ... they are angry about something that has not happened yet," the Reysis offered.

The pair stared at him quizzically. "I'm sorry?" Isolde asked.

Safar smiled at Isolde. "I accept your apology. ," He grinned and then continued. "They are angry for something that has not happened yet, and I do not know what it is because – it has NOT happened yet," he replied.

Isolde squinted and stared at her friend. "Then how ... I ... that," she tried to gather her words and just shook her head. "No ... Seers and spell crafting are strange enough as it is. This just proves the point."

Tulok sat silent for a moment, as if weighing things out mentally. "Strangeness aside, he is right. It is the most expeditious method ... provided they are reliable."

"They are certainly more reliable than that damnable gnomish contraption!" Safar swore.

Tulok nodded his head slightly in thought.

"Gnomish contraption?" Isolde asked carefully. The curiosity of the Witness sparked with the potential for new information.

"No," Safar said firmly.

Isolde looked to Tulok for better information.

"The Conveyance is ... hmmm ... troublesome," the orc offered carefully. Seeing that Isolde would not accept that explanation, he added. "Gnomish engineers cobbled it together with technology that survived the Reaping, but none of them truly understand any longer. Sometimes it works well ...,"

"And other times, the traveler arrives in an unrecognizable state of liquid ooze," Safar scowled. He met Isolde's eyes directly. "It is not safe, and I will not have you use it if other options are available."

Isolde furrowed her brow. "You are deciding for me now, Reysis?" she asked.

Safar paused. He pursed his lips together in frustration. "I will rephrase ... I will not take you to the location, make introductions, or arrangements for you to travel using this unreliable and potentially deadly method of travel. As your Reysis, I am responsible for your safekeeping until you reach your destination." he took a breath and stepped in to take Isolde's hands into his. He placed her hands over his heart and covered them with his own. He stared into her emerald eyes. "I ask you to honor me in this, Island, and not place yourself in needless danger if I can find a better solution," he paused. "Please."

The Witness and the Reysis stood watching one another for a moment, Isolde measuring the intentions of the man before her, Safar asking the Avalonian to respect his station and wisdom.

Isolde looked to Tulok and then back to Safar. "If we get tele-ported inside a cave full of the undead, I am going to be sorely put out with you."

Chapter 21

The night air was pleasant as the priest and knight made their way out of the courtyard of the Guild Hall. All around them were fires and groups of people sitting, laughing, and telling stories. Her time in Setesh allowed Isolde to pick up enough of the language to understand when a bawdy joke was being told or when a spooky story was being woven. She smiled gently as they passed by, enjoying the bustle of the city after nightfall.

Tulok walked quietly at her side. He nodded politely to passersby, eyes occasionally drifting toward the foreign woman at his side. Breaking the silence, Tulok spoke first. "Your letters were being intercepted. Bengt's family were using their pull to find out whether his blood was on my hands."

Isolde nodded quietly and looked up at him, a slight hint of sadness in her eyes at the mention of the late acolyte.

"Bengt was an irritable git, but he did not deserve the end dealt to him," she said firmly. Memories of the remains of their burned campsite in the desert, Bengt's broken body half-buried in the sand. "I cannot blame his family for wanting to know more. At least they will see him send him to his rest."

Tulok nodded. "After we thought you were ... gone, he changed. I told him the full scope of what was going on and he accepted the burden. Part of me wonders if ..."

"No, stop right there. Do not do that," she interrupted. She could hear the pain in her companion's voice, "Wondering about 'what ifs' only causes heartache and undeserved guilt. The entire chain of events happened as they needed, with some very horrible consequences," she said, "Even if he knew what he was getting into – that does not change how things ended up. I would have still fallen into the Iteru and you would have still tried to push forward."

"Arman indicated he orchestrated the events on the Iteru," Tulok quietly admitted.

Isolde stopped and looked up at Tulok, "He did what?!"

The orc nodded. "During my sequestering, I had to relay everything in as much detail as I could remember. The constant questioning allowed me to recall things with more clarity. After they had me bound like a wild animal …" he scowled at the memory of being stripped of every shred of decency at the hands of the Vidria dwarf. "Arman admitted to having a hand in your demise."

Isolde ground her teeth. "That son of a bitch!" She swore and looked up at Tulok. "Does he have to be walking when we bring him in?" she asked.

Normally, the priest in him would have admonished her, yet the orc in him flavored his reply, "We cannot pass judgment on him. That is for the Temple to decide. However, he only needs to be able to talk."

She smiled at him. "You know," she started as they continued walking, "that beard seems to add a lot of wisdom, *your Radiance.*"

Tulok rolled his eyes and just chuckled.

They walked in silence as they approached the archway and entrance to the Temple grounds.

"Well, this is your stop. Or do I need to make sure you make it to the Temple safely?" she said with a smile.

"I believe I will be quite safe, but I appreciate the offer, Ser Knight. I will be at the guildhall by late morning, so try to get some rest. Portal travel is… taxing," he added.

She beamed brightly. "It will be my first time doing so as well. But if it gets scary, I will let you hold my hand."

He looked down at the knight and just shook his head, "I'll hold your hair when you start throwing up."

Isolde laughed and then paused. "Wait – are you serious? Does it make you ill?"

The big priest shrugged, "Guess we will find out tomorrow."

"Oh, I hate you," she said.

"Goodnight, Isolde," he grinned.

"Goodnight ... *bookworm*," she said with a smile and turned back toward the courtyard. Hundreds of colored glass lanterns lit the path back to the guildhall of the Sand Dancers. Tulok watched after her as she walked away, noting the silent figures in guild colors along her path, honoring the promises made by Reysis Safar al-Shifa to safeguard this strange foreigner. Tulok shook his head and looked toward the temple. A few hours of sleep and then jumping through a magical portal to a city hundreds of miles away. What could go wrong?

—

The mid-morning was bustling with activity. The city's inhabitants conducted their businesses after the sun rose and paused at midday. Those in-between hours were filled with commerce that established the capital as the realm's financial backbone, rivaled only by Nahral. While the River Lord's city prospered through its waterway trade and shipping, Ophir's trade came not only from the Iteru and the coast, but from the north as well, providing goods unseen in the region because of its warmer weather. It was in this deluge of traffic and trade that Isolde and Safar spotted their wayward orc making his way through the crowds. His massive size made him an easy target for those seeking guidance from a representative of the Radiant Lord. The ever-faithful priest stopped frequently to politely allow others to pass or was stopped at a request of a blessing or an opinion.

"Do you think if we put a sheet over him, he might get here faster?" Isolde asked Safar.

Completely ignorant that he was being observed, the priest drifted from one conversation to another. First, it was a merchant, then an elderly couple, following that with a mother and her two children. At one point, he lifted the younger of the children up in the air so they could see something on a stall shelf.

Safar stood at Isolde's side, hands on his narrow hips, shaking his head as he watched the spectacle before him, "Possibly, but who are we to deny his Radiance the opportunity to mingle with the masses," Safar said to her and then turn his attention to Tulok and yelled, "WHEN WE HAVE AN APPOINTMENT WITH POSSIBLY DIRE CONSEQUENCES!"

Isolde chuckled and shook her head. Safar just stood there with his mouth open in disbelief, as Tulok continued his oblivious attendance of others around him. He looked to Isolde, then to the priest, and back to the woman. "Why?" was all he could say.

The Avalonian said nothing and just shrugged.

Perhaps through a merciful nudge from The Scribe, Tulok looked up and saw his companions. He smiled and waved. Shaking the hand of the woman he was speaking to, he set the child down and hurried along to the pathway, "My apologies. This was the most direct route here, which was apparently the busiest route."

"Are you sure you want to leave so soon? I thought I saw a line of children forming ...," Safar said with smiling sarcasm.

Tulok turned his head to look behind him, but stopped himself and frowned at Safar and his teasing. "I apologized, but when people are in need, it is difficult to say 'no' to them."

Safar rolled his eyes and sighed. "Well, with any luck," he gazed skyward at the position of the mid-afternoon sun, "our Mazdan should be active now, so their attitude will be less ... volatile."

"Are they normally volatile?" Tulok asked.

Safar mimicked shifting of scales with his hands, as if weighing options and responses. "Six of one, half dozen of another. We will find out when we get there. Barring additional stops along the way to fetch kittens from awnings ...," Safar looked up at Tulok pointedly, "It should take us about twenty minutes. I have already bought their favorite tea. It should at least buy us a foot in the door; the rest will depend on them and how their day has been going."

"Lovely," was all Isolde could add. "Please ... lead the way."

—

Mazdan were spell crafters. Not just the typical spell crafter, these worked with magics considered more dangerous than others. They were considered an oddity within Ophir. While the powers of the Divine provided supernatural results, those that trucked with forces metaphysical were looked upon with caution. While not technically heretical, a Mazdan practiced arts considered "outside" the governing eyes and blessing of one of the existing deities. Concepts like transmutation and teleportation were not directly tied to a deity; this made the reliability of their magics questionable and not a direct concern to the Priesthood. There were, however, rumors of a secretive Divine called simply the Sorceress. The presence of unknown Divine meddling in the ways of those gifted with magic warranted observation by the Temple. Very. Keen. Observation. No one who broached the subject with a Mazdan had anything more about it.

Wise Mazdan, who did not wish to draw the attention of the Everwatchful Eye of the Radiant Lord, still paid homage to the various Divine that sourced the wellsprings of magic across Sanctum. If a Mazdan crafted a spell to elicit a lightning bolt from their hands, it would be customary to thank The Changebringer who held dominion over the storms and weather phenomena. It was better to offer thanks to a deity in order to cover one's mystical behind than risk the wrath of Divine who clearly still roamed the earth.

Because of the unpredictable nature of these magics, Mazdan homes and research facilities were often sequestered from the rest of a City's inhabitants. In Ophir, this was closest to the Northern walls of the City. This allowed them to take defensive positions to protect Ophir if the City came under assault. If anything exploded (as happened with far too much frequency), they were far enough away that most citizens and businesses would not be disturbed. Historical records showed a handful of incidents had led the leaders of Ophir to create a designated space for those citizens who possessed the talent in the magical arts to practice in safety. The Scribe's people had instituted a fifty-yard area of space between this area and the rest of the city for safety. As many locals carried on their day-to-day affairs, all avoided stepping any more than was necessary into the space around Mazdan work area.

The space difference was not lost on Isolde as the three of them approached the 'border' of the work area. She watched as people neatly side-stepped the otherwise empty area, avoiding it with trained skill. She looked up at Tulok.

"Is that why Skavalt was outside of Deneb-aal proper?" Isolde asked.

"Who?" Tulok replied.

"Skavalt. He was the Mazdan who sealed the box originally," she replied, and then was silent for a moment. "You know, it was not until we stopped in Deneb-aal that I had thought of him. The way everything went, I should send word and thank him for what he did."

"That seemed so long ago ...," Tulok added.

Safar just shook his head. "Could have taken another caravan to the north, but no; I choose the one with you two." He gave them both a smile. "And like an idiot, I would do so again. But to answer you Island ... yes, Skavalt took his home up away from town proper in case something went wrong with his binding spells. He is a decent man with a fair disposition. Bay'an, on the other hand ... well, we will see when and where we are."

Most of the homes in the workspace varied in size and decoration. Some were crafted of white clay, others the color of sand. A few sported elegant panes of colored glass. Tulok could see various protection and binding glyphs worked into the decor. Eves, sills, door headers, brickwork; all seemed to carry intricate designs. To an untrained eye, the bindings looked like complex decorations. To one who had spent decades studying in libraries, these designs denoted the magics being woven into the fabric of the building materials themselves.

Following Safar's lead, Tulok and Isolde made their way through the streets of this decorated neighborhood. The home they stopped in front of did not differ from the others, but the glyphs were far more intricate.

"Lots of circles on this one," Isolde noted, looking at the patterns on the door and walls.

"Space within spaces," Safar commented with a nod, "But do not ask about them or you will never leave on time," Safar added and then knocked on the door.

"THERE IS NOT SUPPOSED TO BE ANYONE HERE FOR ANOTHER EIGHT HOURS!" yelled a voice from inside.

"Yes, but this one bears Fire Stem Herbs," Safar called out with a smile in his voice, and on his lips.

"YOU CAN GO TO H ..." There was a pause, a shuffle of footsteps, and a small peephole opened up in the door. "Fire Stem? That's my favor ... SAFAR!"

The peephole closed, and a dazzling figure opened up the door. Their hair was long and dark but streaked with silver, giving the impression of a burst of light in a dark sea. Silks of blue and gold flowed like water off of their statuesque figure. Brilliant blue eyes, set into a smooth, dusky complexion, took in the trio standing at the door. Circular patterns danced in golden embroidery around the hem of their robes, mimicking the patterns on the house. While not as tall as the orc, Bay'an was just slightly taller than Safar and Isolde. As they stood at the doorway, they swayed slightly, as if to music only they could hear.

Smiling at Safar, their eyes drifted to Tulok. A curious eyebrow raised. The priest could feel himself under their polite scrutiny, but tried to give a friendly smile and hoped it looked like such. While not afraid of the Mazdan, treating those who wield dangerous and unstable power with kindness and respect was always wise. After a moment, Bay'an smiled and placed a hand over their chest and nodded.

Leaving Tulok, the brilliant blues met the emerald green of Isolde. The Mazdan and the Witness gazed upon one another for a few moments, each assessing the other. Finally, Bay'an looked behind Isolde as if expecting something to be hidden behind the Avalonian. Isolde turned around and looked as well, but could find what they were expecting.

"Strange … I thought they were always near … Oooohhh. Not yet, not yet, right?" Bay'an said to no one. They turned to Safar.

Safar spread his arms wide, anticipating a hug, but instead, Bay'an reached out and plucked the small bag of tea leaves from his hand. "This will buy you five minutes of time, my lovely backstabber. I have something going on that is time-sensitive."

Both Isolde and Tulok gave each other a sidelong glance, but said nothing.

"You know, you are the only one who has ever called me that," Safar started, but Bay'an cut him off.

"Yes … and as soon as I remember why that is, I am sure it will make saying it so much better. Or worse. One can never tell," they said with a bemused smile. "Enough small talk. You know I hate small talk." Bay'an waved a perfectly manicured hand at Safar and turned to focus on Isolde and Tulok once more. "What does an Avalonian Wanderer… and this beautiful specimen of Orckind … need with me?" Bay'an smiled devilishly at Tulok. Tulok blinked and cleared his throat uncomfortably. "Obviously you need something that is beyond the capabilities of the Radiant Lord or you would not be here. First, the answer is *no*, I cannot get her back to the Avalon. It is impossible; the Incirrata saw to that damned squid people … well, maybe a mile off the coast is a possibility. She could probably use him as a life raft. You can swim, right handsome?" Bay'an asked Tulok, who suddenly realized he was being addressed.

Before the big priest could answer, Safar waved off the question, and interrupted, "No, Bay'an – not exactly. We need to get them to Port Kraken. We believe there is a dangerous person heading to Avalon – if he is not there already. These two can catch a ship there, but it will take them at least three weeks to travel otherwise."

Bay'an sighed and looked at Isolde. "Black roots and dark skies?" they asked.

Wide-eyed in surprise – Isolde nodded her head. "Yes! Exactly! There were visions I had …"

Before she could finish, Bay'an waved a hand and looked slightly depressed. "I had hoped that it would come from the north, like a storm; that the skies would open up and let snow flood through and I could just bask in the chill. That is what I get for hoping. Come with me, good lady," Bay'an said, as they offered their hand to Isolde. "We have to get you prepared."

Confused, Isolde looked to Safar. He nodded at the Mazdan.

"Bay'an is right Island. It will be your first time traveling through a portal. They will take care of you. Go ahead."

Nodding her head, Isolde accepted their hand and Bay'an led them off further inside the house.

Closing the door, Safar let go a sigh of relief.

Tulok still had a confused look on his face. "Were they offering to teleport us to the middle of the ocean?"

"And what handsome raft you would make, my friend," Safar added with a smile and a pat on the orc's arm.

Chapter 22

Bay'an led Isolde into a room where several round pieces of glass hung from the ceiling. Each of these was a different shade and color, and all were catching the light at various angles. A massive shelf of various jars and bottles, all neatly labeled with names that Isolde could not understand, occupied one wall. A few large pots sat on a large cooktop over hot coals, stewing various concoctions. Isolde tried to focus her eyes on them, but Bay'an spun her around and sat her in a chair in the middle of the room.

"Uh Uh. Eyes up here, dear heart; ignore all the things around. They are not for you or your nosy Lord Wanderer. Some things get to stay secret and I need you to pay attention to everything I am going to tell you," Bay'an added with a tone of seriousness.

Isolde could feel the pull of curiosity, but caution won out as she focused on Bay'an's bright eyes.

"Good girl, now drink this," Bay'an added. They placed a cup in Isolde's hand. She looked at its contents. A swirl of greens and golds swam in the small container. Before she could ask, Bay'an motioned with their hands to drink the concoction. Trusting that Safar would not have placed her in danger knowingly, Isolde gave a slight sigh and drank back the cup's contents. It tasted like a mixture of honey and mint, but there was something in the aftertaste; something that made her feel … off.

She felt it in her chest and down in her stomach. She wanted to hold it back, but it felt too painful to hold in, even for a second. Isolde opened her mouth and felt as if she was about to throw up everything. Instead of liquid or solid matter, a swirl of colors blazed out of her mouth. Her eyes opened wide. Blue and green light shot out of her throat like the guiding beam from a lighthouse. She heard screaming all around her and realized that it was coming from her. It was all too much. Too much pain, too much time. How was time painful? She forced her eyes closed and gripped herself tightly. She tried to hold herself without moving, but she could feel ... wind?

Opening her eyes, she was standing on a grassy hillside. The clouds were gray; the signs of a storm coming. She looked around and saw a large lake with a tiny island. There were two figures on the island ... or three ... she blinked.

Blood. Pain. Dear Lord Wanderer, I am so sorry!

She felt tears stream down her face as she brought the sword down on the creature below her. She did not want to do this. It howled in pain as the sword pierced rotted corrupted flesh and let out a final death wail as she twisted the hilt with her tired hands. The tears ran hot down her face. She closed her eyes.

She was in a small, cramped shop. A tiny man was raving about ... something. The little man in front of her was broken somehow ... how was he broken? She tried to focus and could not. She felt it in her heart, and she did not know what to do. She watched as the lucidity faded slowly from his mismatched green and blue eyes. So much pain there ... as she watched him struggle to hold on to who he was ... and then watched the light of self fade away into noth-ingness. Why was this happening to her ... friend? She blinked.

She looked back and saw herself? At least it looked like her. Her face was older, resolute, but something was different, something she could not place. She reached out and nausea took over as the world spun. She was running. She was sitting. She was crying. She was laughing. She was content. She was on the verge of sorrow.

Isolde screamed in the darkness.

And then it all stopped.

She opened her eyes and saw two beautiful blue orbs looking at her. Warm, gentle hands covered hers, patting them gently.

"Avalonians," Bay'an smiled softly, "You always carry so many potential pathways inside you. It's like a pressure cooker.

Have to let some of it out before I send you off, or Heaven knows where you will land."

Isolde was still sitting in the chair in the middle of the room. She felt sweat on her brow and her eyes burned as if she had been crying for hours. Looking around at the light; there was no sign that time had passed, save for a few moments.

Bay'an already had a small washcloth in their hand and was carefully wiping away the tears. "The imagery should fade in a few hours, though it may be longer for one such as yourself," they added with a bit of a smile. "Travel by portal is outside the normal bounds of the Seteshi Gods. They control many things, but this power is outside of their … divinity," they added with a moment of hesitation, watching for Isolde's reaction.

Isolde frowned a little. She remembered hearing stories of other entities outside the Parliament of Heaven. *Orphics,* she remembered. Beings that escaped the Reaping and came to Sanctum as well, but had been denied a seat on the Council of the Divine. Many were single survivors of other Realms, unable to save more than a handful of their own faithful. Lost to the annals of history, but somehow still clinging to existence.

Bay'an continued to gently minister to Isolde. "Spell crafting has rules and order despite its chaotic nature. Sometimes … to get things done, one has to follow pathways outside of the accepted norms. My Mistress can cause a bit of ruckus for some of your Island believers. If it were not for that, I could easily focus a doorway to the shores of Avalon itself. However, the Incirrata's magics and the Keeper of the Crossroads do not always see eye-to-eye," Bay'an said as their gaze wandered away from Isolde.

The title hung in the air: The Keeper of the Crossroads; The Torchbearer; The Sorceress. Isolde frowned a moment. Something nagged at the back of her mind. The wisps of memory, hidden in the cloak of The Morpheum. A cave and a shoreline. A woman and a pair of shears. A golden thread that bound Isolde to … someone. She blinked and shook her head, trying to rid herself of the cotton that wrapped itself around her thoughts.

She remembered stories of blood rites and murder between those who followed the Chaotic Path of Sorcery and those who follow the Natural Order of Spell craft. The magics of the ocean-dwelling Incirrata were a matter beyond even these. Each saw the other as an abomination in the world of Sanctum. While they mostly confined the feud to stories, she could not help but wonder how much salt-driven truth was involved. Bay'an was Mazdan; It would only make sense that they paid heed to something less ... acceptable ... in the eyes of many.

Raising her hands to Bay'an, "The Lord Wanderer tells us to observe the world and tell stories of its inhabitants. He does not play favorites to those who can craft something from nothing, no matter their origins."

Bay'an's shoulder suddenly dropped in a moment of pure relief as their eyes rolled up to the ceiling. "Oh, thank the Mistress! The last thing I wanted was a fight in the middle of eight different projects and explain to your consorts why you were plastered to the ceiling."

Isolde blinked, "I'm sorry, my what?"

"Oh, I'm sorry dear. That is the term you use on your little Island isn't it? Consort? Person of favor? Heartsworn?" Bay'an waved their hand. "Your traditions of Courtly Love are just so quaint. I just assumed you were all involved with each other ... at least Safar, given his predilections and his openness about relationships. Is it just you and Safar ... or the priest or ..." they added with a raised eyebrow, "The priest and Safar? I mean, no judgment. Just curiosity ..."

Isolde shifted in her seat and was suddenly very uncomfortable. Shaking her head at Bay'an, "I ... uh ... um ... I ... well ... uh ... No ... I mean not that, well ... uh ..."

Bay'an's eyes grew wide, and they quickly placed a finger to Isolde's lips, "I am soooo sorry, dear. Choices clearly haven't been made yet. I understand. I will speak of it no more!" They waved a hand in the air as if to shoo away the conversation.

Reaching into their pocket, Bay'an took out a small jar and

opened it up. It smelled like a mixture of rose and lavender, two flowers that Isolde had not smelled for some time. Dipping their fingers into the mixture, Bay'an worked a little into their palm and placed it on Isolde's face.

"To change the subject, the mixture I gave you is something to … *lighten* your mystical baggage," they said, as they smeared a bit of the mixture on Isolde's forehead, cheeks, and nose. With the tips of their fingers, Bay'an worked the mixture all over the young woman's features. "It's taken me a few years to perfect the recipe. The original formula tasted like an old person's sweaty undergarments. I swore to myself that I could do better, and I did. By adding a few earthly ingredients to lighten the taste it brought an unexpected side effect. While not providing a genuine sense of future sight, like, say, an oracle or seer, my recipe provides insight into potential futures. You are my first Avalonian, and I have to say my dear … so *enlightening*."

Bay'an frowned at a random thought, remembering the vision of the small man with the mismatched eyes, then focused once more on Isolde. "So do not place too much stock in what you've seen. The mixture divorces residual spell crafting and magics from your body. The only thing within you is what is naturally attuned to your soul… and you Avalonians are SO full of, well, everything," Bay'an paused as they noted a discernible wrinkle in Isolde's forehead.

"Now, dearie, don't you worry, it didn't divorce you from your leug. That is still in place. You are still every bit the child of your Island as you were when you walked in here. I can tell you were concerned about that."

Isolde nodded a little. "What about payment for all of this? I don't …," she asked, stumbling over her words.

"Tut Tut, that's a conversation for me to have with the Reysis. He's the one that brought you here, so he's the one that needs to pay me. How you settle up with him is between the two of you." Bay'an smiled and winked at Isolde, who flushed a deep scarlet at the insinuation. Bay'an chuckled a little and the knight's discomfort. "Given that you were in a trance for a full minute tells me you were carrying a fair share on your shoulders. Given your ... *friendship* with those two in the other room, I can see why it took so long for the potion to work everything out of you."

Isolde blushed again, but this time not out of embarrassment. Her mind raced to all the divine magic and power she had been exposed to in the last six months ... it all made sense. The visions, as interesting and as terrible as they were, still shook her a little, but she could feel them slowly fade from her mind's eye. Sometimes it was best to not know what was coming, no matter how painful it may seem.

Bay'an smiled as they continued working the mixture from her face to her neck, "Potential paths have no definable taste, but trust me when I say ... it now tastes better by a thousand-fold and will make portal travel much easier from this point forward."

"Will I need to take it every time I travel this way?" Isolde asked.

"Oh, no. Once you go through, the metaphysical make-up of your body and mind will be more ... *accepting,* and will not have to contend with any residual magics," Bay'an answered.

Isolde nodded her head, as Bay'an was applying the mixture to her hands and wrists. "What about this salve? Is this a first-time thing as well or is it something I will need to do each time?"

Bay'an shook their head, "Oh no! Your skin is horrendously dry. Your youthful skin needs to glow like the morning light, not turn into a leather belt! This has nothing to do with travel; this is just self-care, dear."

—

Unable to find a chair that could support him, Tulok simply sat on the floor of Bay'an's sitting room. Staring at the various tomes that lined the walls, curiosity wanted him to pick one up to see what it was about; common sense and politeness rapped his curiosity across the knuckles, so he simply turned his attention to Safar.

The Sun Guide sat in one chair against the wall, leaned back, and closed his eyes. While it looked like he was napping, Tulok could see that the man was keeping an ear out for the other room. He was not eavesdropping; Safar was paying attention to anything that might warrant distress. The orc realized that, in his absence, Isolde and Safar had become close, but he was not sure how close they had become. Were they involved? Did it matter? Should it matter? He frowned at the thoughts and looked at the ground. The events of the seaside town were not spoken of and seemed to have been years ago.

"Your thoughts are as stealthy as a cat wearing bells on its feet," Safar said.

Quickly shoving his thoughts to the side, "Apologies, just worried about her; about Isolde," the orc lied. "My first time through a portal was ... unkind."

With his eyes still closed, Safar nodded. "Island will be fine. Bay'an will prepare her accordingly so it should go as smoothly as possible."

"Have you traveled by portal before?" Tulok asked.

"Me? Oh no, I am a Sun Guide! Portal travel would put me out of business," he said with a smile. "Not only me, but my family!" Safar shook his head with a smile. "No, such things are not for me and mine."

A thought crept up in Tulok's head at the mention of family. He scratched absently at the line of his beard. It was as good of a time as any. "Speaking of family, my friend ... your mother ..."

Safar's eyes opened up and looked at Tulok.

Tulok looked at the honey-gold eyes of the Reysis as Safar studied him carefully. In return, Safar saw that Tulok's own red eyes were doing the same.

"Yes," was all Safar could say.

Tulok simply nodded his head in unspoken acceptance of the single word.

"Does this ..." Safar started, but before he could finish, Tulok simply shook his head. "No."

Safar let out a small sigh of relief and smiled, "I did not think it would." His gaze went to the other room and then back to the priest. "Does she?"

Tulok shook his head again. "Truthfully, I only found out yesterday."

Safar laughed to himself for a moment, and then with earnesty in his eyes, "A favor, then?" he asked.

Tulok nodded. "If it is within reason, of course."

"Do not tell her. Please. It is my story. And if it comes up, I would like to be the one to tell her."

Tulok considered the request, "You wish for me to lie to her for you?" he asked, "Have we not kept enough from her already?"

Safar shook his head. "No. That is not what I am asking," he began. "She is a Witness, Tulok. The eyes of the Divine themselves. Do you know what she sees when she looks at me?"

A dozen possibilities danced in Tulok's mind as potential replies.

"A man. Just a man. Nothing more," His right hand drifted to the scorpion tattoo on his collarbone, the symbol of his Divine mother, The Healer, "It has been ...," His fingers caressed the ink gently, "... a very long time since that has happened." The mirth that so often danced in the Sand Dancer's eyes faded for a moment as a memory graced his thoughts. He blinked it away and focused once more upon the Orc. "I give you my word ... I will tell her. In time. In my own words." Safar promised.

The orc raised his hands. "That is a conversation I will gladly give up responsibility for," he said with a smile.

"Thank you, my friend."

"Practice your dodge and blocking. You will need it," Tulok said with a smile and they both laughed at the thought of the conversation yet to come.

"We leave for a few minutes, and suddenly we're left out of all the fun," Bay'an said as they re-entered the room with Isolde. "Now, if you two are done joking, we have to get you both going. The doorway opened up two minutes ago so we have to get these two moving." Bay'an looked at Tulok seated on the decorative rug, "Come on, Handsome. Flex and lift that fine form off my floor; time to go!"

"Wait, we are leaving right now?" Isolde's eyes darted over to Safar, "We cannot say goodbye, or isn't there a prayer or something?" she said as the finality of the moment set in.

The Sand Dancer's golden eyes were a mixture of emotion. He stood from his chair and crossed the floor to meet her. Offering a simple smile in response, "It is never goodbye, Island. We will all see each other again ... I'm sure of it," he said, and taking her right hand into his, he gently raised her fingers to his lips. "Lady's blessing on your travels," he whispered.

Bay'an looked between the two of them. Their eyes rolled dramatically. "Melodrama time later, Safar. Yes, it's all very *touching*. Come along, right now, my lovely," Bay'an reached to shoo Isolde down the corridor. "You'll be back. Your story is not done on this side of the water."

Accepting this, Safar and Tulok quickly followed Isolde and Bay'an deeper into the house. Down a hallway that seemed longer than the length of the house, the group found themselves in a room large enough to pose as a shop. The room was covered in sigils and circles of various sizes and makes. It radiated chaos and sorcery.

Suddenly, the orc felt very nervous; the Radiant Lord had no place here.

This was entirely something else.

The eyes of the Priest and the Mazdan met briefly. They exchanged an unspoken understanding in that moment of measured silence.

Bay'an moved to the center of the room and stared at a crooked line in the wall. As they drew closer, they saw that the line was not in the wall, but hanging in the air- as if the air were made solid. With hands outstretched, Bay'an rhythmically moved their hands in a circular motion while speaking in a language that none of them understood. The more they spoke and moved, the more they saw sigils slowly appearing in the air, surrounded by purplish eldritch light. The sigils glowed in rhythm with the motions of the Mazdan. The more Bay'an moved, the more pronounced the sigils glowed and the wider the crack opened. Within moments, it was as large as a doorway blazing with purple and golden light.

Bay'an looked at the group; their eyes were glowing in shades of blues and purples. "The time is now, dear hearts! If you are going to go, think of Port Kraken and nothing else. NOW GO!"

Isolde looked back at Safar, who was smiling at her. "Go Island – before that infernal thing closes!" She paused, then nodded and stepped into the rip in space.

Safar looked to Tulok and tapped two fingers to his right breast, "I relinquish my charge, Father."

Tulok nodded and called the favor of the Radiant Lord to his lips as he stepped through.

The last thing they both heard was Bay'an scold Safar, "It's NOT infernal, you uneducated heathen!"

As soon as her head moved through the threshold, everything twisted. Isolde could look behind her and in front of her. Behind her was Tulok, but not Tulok; a melted and stretched concept of the orc followed behind her. His massive bulk became amorphous like a cloud of bright divinity, stretching out like the setting sun along the 'roof' of the tunnel of light. The feeling was exhilarating; it was like standing in the presence of the Divine. She had seen nothing like this and felt awestruck as she felt her body racing forward to … *somewhere*.

Tulok had traveled by portal once before on a mission for the Temple. His first trek had taken but a moment, and he had felt like a beam of light soaring across the heavens. This time, however, was not like the last; there was no beam of light guiding him swiftly across the heavens. Instead, Tulok watched in horror as Isolde's frame twisted and turned in on itself like water and oil being mixed. Her eyes split and multiplied a hundredfold, each blinking and consuming the surrounding sights. Each eye searched the surroundings, gazed within themselves, and back at the orc. The full attention of the Divine, all on him in that single moment. It was too much. All of it was too much.

Tulok roared to make it stop.

For the first time, he roared not in anger but in actual fear.

His voice echoed off the wooden panels in the large room, and he stopped yelling. He could feel a hand squeeze his thumb. He looked down. Isolde was gripping his thumb and looking up at him in surprise. They were no longer in the tunnel of light. They were somewhere else, somewhere real.

Someone cleared their throat.

Looking toward the voice, they both looked over at the gnome, who was seated at a desk across from them. Wearing a pair of glasses with a weary-looking face, he sighed. Above the Gnome was a single sign that read "Welcome to Port Kraken – Harbor Master Registry."

"Ahem …," the gnome asked, "Do you have an appointment?"

Chapter 23

Cold wet mud oozed into the seams of Arman's left boot. He sighed an exasperated sigh and looked at the cloud-covered sky. This island would be the death of him. He closed his eyes for a moment and reached deep to pull on the magics woven into the bones and blood of his people. The earth that oozed between the stitches of his boot solidified into silica stone and formed a small dam. It changed the weight of this foot slightly, but also improved the durability of his footgear. It was not an ideal solution but would do for the moment.

Waterproofing clothing was not something often needed in Setesh. The desert realm rarely saw rain, and the only large body of water was the Iteru. Cloth for sails and tarps for shipping were normally the only thing that was waterproofed. Aside from the lack of need, the use of beeswax and lanolin for waterproofing rarely had a long lifespan in the hot desert climate. Despite being someone who had traveled beyond the desert realm of Setesh, Arman Dah'ay was still a product of the sands.

He had parted ways with Captain Fiske and her crew at the port town of Swansea on the North-Eastern side of the island. Lubri was the capital of Avalon, in the Kingdom of Cadwallon, and hosted most of the Realm's people, but there were still port towns and fishing villages that dotted the coastline. Each of these towns and villages hosted a handful of families and their holdings. Farms, fishing grounds, artisans, herdsmen; simple and self-contained. Each of these was pledged in fealty to a Lord who helped oversee the communities. A handful of landed nobles and High Lords held the fealty of these lesser Lords and those were sworn in service to the Eternal Empress, whose throne was held in Lubri.

Swansea was one of the larger port communities on the opposite side of the island from Lubri, within the kingdom of Oriel. Villages and towns brought their surplus to Swansea, where they would trade with one another for goods and gear their own people needed.

Every able body who was available helped to load and unload ships and wagons as they arrived, or as they prepared for departure. Bags of grain were weighed and measured. Conversations were had about the needs of villages up and down the length of the coast. Lists of needs were posted on various boards along the docks. Tradespeople noted what was needed, posted their own lists, and took their goods to where listing showed they should be dropped off. Information was shared openly and freely. If the shoals of one village were running shy, another provided for them, and discussion was had about what they needed to see them through. If another village had a surplus of grain or their herds had been fruitful, those gains were distributed to ensure no one went hungry or without wool for clothes. Where the Riverlord's city of Nahral prided itself on the statement that "none go without in His Domain" – that statement was made manifest in Swansea, without a single coin ever once changing hands. To a man who had dedicated his life to learning the skillful art of trade among the shrewdest of Sobekites, the altruism of Avalon was an alien and almost offensive experience.

However, it was that same altruism that afforded the Master Cartographer the ability to move within the community as he did. Absent of the native mystical measure of worth, Arman relied on the value of the name of the Guild and Maitresse Lynet. A flash of Guild badge here, a shared missive there, and doors opened to Arman that would have demanded years of dedicated service. Those same doors helped secure a vault in Swansea to store his most precious cargo while acquiring a suitable mount and gear to carry him inland.

He checked the entry in his journal, examining the landmarks and comparing them to the ones he had included the last time he had made this trek. Allowing for seasonal changes, water erosion, shifting landscape, he adjusted his footing and pointed himself in a different direction. Yes, there! In the distance, he could view the tree line and small hill formations noted there. Phaendar had sent word that Arman could find them along this path. If they had been earnest in their words, it would be two days' travel inland along this road until he found them.

"Ugh! Two days in this wet," he muttered to himself and returned to the Folk pony he had acquired. While small breeds of horses existed on the mainland, many were created as working animals and were not suitable for riding. Folk of Avalon had spent generations breeding mounts for the horizontally challenged peoples of the island. These animals were every bit as elegant and attractive as their larger counterparts. They were not wide and stocky. Their gait was not awkward and bouncy. Folk ponies were bred with one thing in mind; to give the chosen people of The Mother a helper animal worthy of their lineage. Arman wondered if that was why The Mother was often associated with horses.

Arman gently patted the neck of the buckskin mare and smoothed her dun-colored coat. She was a fine credit to her breed with a cream-colored coat and raven-colored mane and tail. Black socks ran up into dappled shoulders and hind-quarters. She whickered at him and butted her head into him gently. He smiled and scratched under her chin as he considered his next moves. Phaendar was mercurial on good days. There was a reason the old sage had removed themselves from the community and secreted themselves in the ancient forest in the heart of Avalon. Age affected the long-lived Elven people in different ways. For some, the journey into the aged and wizened advisor was a peaceful transition and one that empowered them deeply. The ancient Druid Matriarch of Avalon, Lady Bellicent, was one of these. Arman had never seen the archaic spell crafter who had stood at the right hand of the

Eternal Empress of the Island for over three millennia. Rumors claimed she wielded the combined powers of the whole of the island and was far older than claimed. Some said she had been one of the original spell crafters who had helped bring Avalon to Sanctum during the Reaping. If that were indeed the truth, the Lady Bellicent may well be a Divine walking in mortal form who simply had yet to ascend. Arman shuddered at the thought of it.

For others of Elvenkind, the weight of millennia (or more) of knowledge, of gains and losses, children born and lovers buried, was too much to bear, and their minds eventually eroded away. The madness that often consumed these ancients was the stuff of legend, both in Avalon and on the mainland. Phaendar's behavior over the course of the last hundred years led Arman to believe that the old elf would not go the way of Lady Bellicent. If there were anyone else on the mainland that Arman could have turned to for the task he needed to be completed, he would have gladly done so.

The Vidria took one more look around to ensure his notes matched his bearings. He nodded and closed the worn journal, wrapping its leather cover tightly closed, and tucked it away securely. In one practiced motion, Arman mounted the little horse and settled comfortably into his saddle. The pony grunted at him and shifted her weight under his. He picked up the reins and clucked at her, urging her forward and on toward their destination.

Above the smaller man, branches creaked and leaves rustled in a pattern unlike the gentle breeze of the area. Arman sniffed once and tilted his head slightly to catch the sounds above and behind him. The tiny hairs on the back of his neck rose. His right hand drifted to the hilt of his sword. The sounds paused as the movements ceased. Arman sucked on a tooth briefly and readied himself. He could not tell if he was merely being watched, or followed, or sized up for supper. His pony snorted and stamped in dissatisfaction. All right, the threat was real; he wasn't just hearing things. His eyes darted to the canopy above him. The branches of the trees reached toward the heavens and then reached for one another, interlocking and providing a secure ceiling above. He searched the shadows above him and could find nothing. Clucking at his pony, he pulled at her reins, directing her to turn about. She resisted momentarily, but eventually gave in. As he changed directions, he caught the glimpse of something moving above him. Whatever it was, it was larger than he was. He was reminded of the words of Captain Fiske; that many things on the island were sentient creatures, capable of reason and thought. Following that thought was also the memory of how many fanciful creatures made their home on this strange land.

Searching the tree line above him once more, he affixed his gaze on the shape that seemed ever so slightly out of place. He was mounted and cut off from direct contact with the soil, so his ability to craft the stone was not as strong as it would be. Arman reached out to sense the soil and earth beneath him, readying himself for assault.

He cleared his throat and addressed the shadows.

"You see me. I see you," he stated calmly. "Shall we speak, or are we to fight? I would prefer the first over the last."

The shadow in the trees waited and did not move. Arman continued to watch it. As he did so, the outline of the shape became clearer. It was humanoid. Whatever else it was, it blended well with its surroundings.

Arman continued, "I mean no harm. I am merely following the path that Master Phaendar gave me."

At the mention of the Sage's name, the figure shifted and spoke.

"You seek the Scholar?" it asked. Its voice was a hushed whisper that almost disappeared into the breeze.

Arman nodded, "I do."

"You have no soul," the figure commented.

Arman paused, considering. He nodded once more. "I am not of the land. No."

"What is your worth, soulless one?" the figure asked.

Arman's horse skittered a little. He pulled her to heel and addressed the figure. "I am Arman Dah'ay, Master Cartographer," he offered.

A pause, as if the figure was deciphering Arman's words. "You map the land?" it asked.

Again, Arman nodded, "I do."

The figure shifted above him and seemed to almost flow down the shadows of the tree trunk and rise from a pool of leaves and twigs. It was bipedal, shaped in the form of a human or an elf. Its skin was mottled and patterned like wood. Where hair would have grown instead was a fall of vibrant, leafy vines. Its eyes were solid black. The tips of its fingers ended in gruesome-looking claws. Arman was briefly reminded of the witch Nebiyre. He controlled a shudder.

The empty, black eyes of the creature examined Arman from a distance. It cocked its head to the side and then to the other in strange curiosity. "They shaped you like Folk, but you are not Hers."

"I am not," Arman replied.

"Little map man, you are in a dangerous place," the creature offered.

"This is the path …"

"The Scholar is mad …," the creature whispered, cutting Arman off, "The Triskele war here. They will kill you. No one crosses."

A flicker of frustration crossed Arman's eyes. He clenched his jaw in thought.

The creature took a cautious step toward Arman. His pony whickered. Arman reached for his blade. The creature held up a cautious hand and uttered words that vanished on the breeze. The pony settled. The creature offered what Arman could only assume was a smile and stepped closer. It reached a taloned hand out and gently touched the tiny horse.

"This is Hers," it spoke, looking at the horse. It leaned forward and breathed deeply, taking in the pony's scent. It froze and slowly turned its black eyes toward Arman, looking up at him through its vine hair. "Map Man is not Hers ... but carries something that is in his bags ..."

Shit. Arman swore to himself. This fey-born thing could sense the scarab amulet and the spark it contained.

Arman swallowed and quickly replied, "It is for Phaendar."

The creature continued to stare at Arman. "Something ... trapped ..."

Arman held the gaze of the creature as his senses tapped into the surrounding land. He might be able to solidify the mud around it and hold it fast. But there was no guarantee that action would not strengthen it.

"It is for Phaendar ... to ... release," Arman spoke softly. Sweat beaded along his brow.

"To ... return ... to the land?" the creature asked, stepping closer to Arman. If he kicked out now, he might be able to plant his boot in its chest.

Or it might rip your leg off and devour you for supper.

Arman nodded once more. "Yes," he lied, "It was trapped in the desert. I have brought it back to be returned to the land." A partial truth.

The creature inhaled deeply through its nose and mouth and then took a step back. It nodded. "It is enough." It bent then, in an unnatural crouch, and pushed off of the wet ground and seemed to flow back into the canopy above them both. It disappeared, and the breeze returned to the leaves above him. His pony whickered and pawed at the ground.

Arman's eyes glanced down at what held her attention. Drawn in the mud, where the creature had stood, was a series of concentric circles and swirls. The symbol of the Triskele Trinity, the Divine that watched the Wilds of all of Sanctum. Watchers of the woods and guardians of the groves.

"The Triskele war here ...," Arman whispered carefully, repeating the words that the Gwyllion had uttered.

He closed his eyes and took a breath. He hated Avalon.

Chapter 24

Ygraine stumbled, catching herself as she fell forward. . The muscles in her legs burned with exhaustion. But she could not stop.

Images of the clearing burned deeply in her mind's eye. The dissolving corpse of a giant cave bear, twitching, re-animating, and standing once more. Chunks of flesh fell off the bones of the creature and onto the green grass of the glade. Everywhere it touched, life seemed to drain from the area. Grass faded and became like ash. Earth dried and caked, cracking as if from drought. It was magic, to be certain, but this was unlike any tale told by the harpers or scops, or even by the elders of the clans; this was alien and dangerous beyond measure.

She filled her aching lungs with a deep breath and pressed on. The Sun God's light broke through the canopy here and there, granting illumination to her dark path. She had to reach the village before dark.

Finding the juniper and nettle that Mael had sent her for had not been difficult. Ygraine had grown up in this area of the forest, and healing herbs were one of the first things that all children learned. In the right mixture, coupled with salt and soot, these could stave off poison and give the body a chance at beating toxins. But toxins did not cause the dead to walk again.

Her feet slapped hard on the path as she continued to crash through the forest. Sweat beaded and dripped from her forehead. There was cramping in her stomach. She could not stop. She could not wait. The village needed to know.

When she had returned to the glade with the medicinals that the Urram Mael sent her for, the scene was far worse than how she left it. A handful of the war party had survived the encounter with the creature. They had been covered in the blood and gore of the creature. Mael had feared that what the bear suffered from might be shared through its blood. This was why she had sent Ygraine to search for medicinals. She was the only one in the group who had not come into contact with the creature.

They had dragged the bodies of the dead into the center of the glade and piled them there. There should have been five. When Ygraine returned, there were eight corpses in that pile. Two additional bodies lay past the pile of dead in the field, their heads separated from their necks. Black ichor oozed from their wounds, seeping into the ground. One body bore the tattoos and markings of the Urram.

They had been a party of twelve when they had departed that morning. Now the only other survivor of the encounter lay pinned beneath the Urram's spear, affixed to the ground and unable to move. Cinioch, the Chieftain's son, cast tired and pained eyes on Ygraine as she returned to the scene. Red blood oozed from his wounds and his mouth. He chuckled darkly at her approach.

"That is far enough, Little Wolf. You must come no further," he cautioned.

Ygraine's eyes widened to see the carnage before her. "What … happened …?" she asked, holding her ground as instructed.

"The Decay came to them," Cinioch answered. His right hand grasped weakly at the haft of the spear that protruded from his midsection. Someone had expertly placed it.

Ygraine looked at the body pile. She looked back at Cinioch.

Cinioch nodded, "Infected, but not risen. I do not know why." He coughed. Bright red spittle colored his lips. He laughed.

"Cinioch …," Ygraine said, her eyes filled with compassion and concern.

"NO!" the young man ordered. He regretted the force used immediately. "I must remain here, like this. Mael fell to the Decay, and I ended her suffering, but we do not know if it will come to me as well," He raised his eyes to look up at Ygraine, "You cannot help me now, Little Wolf," He lowered his voice, "Not in this cycle ... but you can ensure we are not chained to the in-between."

The dark-haired girl nodded and reached to place her hand on the silvered blade that Mael had entrusted her with. Cinioch nodded.

"My father must know what has happened, and a new Urram must be chosen," He lifted bloodshot eyes to hers. He winced under the pain of the spear, "The bodies ... must not ... be returned to the Land ... Little Wolf," he wheezed. "It will ... end ... the Cycle."

Ygraine's eyes widened. Ending the Cycle meant ending the rebirth of the people. It meant remaining in the Summerlands after this lifetime and not returning to the people. It meant the death of Avalon, and its magic.

She nodded. "I will make certain he knows, Cinioch," Ygraine replied.

Cinioch's shaggy head sank forward slowly onto his chest. "... in the next ...," he whispered.

Silence fell on the glade.

"Cinioch ...," Ygraine breathed.

She pressed forward, legs pumping, heart pounding. There was no time to mourn the dead when the living yet needed her. She tasted copper in the back of her mouth and forced herself to breathe in deeply, finding a cadence in her running and breathing.

In-in-in-out-out-out, setting her breath to her steps and the beat of her heart.

Branches broke as she crashed through them, indelicately. She could have followed the path back to the village, but it would have taken twice as long. Cutting through the underbrush would save her almost an hour. The area had been cleared of game recently by several hunting parties. There would be few obstacles of a four-footed nature for her to contend with.

What about more like the bear? The thought came to her. *There could be more.* They did not know where the creature had come from or the source of its infection.

No. The risk is worth it. She countered the voice of doubt in the back of her mind.

If you die, the information dies with you. The voice countered. *And that would be a damned shame.*

Ygraine stumbled slightly at the thought. The words weren't hers. Someone else was speaking to her in the deep recesses of her mind. She shook her head, sweat flung from her dark curls.

"I don't have time for you, spirit," she spoke in her in-out cadence.

You will one day.

Ygraine clenched her jaw and continued on. Voices from the land and its denizens were nothing new to inhabitants of the Island. Trees and rocks, animals and streams; for those keen of wit and clear of mind, the voices were there to be heard. Ygraine had been told that she had the talent if she ever cared to hone it. She never did. Sitting at the feet of the Urram, learning the spirit speech and the ways of the craft, never appealed to the lanky young woman.

Her hand wrapped itself around the hilt of the silvered blade at her waist. Even carrying the silvered blade felt wrong.

Eldest of six siblings, Ygraine, was one of two girls. The rest of her siblings were all rough and tumble boys, but she gave as well as any of them. Her thoughts drifted for a moment to Cinioch. He had been an assuming ass, but his skill with the ax was renowned. She remembered the first time he caught her watching him with it. He had made the mistake of thinking she was appreciating HIM and not his skill with the weapon. That exchange had ended with her on her backside in the mud and Cinioch with a busted nose.

He had agreed to teach her in private after that.

Not that women could not study martial skills in her Clan; indeed, every able-bodied member of the Clan knew how to handle at least one weapon of war. They were nomadic people;

survival depended on each of them being able to defend themselves. No, but for every score that wielded a weapon, one was needed to tend the wounded and learn the way of the Craft. Urram Mael had seen something in Ygraine at an early age and called her to serve the Clan differently.

It had been shortly after Mael called her to serve that Ygraine had "lost her way" in the forest and been separated from her hunting party. A nobleman had found her, while he and his people were beating the bushes for pheasant and rabbit. She couldn't have been more than eight. Covered in mud and thorn berry scratches, hiding in an abandoned wolf's den. Niall Whitebrook, husband of the Lady Whitebrooke, coaxed the all-but-feral child out of her den and helped her back to his home. Lady Whitebrooke had opened her hearth, her home, and her heart to the young Ygraine. They had welcomed her as family. Giving her a place to stay, food, and shelter, more comfort than she had ever known in the Wilds. Lord Niall had sent scouts into the wilderness to look for Ygraine's people, to reunite the child with her people. It had taken several seasons to find them.

Urram Mael and Cinioch had come to Council Whitebrooke and collected Ygraine. Cinioch had teased her mercilessly the whole way back to the winter camp. Calling her "Little Wolf" for hiding in the den where she had been found. Mael had watched their exchanges, and on their return, eased her requirements of Ygraine. She allowed her to train as a tender of the dead on the field while waiting for the girl's calling to make itself known. She hoped Ygraine might someday change her mind, but one could not force the Craft on a soul. It must be embraced willingly.

They were both dead now. Cinioch and Mael. Fallen and rotting in a field behind her. Decay and rot, refusing their bodies to be returned to the land.

Her breath became caught in her throat for a moment. She coughed. Her eyes watered. She blinked it away, swallowing the grief down. A slow pit of fire burned deep within her.

Anger at whatever had caused this. Fury at the senselessness of their sacrifice. Rage burned in her soul, powering her forward. A slow, red haze danced around the edges of her sight. There was power in that anger that burned so hot. The power that gnawed at the back of her mind. A peal of dark laughter, devoid of mirth, and filled with hunger, teased her mind.

She crashed through the tree line and broke free into the edges of the Autumnal encampment. Startled voices arose at her appearance. Hands reached for weapons; warriors stood in defense. She stumbled forward, tasting copper and bile, and fell forward onto her hands and knees.

"Dark ... spirits ...," she coughed.

Eyes darted back and forth, whispered voices exchanged hushed words.

A towering figure lumbered toward her. Covered in leathers and skins, his forest hazel eyes stared down at the young woman from his great height. Chieftain Cynfael Aerfyn crossed his massive arms across his broad chest. He was a giant of a man, standing nearly seven feet tall, solid and sturdy. Much like his son Cinioch, he wore his dark kinky hair pulled back and braided in intricate patterns. Beads of bone and lapis decorated his braids and his beard. The left side of his face was covered in a deep blue tattoo of swirling triskele patterns that seemed darker against his cornflower blue skin.

"Speak again, girl," his deep voice rumbled.

Ygraine responded by pulling the silvered blade of Urram Mael from her belt and slamming it onto the earth before her.

Aerfyn raised his eyebrows, then scowled darkly.

"What is the meaning of this, Ygraine?" he demanded.

The exhausted young woman lifted her head to meet his eyes with her own. Her dark curls matted to her face in heavy sweat and soil. Her eyes glistened brightly, with the hints of pain and mania. The hint of a smile tugged at the right corner of her mouth.

"The hunting party is dead," she spoke.

A hush fell over the encampment. Many cast signs against

evil.

Aerfyn's right eye twitched.

"The Urram ... and your son ... sent me ... to warn you," she continued.

"My ... son ...," Aerfyn repeated carefully, his voice cautiously guarded.

"Gave his life to save this Clan, my king," came the reply.

Cynfael Aerfyn's teeth pulled back into a hideous snarl. "Warriors, to me now!" he roared.

Around him, the entire encampment sprang to life. As each warrior grabbed armor, shield, and weapons, a silent figure walked slowly through the chaos. Robes of linen dyed dark and embroidered with colorful sigils, their face was covered in scars and ink. Ignoring Aerfyn, they approached Ygraine and knelt before her. Bone-thin fingers took the girl's face in their hands and stared deeply into her eyes.

"Show me," they spoke. Words burned in the air and in her mind as the Seer pulled from Ygraine what was needed. She screamed as the visions came flooding back to her. Around the edges of the visions, a dark shape danced, clothed in rage ... and laughter.

Soon.

Chapter 25

Securing passage from Port Kraken back to Avalon had been a simple task ... for Isolde. Away from the strangeness of the desert and standing on the docks of the harbor, Isolde had become a wholly different person. She moved with freedom and confidence that Tulok had seen only once before; on the *Gnomes All*. That was the day she had gone overboard, and he thought he had lost her. The Wandering Knight had displayed such comfort and confidence among the crew of that barge on that day. Tulok pushed his anxiety out of his mind. This was going to be different.

Tulok remembered watching her as she approached the Captain of *The Loyal Knave*, standing tall, all smiles and confidence. The Captain had been more than happy to take the Knight and her healer onto his ship for the trek across the water. Tulok's size had been an issue for the river barges along the Iteru; but *The Loyal Knave* was a four-masted Carrack, designed for the open water between the Mainland and Avalon. Merchants traveled between Port Kraken and the capital city of Lubri at regular intervals. Once a week, ships arrived and departed from the docks on either side of the waters carrying people and trade goods. It was a lucrative industry.

"The cost of our passage is ... what?" Tulok asked.

Isolde finished tying off the long braid of her dark hair and tossed it over her shoulder. Loose long hair on a windy sea was a recipe for a shaved head, and Isolde enjoyed her long locks. "Huh?" She looked up at Tulok, "Oh ... uh... Help load crates and tend to any injuries along the way," she replied absently.

The big orc frowned and looked up at the enormous ship. It had cost most of their shared allowance to traverse one bank of the Iteru to the other back in Nahral. How was there no exchange of coin?

Isolde noted the confusion on her companion's face. She smiled and patted him on the shoulder, "Captain Hywel is Lubri-born. He's from the island. He won't take my coin, Tulok. My leug is great enough to earn us passage, with a little extra help here and there."

Tulok stared down at Isolde, up at the ship, and then back down at her. "I ... but ... how?" he blinked. Management of costs and coins was one charge of the Radiant Lord's people. They often excelled in means of money management. That coin exchange did not exist for an entire civilization still baffled him.

Isolde sighed, "I'll explain it all on the trip across."

Tulok nodded and rubbed his bearded chin. "How long will we be on the water?" he asked.

Isolde shrugged. "Provided we have pleasant weather?" Isolde mused. She chewed her lip briefly in thought, "Depending on how heavy she is ... probably somewhere between five and eight days," she replied, smiling up at him.

Tulok blinked at Isolde. "How ... how do you know all of this?" he asked.

Isolde smiled warmly at the priest, "Don't feel bad, Father ... I grew up on the Island and ... well ..." She reached for the broken compass that hung around her neck, the symbol of her God, "I may have some inside information."

The priest's eyebrows lifted as understanding came to him. "Ah," he nodded, "Yes, I suppose that would make sense."

She smiled at him, "I may have also asked the Captain what he expected."

"Ahhhh," the orc nodded.

Isolde regarded the big priest for a moment, a flicker of concern in her green eyes.

"Some problem?" he asked.

"I ... uh ... I don't suppose you learned how to swim while you were in Ophir?" she asked.

Tulok scowled at her. "I did not."

Isolde nodded. "No matter. We'll get it handled."

"I *have* been on boats before, Isolde," Tulok replied indignantly. "I traveled from Kef-aal to Ophir without incident. You should grant me more faith than you do," he huffed.

—

Four hours later, the Radiant Father was bent over the railing of *The Loyal Knave*, feeding the fishes the contents of his stomach.

"How is he?" Hywel asked. His sun-bleached blonde hair was pulled back into a fastidious knot at the back of his head. Dark scruff colored his cheeks and his broad jawline. Three golden rings decorated the upper cartilage of Hywel's right ear, denoting his years of command. He was a strong and weather-worn man. Isolde guessed him to be in his late twenties or early thirties. Hywel looked past Isolde's shoulder at the massive figure of the orc priest who was so clearly not handling his ocean-going voyage well.

"Well enough, Captain. He'll get his legs soon, I'm sure," Isolde reassured. "Thank you for this. I'm sure it will help," she replied. In her hand was a small bottle of green-colored liquid.

Hywel shrugged and pulled his eyes from Tulok and let them fall on the figure of the Wandering Knight. "I can't very well have a member of the priesthood dying from dehydration on the crossing, now, can I?" he offered.

Isolde chuckled a little and nodded. "I'll be certain your generosity is known," Isolde replied.

Hywel nodded once more. He sucked on a tooth in thought for a moment and then looked out at the horizon. "Gonna be clear sailing into the night. Make sure they set the two of you up beneath the canopies. Should keep most of the wet and cold at bay," He looked back at Isolde, he eyed the compass around her neck, "Forgive the ask, Ser Knight ..." He rubbed at the side of his nose with his left thumb," But ... you seem awfully young for a Wanderer to be returning home ..."

Isolde's eyebrows rose. "Oh ... yes. That ..." She stumbled

189

over the words a moment. "It's not my returning home if that's what you are asking, Captain."

"No?"

She shook her head. "Oh no, not at all. We are ...," She scowled and looked back over her shoulder at Tulok. He was bent over and resting his forehead on the railing of the ship. "We're trailing a criminal, to be honest," she blurted.

Hywel folded his arms across his chest, "Not something the Lord Wanderer often sends his people to do ...,"

"No, I suppose it's not ... but there we are," Isolde shrugged. She offered the Captain a smile.

"This fugitive from the Sun God's justice have a name?"

Isolde nodded. "Arman Dah'ay. He's a Vidrian stone shaper, and a merchant. Do you know him?" she asked.

Hywel shook his head. "No, I can't say as I do. But I will put the word out once we make landfall." He looked over at Isolde. "May I ask what he is wanted for?"

Isolde's eyes darkened for a moment. She set her shoulders and her jaw and met the Captain's gaze. "Kidnapping ... attempted, and successful murder of members of the faith," she replied flatly.

The Captain's eyes widened. He looked between Isolde and Tulok and slowly nodded his head. "Understood. I hope that elixir eases his journey," he replied, then excused himself to return to the stern of the ship.

Isolde watched Hywel depart, then turned and walked back across the deck to where Tulok was still leaning on the rail.

"How are you doing?" She asked.

"I'm not sure that I will eat anything again ... ever ...," the orc priest groaned in his misery.

Isolde rested her hand gently on the big man's arm and gave it a gentle squeeze. "I asked Captain Hywel for the remedy my people often use for new travelers."

Tulok shook his head, "It will just come back up."

Isolde smiled. "Well, it goes in your ears, so ... that would be impressive."

He looked askance at her and remained bent over, "In my …"

"Ears," she finished. "Yes." She pulled the cork out of the tiny bottle and motioned him to turn his head to the side. "I am really surprised you didn't know that," She smiled a little as she poured a couple of drops of the green elixir into his slightly pointed ear, "Wait for a minute then we will do the other."

"There are few cases of … sea … sickness in the middle of the desert, Isolde," he countered. He waited a moment and then shifted to turn his head to the other side and present his other ear.

The knight nodded. "I suppose that would be true," she replied and administered relief to the other ear. She stoppered the bottle and patted Tulok on the shoulder. "Give it a few, and the nausea should subside. You'll want to use it every day until you acclimate. If … you acclimate," she added.

"IF?!" Tulok asked a moment of horror on his broad features.

Isolde shrugged and placed her back against the railing next to him. "Some folks never get used to it. No shame in it, Father. Not everyone is born for long voyages on open water … especially the sand born." She smiled at him.

Tulok turned his face back toward Isolde and scowled at her, "Point taken."

They remained there for several minutes, silent in their shared space. Isolde was the first to break it. "Thank you for coming with me," she offered.

Tulok nodded from his bent position. "Our assigned duties are apparently still aligned along the same path," he replied.

She shook her head and chuckled a little. "I could think of worse traveling companions …"

Tulok slowly stood, expecting waves of nausea to take him back down. He was pleasantly surprised. "Or better?" he asked.

"Better?" she frowned and thought about it. "No, not offhand." The ocean waves splashed against the side of the boat, giving it a gentle rock. She looked down, and Tulok gave her a small smile.

He gave a nod and paused. Laying a hand on his stomach as

if checking something, he eyed the bottle in Isolde's hand. She offered it to him and he held it aloft to gaze at the color. Dissatisfied at his observation, he opened it to sniff the mixture.

She nodded at the bottle. "I think it's mostly just olive oil, chamomile, some belladonna, and clubmoss."

Tulok raised an eyebrow at the ingredient list, "This bottle would be worth a month's allowance based on the ingredients alone." He carefully tucked the tiny container away.

Isolde looked at Tulok with confusion, "Why ... oh ... Ya ... clubmoss won't grow on the Mainland. I forgot." She looked over at the big priest. "Feeling better?"

Tulok paused and took an assessment of himself, then nodded appreciatively, "Indeed," He looked down at Isolde, "Thank you." he offered her a gangly tusked smile.

She nodded once again. "Of course."

Tulok placed his hands on the railing for balance and looked out across the vastness of the wide sea. There was no land in any direction. The water stretched before them and around them. Blues and greens, with the occasional cap of white in the waves. On the far horizon, a line of dark blue separated the sky from the water. White clouds, round and fluffy, painted the skyline. It was all at once peaceful, awe-inspiring, and terrifying. He suddenly understood the vacuum of power that must be present in the heavens with the absence of the Ocean Lord. It was the Crafting of Avalonian and Incirrata magic alone that made this journey even possible. He squinted his red eyes and looked skyward in an attempt to determine the position of the sun above them.

Isolde tapped Tulok's arm and pointed behind them. They were sailing east, away from the sun, so it was past midday. The priest of the Sun Lord nodded in silent thanks to the knight.

"Five to eight days, you said?" Tulok mused, remembering Isolde's estimates about their length of travel.

She shrugged and reached for her compass medallion. "Captain Hywel says he should be able to make it in six. Weather reports from the island are favorable and there are fewer storms this season."

Tulok pursed his lips in thought. "It is … very wet," he commented, noting finally that his face and forearms were covered in salt spray.

Isolde laughed out loud then. It was a warm, rich, and full thing. Several members of the crew glanced in her direction. "Yes, Tulok. I suppose it is," she smiled brightly, then turned around to look out at the ocean, standing next to him.

"And … none of it is drinkable?" he asked.

She shook her head. "No more so than the water off the coast of Ophir is."

"Seems a waste," He frowned.

Isolde nodded a bit. "I can imagine that it would. Have no fear, my friend; the water on Avalon is potable and aplenty."

"Hmmm," the orc mused and folded his arms across his chest. The ocean breeze tugged at the corners of his white and gold tunic, it fluttered effortlessly. "Are you quite certain you would not have preferred Safar's company on this journey?" he asked her quietly.

There. It had been said. The question that gnawed in the back of his mind that wanted an answer.

Beside him, Isolde frowned, her eyebrows furrowed in thought. "Safar is a Sand Dancer and knows neither the ocean nor Avalon. Why on earth would I want to drag him out of Setesh for … ohhhh …" She paused and pursed her lips, then sighed. She looked up at Tulok and away once more. They stood there in uncomfortable silence for a few moments, watching the horizon.

"I think you would be quite handsome together in matching sand gear …," Tulok offered, the hint of a smile tugging at his lips.

Isolde glared at him. "I hate you," she quipped and shoved into him with her shoulder, though he did not move.

He looked down at her and pursed his lips a little, "Mmm hrmmm."

The Wandering Knight shook her head and sighed at the priest, who leaned solidly on the railing. Shoulder to shoulder, they stood staring out at the endless waves of water before them.

Chapter 26

The concept of leug was difficult to explain to someone not born of the island. Avalonians were tied to its land in a way that no other were in all of Sanctum. During the Reaping, many of the Divine brought their surviving people to this small pocket of protection. However, it was the combined might and magic of those Divine beings beholden to the Realm of Avalon that caused the entire island, its people, and its culture to be transported from its place of origin to Sanctum. Avalonians alone held such a claim. How this was possible was steeped in a myriad of theories and conjectures. Perhaps it was the residual magic that linked the survivors and their descendants in such a fashion. Or maybe it was something that happened in the transport itself, something that infused them all with magic tied to these lands. It was also possible that one or more of the Divine who was lost gave their essence to ensure the safety of these people, and it imbued this within them all. It was this last thought that a great hero or forgotten Divine had sacrificed themselves to save the Realm of Avalon, that seemed most prevalent in the books Tulok had read about while hidden away in temple libraries.

The people of the island had always been a subject of great interest so, when one of their ilks found their way to his humble village of Tarf-qua, he had secretly hoped that his questions might find answers. Now, as he sat on the deck of *The Loyal Knave* surrounded by the people of the Island, he had more questions than answers could ever solve.

The darkened night sky spread above the ship, the only light being the four lone stars in the firmament. Darkness and the sound of the waves surrounded them. In the desert, there was at least the hope that runners had placed torches or other light sources along the traveling paths. Here, there was no such hope. The orc felt he should be walking the length of the ship, keeping watch against the darkness, as was his calling. Yet Captain Hywel had confined both him and Isolde to the canopied section of the main deck and aftercastle, where the Captain's quarters and cabins were located.

"I understand full well, Father," Hywel said. "We all answer to the Divine. But you are a valuable passenger and should harm come to you on this voyage, the damage it would do to my leug may well be irrecoverable. If you have need to stand your watch, you may do so here, or walk the below decks, check on the crew and the other passengers. Hell, go sit a spell in the infirmary if you need to, but I cannot spare the crew to monitor you with no light in the sky. It's too big a risk. I'm sorry."

The Captain's words had stung. In Setesh, the faithful of the Sun Lord were often given deference in many things; but they were no longer in Setesh.

"Don't mope. I hate it when you mope," Isolde commented, and sat down opposite him. She held out a large bowl of something that smelled amazing. Tulok took it from her and eyed it suspiciously. "Fish stew. Eat up." She smiled and tipped the brim of her own bowl to her lips, and slurped at the salty broth. Tulok gave a disapproving look to Isolde in her manner of supping, "Don't look at me like that. When we are eating at the Captain's table we can worry about serving ware, until then … there's a spoon in your pack, or you can use the bread and your fingers. It's like my first night eating at the table in Tarf-qua!" She grinned over her bowl at him.

Tulok sighed and lifted the bowl to his lips and poured the broth carefully into his mouth, pushing his lips farther out to circumvent his tusks. Humans often forgot that eating and drinking for his people was more challenging in a civilized setting. And Tulok always endeavored to appear civilized. Broth dribbled down his chin. He scowled and wiped it away with his thumb.

Across from him, Isolde chuckled, "Relax. We are among friends, and no one here is going to judge you." She nudged at him with her booted foot.

"Hrmmm. An easy enough request for one born to the people," Tulok mused. He looked behind him, reached for his leather pack, and fished out a hand-carved wooden spoon. He returned to eating the stew, happier for the tool.

"I suppose that's fair," Isolde nodded. "I saw Hywel speaking with you earlier. Everything all right?" she asked.

Tulok harumphed. "The Captain has confined my nightly patrols to this area and the crew deck. If I am to stand my duty for the Radiant Lord while on this vessel, it will not be to the full extent."

Isolde listened and waited for there to be more. When there was not, "Oh! Well … sure … I mean …, "she peered out from under the canopy that covered the main deck. "It's really hard to see out there, and he's probably already got his night team on duty, scanning the water … so pulling one of them off duty to make sure you don't go overboard is probably taxing on them …,"

Tulok sniffed in irritation as a reply.

"Which … I can see is very difficult for you," she added. Sighing, she set her bowl aside and casually wiped her mouth on the sleeve of her shirt. Tulok rolled his eyes. "Ok, so. You remember how we both have to defer to Safar when we are on caravan?" she asked.

Tulok nodded. "He is Reysis, the Sun Guide and King of the Sands while on caravan our lives are in his hands. Of course."

"Right!" Isolde exclaimed and smiled. "So, on the open sea, Captain Hywel is essentially Reysis. He is responsible for every life on this ship. If something bad happens to a caravan, the Reysis is held accountable, and his standing in the Guild is affected … or at least, that's what Safar explained. The same holds true for Hywel. Except …," she reached back for her bowl. "And here's the part that may be more difficult for you. His leug is also affected, and every Avalonian will know it."

Tulok furrowed his brow and continued to eat. "Respecting the secrets of your people as best as I can ..."

"Of course,"

"How?" he asked.

Isolde scratched her forehead and thought about the question. Tulok was already aware of the connection that Avalonians held with their land. It was the secret he held while she held the secret of the location of Ashal. The details of her people's tie to the land were one of the more closely guarded secrets they possessed. As he already held this knowledge, the explanation of leug would be a little easier; but others might not appreciate the sharing of information.

She shrugged, "We can ... see is not the right term. And ... It's more than feel ... hrmmm ...," she thought about it a moment more, "We ... each ...," she began carefully picking through the words, "instinctively know ... each other's inherent value as it pertains to their weighted name and honor?"

Tulok frowned, contemplating the words. "Inherent value to ... whom?" he asked.

"Avalon," she replied.

"To the island?"

Isolde pondered and nodded. "And the people?" she scooped out some of the meatier sections of fish from her bowl and stuffed them into her mouth.

"You have a spoon," Tulok scolded.

"It's put away. My fingers work fine, Mother," she teased. "Ok ... look. Uh ... oh, I know! So ... "she looked up at Tulok. "You play Chatrang, right?" she asked.

Tulok continued to spoon broth and fish into his mouth carefully. "The board game with the opposing armies? Yes, of course."

"Each of the pieces has an unspoken, but understood value, right?" Isolde continued.

Tulok nodded. "To one degree or another, yes. A Minister has more value than a Chariot because it can travel on more squares."

Isolde nodded. "And a soldier has more limitations. But … if it makes it across the board …"

"It can become any other piece on the board except Imir …" he paused for a moment as if the light of dawning knowledge were upon him. "All of your people hold intrinsic value to their established armies, but even the lowest soldier can become a Minister … and leug is how that is shown."

Isolde smiled and said nothing.

"Which is why you each take care of one another as you do."

"We all succeed or fail together, Father. Some of us simply have more defined roles. Abandonment is never an option."

Tulok rubbed his broad jaw in thought, scratching at his beard. "Thank you. That helps."

Isolde continued to smile at Tulok. "Good! It's really the best explanation I can offer. If you aren't part of the people, you can't really understand how it all works … but, ya … that's pretty close."

Tulok mused on this new information for some time, continuing his meal. He finally raised his red eyes to regard Isolde. "Isolde … when you made arrangements with Captain Hywel, you had to arrange for my passage as well."

"I did, yes," she answered.

"But I have no leug. How was I valued?" the big priest asked.

Isolde took a deep breath and set her now empty bowl aside. She leaned back on her hands and regarded the sun priest. "You are a valued member of the faith," she offered.

"But what does that mean to your people?" he asked. "Once upon a time, you were in my care, and I had to handle the costs and coin exchanges while you were in Nahral and beyond. I have no coin to hand over to you to manage for this journey, Isolde."

"We travel on my leug while in Avalon," she said quietly.

Tulok took a deep breath and blew it out, as he processed that statement with his new understanding. He lifted a beefy hand and rubbed the back of his shaved head. "So, anything I do …"

"Reflects on me, and my value. Yes," she replied.

Tulok sucked on his empty spoon and set it aside in his bowl as he contemplated the Witness's words. He leaned forward and placed his hands on either side of her knees. His deep voice lowered noticeably.

"You were going to tell me this when?"

She shrugged in response. "When it became important for you to know."

"And you did not think that I might care to know that my actions could have a negative impact on the value you hold among your own people?"

"They can have a positive impact as well," she smiled.

"That is not the point and you know it," he chided. "What else do I need to know?"

She chewed on her bottom lip for a moment.

"Isolde ..."

"The Mother is the main Divine on the Island," she began, "There are no massive Temples like what you are used to. The ... *opulence* of the Radiant Lord does not really exist on Avalon. We find beauty and value in other things, so ... maybe lower your expectations for lodging?"

He nodded slowly, then carefully asked, "Is there a place of worship ascribed to my faith on your Island?"

Isolde shook her head gently. "No more so than there is mine in Ophir."

Tulok took a deep breath and sat back, thinking about those words and what they meant. He was silent for several minutes. Then he raised his eyes to meet those of Ser Isolde.

"Then I suppose I will depend on the good graces of the Landless Lord, and endeavor to be an Honored Guest in a foreign land."

Chapter 27

On their second day at sea, Captain Hywel watched his two important passengers go back and forth in some sort of debate. He watched as the Knight Wanderer threw up her hands and strode over to a deckhand, who pointed her to a storage locker. He watched as she pulled out a deck tarp and hefted it back to where the large priest was. Curious, the Captain chewed on the inside of his cheek as everything transpired. He saw Isolde shake the dust and sand out of their possessions and onto the tarp. It looked like a small sand dune. The pair looked at each other, the small dune, the ocean, and then back at each other. Promptly picking up the tarp, they threw the sand overboard and watched as some of it splashed into the water below while the rest seemed to fly on the wind ... as if heading back home.

From his vantage point, the Captain watched as they gestured at their belongings and each other. While he was not expecting any trouble, he watched with interest as the orc picked up one of his robes and shook it to show that there was no more sand ... only to lose his grip on it and watch as the wind carried it away and it floated out to sea. They stood there, dumbfounded. Then the Witness started laughing and just patted the orc on the shoulder. Hywel could only shake his head and laugh.

They were not the oddest passengers he had, but they were by far the most entertaining to watch. He had assumed that the orc would be the one in charge but, the more he watched and observed, the more he realized that the massive being was deeply out of his element. He had taken orcs on as passengers before. Some tended toward a bullying nature among their own kind, but not so much with anyone else aboard (for which he was thankful for). Others bore a high level of stoicism and probably lacked a decent sense of humor.

The captain saw the priest as an oddity. Occasionally, a member of the Sun God's faith visited Lubri, but they were always men or elves. This one was somewhere in-between all of that. His mind wandered to the great northern tribes of orcs who called Avalon their home. He wondered what they would think of him, and he of them.

He smiled to himself and continued on his rounds.

—

Though he was still using the tincture, Tulok felt better than he did on the first day. The one thing he could not adapt to quickly was the shift in temperature. On the third day he layered his travel robe on top of his normal robes.

"Is it always this chilly in the middle of the sea?" he asked Isolde.

She raised an eyebrow at him. "What are you talking about? It is beautiful out, and the sky is gorgeous!" She took a deep breath of the crisp sea air, feeling it wash over her skin. Gone was the stickiness and muck of the desert, where clothing and grit clung to the body. Here it was different; the air and the sea spray made her feel more alive than she had been in a long time.

"Well, to me it's chilly," He gave a slight sniffle and wrinkled his nose.

"Maybe the cook will let you sit on the stove?" she teased.

He harrumphed and shook his head as slowly made his way back to the canopy.

Desert things are Desert things.

She frowned at herself and turned back to her friend. "I know being on the sea is not the most comfortable if you are not used to it. I complained a little to Reynard when we first noticed that grass had disappeared the further south we went. Go below and ask the cook for some hot Giber Tea. It will keep you warm inside and help you with the rest of the journey. Let me figure the rest out."

Tulok nodded his head with thanks and went down below deck. He returned not with a cup, but a carafe of warm liquid. "The cook said it was probably better for me to drink out of this."

Isolde smirked. "Well, when we get to the mainland, you will not have to worry about utensil size. In fact, it may be the least of your worries."

"Oh?" he asked with a bit of caution.

"So, to *me* and most non-desert people, this is a nice day. The Radiant Lord is doing his thing, the sea breeze is alive, and the air cool. The closer we get to the Island, the cooler it will get," she added slowly.

Tulok raised an eyebrow and sniffled, "How much cooler?"

Isolde gave a worried smile, "Well ... is there anything against the Radiant Lords' chosen from wearing breeches and boots?"

His brows furrowed in thought. He had not really considered it. Tulok had worn his assigned vestments for years and never questioned it. He shook his head as if to say no but stopped and his eyes widened in an understanding of the question, "No, there isn't a prohibition against what I wear – save *this*," he said motioning to the sun medallion on his chest. "I have to keep it displayed at all times to let people I am there if they are in need. However, ...," He sat down and looked at his robes, "I will need to find something more ... suitable."

"And in the meantime, your Radiance should spend time with this over your shoulders," she said as she draped a heavy blanket over his shoulder, "... and sit a bit more in the sun. You are going to want to take in as much warmth as possible.

Before he could protest, he sniffled loudly. Isolde put another blanket over his lap. "Please. For me?"

Tulok sighed and sipped his carafe, "As long as I can see the morning light, I will be fine."

Isolde pursed her lips, "About that ... how are you with rain?"

—

On the fourth day, they found themselves on the bow of the boat, watching the horizon line and the darkening of the clouds. The captain had assured them it was clear sailing, but the clouds worried the priest. He could barely handle being at sea. Being on a boat during a storm seemed akin to a dizzying nightmare. Instead, he focused out at the northern horizon and could see something from this higher vantage point.

"Isolde, do you see the water over there?" he asked as pointed outward.

She looked out, "I see a lot of water over there."

Tulok made a face. "No, I mean further out. Look at the color. It has been gnawing at me for the last few days. The water closer to the boat is ... clearer than the water further out. Is that the 'edge' of the Corridor?"

She focused her eyes outwards and gave a nod of her head. "Yep! The corridor is roughly a mile wide. It's the only safe way to travel between the two continents. I have heard stories of ships who dare to skim outside of the Corridor, only to be pulled down below by giant serpents or things with tentacles the size of ship masts. You do not want to think about it too much. There is a lot going on beneath the waves, and most of it is not our business," She looked up at him and patted his arm, "I'm going to get something to eat. I will see you over there."

He nodded and stared out at the darker water on the horizon. No one knew how deep the oceans were or what held power in the water's darkness. The River Lord's influence was without question within His Realm, but outside of Setesh, and freshwater, the god had little power. Even the water that ran along the coast, while safe to sail, was outside of the River Lord's influence. He wondered if there was a library or something similar in Lubri. His spirit perked up at the thought, and then he saw something in the corner of his eye. It was quick and broke the far water in a flash. It was long ... longer than the ship. Just as quickly, it was gone. The scene was less than three seconds and he felt chilled to the bone.

He clutched his medallion and steadied himself.

It was not until the fifth day that Tulok felt his legs and stomach more at ease. He had been using less of the tincture each day. During the trip, one sailor had mentioned to the priest that if he kept toward the center of the ship and his eyes on the horizon, he could break the trick that the sea was casting on him. While not fully sea-worthy, the orc felt a bit more confident walking along the center of the deck and enjoying the view. He had taken to wearing a few blankets on his person while he took his walks along the desk. The crew paid him no mind, even though he looked like a creature formed of warm fabrics. In fact, many of them began wearing long shirts, vests, and boots as they got closer to their destination. The chill in the air was always present, no matter the time of day. The clouds also seemed darker and grayer.

He stood next to Isolde, and they gazed at the eastern horizon. They could see a small green and white "pebble" in the distance. They were a day or so out, but they could see their destination clearly.

"What is that mass of white in the distance?" Tulok asked.

"The Great Sea Walls. Stories differ depending on who's telling it, but that's the way of stories," she smiled as she thought about it," When the Gods brought Avalon over to Sanctum, they wanted to ensure that everyone was protected, you know, just in case things got bad again. So, they carved out a mighty wall of white stone and placed it around the island, like a barrier. However, since they were hurrying away from the Reaping – one of them accidentally lost their grip and dropped their share. It was because of this, the protective wall hit the ocean rock and cracked in two," she said as she smiled into the distance. "And that created the channel to Lubri. At least I like to think so. It was the story my parents told me when I first saw the Sea Walls. The walls stand hundreds of feet tall, and the channel is the only entrance for a large ship to access the port to make easy landfall on Avalon. The genuine beauty is when we go through it."

"I'm listening," Tulok said as he looked out at the pebble.

"Oh no, it is better for you to see. Trust me; it will be amazing. I mean, the Eagle's Rest was amazing, but I think this might make you think twice." She spoke with a brightness that he had not seen in some time.

He smiled. "Then I will take your word at it. Is there a plan for once we make landfall? Do you have to check in with your Order or your own temple? How does that work?"

She made a face as she chewed the inside of her cheek, "Well ... not exactly? There really are no temples dedicated to the Wandering Lord – because he, you know – wanders. The closest thing would be the homely houses."

Tulok's face bore confusion. "Homely Houses?"

"Um ... think of an inn run by priests. You see, Witnesses travel across the world. We see all the things and all the sites Sanctum offers. We are His Eyes and His Hands within the world. However, even our feet get tired, so there are Homely Houses. They are usually spread out across the land–many times in out-of-the-way places. There, we can share our stories of what we have seen and done. They are usually near a well or lake of some sort ... which may explain the lack of them in Setesh."

"Any place with a well or an oasis would have instantly been populated no matter how out of the way they were," the priest said with a bit of a smile. "Perhaps there is one hidden on the eastern side waiting to be discovered."

Isolde gave him a sidelong glance and shook her head. "Stranger things in that desert of yours ... but yes, homely houses. There should be one just outside of Lubri that we can go to. From there ... we will just have to trust in Him to guide us where we need to be."

Tulok sniffled and tried to discretely blow his nose, which was anything but. Isolde pursed her lips together as a slight sense of guilt hovered over her. She was going to need to get him bundled up for the cold weather.

—

The last day of the journey was both terrible and magnificent. The last of warm weather faded with the sunset the day before. All had awakened to dark gray skies with cracks of blue peeking out. Behind them, a white-yellowish disc could be seen breaking the line across on the horizon. The abrasive chill in the dawn air was the coldest that Tulok had ever experienced in his entire life. Wrapped in as many blankets and coverings as possible, he completed his sun-rise oblation with as much dignity that his chattering teeth allowed. At one point, the wind picked up and added to the cold, which made his ritual its own trial. It was so cold that he almost thought he saw his very prayers leave toward the heavens in frozen puffs.

Finally done, he shambled back below deck and took his place by the stove in the galley. He had been a frequent visitor to where the cook simply worked around the big priest when he was there.

Isolde found her friend, with teeth chattering away, holding the carafe of warmth to his chest to take in the heat. "The first thing we are going to do is get you outfitted properly. I swear, okay?"

Tulok forced a chattering grin. "Whatever fo-fo-fo-for? Itss brissssssssssk... re-re-refreshing."

Taking off the blanket she was wearing across her shoulders, she placed it over the top of the orc, covering him up like furniture. Before he could protest, "No, do not take it off. I am fine; you are out of your element here. Just accept it, nod your head, and warm-up, okay? I want you to be ready to brave the cold in an hour. Meet me out on the bow, okay?"

The teeth chattering, while not completely gone, was replaced by a slurping sound, and then the covered bundle nodded in agreement.

"Good. Now drink your Giber," and she patted him on the shoulder.

"Thank ... you ...," said a muffled voice.

She sighed at the bundle with a small smile and then turned to walk up the stair toward the deck.

—

An hour had passed and the shambling fabric creature made its way from below deck and came to a dead stop on the deck. His gaze was met by a massive, towering wall of gray-white stone that seemed to reach high into the heavens and stretch for miles in either direction. It seemed as if the ship was heading on a collision course with the massive structure, but there was no panic aboard. None of the crew was doing anything other than their normal duties. Across the way, he could see Isolde waving at him. Giving the surrounding area one last look, he made his way over to the bow of the ship.

"Amazing, right?" She was filled with both excitement and pride.

"It certainly is … tall?" was the only thing he could think of to say.

She rolled her eyes and motioned him to look forward. "You have to learn to open your eyes, Father. Look straight ahead, but do not focus on the wall; focus on the imperfections of the wall. When you see them, you will understand. Okay?"

Tulok frowned at her and sighed, "Very well."

Staring again at the massive structure, he noticed how much closer they were than before. He could almost feel the speed of the ship race with the waves. Panic was still bubbling in the back of his mind, but he needed to be calm. He knew she would be the first to act if something was wrong, so if she was calm, things were fine.

He took a deep breath and closed his eyes.

Opening them slowly, he ignored the massiveness of the white chalk wall and focused instead on a wide crack ahead of them. Its shape followed the natural formation and body of the wall, but something was off. There was a … shadow to it. He slowly craned his head to the side as his eyes scrutinized the cracks more and more. Shifting his head from the side to side … there was some sort of illusion. Slowly, he pieced together the puzzle in front of him. It was right there in front of him the whole time; the crack in the wall from the children's story

Isolde had told him. The difference was that the 'crack' seemed to be half a mile wide.

"Is it ... magic?" was all he could ask, partially awestruck.

"Sort of ... yes ... no? Most outsiders will only ever see a stone wall. It essentially could keep an invading force from hitting Lubri directly. From the stories we were told as children, that used to be the original purpose ... when there was war between the two continents. However, trade changed all that, made people a bit more civil. However, only ships that are crewed and captained by Avalonians ever make this trip. It is the only way to get to Lubri, and it is the only way for those in Lubri to get to Port Kraken."

After all these centuries, they were still so isolated.

Taking it all in, Tulok watched as they slowly entered the mouth of the crack. The light dimmed all around them and, for a moment, it almost seemed like they were going to get full shunt into the darkness. Then there was a soft glow that almost pulsed before them. The speed of the ship slowed down significantly as they slowly rolled towards the curve of the light.

"This was always my favorite part ..." The sense of joy brimmed out from Isolde as she laid an excited hand on his arm. Tulok looked down at his friend and then back up and saw them:

Lanterns.

Hundreds ... no ... thousands of lanterns that hung from the walls on both sides! There were lanterns of all shapes, sizes, and colors. The light was not just the soft yellow glow but mixed in with colors of greens, blues, reds, and oranges. Each was providing light in the darkened space between the massive stones. Even more astounding was the action around the various sources of light. Among the lanterns, he could see people! People hanging from ropes and moving from space to space. Each was tending to the lights and keeping them lit.

Isolde gave a shallow sigh as she felt her eyes water a little. A single tear fell down her cheek.

She was home.

Chapter 28

The warmth from the firelight was a blessing to those gathered around it that evening. The threat that Ygraine had seen in the glade demanded attention and immediate action. Now, as the few stars that remained in the heavens began to light, the moans and cries of the injured carried across the encampment. The voices of the dying.

The Triskele were at war.

It was to be expected. This battle between Clans and Kingdoms. It was part of the Cycle of the Island. But now there was something new in the mix. Something unknown to the people of the Realm. And it threatened the Eternal Cycle of rebirth.

Cynfael stood at the outside edge of the firelight, his arms folded across his chest. Mud and blood covered his face and hide-bound armor. He had taken the warriors of his Clan into the forest and back to the area where Urram Mael and his son had fallen to some creation of unholy powers. An unnatural curse had infected the blood of the band that encountered the beast. They had found the remains of the creature and the war band in the clearing where Ygraine had indicated. A pile of bodies in one area of the glade, the decaying corpse of what appeared to have once been a great cave bear, the headless body of Urram Mael, and Chieftain's son, Cinioch.

To all accounts, Cinioch had braced a spear and impaled himself upon its sharpened end to pin himself to the ground in death. According to the story shared by the only survivor of the encounter, the creature that lay in the glade had walked upright even after death. If this was indeed the case, the work of The UnSleeping walked the lands of Avalon. Something that could not be permitted to stand.

"… my King?" one man at the fire spoke.

Cynfael's eyes pulled from their thoughts and fell on the scout sitting at the fire, who was addressing him. Gruffydd Marestongue looked up at his Chieftain with questioning eyes. Gruffydd's woven leather cuirass creaked as he moved and adjusted his position.

"Repeat the question," Cynfael said.

Gruffydd nodded simply. "I think it would be wise to send runners to the other encampments to ensure they know the extent of what we are facing. To ensure they do not return their dead to the earth?" the scout repeated.

Cynfael grunted in response, "Agreed. The Crafters and Healers confirm Mael's …," He paused, "*May her spirit be returned to the Cycle …,*" he invoked the blessing for the dead, "… assessment of the infected. It cannot be allowed to spread."

Several of the others seated around the fire nodded and uttered similar comments of blessing and security. A couple made gestures designed to ward off bad omens. Chieftain Cynfael dropped his arms and gestured at a young woman standing in the shadows. She stepped forward. Dark curly hair surrounded her face in an unruly mop. She was covered still in the mud and blood of the fallen that she had pulled from the battlefield. Her arms were covered in bramble thorn scratches that had just begun to scab over. She turned her green eyes up to meet the gaze of her King.

"You go with Gruffydd," the big man spoke to Ygraine.

Ygraine nodded simply and glanced over at the lead Scout. She knew Gruffydd; he was a demanding man who preferred the freedom of the wilds to the company of an encampment. He and his Scouts were the first line of defense the People often had. It had been one of Gruffydd's messengers that brought word back to Cinioch of the fell beast that would ultimately become the warrior's end.

Gruffydd assessed the young woman with a trained eye. "Has she been marked yet?" the Scout asked.

"She is standing right here," Ygraine commented defensively to the Scout.

Gruffydd scowled at the open challenge and disrespect.

Cynfael chuckled deeply. It had been a sorely missed sound. He gestured to Ygraine. Gruffydd bristled a little and turned his gaze to Ygraine.

"Well, girl. Have you been marked yet? Have the gods divined your path and protector?" Gruffydd demanded.

Ygraine met the eyes of lead scout Gruffydd. She straightened her back and shoulders and stood to her fullest height. She was broad-shouldered but lanky of limb. Her reach had proven useful in training her on the bow and her natural strength aided in tending the fallen on the field. Her body was still changing from youth to adult. She was gangly and lean, not yet blossomed fully into womanhood. Despite her youth, there was a sense of both strength and defiance about her.

Knowing the name of the Divine that watched over the soul of each of the People was vital to the health and wellbeing of them all. The Mother placed Her mark on those gifted with Healing Aptitude and those gifted with skill with the soil. Their calling would ensure a clan's people did not go hungry through a lean winter and ensured that ailments did not overtake a settlement. A company of those dedicated to The Huntress would have greater success in felling quarry than one dedicated to the Stag Lord, as one was more gifted to hunting and the other toward speed and evasion.

Almost all of Gruffydd's Scouts were Stags for this reason. Swift of leg and keen of eye, the chosen of the Stag Lord were natural runners and Scouts. Crafters could come from the ranks of any, though most were more deeply tied to the land than many. Urram Mael had seen the ties of the land in Ygraine and had thought her to become a Crafter, but Ygraine's spirit proved too wild for the focus needed to Craft the magics of the world. Indeed, Mael and Cinioch had to venture into Whitebrook several years earlier to recover the recalcitrant young woman and bring her home. So firm was she in her refusal of the Mother's call. She would rather run away than be fitted for a Crafter's role. She remained unmarked.

Ygraine shook her head. "No Scout Gruffydd" she replied.

Gruffydd narrowed his eyes to look at Ygraine once more. "You understand the importance of that question, girl?"

Ygraine nodded. "I do," she replied and then continued. "A scout must be able to move swiftly and freely. They cannot be distracted from the run of a message."

"Are you going to run back to Whitebrooke, Little Wolf?" Gruffydd asked her.

Ygraine set her jaw and glared at the Scout. "Only if a message needs to be carried there ...," she paused and added, "Even then, there is no cause for it. Council Whitebrooke fell to raiders two years ago."

Cynfael's bushy eyebrows raised in surprise. He looked over at Gruffydd. "Were you aware of this?"

Gruffydd's skeptical eyes were locked on Ygraine. "I ... was not."

Cynfael folded his arms across his chest and stared at Ygraine. In the fire's light, her muddied features gave her the appearance of a forest spirit. "Well, explain yourself," he spoke.

Ygraine looked between the two men and considered her words for a moment. "Lord and Lady Whitebrooke took me in when I ... was elsewhere," she began.

"Yes, we all know that child," Cynfael commented.

"Their daughter ... she was to have been married ...," Ygraine commented quietly. She remembered the tall girl who had taken care of her in her time in Whitebrooke. She had been filled with smiles and warmth. They had shared stories in the apple orchard that fall and watched the fireflies dance in the fields.

Ygraine continued. "I ... could not attend the wedding. Urram Mael ... *may her soul be returned to the Cycle* ... forbade it, but a message came to us to tell us that the wedding feast had been assaulted and the village was razed."

"You didn't think we might need that information?" Gruffydd demanded then. He stood and approached the young woman. They were of equal height. She met his eyes, unflinching.

"Whitebrooke is outside Blaidd Drwg territory. They are Village-born … tied to Court and Castle … not hearth and Clan. They are not of the Free People. It was the Urram's decision. I am, as you recall, unmarked," Ygraine countered as she met Gruffydd toe-to-toe and eye-to-eye. A fire burned gently in the pit of her stomach and along her spine.

"Leave off, Gruffydd," Cynfael said quietly in his deep voice. He looked down at the two from his great height. "It was two years ago. There is nothing to be done for it now."

Gruffydd sniffed and spat. "Village-born," he swore.

Ygraine bristled at the insult and stood taller for a moment. Cynfael placed a powerful arm on her shoulder. "Stand down, or stand aside," he cautioned.

Ygraine growled slightly but eased back off of her toes. She snorted at Gruffydd.

Cynfael fixed his gaze on the young woman. "Whitebrooke could have served as a solid encampment for the people. We could have maintained its lands, its fields and its memory. Do we know who keeps the lands now?"

Ygraine shook her head and lowered her gaze. "No, my King," she replied.

Cynfael looked down at Ygraine once more. "Were there any who survived?" he asked.

Ygraine nodded, "Lady Whitebrooke's daughter, Isolde."

"So, there could still be a Council Whitebrooke …," Cynfael nodded absently.

Ygraine shook her head. "No, my King."

Cynfael frowned. "What do you mean 'no', girl?" he demanded. "If Whitebrooke's daughter lives, Council Whitebrooke falls to her care. That is the way of things."

All eyes fell on Ygraine. She looked around at all of those gathered, each waiting for her reply.

"She … was … called to Witness," Ygraine replied quietly.

Cynfael chewed on his bottom lip and smoothed his mustache into his bushy beard.

"The Landless Lord?" he asked.

Ygraine nodded.

Cynfael took a deep breath and uttered several unpleasant oaths in quiet tones. "Very well then," He looked at Gruffydd and pointed at Ygraine, "Until the Gods speak otherwise, she runs with you. I want a band out to Whitebrooke in the morning. We need to know if this is linked."

"It was two years ago ...," Gruffydd began.

Cynfael fitted the scout with an icy stare. "Have you suddenly joined the Crafters, Scout Gruffydd?"

Gruffydd lowered his eyes. "No, my King."

"Then the Lady of the Crossroads has certainly given you some insight into this matter?" Cynfael inquired.

Gruffydd remained in his position of submission. "No, my King."

The towering figure of King Cynfael loomed over his lead scout. "Then until you have a significant insight on these matters ... do ... as ... you ... are ... bade."

"Your will be done, my King," Gruffydd replied and bowed his head deeper.

Ygraine looked up at the giant of a man, who was King Cynfael Aerfyn. The swirl of the Triskele Trinity proudly tattooed on both of his shoulders. Woven vines entwined down both his arms, signifying his duty to the Trinity as Chieftain. It was the great mark on the left side of his face that denoted his patron. Intricate tattoos wove a circular pattern on the King's face. Swirls of blues, blacks, and greens. This ornate mark had been added to over the years, but beneath it was the shape and form of the mark of the Shepherd. The Mother's opposite and balance.

As the Urram would be chosen from the ranks of those who had been called by The Mother, so too would any who lead the People of the Wilds as Chieftain and King be chosen from those marked by the Shepherd. No matter how deeply he may have wished it, Cynfael had always known his son Cinioch would never succeed him in his seat. The Shepherd had not chosen Cinioch to patron; he had been marked by The Huntress and had fulfilled his role to the People even in death.

Cynfael watched Ygraine in the firelight. No divine had claimed her yet as their own. Mael had seen the strength of the Island in her. She had wanted Ygraine to follow in the path to Urram, but Ygraine had walked away from the calling of the Crafters.

Perhaps?

A chill breeze danced across the encampment, carrying leaves and debris, as well as the cries of the wounded and the sound of music used to ease their pain. And for a moment ... laughter.

Chapter 29

"Sweet Wanderer's beard, Tulok, you would think you have never been cold a day in your life!" Isolde chided the big orc standing next to her.

The Radiant Father stood on the dock of the Lubri port, clutching a blanket and his gear to his body to keep warm. His teeth chattered, tusks threatening to pierce his upper lip.

"Th – the … chill … of the desert … is dry. This … *wet* … goes … to … the bone," he replied through his shivers.

Around the two of them, the Capital City of Lubri bustled with life and activity. Workers and traders, messengers and artisans, gathered to unload the ships from the mainland and take goods to their assigned destinations. Captain Hywel stood on the dock, overseeing the unloading of his crates, goods, and gear. The lean Avalonian looked every bit at home here, as he had on the ship itself. The breeze carried Tulok's words to him and he turned a concerned eye in their direction.

"Anything I can assist with, Ser Isolde?" he asked.

Isolde smiled brightly over at the Captain. "Oh! Thank you, Captain Hywel!" she answered. "The Radiant Father and I merely need to make our way to Homely House for a warm meal and discussion on where to acquire appropriate warm-weather gear for His Radiance."

Hywel quirked his eyebrow in Tulok's direction and looked skyward for a moment, "The weather is clear and almost balmy …"

Isolde nodded and shrugged. "His Radiance is desert-born, Captain," she explained.

Tulok watched the two of them speak around him while he stood there. He wondered if this was how Isolde had felt in

Setesh when he and Safar had spoken originally. Part of him suddenly felt a twinge of guilt.

"Ahhhh ... of course!" Hywel nodded and left his position on the dock to stand next to the pair.

Several sets of eyes watched them all from the assembled group. A mixture of anxiety, curiosity, and judgment danced behind their depths. Hywel surveyed them all and gestured to one young Elven boy.

"Lucan! Come here, boy!" he called.

The lithe Elven figure hopped down from a pile of crates and bounded over to Hywel, all smiles and eagerness. His blue woolen cloak fluttered effortlessly around him as he moved. "Afternoon, Captain Hywel! You need something done today?" His almond-shaped silver eyes fixed firmly on the Captain.

"Aye, lad," Hywel replied. He nodded to Isolde and Tulok. "You recognize this Knight's calling?" he asked the boy.

Lucan turned his silver gaze on the towering figure of the Orc first. Beneath his gear and blanket, Tulok still wore the vestments of a priest of the Radiant Lord. White robes with gold embroidered embellishments around its edges. Around his neck hung the mighty golden emblem of the Eye of Heaven. The symbol of the Divine. Lucan frowned.

"Erm ... no?" he offered, blushing slightly.

Hywel scowled. "Not the priest, boy. The Knight!" he gestured to Isolde.

"Oh!" Lucan blushed deeper and stumbled over himself in his embarrassment, "Apologies, my Lady ... I mean ... Ser Knight," His eyes landed on Isolde fully and at that moment the weight of her leug imprinted itself upon his senses, along with the importance of the broken compass around her neck.

"A Witness returned home ..." he whispered in shock. His eyes rose from the compass to her face. Confusion and honor filled his eyes. "A Witness returned home!" he called out.

Isolde held up her hands. "No. Wait ...," she began. But it was too late.

The call bounced from mouth to mouth and ear to ear across

the entire dock. "A Witness returned home!" Where there had been a dearth of attention, they were now surrounded by dozens of people, all clamoring to get a view of the Knight returned from her Wandering. Men, women, children, race of birth did not seem to matter; all made their way to the dock to welcome the returning Knight.

"Welcome home!"

"So glad you made it back!"

"Thank you for your journeys!"

"How exciting!"

The cacophony of voices was reminiscent of the scene in the market square in Ophir; only this time, it was Isolde, that was in the center of it all. She smiled and shook hands and nodded gratefully to everyone. Tulok found himself in a situation that he was very familiar with. Managing the crowds and onlookers for Ahsom Ibris had been one duty assigned to him while at the Temple. Without being bidden, the huge priest shook off his gear and blanket and assumed a position of quiet protection at Isolde's side. Soft luminescence glowed from his being. The onlookers blinked in awe to see a member of the Orckind so blessed by the presence of the Divine – even if it was one that had no home here.

Hywel beamed brightly and clapped Isolde on the shoulder. He leaned in and spoke into her ear, "Welcome home, Champion. I'll go see about that bit of information you shared with me. If I'm in port when it comes time for you to return to the mainland … come see me," and disappeared into the crowd.

At home in Ophir, crowds of this size warranted concerns for attempts on the life of the Champion, or theft of goods. As Tulok watched the gathered crowd, he gleaned no such intent from any of them. Despite this being a prime opportunity to steal their gear, not one person seemed interested in making such an attempt. One more oddity to ascribe to the Avalonian culture.

"All right, all right, that's enough now!" a rough voice sounded from the back of the crowd.

Tulok's red eyes lifted and began searching for the source.

"The Landless Lord thanks you all for the warm welcome of His charge back to the island. Now let us get them home," the voice continued.

Slowly, the crowd parted like the sea before the bow of a boat. Making their way through the gathered group was a small man. No … Tulok corrected himself; the person was too broad of shoulder and short of stature to be human. Most of his face was occupied by a large, white, bushy beard and mustache. It flowed down from his upper lip and jaw and ended in a large braid, held in place with several decorative golden beads and crimps. He was dressed in the blues and whites that Isolde ascribed to the faith of her people. Heavy steel pauldrons sat on the shoulders of his white leather gambeson that was decorated with ornate blue silk stitching along the edges. Much like Tulok's own vestments.

A dwarven priest of the Knight Wanderer.

The broad dwarf waded through the crowd and up to the pair standing on the dock. He cast a quick glance in Tulok's direction, his eyebrows raising slightly, then turned to look at Isolde. He frowned a moment and seemed to look past Isolde as if looking for someone else. Then his gaze settled on the young woman. He folded his arms across his chest.

"Whitebrooke. Where's Reynard?"

Chapter 30

"Well, that's a damned shame," Farnak said. The old priest cradled a cup in his weathered hands and swirled its hot contents around in thought. "He was too young," He nodded to himself and raised the cup to his lips.

Across from him, Isolde sat in measured silence, leaning forward, elbows resting on her knees, head bowed. She nodded quietly, as the weight of her Knight's death came crashing down on her once more.

Farnak set his cup aside and moved to stand before the fireplace. The heat from the flames warmed the simple structure from the chill outside. Homely Houses were the only edifice that might qualify as a Temple to the Wanderer. The Divine of the Island had no need for the grand buildings on the mainland. Here, they were one with their people. They could be felt in the home and witnessed in the field. They were not relegated to Temples and Shrines. The call of the Wanderer often left their people without homes and families, and so it was that the holiest of places for Him was the way stations of travelers. A place of welcome, with a soft bed and a hot meal, was all that many travelers ever hoped to have. A respite for the road-weary. If they could meet it, no request was too great to those who bowed their heads at a Homely Hearth.

The broad-shouldered dwarf held his hands out to the fire and considered Isolde's words. Behind him, the young Knight sat quietly. Tulok stood, arms folded, at her side. His towering figure bathed in reds and yellows of the firelight. His eyes followed the line of the room, taking in the details of what served as a place of faith for his friend.

"And you ... what do I call you, priest?" Farnak asked. He

turned around and warmed his back and thighs against the fire.

Tulok looked down at the smaller man. "I am Tulok, Priest of the Dawn of the First Order to the Lord of the Skies, Bringer of ..."

Farnak waved a calloused hand at the orc, "Yes, yes, we could both go on for the next five minutes in an exposition of titles if we really wanted to ...," He sighed. "Is it Father? Brother? What did I hear dockside ...? Your Radiance?" he chuckled with a scoff and looked Tulok up and down, "Your sun god loves His titles, doesn't He?"

Tulok scowled a little at the irreverent comment.

Farnak ignored it.

"This has to be quite the change to what you are used to on the Mainland. No pillared Temple with a grand walkway of polished marble, ornamented and embellished with gold," the old dwarf commented, looking up at Tulok.

"It is ... different," Tulok agreed.

Farnak glanced at Isolde and grunted, "Well, he's polite. That's unexpected."

Isolde raised her head from her seated position to look at Farnak. Her eyes were red-rimmed. She swiped her left hand across her eyes and face. "His Radiance is a loyal companion and Temple scholar, Farnak," she quipped.

Farnak pursed his lips and looked Tulok up and down once more, assessing him. "We don't see many Orckind in Lubri. They usually keep to the Wyldlands and hills... and they are rarely called to serve," He narrowed his blue eyes a moment and Tulok could feel himself being weighed and measured by the smaller priest, "But the Lord sees you as worthy, so I suppose that makes you all right," He huffed a little and looked back at Isolde.

The younger woman sat up. The metal of her pauldrons glinted in the firelight.

"What the hell are you wearing, Whitebrooke?" Farnak shook his head and stepped in toward her. Reaching out, the dwarf looped a finger inside the collar of her leather chest plate and pulled her toward him. He examined her gear. "You look like you killed half a dozen people and scrapped together whatever fit ...,"

Tulok dropped his arms and stood up straight, fighting the urge to fend the smaller man off of Isolde.

Isolde turned her face away from Farnak and raised her hand to push him away.

"That's because I did," she replied coolly.

The old priest stopped and looked at the Knight a moment, considering her words. "Ah, damn. I'm sorry, girl. That can't have been easy."

Isolde met Farnak's eyes. "It needed doing," she replied and stood.

Farnak's bushy eyebrows rose at her reply. He watched her as she walked away from the hearth and over toward the kitchen area. Tulok remained where he stood, his eyes following her.

"I see you are wearing Reynard's compass ...,"

Isolde nodded. She ripped a chunk of bread off of a loaf on the table. "He gave it to me before he died."

Farnak nodded. "Well, you're home now, so you can leave it with me and I'll make sure it gets to the next Champion."

Isolde froze.

"And the blade, that will be important," the priest continued.

"Excuse me?" Isolde said from the kitchen. Her voice was hard.

Tulok frowned and looked between the two of them. He wanted to interject, but this was clearly a matter of faith between the two.

"Your time of mourning is over, Whitebrooke. You have duties that need fulfilling," Farnak said.

"Stop calling me that," Isolde said firmly.

"What? Whitebrooke? That's yer name, girl," Farnak replied. He folded his arms across his broad chest and stared at Isolde from across the room.

"No, it's not," she replied.

Farnak shook his head and scoffed. "You don't get to cast aside a Founder's name, girl, because you decided you don't want to wear it anymore."

"There is no Council Whitebrooke, Farnak. They are all dead."

Farnak sucked on a tooth and nodded, "Aye. That they are. Except for you," His eyes slid over to Tulok a moment and then back to Isolde, "And that's why we let Reynard take you on. You both needed lookin' after, and you were good for each other. Made certain he didn't lose his way and fall into despair. Nathaniel was important to both of you."

Isolde turned to face the priest. "Let ... him ... take me on?" she repeated.

Farnak nodded and continued, "Had no idea he would actually take you off the fekkin island!" He shook his head. "Idiot boy."

Isolde stood in shocked silence as she listened to the old priest. Disbelief clouded her pale features.

Farnak looked up at Tulok, "So, I suppose we owe you a gratitude of thanks for bringing her home, yer Radiance."

Tulok frowned and looked over at Isolde, pain clearly coloring her entire demeanor. He looked back at the dwarf and held up a broad hand to ask for a moment of pause. "Forgive the interruption, Father Farnak," the big orc began. His deep voice rumbled in his chest, "... but you misunderstand my involvement in this matter."

Farnak turned his attention to Tulok and glanced at him skeptically, "Oh?"

Tulok nodded, "Ser Isolde ..."

"Lady Whitebrooke," Farnak corrected.

Tulok's left eye twitched slightly at the correction. He held his stance. "SER Isolde," he continued, "... has served the Lord Wanderer in a most loyal and righteous fashion. I have personally witnessed His hand in her actions."

Farnak placed his hands on his hips and looked up at the

other priest. "Have you now? And what exactly have you born witness to that makes you feel that way?" He paused. "And I would caution you, yer Radiance ... you are speaking about the chosen of a Divine who serve as witnesses to the world ... so choose your words wisely."

Tulok squared his shoulders and narrowed his eyes as he stared down at the smaller man. He maintained his position, towering over the dwarf. "One assumes you do not mean to accuse a priest of the Radiant Lord of falsehood ...," Tulok began, a dim light emanating from around him.

"Oh please, boy," Farnak answered, squaring off against Tulok, "Under MY roof?"

Both priests stood glowering at one another, the air between them crackling with energy as they met one another, faith against faith.

"I've already taken the Oath," Isolde's voice interrupted from the kitchen.

Farnak blinked. "What?" He turned his attention from Tulok to look toward Isolde.

"I said it doesn't matter. I have already taken the Oath," she repeated. She reached for the gloves that hung from her belt and tugged them on. "So it doesn't matter what the Council wants ... or demands of me. I belong to the Wandering Lord," she turned to face Farnak, "And you would do well to not deride the name of one of his fallen Champions in my presence again, Farnak. His name is Ser Reynard the Swift, not idiot boy, and I set his soul to rest at the crossroads myself," she said coolly and headed for the door.

The old priest shook his head in disbelief, "Whitebrooke lay fallow because you walked away from it!" he said and gestured behind him, "The land needs a steward, girl, and like it or not, your blood is still bound to these shores!"

Isolde paused, door pull in her gloved hand, "They can find someone else," she said quietly and stepped out into the chill.

"Dammit, girl!" the old priest swore. He turned his gaze on Tulok and pointed a thick finger at him and then just shook it in exasperation, "Bah!"

Tulok watched as Isolde walked outside into the fading light, then turned his gaze back on the dwarven priest, "She survived an encounter with the River Lord and trekked across the Seteshi wastelands with nothing but rags on her feet, that compass, and her faith to guide her. Perhaps you should give her a little more respect, Father," he said quietly. He inclined his head and tapped his left breast with the tips of the fingers of his right hand in respect, "Please excuse me."

Farnak watched the Radiant priest depart, his words and their meaning sitting uncomfortably in his ears.

~~~

CRACK!

The branch slammed against the side of the tree trunk with a resounding blow. She drew her arm in and set her stance once more, preparing to strike once more. With a shift of the weight, a twist from the hip, she flung her arm out and snapped her wrist, bringing the wooden stick in her hand back against the trunk once more.

CRACK – SNAP!

It shattered in her hand.

She let out an exasperated and angry cry, turning her head to the heavens.

"You are absolutely correct in your assessment," Tulok said as he approached. "The tree had it coming."

Isolde scowled and rolled her eyes at the comment, "Go away, Tulok."

He shook his head in reply, "I am afraid that really is not an option currently."

"Because I need a stern talking to?" she asked and looked around for another section of wood that she should use.

Tulok watched Isolde and wandered over to the support beam on the back porch. He leaned against it and folded his arms. Shaking his head, "No."

"Then what?" She asked. Finding a suitable length of wood, she hefted it twice and swung it around to test the grip and weight.

"I am a foreigner to your land, Isolde. I have nowhere else to go," he offered.

She paused at that and looked over at him. Nodding, she looked away and at her feet. "No … that …," she sighed, "You are right. I am sorry." She swung her makeshift sword twice.

Tulok nodded and watched her from a distance. "What did he mean? The land lies fallow because you walked away?" he asked.

Isolde's brow furrowed, and she snapped her arm out again to slap the trunk of the tree a couple of times. "It's … complicated," she replied.

"So … uncomplicate it for me," he offered. "Help me understand, Isolde."

She frowned again. "I … can't," she replied with some reluctance.

Tulok's eyebrows rose a little, and then he nodded. "Ah. Is this relating to … our shared bond?" he asked carefully, referring to the shared secrets they were both sworn to keep.

She nodded. "It is," she sighed in frustration and ceased her angry flailing. They had cut a barrel in half and placed face down by the tree to serve as a seat. She flopped down on it and tapped the ground with her stick.

Tulok nodded, considering her words. "Very well." He pushed himself off of the support and walked over to her. Lowering himself to the ground, he sat in front of her. Even sitting with her on the barrel seat, he almost met her eye level. "Tell me what you can," he offered.

Isolde looked up from the ground and into Tulok's eyes, so full of caring and compassion. Yearning to understand her pain so he could ease it.

"The Whitebrooke's were one of the Founding Families of the Island. They came here, with the island … during the Reaping," she began. "Because of that, there are … *responsibilities* assigned to them … and their lineages."

"Because of …," Tulok waved the fingers of his right hand,

indicating there were words he could not speak of that related to the magic of the island and its people.

Isolde nodded. "Yes," she replied and drew absently with her stick in the dirt between them.

"Mm mmm," Tulok nodded, "And you are the last of your line now?" he asked quietly.

She nodded once more. "Yep. Hooray for me," she said sarcastically.

Tulok sat in silence, listening and pondering, "Can you not … assign the duties to someone else?" he inquired.

She laughed a little sadly at that. "If I were a man? I could sire half a dozen children and be done with it, and leave the lineage to them and their mothers." She sat back and gestured to her feminine frame, "Alas."

Tulok pursed his lips and considered, "Ah," He sat quietly for a little while, drawing circles in the dirt with his finger, "Does … The Wanderer require something from you where that is concerned?" he asked carefully, almost tripping over the words as he asked them.

Isolde stopped and looked at Tulok. She sighed, "No, Tulok. He does not," she replied. "The Lord Wanderer has a dozen lineages across this Island that He Himself helped to found. No. He has no issues with … issue," she replied, referring to the siring or bearing children while in His service. She went back to poking at the ground with her stick, "I was pretty sure we covered that back in Kef-aal," she said quietly.

Tulok blushed deeply at the mention of the city where they had shared the ZinHisal. He cleared his throat awkwardly, "Yes, of course."

The pair sat quietly in their awkward silence, avoiding discussion on their shared history, both poking at the earth and not looking at the other.

Tulok broke the silence first, "Does …," he cleared his throat, "Does the land suffer for your absence then?" he asked her.

Isolde shrugged, "I took the Oath; it is understood that I would probably not remain here to simply bear Witness to the comings and goings of every Fishing Village and Faire." She drew a lazy river on the ground with fish beneath the waves. She scribbled it out with her stick.

Tulok nodded, watching her drawings, "And does the Oath hold greater power than your ... lineage obligations?" he asked. He drew fluffy clouds and a sun in the dirt with his finger.

"They come from the same source," she replied. She reached out and drew several stick figures under the clouds and sunlight.

Tulok watched her actions and nodded. He drew a fire next to a pair of the stick figures, "Then surely the Divine understand?" he asked.

"That would be the thought ..." she answered. She drew a rudimentary house shape in the background, behind the pair of figures.

Tulok stared at the images in the dirt, contemplating their meaning. He glanced up from the ground to find Isolde staring at him. She smiled gently and then looked away once more.

An idea slowly took root in the orc's mind, born of years of dedicated service to the Temple in Tarf-qua. He reached out and drew several smaller figures next to the pair by the fire. Isolde frowned and reached to scribble them out with her stick. The big orc dashed his hand out quickly and stopped her actions. He looked up at her and met her eyes with his own.

"Must they carry your blood to carry your name?" he asked.

Isolde frowned, "What?"

"Must they carry your blood, to carry your name? Must you birth them to name them as your heir?"

Isolde blinked and stared at Tulok, then looked back at the sketch in the dirt.

Tulok released his grasp on the stick and looked up at Isolde. "Surely sometimes in the past where children did not result from a union," he gestured around them, "... and yet the island stands firm."

Isolde contemplated Tulok's words and the implications behind them. A flash of a memory darted across her mind. A vision, something from somewhere else. A promise made. Blood in the sand. A Smiling God.

She paused and shook her head and stood. The stick fell from her hand to the ground.

"Isolde?" Tulok asked, concern crossing his red eyes. "Is there something wrong?"

"I ...," she rubbed the bridge of her nose. There was a sharp pain behind her eyes as a headache flared.

Tulok pushed himself up off of the ground and reached for the dark-haired young woman, "Isolde ...," he extended his arm to steady her. She placed her hand on his arm, welcoming the healer's support. Tulok watched her carefully. "How can I help?" he asked her, concern flavoring his voice.

She shook her head. "It's nothing, just a headache," she replied, "And ... a memory." She took a deep breath. The headache subsided.

Tulok remained where he was, supporting Isolde and watching her. "A memory?" he asked.

"Something from ...," she thought for a moment, but the memory was already fading, like wisps of mist in the morning light. "I ... can't recall." She shook her head. "It's gone," Blinking, she patted Tulok on the forearm, "Thank you."

Tulok nodded silently, still watching her.

She smiled up at him. "I'll be fine, Mother," she teased.

He harrumphed at her in response.

"We should get some supper and some rest. Tomorrow we need to see if anyone on the dockside has news about our little friend or information on these visions." She offered.

Tulok nodded in reply and slowly lowered his arm. "And Farnak?"

Isolde furrowed her brow for a moment, her right hand raised to grasp the compass medallion at her neck. "Farnak and I are going to have a conversation."

It did not sound like it was going to be pleasant.

Chapter 31

Tulok tried to not think of it as an insult. The dwarven priest explained matter-of-factly that no beds within the Homely House could support "his Radiance's proportions". Biting his tongue for the sake of argument, he simply nodded his head in agreement. Instead, he was provided thick fur to spread on the floor near the fireplace and several blankets "to deal with the night chill", Father Farnak added with a nearly condescending smile. Part of him wondered how long the dwarf's bravado would last under the mid-morning sun, but he shook off the thought. It was not his place to be petty, even if the other party were rude. The Radiant Lord was not in charge here. This was the house – no, this was the *land* of the foreign gods. He just had to take things in stride. He had no way of support here and there were no other of his kind to rely on. There was a level of curiosity about that, though; Farnak had mentioned that the orcs native to Avalon lived to the north and rarely dealt with the people of Lubri. Based on his first meeting with Isolde, they probably regarded their presence with suspicion, fear, or even contempt.

While Farnak said it was unnecessary, Tulok stood outside of the homely house for a few hours to keep his Watch. It was the one duty he could not let go of, even in a foreign land. While he did not wander past the yard, he saw very little movement from people. He wondered if he was the only person awake in this land of lanterns. After a few hours spent listening to the strange nightlife, he felt his obligation honored. Making his way back inside, he sighed and looked at the fire. The looks that people gave him rarely registered with him, but here it felt different. The orcs on the island were feared, but he presented a new twist to that old fear.

"Children fear monsters, but men are terrified of monsters who think," he said to the embers.

The embers crackled back at him in either laughter or agreement. Turning his back to the fire, he closed his eyes and let the weariness and warmth take him over.

—

The bed linen smelled a little stale, but with a few well-placed smacks, and some snapping of the bedsheets, they gathered the scent of the night air.

"Better," she said to no one.

Isolde stood up and looked out the window. Lanterns of various colors dotted the nighttime landscape. It was a sight she had forgotten. The lights, the coolness of the night, and the taste of moisture in the night air; all the things that touched her deeply as she realized she was home again. She was no longer dealing with the grit of the sand on her skin, the dryness of her cracked lips, and the constant sensation of sweat dripping down her back. They were two different worlds, but she suddenly missed the rich scents that spices colored the air. Setesh had its positive points as well, but it was not home.

She frowned, "Yet … this does not feel like home, does it?"

A deep rumbling purr rolled across her ankle as soft fur brushed off her skin. She looked down just as a large calico cat jumped up onto the bed to join her. It was a large thing, more orange than white or black, with green eyes and a round body. She trotted across the bedsheets to Isolde and bumped against her affectionately.

"Well, hello there to you too!" Isolde smiled as she reached down to scratch the cat's ears and then rub under her chin.

The cat closed her eyes and rubbed on Isolde's hand in glee. It had been a long time since she had enjoyed the company of a cat. There had been a few animals at the Temple in Setesh, but most of those had been goats, sheep, and dogs. She remembered seeing two cats in the time that she had been there; both had been unfriendly to the foreign knight. Safar had suggested rubbing her hands with animal fat, but that only made her smell rancid; though the dogs seemed to appreciate it. Safar had offered to bring her a kitten from one of his trips, but Isolde had not thought it fair to bring an animal to her if she were not planning on remaining for long. Taking an animal as a traveling companion was a responsibility, she was not ready for, especially something as small and easily injured as this. She smiled again, turned, and sat on the bed. The calico immediately jumped into her lap and assumed a position for petting.

Isolde watched the animal as she gently stroked its fur. "Farnak is very lucky to have you as a companion," she said. The cat purred louder, as if in response. "He's not thrilled with me right now," she continued. The cat reached forward slightly and began to gently knead Isolde's thigh. "He says I need to give all of this up, turn it all over, and take up my family's place in Council Whitebrooke once more," She sighed and looked up at the ceiling as she continued to pet the cat in her lap. "I just don't think I can do that, kitty," she said quietly.

The cat made a gently "meowing" sound in reply.

"Mmm, exactly," Isolde replied, and continued to stroke the feline as she sat quietly in the dim light of the room.

The lantern's glow added a gentle warmth to the area, even as the chill of the evening took hold. She hoped Tulok would be warm enough. He was by the hearth. It should help. Isolde furrowed her brow, thinking of the exchange she'd had with Farnak about where to put the Sun Priest for the evening. A rush mat and furs coupled with heavy wool blankets by the fire was a far cry from the opulent room and bedding that Tulok had been accustomed to in Setesh. It was insulting, truth be told.

Isolde looked down at the cat, who had ceased her kneading and settled in to snooze, "He could have pulled a couple of the straw ticks together for him, kitty. That's all I am saying," she offered. Hospitality was demanded of the Homely House, but the quality of its gifts was apparently up for some debate. It did not sit well with Isolde.

Have we always been like this? She wondered, though she

knew the answer immediately; the Island preferred its privacy. Outsiders, regardless of race or origin, were frowned upon and rarely left the City of Lubri when they arrived on Avalonian shores. Arman was here ... somewhere. That there were those willing to transport him to the far side of the land spoke volumes. Now another outsider had arrived with intent to traipse deep into the sacred groves of Avalon, and potentially unearth more of her deepest secrets. That he had been bound in secrecy once already might garner some leniency, but Tulok was also not only a priest of the Radiant Lord but an Orc. And the Orc-kind were not popular in Lubri.

Isolde shifted under the weight of the cat, who meowed her displeasure at the movement of her new bed and slowly lay down. The cat adjusted herself and walked up Isolde's lithe frame to settle on her chest and began purring once more. Isolde watched the creature and continued to gently pet its soft fur, slowly relaxing into the bed beneath her tired form.

It was a battle for the morning.

With the warm, purring weight of a calico cat on her chest, Isolde closed her eyes and drifted off to sleep.

—

The sun had not risen yet, but he could see the dunes clearly. They were an endless sea that went on for miles and miles all around him. How did he get there? Looking behind him, he saw no footprints in the sand. He did not walk here, did he? Tulok closed his eyes and ran his hand over his head. Was he checking ahead and scouting? If he was scouting, then where was the caravan? He looked around and realized he was alone. He looked down at his other hand and saw that he was holding on to a scroll. Unraveling it, he saw words form and then slide off the parchment-like ash, leaving it blank. Looking up into the night sky, he looked for the lone stars that dotted the night, but they were not there.

On the horizon – something flicked off in the distance.

He narrowed his eyes, trying to focus on the source when everything shifted.

He was sitting in front of a fire laughing with several people, but he could not remember why he was laughing. He did not recognize any of these people. The group comprised humans, elves, and dwarves. Slowly, they stopped laughing and turned their attention toward him. They stared at him with contempt. Tulok could feel the weight of their gaze and it was not friendly.

"You better run, big man. I think it is going to get ugly real fast," a voice behind him laughed.

"Run you, dolt! You have no claim here!"

He could feel the panic well up inside as he stood up and backed away as others rose in tandem, and moved forward. He turned and ran away from the fire. The last thing he saw was the silhouette of a small man smiling with white teeth. Tulok pushed himself hard as he ran further into the darkness, away from the people behind him, giving chase. His heart pounded in his chest as he ran from the thunder of voices. He fell to his knees, breathing hard. The sweat that ran down his face felt cold. His knees were damp, and he realized the ground was wet. He looked up and there was a massive river in front of him. Looking up in the night sky, he could see the sun, but it was not warm with light. This was a silvery orb that brought no warmth of its own. Its reflection shone brightly along the water.

Cold and lonely.

Tulok reached forward and scooped up some of the water in his hands and splashed it on his face.

He felt nothing.

He reached forward to do it again when he saw a longboat in the distance. There was a single light on its bow. Its deep yellow hue was the only color he had seen. He watched it as it continued down the river. Then the light 'blinked'. The focus of the light was almost like a cat's eye, a long thin sliver. It blinked again and he could hear a voice call out,

"I would not do that if I were you. These waters bear a different toll, Sun Child."

There was a familiar smugness in the voice that he could not place.

The water splashed at his knees, and the chill was unsettling.

"Too late, Sun Child ..."

He tried to stand, but a wave surged from the edge of the water and knocked him on his back. It cold was painful and he felt its weight press down on his chest. The silvery orb was gone. The water was black and thick as it slammed down on him. He struggled to stand and push himself back from the water, but it was all too much. A sense of failure, doubt, and fear washed over him with wave after wave as he struggled to breathe. He flailed until he could not feel himself anymore.

There was no more time. There was no more fight.

He went under the water and felt the cold filling him up inside. His pain and his tears flowed as he felt himself being pulled further into the darkness and nothingness.

The river water lapped on the shore and the landscape dimmed more and more ...

Suddenly, bluish-white light exploded across the night sky overhead. A thunderclap echoed across the dunes so loud that the sand shook and shifted.

The bluish object fell with purpose as it impacted the river water. The force of the object blew a wide hole in the surface as the light engulfed the scene. The water seemed to fight back at the intrusion, but the light just became brighter until it hissed in frustration. Like hundreds of snakes, the water sizzled as it parted.

Tulok's red eyes slowly opened. There was a light in the distance that seemed to come closer. He wanted to move, but it took all his energy to even open his eyes.

The light approached. A face came into focus. The features reflected icy determination. Hands reached for him. He felt the chill recede from his body slowly.

Something struck his face hard, "WAKE UP, TULOK!"

The white light struck him again.

Isolde struck him again, "YOU ARE DREAMING! WAKE UP, YOU DAMN IDIOT!"

He felt pain and shame, all at the same time. He sluggishly tried to move, but only raised an arm up.

He felt a hand grab the front of his robes, and a hot fist struck his jaw. "WHERE IS THAT DAMN GURKH YOU COWARD?!"

Pain, insult, and challenge awakened something forgotten and primal in his chest. He roared back in defiance; his body burned like the noonday sun. The hiss became loud and aggressive as he swung free from the thinning water.

—

Isolde was covered in sweat as she sat on the floor next to the orc. She struggled to pull him out of the darkness that tried to engulf him. She was angry at herself. How could she have been so stupid? Tears and sweat fell down her face as she looked over to the dwarf who was re-lighting the hearth.

Farnak said nothing. He was as guilty as Isolde in this error.

He turned to her. "I'll get some water. He will need the tea." He tossed another log into the fire and walked toward the kitchen.

Tulok stirred slowly. Everything hurt.

"Easy. Relax. But do not fall back asleep, at least not yet," she said gently.

The orc turned his head towards her voice. Everything was blurry. Slowly trying to find focus,

"What ..." was all he could say. He was exhausted and wanted to close his eyes again.

He felt his head raise up, and a hand slapped his cheek, forcing his eyes to open again.

"No, you cannot fall asleep yet. You are not ... ready. I'm ... I'm sorry. This is my fault. I should have remembered this. Of all the mistakes to make ..."

"You are not alone in your mistake, girl." Farnak stood at the doorway, looking at them. "Do not be bearing all that weight yourself. I will not have it. Sit him up, and we will sort him out."

Isolde nodded and urged the orc to a seated position. Reluctantly, Tulok slowly turned his body toward the fire and forced himself to his side, then on all fours. Pushing himself up onto his knees, he rubbed his face. The pain on his jaw spiked his awareness, and his eyes opened wide.

Farnak held a large tankard toward him. "Drink this ... slowly."

The black drink had the earthy scent of tea, but the taste was bitter and without flavor. He made a face but took another sip. Far be it for him to reject bitter medicine or whatever it was.

Isolde stood and took a seat by the fire.

"Dreams here in Avalon are different ...," she started but looked to Farnak.

The dwarf nodded his head to her, and she continued.

"If you live in the wilderness, you will see all kinds of animals that live there. Over time, the animals acknowledge you are not a threat, and eventually, you can walk further and further into the forest. However, there are things in the forest that will see you not as a threat ... but as prey. Dreams in Avalon are like a forest ... and as children, we are taught to respect them and not venture too far. There are places we are not meant to go ... because even the darkness has hunger."

"The tea will let you sleep, Father, but not dream. You are not ready yet," Farnak said as Tulok looked at black brew and took another deep sip.

It was only the first night.

Chapter 32

Nightfall on the island was not like nightfall in the desert.

In Setesh, caravan runners made efforts to place guide lamps along trusted pathways; they offered some sense of direction in the otherwise blank canvas of night. The faint light from the sacred stars was almost always visible, and the only gift that illuminated the wastelands. A skilled Reysis could see the shifts in light on the horizon from township to township and guide the path of their caravan safely.

There were no guiding lamps on the pathway that Arman was on.

The heavy canopy of trees above him covered any hopeful glimpse of starlight above, leaving him no sky-bound anchor to gaze upon for direction. Instead, he had been forced to rely on skills learned in his earlier years of Guild studies in direction-finding. Noting which mosses grew on which side of which trees, sighting the bend in flower stalks whose heads had followed the sun overhead during the day. He reached down and placed his hand on the flat surface of the rock, and closed his eyes. Calling on the magic in his blood, he reached into the stone to gently gauge where it was warmer and where the chill of the air was more pronounced; the warmer area would have felt the sun's light more recently. He had adjusted his trek accordingly until the darkness grew too great for his pony's comfort. While he could have continued in the darkness for some time, the animal had no such connection with its environment and would no doubt stumble and break its leg in the darkness. That was not something he could allow.

He gathered what dry wood and tinder he could find and selected a place of relative security for his encampment for the evening. There was a risk of being alone in the forests of Avalon, but there were no villages where he was going. It was possible he might come across one of the wandering tribes that made the Island their home, but there was no guarantee what form of reception they would give him. If he were lucky, he would run into a human band and be able to negotiate with them. If he were unlucky, it would be one of the many bands of Orckind that claimed the Wyldlands for their own. Those may be just as likely to kill him as to speak to him. He shook his head and muttered to himself. The orcs of the Island were nothing like the orcs of Setesh. There they built settlements and engaged in merchant trade. Some even served in the grand Temples as missionaries and keepers of the faith. Here? The Orckind of Avalon were still trapped in roles and superstitions of a time long passed. They were often little more than brutish thugs, raiding the villages and land for what they wanted.

Arman wondered at that. With the strange balance that seemed to exist between the people of the Island Nation, why were the orcs permitted to do as they did? What purpose did it serve to allow such brutality to exist in such a place? He frowned and poked at the fire with a long stick; turning the logs slowly and nudging the coals to life once more. Under different circumstances, he might have enjoyed engaging someone in a dialog on the subject. Now, however, was not the time.

The pony whickered and swished her dark tail impatiently, drawing his attention to her and pulling him out of his thoughts. The animal stood with head raised, nostrils flaring, ears twitching in an alert position.

"Damn this island," he muttered to himself. Narrowing his eyes, Arman reached for his blade and slowly stood, readying himself for anything. His senses reached out to touch the earth beneath his booted feet, and in doing so sought to feel the presence of anything else in the area.

In the distance, tiny blue-white lights flickered around the tree line. Dozens of lights illuminated the darkness of the forest, dancing silently. Arman's grip on his sword tightened. Nothing was as it seemed on Avalon, and dancing lights were rarely simple fireflies.

The pony chuffed and stamped. Arman held out a careful hand and lay it on her neck, soothing her. His eyes continued to watch the tree line and the strange lights.

A soft breeze blew through the trees. Leaves rustled with the wind. The creaking of branches overhead and around him could be heard. Lights in the distance remained where they were, steady and almost fixed in place. Around them, bioluminescent moss glowed faintly on the trunks of the trees, the not-fireflies were giving off enough light for them to awaken in the darkness. A shared light source seemed to grow and expand away from Arman, deeper into the tree line across from him. The not-fireflies danced in the darkness. Their number seemed to increase as the tiny swarm split into two. One swarm remained where it had been, the other floated lazily into the trees. Moss came to rest on the trees as the swarm passed; forming what appeared to be a trail in the darkness.

Arman watched the not-fireflies in the darkness with a wary expression. It could be Phaendar's actions that he was witnessing. Some strange messenger that the old Sage had tasked with leading him to their location.

Or it could be willow wisps leading you into a marsh, where you will drown and they will consume you, Arman warned himself.

Beside him, the pony snorted and chuffed with displeasure.

"Your opinion is noted," Arman commented to the horse as he continued to pat her neck. He remained where he was, standing at the fire's edge, watching the lights in the distance. His hand rested on the pommel of his sword, ready to draw it and engage if needed.

The lights in the distance continued their silent dance in the darkness. A very clear pathway slowly came into sight, formed by the not-fireflies and the moss. It continued deep into the tree line and disappeared beyond Arman's sight. The chill of the forest seemed to intensify briefly around him. The pony snorted and pulled away.

Arman drew his blade and quickly took a stance of readiness. Across from him, a figure stood by the firelight. Shadows seemed to ebb and flow around them, softly caressing the figure with velvet darkness. Arman had seen this before when in the presence of the witch Nebiyre. A moment of fear gripped the dwarf's heart as he remembered leaving her to die in the ruins of the wastelands. The palm of his hand began to sweat slightly.

Clearing his throat, he whispered softly, "In the beginning …"

The figure lifted its head and looked at Arman from across the campsite. A thin and ageless face with deep-set dark eyes gazed back at him. The voice that answered was like a gentle song, carried on a nightbird's wing … "There was only Chaos."

~~~

"There's nothing here but graves," Gruffydd said. The scout stood in the center of the clearing and turned in a simple circle, looking at the area. Around him, the earth rose and fell in a neat concentric circle of berms. Stones stood at one end of some berms. Once neatly piled, they lay scattered around the field now, their denoted markings lost.

Ygraine knelt at the side of the berm, her fingers dug deeply into the earth. Green grass had covered the gravesites as the island reclaimed its lost. The hilt of a weapon emerged slightly from the ground; its blade buried deep beneath the surface. She hovered by the graveside; her head bowed in reverent memory.

"What have you there, girl?" Gruffydd asked. Minding his steps, he made his way over to Ygraine and squatted next to her.

"Alderman Whitebrooke," she replied quietly. Her mind replayed the memory of the kind gentleman who had taken her in and given her a roof over her, a place to live when she had abandoned her Clan. His eyes were always full of laughter.

"Mmmm," Gruffydd nodded and sucked on a tooth. His hand clapped down on Ygraine's shoulder. There were no other words on the matter.

"What in Trinity's name happened here?" one of the other Scouts asked, a young man, barely blooded. They stood in awe of the clearing and the number of deceased that surely lay here. There had to be fifty souls that were committed to the earth here.

Gruffydd watched Ygraine, waiting to see if she had an answer. When nothing was forthcoming, he nudged her. "What do you know?" he asked.

Ygraine shook her head and pulled her hand out of the earth. She rubbed her hands together; the soil falling to the ground. "Nothing," she replied. She turned her eyes skyward and looked at the trees.

"Nothing?" Gruffydd repeated. He stood slowly and looked down at her. Gesturing broadly, he took in the whole of the clearing. "This is a wide stretch of nothing, Little Wolf, to have taken down the whole of the Council Whitebrooke."

Ygraine stood, her eyes still on the tree line. A dozen ravens sat in the branches above them. Their dark eyes glittered as they watched the tribesmen examine the graves. She wondered at their presence.

The young woman shook her head once more. "Isolde was not …," she paused and frowned, trying to remember. It was only a couple of years ago. Why was it so hard to remember? She cleared her throat. "She didn't go into details when we spoke last."

Gruffydd eyed Ygraine and scratched at his dark, patchy beard. "When was this? That you spoke to your village-born?"

Ygraine bristled at the term and stretched her neck from side to side. A warmth slowly spread at the base of her spine and up her back. She shook it off. "Not since she left the island with her Knight."

"And … that … would … be …," he continued. Irritation dripped from his voice.

"It's been a little more than a year since we spoke last," she replied.

Gruffydd sniffed in displeasure and looked up at the tree line. Black-winged birds flapped and cawed and watched them from their perches aloft. He narrowed his dark eyes.

"We have company," he whispered. His eyes remained on the ravens in the trees.

"I see them," the younger Scout with Gruffydd replied. He continued to walk the glade, counting berms, one eye on the treetops.

Ygraine looked up at the ravens and glared at them, then back to Gruffydd. "What does She want?" the young woman asked.

Gruffydd snorted. "You want to ferret information out of a keeper of secrets? Be my guest ..." he shook his head, "If Her eyes are here, they are watching it for a reason," He looked around the glade and the graves once more. "And I am not about to disturb the dead to uncover it." He gestured broadly and whistled, then pointed out of the glade. "Let's go check the settlement. Maybe we can find something there."

The group slowly departed the gravesite, three Scouts and Ygraine. All watching the tree line and the glade behind them. Raven's cries followed them as they walked away.

As the canopy closed in over them, Gruffydd looked to Ygraine. "Did she say anything that might give you an idea of what happened here? Anything at all?"

Ygraine shook her head and stared at her hands. They were covered in grave soil. "No. Only that the wedding feast had been attacked by a larger force," she replied. Her heart ached for the loss of the family and friends she had once known. Their interactions had been brief, but they had touched her deeply with their warmth and love. It was one thing to hear the news. It was something altogether different to see what had happened in person and stand at the graveside of people you knew.

Gruffydd frowned. "That makes no damned sense," he growled.

Ygraine simply shrugged in reply.

"Orcs? Did she mention orcs?" he asked.

Ygraine shook her head. "No."

He grimaced and continued to trek through the woods toward the village.

They had established Council Whitebrooke during the foundation of the Island, after their arrival on Sanctum. It was one of the oldest settlements on its shores. Built on the edge of one of the larger sources of fresh water on the island, Whitebrooke served as a center for fishing, hunting, and farming. The lands were rich with life and had supported several families over the centuries. They had always been careful not to overfish, rotate crops, and thin herds as needed. Surplus from Council Whitebrooke always made its way across the island to other settlements in need. How the absence of Council Whitebrooke could go unnoticed for two years baffled Gruffydd. Did no one have need of the resources from the Council's lands?

Or had they suffered similar fates and not been able to send word to anyone?

Was the massacre at Whitebrooke an isolated incident, or perhaps it was a precursor to what was being experienced in the Wylds. The implication nagged at the back of Gruffydd's mind.

The tree line broke and revealed the settlement of Council Whitebrooke.

Buildings stood along a simple cobblestone path that led off into the distance to join the larger trail that would eventually lead to Lubri. Stone and wood, brick and mortar. Thatched roofs now home to birds and rats. Colorful clay-tiled roofs, now broken and scattered on the streets below. Shuttered windows, some open, others closed. Windowpanes covered in dirt and age. Ivy and other trailing vines climbed the edges of many of the buildings, weaving their way into the stonework. A village of over a hundred people, empty, abandoned, and silent.

"Everyone on their toes. Eyes and ears open wide," Gruffydd cautioned. The group nodded quietly and slowly began their advance into the abandoned settlement.

"Which house was the Alderman's?" Gruffydd asked quietly. He slowly drew his weapon from its sheath. The two Scouts with him followed his lead, both notching arrows and making ready.

Ygraine paused for a moment to survey the scene. Her stomach sunk. She remembered running on this cobblestone street, chasing after Isolde and two boys. One was Isolde's intended, the other would become her knight. Their laughter echoed in her mind. Shaking her head free of the memory, she looked around and nodded in the distance. A large two-story home sat back from the main square. Its white stone walls were covered now in vinework. Multi-Colored tiles decorated the roof and stained-glass window panes adorned three of the remaining sashes.

"There," she replied.

Gruffydd snorted his derision, scoffing at the waste of land used in such a fashion. He gestured to the two other Scouts with him to go out and search the ruins. They nodded in unspoken understanding and darted off to do as bid.

Scout Gruffydd approached the gates to the main house and crouched to examine the soil and the hinges of the heavy gates. He gazed skyward and around them.

"Not been used in some time," he replied. He looked at Ygraine. "Two years you said?" he asked.

Ygraine nodded.

Gruffydd stood and looked around. There were no signs of forced entry. No windows broken inward by physical assault. The door before them remained closed without evidence of an attempt to break it down. Mud caked around the edges of the frame.

"Makes no sense," he muttered once again. "Where the hell did they all go?"

Ygraine watched the eves and the windows of the house. Nothing but memories and phantoms of memories answered her. "I don't know."

Gruffydd readied his hand on the door and nodded to

Ygraine to make ready. She nodded in reply and readied her weapon. Sliding his hand down to the lever of the door, Gruffydd slowly pushed down and kept pushing as the handle disintegrated in his hand.

The Scout started and jumped back and away from the door as the metal fixtures that held it in place lost their cohesive shape and fell away. The door shifted with their absence and fell backward through the doorway. It landed with a loud and resounding THUD. A puff of greyish-blue smoke surrounding the door and floating away in the air.

"Morpheum touched," Gruffydd swore under his breath.

Gruffydd's Scouts darted from the shadows and bolted toward the sound, ready to defend him from whatever enemy had presented itself.

Ygraine nodded, following Gruffydd's eyes as he examined the fallen door. "Are you sure?" she asked.

The Scout leader nodded gravely, his keen eyes sighting the room beyond them. A thin layer of blue-gray dust settled on the whole of the scene. It sparkled slightly in the light that shone through the open doorway, like some strange snowfall.

"Someone opened a gate here, and left it open ...," he said softly. To his right, a large staircase rose to the second floor. To his left, open doors led to what appeared to be a sitting room. A large table occupied most of the room, along with several chairs. He looked back at the staircase and shook his head. "If that door is any indication, I don't trust those stairs to hold weight."

There were no objections.

"Touch nothing. Trust nothing. The dreamscape flooded this place. There is no telling what is and isn't Realm material here," he cautioned and carefully stepped through and into the home. The blue-gray dust crunched under his booted feet, like snow; but no footprints were left in his wake. The magic of the otherworld still had a hold here then. Looking into the far room, Gruffydd spied a large table with what appeared to be several parchments laid out on it. Gruffydd frowned and stepped over to the table. Everything was covered in that same sparkling dust. He squinted against the darkness of the closed room.

"Flint and tinder; I need light over here," he said to anyone listening. A moment later, a small lantern was passed over to him. He approached the table and held the lantern aloft to look at the parchment on the table. It appeared to be a map. Stepping closer, Gruffydd leaned in to look at the markings on the parchment. It seemed familiar, but the language was not something that he could read. He grunted at Ygraine.

"Your village-born taught you letters while you were here?"

Ygraine nodded and stepped up next to Gruffydd. Reaching back, she pulled her long hair out of her face and knotted it at her neck. She gazed down at the map and its markings, careful not to touch anything.

"It's a map of the Island," she commented and moved to get a better look at the markings. The island of Avalon lay marked out on parchment before them. Its forests and mountains in a fine pen, sprawling rivers and creeks colored the parchment in faded blues. In the center of the Island loomed a dark shape, like a crescent wave. In the crescent's curve was drawn a lantern. A pathway appeared to wander from the northern seashore to the mountain.

The map shimmered and seemed to lose cohesiveness for a moment. Letters flipped and changed, making it impossible to read.

Gruffydd swore and hissed as the Morpheum warped the image before them. "Someone manifested something…"

The Morpheum sang in the blood of the trueborn of the Island, magic, and dreams and the realm fantastic, often nothing more than a thought away. It was different for each. For Ygraine, it was the ability to find the places and things that slipped between worlds and call them into better focus. Ygraine nodded and tried to concentrate on the item on the table. Her sense of self blurred momentarily as the inherent magic in her blood synced with the area and the scene solidified for a split second of clarity.

The Alderman and Isolde's intended ... *What was his name ... she should remember* ... standing and examining a map of the island ... Nathaniel? That was his name! A strange figure stood in the darkness, just out of sight, watching them, waiting for ... something ... glowing amber eyes filled with hunger. They could not see the figure, could not sense it. Here, in the moment's memory, Ygraine saw them. Tall, lithe, lean to the point of almost skeletal; wide, deep eyes gazing from the in-between place with an almost ancient desire. The figure's mouth moved and words flowed across the air, lilting like music.

The Alderman nodded with a smile and handed the younger man a bag that was tied shut. The younger inclined his head politely and tucked the bag away into his pouch. They were making an exchange. Finalizing Isolde's bride price? Perhaps.

The Alderman smiled and clapped Nathaniel on the shoulder. He produced a silver key from his pocket and gestured at the map on the table. It was a simple key, well-worn from age. Here in the space between the worlds, it seemed to almost hum as it was made visible. Ygraine could feel the vibrations in the air and in her bones. There was magic associated with this key.

They exchanged words that Ygraine could not understand; they were lost to the dreams and time. Nathaniel nodded solemnly to whatever had been said and turned his eyes on the map once more. Alderman Whitebrooke gestured toward a cave at the base of Mynydd Mawr: The Great Mountain. The Heart of the Lady. The two men met eyes and then clasped hands over the table. As they did, the figure in the darkness smiled and stepped away, the air around them shimmering blue-gray as they vanished. The scene ended.

Ygraine blinked as she was thrown from her reverie, back from the realm into the real. She gasped deeply for air and swung at nothing. Gruffydd ducked her wild punch and grabbed her arm, securing her.

"What was it? What did you see, girl?" Gruffydd demanded.

"Mynydd Mawr," she whispered.

The other two Scouts uttered words of protection at the name of the mountain at the heart of the island. Ygraine looked into Gruffydd's eyes.

"Alderman Whitebrooke held a key to Mynydd Mawr. I think … I think they were killed for the key."

Gruffydd stepped up and met Ygraine's eyes. "Be damned sure of what you saw, girl," the Lead Scout growled. "That's a thing once spoken what cannot be unspoken …"

A fire burned in the pit of Ygraine's stomach at the singular challenge on Gruffydd's lips. Her eyes narrowed, and she straightened her shoulders. Stepping in, she met him, nose to nose, eye to eye.

"*Mynydd. Mawr,*" she said each word slowly and clearly.

"Then may the Lady have mercy on us all," Gruffydd replied quietly.

A light breeze blew across the courtyard. The sound of tiny silver bells dancing on the wind. Ygraine thought it sounded like laughter.

Chapter 33

Lucan straightened his vest and tugged at his cuffs to improve his outward appearance. Reaching back, he quickly fastened his long dark hair with a leather thong, tucking it behind the tips of his pointed ears. Straightening his shoulders, he rapped solidly on the door of the Homely House and waited.

There was no answer.

Lucan's finely arched eyebrows knit together on his brow. Someone was always in attendance at the Homely House. A soft bed, a warm meal, and a welcome hearth were part of the Lord Wanderer's promise to every traveler. Lucan raised his hand and knocked once again, politely awaiting a response.

Once more, there was only silence.

The Elven boy chewed on his bottom lip in disquiet and reached for the door pull. Pressing down on the latch, the lever came free ... as it should; Homely House was never locked. He breathed a little easier at that and pushed the door open.

"Farnak?" he called as he peered inside.

A warm fire glowed with a welcome at the hearth, a loaf of bread on the bricks, and a kettle of morning oats on the fire. Lucan smiled and took a deep breath. He thought he smelled apples and cinnamon. Stepping inside, the runner looked about and walked over to the hearth. A handful of wooden bowls sat on the mantle, along with cups and spoons. He reached up and pulled down a bowl and spoon and moved to the fire to ladle out a helping of warm morning cereal. The sweet scent of maple, apples, and cinnamon filled his nose. He closed his eyes and sighed a contented smile and raised a spoon to his lips.

"Lucan, what are you doin' here this morning, boy?" Farnak's gruff voice asked from the doorway.

Lucan jumped and bobbled his bowl of hot cereal, nearly dumping it all over himself and the floor. His Elven reflexes saving both from certain disaster.

"Hearthkeeper!" he exclaimed, turning around quickly.

Farnak sniffed and watched the boy's actions. He scratched absently at his beard and lifted his chin at the bowl in Lucan's hands. "Well, how is it this morning? Whitebrooke insisted on making it. Claimed it was how her mother made it."

Lucan's eyebrows raised, and he looked at the bowl and then back to Farnak. "I, uh ... I haven't ..."

"Oh, sweet Wanderer's beard, boy. You came into the House; you get to eat from the kettle!" Farnak shook his head and walked past Lucan and into the kitchen. Grabbing what appeared to be a worn apron, he tied it around his stout form and reached for a knife and an apple. He cut the fruit up and watched Lucan.

"Right, of course," Lucan nodded, and tucked into the cereal. It was filled with flavor. Morning oats were robust and often accompanied with butter and milk. Sometimes you might get honey. The Witness had added more than these to her offering this morning. Lucan smiled around the spoon and nodded. "It's really good!" he replied and continued eating.

Farnak grunted and continued to dice apples. "Council Whitebrooke's always had good luck with their orchards. Makes sense. The Lady would have added them into the pot." His gnarled hands made quick work of the white-fleshed fruit. "I'll have to grant the girl that at least," he said with a note of reluctance.

"Is she here?" Lucan asked around the spoon.

"Whitebrooke?" Farnak asked. He eyed Lucan suspiciously. "Aye. She's in the back with that Mainland priest, trying to teach him how to not fall into his dreams again." The old dwarf shook his head. "Idiot."

Lucan's eyebrows rose. "The orc? Is ... is he alright?" he asked, licking the spoon clean of its contents.

"Aye, he's fine, thanks to Whitebrooke." Farnak wiped his hands on the apron. "Can't say the Wanderer didn't choose her. Girl's not got an ounce of fear to her soul … or sense in her brain." He sighed deeply and shook his head. Looking around for a moment, his eyes landed on a cup. He reached for it and drank down the contents, then wiped his mouth with the back of his hand. Setting the cup down, he looked over at Lucan. "Well, what do you need? I assume you've been sent on someone's errand."

Lucan finished cleaning the bowl of its contents with his index finger and nodded, "Captain Hywel sent me with a message for the Witness."

Farnak rolled his eyes. "What does that troublemaker want with Whitebrooke? She's got a calling to fulfill. She ain't got time to entertain anybody right now."

Lucan frowned, "No, no; Nothing like that. This is about the man the Witness came here in search of," he replied. He glanced around and found a large wooden tub by the hearth. He deposited the bowl and then the spoon into the tub with a polite "Thank you," uttered to no one specific.

Farnak folded his arms across his chest and watched Lucan. "Go on."

Lucan chewed his lip and tugged at the hem of his vest.

"Oh, fer the love of The Mother, boy! You can either tell me and I will tell her, or you can go out back and deliver your charge," Farnak huffed.

Lucan's eyes brightened, and he nodded quickly. "Thank you!" he smiled and darted out the back door.

~~

"You have to try again," Isolde said to Tulok.

The orc sighed and grumbled and stretched his neck from side to side, "I feel ridiculous, Isolde."

"Well, I'm sorry that your Mainland sensibilities find the ways of my people … ridiculous," she countered.

The Witness folded her arms across her chest and frowned at the big priest, who stood on one foot with his left hand pointed at the sky and his right arm hugging his side. Tulok looked down at her and scowled, "That is not what I meant."

"Prove it," she replied, and remained where she was.

Tulok pursed his lips and closed his eyes. His massive body swayed, off-balance, and he started to fall forward. His eyes sprung open and his hand flailed out to stop his forward motion.

"No!" Isolde yelled at him. She pushed off of the tree she had been leaning against and tromped over to him. "You have to hold your position for the count of ten!"

Tulok pursed his lips and stood up tall and looked down at the smaller woman. "This exercise makes no sense, Isolde," he glowered at her.

Isolde rolled her eyes skyward and then focused back on Tulok. Reaching out, she placed her hands carefully on the big priest's arms and looked up into his eyes. "It's part of attuning yourself to the island. So you don't fall through a dream gate in your sleep," she explained.

"So you have said," Tulok answered looking down at her, "That does not help to explain the WHY of the thing."

Isolde's face softened, and she offered him a gentle smile and patted his left arm, "Many things here do not have a WHY, my friend. They just have a ... How," She shrugged, "It is the way of things."

"You realize that makes no sense at all?"

"You realize that your insistence that everything has a reason makes no sense to ME?" she asked in reply.

They stood there, Priest and Witness, staring at each other in the morning sunlight, each refusing to budge. Movement from the back porch caught Isolde's eye. She released Tulok's arm and nodded toward the figure of Lucan. Tulok turned to look over his shoulder. His eyebrows rose as he recognized the lithe Elven boy from the docks.

Isolde waved him over. "Lucan?"

Lucan's eyes widened in amazement and slowly approached the pair. His silvered eyes glanced upward at the massive figure of Tulok and then back at Isolde. Giving the orc a wide berth, he directed his attention to Isolde.

"Oh stop, Lucan. Father Tulok is a friend; he's not going to eat you," Isolde offered as she reached over to place a welcoming hand on the Elven boy's shoulder.

Lucan nodded. "Yes, of course," He looked up at Tulok and nodded a little uncomfortably, "Father."

Tulok grunted and nodded in polite reply to the youth. Offering him a smile might have frightened him to death at this point.

"What can I do for you, Lucan?" Isolde asked.

"Captain Hywel sent me," he answered.

Lucan's words caught the attention of both Isolde and Tulok. They exchanged careful glances.

"Did he find Arman?" Isolde asked. Impatience flavored her words.

Lucan nodded and then shrugged, "Well, yes ... and no."

Tulok frowned at the response. Lucan shifted his weight back and forth uncomfortably.

"Yes, he found where Master Arman was headed. No, he does not know his final destination," Lucan clarified.

"Master Arman?" Tulok asked.

Lucan nodded and looked up at Tulok. "Arman Dah'ay, Master cartographer and stone shaper from Port Kraken and Setesh."

Isolde and Tulok exchanged glances. Tulok nodded. "Well, he's Vidria. The stone shaping is a close enough description ..."

"He's not Folk?" Lucan asked, a confused look on his face.

"Ah. No," Isolde answered. "Arman is ...," she hrmmed and thought how to describe the merchant that had caused such trouble for them both.

"He is a Vidria dwarf, native to the sands of my homeland," Tulok replied as Isolde searched for words, "Their people are similar in form and talent to the other dwarven peoples here on Sanctum, but they shape sand instead of stone."

Lucan blinked, "I ... had no idea." The Elven boy thought

about it for a moment.

"Master Cartographer, you said?" Tulok asked.

Lucan returned his focus to the conversation. "Yes, Father. The Guild has several of Master Dah'ay's works in their library."

Tulok folded his arms across his chest and looked down at Isolde. "That explains his interest in the ruins ..." he said quietly, referring to the ancient map they had discovered in the Ruins of the Temple of Silence. A map that seemed to display the locations of all the original settlements on Sanctum, from the time of their arrival after the Reaping. A map now buried in the sands and guarded by Safar's people.

Isolde nodded at Tulok. "And it would appear our tradesman has been building a business on the island for some time if the Guild has examples of his work." She fixed Lucan with a direct gaze. "What else?"

Lucan pulled his eyes away from the towering figure of Tulok and back to Isolde, "Only that Master Dah'ay took passage with Captain Fiske, who was headed around the northern part of the island. He thinks the Master was debarking at Swansea, but he's uncertain."

Isolde closed her eyes and rolled her head toward the sky. An exasperated noise escaped her lips.

"When is Fiske due back to port?" Tulok asked as he allowed Isolde her moment of frustration.

Lucan shrugged. "She's logged to be making the circuit. Not for at least a fortnight. Maybe longer, depending on who has cargo to bring in."

"We don't have that much time ..." Isolde said quietly.

Tulok turned concerned eyes on his friend and then back to the boy. "Thank you, Lucan. Can we call on you if we need you further?" he asked. The orc's deep voice rumbled in his chest.

Lucan stood up straight and nodded, a bright smile on his delicate features. "Of course!"

Tulok nodded in thanks, adding, "Please send my words of commendation to your Guild for your service to the Radiant Lord in this matter."

Tulok's words caught the boy off guard. He paused and thought about it and then nodded slowly, "I ... shall, Father. Thank you," he replied, and then darted away.

Isolde paced at Tulok's side, her head lowered, rubbing the back of her neck and muttering to herself. Tulok's firm but gentle hand came to rest on her shoulder, ceasing the wandering steps of the Witness. She blinked and looked up at him.

"What do you mean?" his deep voice asked gently.

Isolde forced a smile, reaching up to pat Tulok's hand. "He's already at least a week ahead of us and on the north side of the island by now. Fiske might not be back for weeks. We can't wait for her to get back to Lubri and tell us where she dropped Arman off. The damage he could do to the island in that time could be irreparable."

Tulok watched Isolde and nodded in understanding. He pulled his hand back slowly and folded his arms across his chest in his standard resting position. "What do you recommend then? It's a big island," he asked her.

Isolde stretched her neck and nodded in agreement, "It is, but ... there are ways to find him," she said softly.

Tulok's right eyebrow arched in critical assessment of her comment, "Why do I not like the way you just said that?"

Isolde shot Tulok a wry grin. "Aw, come on, big guy. Have a little faith ..."

Tulok harrumphed at her indignantly, "I assure you; I am perfectly secure in my faith."

"In me," she added.

"Ah," Tulok replied. His arms dropped to his sides, and he pursed his lips in thought.

"I ... hmmm ...," he looked away from the woman standing before him for a moment and then his eyes returned to gaze on her, "I did not mean to imply that I lack faith in your abilities, Isolde," he began, "Your ability to locate myself in the middle of the Seteshi wastes, alone and without proper gear, still baffles me. I ..." he stumbled a little over his words. "I apologize, my friend," he finally managed.

The Knight of the Wandering Lord stepped up to the Radiant Priest and looked up and into his broad face. Tulok was reminded of how awkwardly tall Isolde was compared to many human women. While not as tall as himself, she was still only a head shorter than he was. She reached up and placed her right hand on his shoulder and squeezed it firmly as she grasped her compass medallion in her left.

"When it counts, they work," she said of her medallion, "We just have to hope that He ..." she glanced skyward, "Agrees that this is a worthy Quest."

Tulok nodded. "And how do we accomplish that?"

Chapter 34

The faith of the Island was nothing like what Tulok was accustomed to. There were no Temples to the Radiant Lord here for him to perform his daily oblations. Privacy was also something that seemed an often-odd concept to the people of Avalon. As Isolde spoke with Farnak on the best way to negotiate with Lord Wanderer on how to find Arman, Tulok was left to clear a space at the noon hour and pay homage to his God. A space in the open, with no walls and nothing but gray cloud cover for a ceiling.

There are no secrets in a sea of tents, Safar was wont to say. The openness of the desert and the thin walls of tents often prevented any form of privacy among the Sand Dancers. Tulok wondered if that was one reason Isolde and the handsome Reysis seemed to get along so well; similarity in culture.

The presence of an orc in the city of Lubri was an oddity by itself. However, an orc that wore the vestments of a Mainland god was truly unique. It should not have surprised Tulok that a small crowd had gathered while he performed his afternoon prayers, and yet it did. As he rose from his position of humble supplication, head to the ground, to raise his face to the sun overhead, his eyes glimpsed the audience that had gathered to bear witness to this strange occurrence. He took a deep breath and focused his attention inward, not allowing the onlookers to distract him from his duties.

He heard a pair of hands clapping. Irritation welling inside for a moment. He swallowed it down as he realized the sound was not one made when one was applauding a performance, but more that of an adult clearing a room of children. Tulok pressed his eyes tighter and took a deep breath in, clearing his mind and focusing on his prayers once more. He reached outward to feel the warmth of the sun on his face and his bare head, the chill of the island fading from around him for a moment as he took in the glory of the Divine.

He bowed his head and touched his hand to his heart and his forehead. "Thank you," he said softly and opened his eyes.

Seated before him was a small child.

No. Tulok corrected himself. This was not a child. He focused his attention downward at the smaller figure, noting the wisps of steel gray in her dark hair and the weathered lines around her brilliant blue eyes. She wore a simple tunic of faded green and leather pants. The left half of her face was covered in an intricate tattoo of leaves and entwined knotwork. Around her neck was a fashioned torc of brightest silver whose double ends bore elegant horse heads.

"Blessings of the Mother be on you this afternoon, Your Radiance," the little Folk woman smiled up at Tulok.

Folk. Not Vidria, Tulok reminded himself. The people of the Mother, fashioned from the clay of the Island here on Sanctum. He had seen a few of them in Setesh; they were often given to wandering and exploration as well as maintaining hearth and home. He inclined his head politely to the small woman.

"May His Brilliance light your path always, Mother," Tulok replied formally, using the Seteshi title.

There was an uneasy truce between the followers of the Radiant Lord and those who embraced the bounty of the Mother. Long before their arrival in Sanctum, each had led their respective Pantheons with a strong, parental hand. Neither had been willing to relinquish that lead among their people even when the Reaping brought them to Sanctum. While they were not each other's direct opposition, the push and pull against the divine masculine and feminine often made itself manifest in the followers of their faiths.

"You had quite the audience, Father. I hope you do not mind that I shooed the children away so you could attend your Lord in some manner of privacy?" the priestess asked politely.

Tulok inclined his head, "I thank you for your pains."

She nodded and continued to watch the hulk of a priest before her. Tulok remained where he was, still kneeling, suddenly very self-aware of his place and position. Kneeling for hours in one position was not something Tulok was unfamiliar with, but he was uncertain if that would be appropriate currently. He cleared his throat a little uncomfortably and gestured at the ground.

"May I?"

The Folk woman smiled warmly up at him, "Of course!"

Tulok nodded in thanks and shifted his great bulk to take a seated position opposite her.

The priestess continued to watch Tulok, a warm smile on her round face. After a few uncomfortable seconds, she began, "Let us dispense with formalities and titles, shall we?"

Tulok began to protest, and she held up a hand for him to pause.

"Yes, Father, I know. The Radiant Lord loves his titles and ceremonies, and I am certain that yours are very impressive and carry significant weight and respect ... as do my own ... but neither of those is important right now, are they?" she asked.

Tulok bristled slightly at the smaller woman's dismissive tone.

"I am Speaker Iscaria, and you are Father Tulok, yes?" she asked simply.

Tulok's bushy eyebrows knit together. He nodded slowly, "I am."

"Excellent!" Iscaria replied. "Now then, are you here to recruit for your Temple?"

"What? No, I have not been sent ..."

"Good." she nodded. "Are you here to scout land to build on our shores?"

"No!" Tulok protested.

She nodded once again and continued to smile, "Excellent!" She looked at Tulok with a critical eye, "You are desert born.

Have you come to visit with the orc tribes then?" she inquired.

Tulok sighed in frustration, "Speaker Iscaria," he began. He took a breath, calming the irritation that he felt nagging at the back of his mind. "I am here in the company of Knight Wanderer Isolde duAvalonne. We are here together in search of a fugitive from Setesh," he said calmly.

Iscaria's eyes widened at the news, which had apparently not yet made its way to her ears. "A fugitive from the Mainland?" she repeated. "Well, good heavens, man, why didn't you say so?" she exclaimed. "How can I help?"

"Do you happen to know anyone going to Swansea?"

~~~

"I don't think He's going to care," Farnak sniffed.

"So you are suddenly the Wandering Lord's Voice?" Isolde countered.

The dwarven priest straightened his shoulders and puffed up his chest, "Now look here, Whitebrooke …," he held up a thick finger and pointed up at the tall woman. She met his gaze and his gesture, standing over him and looking down, hands on her narrow hips. Farnak adjusted his gaze and glared up at her, unmoved, "I was tending the flames of this hearth before you were even a gleam in your daddy's eye …,"

"Then maybe you ought to … Ewww. That's … ewww," she stopped and stepped back.

Farnak raised his eyebrows a little at her response and then chuckled, "Give an old man the respect he deserves, Whitebrooke," he offered.

Isolde sighed and nodded and grabbed a chair. Turning it around, she straddled it and rested her arms across its back, "I'm sorry, Farnak this whole situation is just …," She leaned her chin on her forearms.

"A pain in the arse?" he asked.

"Mmmm."

The old dwarf strode back into the kitchen and draped his worn apron over one shoulder and leaned on the counter, "How long you been havin' the dreams?" he asked her.

Isolde shrugged, "I dunno. They started before we came here. Maybe a month?"

Farnak sucked on a tooth and tugged on his beard in thought, "Triskele went to war about a month past ... but I don't think that's related."

Isolde shot Farnak a surprised glance. "Triskele's at war again? Dammit, that means the trailhead is going to be closed off while they renegotiate their territories and figure out who's in charge of this Cycle," She buried her head in her arms.

"You could pay them tribute to cross ...," Farnak offered.

"Sure. What's the going rate these days for clear passage during their negotiations? Lock of hair, a secret no one knows ... firstborn child ...," she grumbled.

"You know how this works, Whitebrooke," Farnak chided, "Triskele Trinity and the Fae-Touched renegotiate every century. It's part of the Cycle. Traversing their lands right now means paying a toll to one of them."

"Mmmm," she groaned, "I don't even know for certain he's IN their lands ..."

"Then go around."

"Then he could poison the land further."

"Then pay the toll."

"Augh! I hate this!" she exclaimed and kicked up out of her chair. It skittered across the stones and toppled over. Farnak folded his arms across his chest in displeasure.

"You breakin' my furniture now?"

"No. Sorry," she replied, chastised. She walked over to the chair and righted it, then stared out the window. Tulok was seated before a Folk woman in robes of the Mother. Isolde frowned.

"You expecting a visit from one of Mother's people?"

"Hrmmm?" Farnak turned and looked out the window. "That's just Iscaria," He watched the pair talk for a few moments, then chuckled. "She's probably making sure the Radiant Lord doesn't have plans to expand His temples onto the island. They're territorial, you know, those two." He jerked his head toward the window.

Isolde nodded, something nagging at the back of her mind. A wisp of a memory. Words spoken in a distant desert, a knife, a handshake, blood on the sand. She shook her head.

"You ok, girl? You just turned white as snow?" Farnak asked.

She nodded and rubbed her eyes. "Ya. Just ... a memory. I think ..."

Farnak continued to regard Isolde carefully. He scratched absently at his beard, "If you say so," He looked between Isolde and outside to Tulok and back again, "Your big fella know anyone locally?"

"What? No, Farnak," Isolde commented, "Do you know every Mainland dwarf simply because you share a common ancestor? Do you have any idea how ridiculous that sounds?" she chided the priest.

"I don't know how his people work," Farnak grumbled quietly.

"Though, now that you mention it ...," Isolde pondered the priest's words. There could be some merit to talking to one of the local clans. They could assist with traversing disputed land and might have a better idea of what has been going on in the area. They might have even had contact with Arman.

"And don't you have kin with the Wyldfolks in the Eastern Range? Yer father took one of em in for a spell, didn't he?"

Isolde nodded. "Ygraine." She hadn't heard from the young woman in some time. She'd been able to send messages via courier across the passage but had been lax in doing so of late. Isolde was uncertain where Ygraine's people were wintering this season, though they could be an excellent resource as well. They were a Triskele Clan, if she remembered correctly.

And your mother named her family.

She frowned slightly at the voice.

Widen the scope of your mind's eye, child.

Farnak's voice pulled her from the internal dialog.

"Well, yer not going anywhere unless that lug can get a better handle on his dreaming. A loose dreamer, while the Triskele is at war, could open a gate to Lords know what right now and I don't know about you, but I don't want a horde of Morpheum critters running rampant through the villages. There's only so many of us, after all," he said, referring to himself and Isolde.

"I brought him. He's my responsibility," Isolde commented.

Farnak made a rude sound from across the room. "Not good enough. Put a bell on him."

"I most certainly will not!" Isolde exclaimed, "Tulok is not a child, Farnak!"

Farnak glowered at Isolde, his bushy eyebrows knit together in displeasure, "Child or not, he's a danger until he masters his dreams, and that may take a good long while that you do NOT have. You put a bell on him, you buy him the time he needs," the old priest reasoned.

Across the room, Isolde fumed.

"Look, Whitebrooke, I don't mean any disrespect," he began. "It's clear he can handle himself ... *on the Mainland.* But this is home, and you know as well as I do that Mainland minds and the Morpheum ...," he left the rest of the sentence unfinished.

Isolde frowned and looked down at her boots as she considered Farnak's words. The people of the island were tied to the realm of dreams like no other people on Sanctum. Stepping into and out of the Morpheum was something that was learned at an early age. It was instinctive. And for the untrained, it was potentially deadly. They gifted infants born on the island with bracelets of tiny, elegant silver bells that served as a ward against the gates of Morpheus. They wore these bracelets until they were of an age to understand how to control the stuff of dreams that surrounded them.

Those who walked the Wanderer's Path also held the responsibility of policing the Real and ensuring that creatures who had wandered past the Gates were returned, willingly or not. Isolde had brought Tulok, an untrained dreamer, to Avalon. His first night on the island, he had almost been lost to the Realm and its denizens. He showed no signs of being able to master even the most basic of rituals and keep himself rooted in the Real and not the Realm. Farnak was right; to keep him safe, she was going to have to outfit her friend with a child's trinket and hope for the best.

Isolde rested her hands on the mantle of the hearth and leaned there for a few moments, head hanging as she considered her options. The presence of another body standing next to her roused her from her thoughts. Turning her head to the side, Isolde saw the wide figure of Farnak standing beside her. The old priest offered a guarded smile and held out his hand. Laying across his palm was an intricately woven bracelet, as fine as silk, but as strong as steel. Along its length, tiny bundles of round beads gathered together. When lifted, the beads hit against one another, and the lilting tinkle of bells sounded.

"I'm sorry, Whitebrooke. You know this is for the best," Farnak said gently and offered the bracelet to her.

Isolde eyed the helpless piece of jewelry carefully and then with some reluctance, nodded and accepted it from the old priest.

She hoped in her heart that Tulok would understand.

Chapter 35

The fire's warmth was a welcome reprieve from the chill of the island night. Arman stretched his hands out to the red-orange flames as they danced in the hearth and welcomed the heat that loosened stiff muscles and joints. He was not built for the cold and the wet of this damnable island. He missed the heat and dry of the Seteshi sands.

Gentle lights illuminated the room of the small home he stood in. Arman was familiar with stonework and crafting bricks of clay to create dwellings. The desert provided ample supplies for such brickwork buildings. Here, powerful beams of timber were used for braces for wattle and daub walls and provided a framework for gabled roofs. Limestone plaster covered the inside and outside of the building, giving it a fresh, crisp, white color. Elegant stained-glass panels occupied the window sills, depicting scenes of hunters, stags, hawks in flight, and hunting parties in regal attire. In the left corner of every image, etched and embossed was a single gold coin; an image that seemed well out of place in a society that had no use for money.

The home was well-appointed, bright, colorful, comfortable, and welcoming. There were no soot stains from lamps or candles. No red mud was tracked along the floors. The chairs were padded and high-backed. The wooden tables were polished and smooth. Plates and cups of elegant bone china and fine blown glass accompanied serving ware of silver. A single wall in every room was appointed with floor-to-ceiling shelves filled with books. It would take him years to read the contents of these shelves. It was a home that sang of wealth in a culture that spoke of modesty.

"The meal was to your liking?" Phaendar's soft, lilting voice asked from across the room. They were settled into one of the high-backed chairs opposite the hearth fire.

Arman nodded. "It was. My thanks for your hospitality."

The sage inclined their head, the hint of a smile tugged on their lips. Light played with the shadows of the tattoos on their face. Delicate and interwoven ink branches seemed to move on his face by their own volition – though it could have also just been a trick of the light. Down the sides of his face, along the edge of his silver-white hair, images of tiny leaves seemed to float downward past his jaw and along the sides of his neck. Around his throat was worn a thick chain that appeared to be fashioned from dark metal.

The strange Elven figure watched Arman from their position in the room. Eyes the color of soft violet forget-me-nots watched him with the training of an observer. He was beautiful and dangerous.

"It was the least that I could do, given the distance that you have traveled," Phaendar replied casually. His eyes broke from watching Arman and drifted to the saddlebags that sat on the table.

Arman watched Phaendar's eyes and nodded. He pursed his lips and pulled his hands back from the fire's warmth. He placed them behind his back and walked toward the table. Phaendar remained where they were, their body unmoving, but their eyes following the Vidria's every move.

"The Guild loves their mainland … spices," Arman replied. Trade from the Mainland to the Island was something that Arman was well versed in. There was a market for everything if one looked deeply enough.

"Mmm, yes," Phaendar agreed, "The … samples that you sent me on the previous delivery have proven to be very useful," they said and turned their attention back to hearth and away from the merchant.

"Happy to oblige," Arman nodded. He reached for the saddlebags. Whispering a few words under his breath, he traced a small sigil over the clasp on one of the bags. It glowed red for a moment and then the light faded. Nodding to himself, he quickly unlatched the clasp and flipped open the bag.

Inside the deep leather bag were two boxes, both the length and depth of a loaf of bread. With skilled hands, he carefully withdrew both boxes and set them on the table, side by side. One box was covered in intricate designs, inlaid with metal and abalone. The other was a simple box of smooth green stone.

"I hope you find these to your liking," Arman offered. Nimble fingers pressed on several areas on the inlaid box and a hidden latch clicked open. He flipped the lid open and stepped back, pulling his hands away and placing them behind his back once more.

Within the box lay two small bulbs, the shape of apples, and covered in wicked-looking thorns.

Phaendar stirred in their chair and slowly rose. The fabric of their robes flowing gracefully and silently around them as they moved across the room to the table. They towered in height next to the smaller man and peered into the box at its contents. Their violet eyes gleamed with sudden focus and interest.

"Desert Thorn Apple. As promised," Arman offered, watching the lithe figure examining the box. Acquiring two whole fruits had required more than a handful of less-than-savory trades on Arman's part, as the entire plant was poisonous. Common enough in some areas of Setesh, it was unknown here on Avalon. Transporting a non-native species like this one to Avalon was a hanging offense if he was discovered. Ordering it for transport would garner the same punishment. He had provided a handful of dried leaves to Phaendar months ago to pique the sage's interest, hoping to convince them to help him with the amulet in his possession. Now he would see if his investment paid off.

Phaendar gently stroked their lower lip with their elongated thumb and forefinger in thought.

"They are lovely," Phaendar's soft, lilting voice replied. They blinked slowly and then turned their attention to Arman, "The leaves alone have begun the delivery of the theme for this Cycle. I expect these shall ensure all well understand the message."

Arman pursed his lips and watched Phaendar. "I can't promise they will grow here. Non-native plants and Avalonian soil …"

The Elven sage chuckled; it sounded like discordant silver bells. "Oh, leave that to me, my friend. I know exactly where to take them."

Arman met Phaendar's gaze and reached over to flip the lid on the box closed. Several clicks were heard as it sealed shut once more. "Tip for Tap," he said carefully.

A sour look crossed Phaendar's face, as if a foul odor had entered the room, "You Mainlanders are so … direct".

Arman shrugged lightly. "And you Avalonians are so quick to ask for what you don't have, but not want to recompense anyone for it," they replied coolly.

The Elf and the Vidria stood across the table, staring at one another, unyielding in their positions. Phaendar's too-thin features lent no emotion to the exchange, his violet eyes studying Arman carefully. They were a strangely perfect statue, brought to life by the will of their creator. They blinked their eyes slowly.

"Very well," Phaendar sighed deeply and held out their left hand, unfurling their long fingers and exposing their open palm.

Arman's right eyebrow twitched slightly, and he inclined his head in polite thanks. Reaching out to the second box, he made a series of similar gestures as before. A sigil appeared in the perfect stone of the second box and a seam materialized where there had been none before. Skilled fingers lifted the lid from the box and carefully set it aside. Within the stone-shaped box lay two items: The first, a jar of earthen clay topped with the figure of a horse's head; The other, an intricately crafted and bejeweled amulet fashioned in the figure of a scarab.

Arman's eyes hovered over the amulet for a moment, remembering the trouble this little trinket had caused in Setesh. It should have been a simple thing; deliver the item to the indicated party and walk away. The magics would do the rest. But the original messenger had traded his contract off to a Knight Wanderer and his Squire, who were looking for a Quest. That unforeseen exchange had led to multiple deaths, including said Knight Wanderer and Arman's initial partner, Nebiyre. It had also earned Arman the enmity of the Temple of the Radiant Lord, the Guild of the Sand Dancers, and one very dedicated young woman who had taken up her Knight's Quest as her own.

Arman carefully lifted the amulet out of the box and placed it into Phaendar's outstretched palm. It glowed with warm light at their touch.

"And this is what Nebiyre died for?" Phaendar asked coolly as they looked down at the item.

"It is," Arman replied.

Phaendar lifted the amulet to gaze at it closely. Their spindly fingers traced the outline of the scarab slowly. They paused; their eyes narrowed and then slid off of the amulet and over to Arman.

"You are aware of the contents of this … bauble?" they asked.

Arman nodded. "I am."

Phaendar's eyes hardened at the response. "And you are aware of its value to this island?"

Arman paused for a moment, watching the alien being before him. It was only through years of trade with the Avalonians that he had learned anything of their people and the rumors of their mystical ties to the lands of their birth. It had been those rumors and stories which had led him down the path he was currently upon. A path that was no longer his own.

Arman nodded once again. "It has been explained to me, yes," was his reply.

There was no movement from the statuesque figure across from Arman. While he understood that the sage only had two eyes – Arman felt himself being examined by strange, obfuscated features. It felt almost alien as those eyes, and not eyes scrutinized him – eyes that had been trained for centuries to discover information. Suddenly, the left side of Phaendar's mouth twitched upward. Their cheek and mouth 'dancing', breaking the serene and controlled facade. The chill in Phaendar's eyes fled, replaced with something far more sinister. Their lips pulled back from his perfect teeth in a terrifying smile.

"Oh, this will do quite well," the sage's voice spoke. Gone was the soft lilt that had met Arman in the woods, replaced with a tone akin to discordant strings on a poorly tuned lute. Phaendar chuckled to themself and turned the amulet over in their long-fingered hands, their violet eyes searching every crevasse and curve intently. They nodded to themself. "Yes ... combined with the fruit ... yes ...," Their eyes darted up from the amulet to focus on Arman, "Normally, I would kill you for even being in possession of something like this." they paused.

Arman felt his heartbeat quicken as Phaendar's countenance changed before him. This was what they had warned him of. Practical immortality did not always weather well on a mortal mind. His right hand drifted slowly toward the blade on his belt, as his eyes glanced toward the door, assessing how quickly he could reach it if needed.

"But not tonight," Phaendar continued. They giggled and glanced back at the amulet, stroking it lovingly, "Oh no ... this ...," They paused and looked at Arman, "You want to take it with you, yes?"

The question hung in the air between the two. Arman could hear the beat of his heart in his ears and feel the singing of adrenaline in his blood. He inclined his head slowly.

"Excellent!" Phaendar almost cackled with delight. They gestured at the mud-formed vase. "Is that the vessel, then?" They wiggled their fingers at it. "Give it here."

Arman reached for the vase and lifted it carefully out of the stone worked box. It was smooth and almost warm in his hands. The carved horse's head gleamed in the hearth's firelight. Reaching across the table, he placed it in Phaendar's grasp.

Phaendar's eyes widened as the vessel was placed into their open palm. They turned their gaze from the amulet to the vessel. Violet eyes mad with fascination. "Oh, you have outdone yourself, Master Shaper. This is indeed a vessel worthy of a Founder's soul ..." Phaendar's lips cracked into a disturbing grin as they held the amulet and the vessel up and gazed upon them both.

Arman watched the Sage, now clearly lost to his madness, fondling his life's work in the firelight.

"Can you do it?" Arman whispered softly.

A palpable hush fell across the room. From the corners of his eyes, Arman saw the shadows slide in a soft, undulating dance. He has seen this before. In Ahsal, the Temple of Silence.

Phaendar closed their wide violet eyes and folded their arms across their narrow chest, pressing the items close to them in an embrace. For a moment Arman thought he heard whispers from the shadows, crooning in a language he could not understand. Under those whispers was a heavier sound, almost metallic, like the rattling of chains.

Phaendar's eyes opened, no longer violet, but filled with shadows that swirled in their orbs.

"The Jailer thanks you for your tribute," a voice that was not Phaendar's whispered in reply.

Arman swallowed hard and averted his eyes, lowering his head. His hands began to sweat. His heart pounded in his ears.

The firelight lowered, and the shadows rose. Along the edges of the stained-glass windows, the finely etched gold-work on the tiny coin emblems glowed softly.

"Thy will be done."

Chapter 36

Iscaria's arrival proved both bane and balm to Tulok's situation. The little folk priestess was more than happy to provide the information that he was seeking about Swansea and how to get there. She advised him of the direction, path, number of days it would take up and even suggested who he should speak with to ensure they properly equipped him for the journey. It was when she added that he would have to wait until the turn of the season had passed before undertaking his trek that the situation had become sticky.

After a testy and irritable exchange, Tulok finally excused himself to walk away and wrestle with his Gurkh, lest his passion get the better of his reason. Farnak invited Iscaria into the Homely House to talk while Isolde wandered out back to check on the priest.

"Safe to approach?" she asked from a distance.

Tulok rubbed the back of his neck and exhaled with a nod. "Yes. My apologies. I had not thought to become quite so irritated at hearing that we would be limited in our ability to travel because of the actions of others. It is not something we often encounter back home."

Isolde nodded and stepped closer to Tulok. She'd been on the receiving end of his unbridled rage once before, and while she had talked him down then, she did not relish the idea of ever having to do it again. "Probably something Safar deals with on a fairly regular basis, having to factor in alternate routes for caravans. Not something that the travelers get to see, yes?" she asked. Isolde leaned her back against a railing and rested her hands on either side of her hips on the wooden surface.

"Mmm. A fair point, but the Reysis is not here to navigate

for us this time," Tulok offered. He sighed and looked skyward, examining the position of the sun as it peeked through the overcast clouds. He rubbed his hands together absently.

"Cold?"

"Hrmmm? Ah. Yes, a little. Your Island is a far cry different from home, though ... perhaps only as chilly as a night in the desert if one stops to think about it," he reasoned.

Isolde nodded and watched her companion. She pondered her words. "We don't have ... to wait for the Triskele to finish ... whatever they are doing," she offered.

Tulok eyed Isolde carefully, noting the hesitation in her voice. "You have an idea that I will not like. I can tell."

She shrugged a little. "I'm not terribly fond of it myself, being honest," she admitted.

"Alright, let's hear it."

"We have a couple of options, once the Lord Wanderer points us in the right direction," she said and tapped her broken compass. "One: We pay for passage through the disputed territory."

Tulok narrowed his eyes. "That you have hesitation about paying for passage somewhere on your own island makes me worry about the cost."

Isolde nodded and shrugged. "It could be problematic, depending on who we have to negotiate with ..."

"Like the River Lord's domain?" he asked her quietly.

Isolde frowned a little at the memory of the River Lord and the price she had paid at His hands. Most of the experience was held in fits and starts, snatches of dark dreams and wisps of remembrances. The Witness struggled with the holes in her memory over the experience, a flaw in her ability to fulfill her duty.

"A little. Fey-born Triskele ... those born to the magic of the Island have no use for coin," she mumbled.

Tulok tugged on his beard in thought and nodded. "Something I had not considered. They traffic in other things then?"

Isolde chewed on the inside of her cheek in thought and

nodded. "Dreams, memories, if we are lucky. Stories ..." She looked up at Tulok. "You are a Librarian, right?" she asked.

He scowled. "You know the answer to that question," he grumped.

"You have read the old stories and legends of people trading away their firstborn child to some malevolent force for personal gain, or prophecy?"

Tulok straightened his shoulders and stared down at Isolde. "You allow such things to happen here?" he demanded. The irritation that nagged at the back of his mind was now whispering angry and insulting thoughts – priming the embers of anger in his chest.

Isolde looked up at the orc and met his irritation with her own. "You allow people to starve in the streets for a lack of metal pressed into the shape of a flattened circle?" She eyed Tulok. They each met the unyielding gaze of the other, Priest and Witness, unyielding in their irritation. Isolde was the first to break the tension. "We could have this argument for weeks and neither of us be any closer to Arman."

Tulok closed his eyes and nodded slowly. "You are correct." He paused and then opened his eyes once more. "And we do not know what they may ask for in trade?"

Isolde shook her head. "No. They are capricious people. It will depend entirely on who we run into."

Tulok's left eyebrow quirked. "Capricious?"

"Yes."

"Good word," he nodded in appreciation.

"Oh, shut up!" She teased him and pulled one of her gloves from her belt and threw it at him, hitting his broad chest, the hint of a grin on her lips.

Tulok caught the glove. "You challenging me?" he asked, eyeing the leather and then Isolde.

She scoffed in response. "Hardly."

Tulok pursed his lips and nodded, then tucked the glove into his belt, holding on to the item. "So option one is wandering into the middle of the fray and possibly trading away our souls to find Arman."

"Extreme ... but potentially accurate," she agreed.

"What is option two?"

Isolde looked at the ground and kicked at a stone absently. "We go talk with Maelona Blodwen of Clan Baedd Gwyllt and see if they will escort us through the area. They have a treaty."

Tulok recognized the name Baedd Gwyllt. It was Tribal, but not desert Tribe. Tulok's lineage came from Lan-not, the Bat Clan of the Sandborn orcs. Baedd Gwyllt was the name of one of two island-born orc clans.

"Wild Boar Clan?" he said.

Isolde nodded in reply.

Tulok had heard of the island-born orcs but had encountered none of them. In theory, they all shared a similar ancestry, but the stories said that the orcs of Avalon had departed the heated sands of the Seteshi desert early in the migration of the people from their homeland. They were still children of the Scribe, having been blessed with reason to combat the rage within their souls; but how much of that had they embraced?

"I couldn't just decide without talking to you about it," Isolde replied.

Tulok nodded. "Thank you for that."

Isolde shrugged in response and said nothing. Growing up on the Island, orcs were not something that one actively sought. They, along with many other more barbarous clans on the island, were often responsible for looting and pillaging settlements and villages. Orckind tended toward more violence than their human counterparts, but both were responsible for hardship on Avalon. Isolde did not relish having to negotiate with them, but they were a better option than the Triskele Fey-born while they were at war.

She had been asked if orcs had been responsible for the demise of Council Whitebrooke. As much as she would have liked to have said "yes" and had reason for the slaughter of her kith and kin, the Orckind had not been present on that day. No, the violence that was wrecked upon her home was done at the hands of humans.

And the Morpheum, a gentle, patronly voice, reminded her. She smiled inwardly to hear it, glad to know that He was still with her.

"Wandering already?" Tulok asked her softly.

She blinked and looked up at the big priest, her eyes meeting his. "Oh! Sorry," she apologized and shook her head to clear it of the distractions and wisps of memories.

Tulok shook his head and waved it off. "No need," he replied and watched her face for a moment. There was a darkness to her eyes that belied something hidden. "What troubles you?" he asked her.

Isolde offered Tulok a pained smile. "Many things," she replied and looked away, her brows knit in both thought and concern.

"Mmm hm," the orc replied, and turned to rest his hip on the hitching post next to her. She stared at her feet in thought. He turned his gaze toward the heavens. "What, of the things that trouble you … have you control over?" he asked, not looking at her.

Isolde kicked at a rock in the dirt. "A couple of things, I suppose … and many that are well outside my ability to do a damned thing about at present," she said.

Tulok nodded, noting the irritation in the Knight's voice as she spoke. "I understand that frustration," he said and continued staring at the sky. "The Radiant Lord thrives on order: Everything in its measured pace; everything with its reason and justification. It is the way of things."

Isolde inclined her head in silence.

"Everything on your island is at odds with what I know," he offered, and turned his gaze down to look at her once more. "And yet I have complete trust in you to make the right decision for us both."

Isolde blew out loudly and groaned. "Ugh!" she exclaimed and looked up from the ground at the sky for a moment. She lolled her head to the side and gazed upward at Tulok. "Is this what it was like when we were in Nahral?"

Tulok pondered her words for a moment and shrugged. "Perhaps." He leaned over and nudged her with his massive shoulder. "We are speakers of the faith, Isolde. We can pretend to know what needs doing, but ultimately we will walk whatever path He …" he jerked his chin at her compass, "… sets us on when you ask Him where Arman is, yes?" he asked.

Isolde chewed on the inside of her cheek and pondered Tulok's words. He was right. She was allowing herself to become irritated about things she had no control over. They would be directed into the fray of the Triskele or elsewhere, depending on the will of the Heavens. They could attempt to go against it; but what would they gain? They did not know where Arman was or what he was about here on Avalon.

It is called faith for a reason, child. The voice whispered in her mind once more.

Believe.

She reached up and scratched absently at her scalp, her eyes glimpsing Tulok staring at her. She looked around awkwardly. "What? Have I got lunch on my face somewhere?" she asked and wiped at her lips with her fingers.

Tulok chuckled and shook his head. "No," he said, and pointed above her head.

Isolde scowled and followed Tulok's direction. Above her head were a handful of tiny lights, like fireflies, that danced on the edges of her aura. Her eyebrows shot upward. "Mother's apron …" she swore in a hushed voice. The lights slowly danced off and away in a north-easterly direction, toward the Wyldlands and Swansea.

"It would appear we … or you … have your answer," Tulok offered.

Isolde watched the lights as they danced off into the distance. Her eyes focused on them and the trail they mapped out before her. She reached into her pouch and pulled out a string of silver bells and handed it across to Tulok. "Put that on," she said, absently.

Tulok eyed the tiny band of silver bells suspiciously, but accepted it. He looked to watch where the lights had danced off and away, but they were gone. "What is it?" he asked of the bells.

"Huh?" Isolde asked, "Oh. Uh … it's a warding charm. Wear it and it will keep you from falling through your dreams again." The lights vanished into the city and into the crowd. Isolde blinked and turned her attention back to Tulok, who was peering at the string of bells with both curiosity and suspicion.

"It's magic?" he asked.

Isolde rolled her eyes and grabbed the bells out of his hand, wrapping them around his wrist. "It's part of a pact that was made before we were here. It's … complicated. Just wear it," she finally managed. Securing the item around Tulok's wrist, she patted his arm and smiled up at him.

Tulok examined the string of bells around his wrist. It made a soft, tinkling sound when he moved. "You know, Isolde," he began in his best Librarian voice, "In some cultures, an exchange of jewelry is reserved for very special relationships …"

Isolde narrowed her eyes, balled up her fist, and punched Tulok squarely on the shoulder, and snatched her glove back from him. He winced and pulled away, chuckling the entire time.

In the distance, Speaker Iscaria watched a group of lights dance off into the darkness and looked back toward the Homely House and its occupants.

"Interesting."

Chapter 37

"You are full of shite Marestongue!" the insult rang across the firelight.

Gruffydd ground his teeth at the accusation and stood abruptly to answer it, sea-green eyes flashing with anger. Crossing the space between himself and the speaker, he met them nose to nose. "I know what I saw! Council Whitebrooke fell to the Morpheum!"

The accuser was a burly man almost twice the width of the scout and easily 5 inches taller. He looked down at Gruffydd and smiled wickedly at him. "You want to take this to the mound, little man? I'm more than happy to oblige..." he replied.

"Someone separate them." the deep and commanding voice of Chieftain Cynfael Aerfyn commented. Several members of the tribe stood to answer the call of the Chieftain. With no physical intervention, the combatants stepped apart from one another. The bigger man smiled widely at Gruffydd.

Cynfael watched the two men for a moment, his eyes searching the attendees at his fire. A score of people gathered around the Chieftain's fire this evening. Many were of his own Clan, but there were representatives from the other neighboring tribes present as well this evening. This was a matter that called for a moot, but Cynfael's voice was only one among many. He hoped that the information shared tonight might move the other Chieftains to action.

He turned his attention to the burly accuser, thickly built with dark greasy hair that was bound into several heavy braids. His chin was bare, but his upper lip sported a thick mustache that grew down the sides of his mouth. An intricate raven tattoo decorated the space between his eyebrows and spread across his forehead, disappearing into his scalp. The tips of feathered wing tattoos emerged from behind his ears and wrapped around his neck to meet in the center of his throat.

"That is enough, Cadfan, "Cynfael said to the dark-haired stranger. "There will be no slaking of blood tonight. We come for conversation, not battle."

Cadfan snorted and spat. "Of course not." he looked around the circle and then lifted his voice to sound loudly, "You are not Fwyalchen!" around him four other men howled and hooted in support of their speaker.

Cynfael narrowed his eyes at Cadfan, recognizing the challenge and insult. He sucked on a tooth and met the dark-haired man's eyes. "But I will happily meet you on the mound when we are done... if you persist."

Silence fell around the circle as both men regarded one another across the fire. Cadfan was younger, but Cynfael the more experienced of the two. It would not go well for either of them, should they draw down. It was clear to the raven-marked Cadfan that Cynfael was not in a mood to be tested this evening. He sniffed once and nodded simply, then gestured to the fire.

"We are here to listen. Let us hear why your Scout believes the dream creatures are to blame for losing Council Whitebrooke and what that has to do with the blight that has befallen us all."

Heads nodded around the fire circle.

Cadfan continued, "When has the Morpheum cared to become involved in the Triskele wars? Their place is not ours, and ours not theirs. Even for those who may be closer in bond to the land than others." he looked around the circle. Shaking his head, "No. The dream creatures have no role in the warring. They serve all and none since the death of their Cyning. They have their own battles afoot. Why would they meddle here?"

Cynfael nodded in agreement. "You speak true, Cadfan." he

turned to look at Gruffydd. "What proof have you that the dream creatures were involved in the destruction of White-brooke?"

Gruffydd met the eyes of his Chieftain. Cynfael nodded at the fire. Gruffydd lowered his eyes in respect and stepped into the firelight. He held his right hand aloft, a small leather pouch sat in his palm. The light from the fire danced across his face and in his eyes. His leather armor creaked slightly as he walked around the circle. He stopped before the towering figure of Cadfan.

"The breath of Morpheus!" he said firmly and shoved the pouch toward Cadfan. The burly man pulled back slightly; his eyes suddenly fixated on the pouch. Gruffydd grinned and turned to the assembled around the fire. "The whole of the village is covered in it."

Whispers moved across those gathered as persons leaned in and whispered to one another. A tall woman, dressed in the greens and russet tones of the Mother nodded toward Gruffydd.

"And this is why we have not thought to worry about their disappearance, or even noticed they were missing?" she asked.

Gruffydd nodded toward a strange, willowy figure standing in the shadows behind Cynfael. "That is what our Seer believes to be the truth, yes."

The figure stepped quietly forward and inclined their head to those gathered. They bore the too-thin figure of the fae-born elves, limbs that seemed too long, eyes set slightly too far apart to be comfortable to gaze upon for too long. They moved with an unnatural and effortless grace. When they spoke, it sounded like the soft rustle of a breeze in the trees.

"Covered in such a blanket, Whitebrooke has become a memory, lost to many. A wisp of a dream that fades upon waking." They said carefully.

"Why now?" a clear voice asked from the darkness.

The Seer turned their silvery eyes toward the newcomer, who remained hidden in the shadows. They were of a medium height, leaning toward tall. Their cloak sat on their broad shoulders comfortably, hood pulled up to hide their features from enquiring eyes. The flash of metal could be seen in the figure of buckles and the hilt of a peace tied weapon at their side. The voice was deep, but not masculine.

Cynfael and Cadfan both turned to look in the direction of the speaker, who stood just outside the fire's light.

Remaining where they stood, they repeated, "Why now? What is it about now that Whitebrooke comes to our minds and we know about this?" they asked. There was a pause. "What changed?" they clarified.

Cynfael and Gruffydd exchanged meaningful glances. Cynfael gestured for Gruffydd to answer.

"My Scouts received word that Whitebrooke had fallen. We had heard nothing, so we investigated."

"But why now?" the cloaked figure asked again.

There was an uncomfortable silence around the fire. Cynfael considered the question and then stepped into the light. He gazed outward at the shadowed figure. "I do not think I know your voice, stranger. Step into the light and join the circle that we may discuss this matter openly."

Heads turned to look at where Cynfael directed his words. The figure remained where they were and did not step forward.

"You may call me Blodwen, Chieftain Cynfael Aerfyn." they replied clearly and respectfully.

Several of the attendees shifted uncomfortably at the mention of the name. Cynfael narrowed his eyes. His beefy hand came to rest on the pommel of his blade. "That is a Baedd Gwyllt name." he said carefully.

"It is." the figure replied. They raised their hands to show they were empty. The hands were powerful and calloused, the skin the color of dark walnut bark.

Cadfan swore and spat, straightening his shoulders and standing tall. Murmurs ran around the ring of firelight. Some hissed. Others swore. Gruffydd took up a defensive position before Cynfael, as the Seer slipped back into the shadows.

Cynfael's heavy hand came to rest on Gruffydd's shoulder. "We are all born of the island's blood," he said quietly, but firmly. "And this affects the whole of us."

Cadfan's group growled audibly at Cynfael's allowance and turned narrowed eyes on the newcomer. "One wrong move, and the mound will not contain the blood that is spilled." He threatened.

The figure slowly raised their hands to the hem of their cowl and carefully lowered it. A woman with broad features and thick black eyebrows stood outside of the fire's light. Deep red eyes turned to meet Cadfan's. The right edge of her lip lifted slightly in what served as a smile but seemed more a sneer, courtesy of the pair of upward-facing tusks that emerged from her lower jaw.

"Orckind." the word hissed from the lips of many of the attendees.

Unflinching, Blodwen turned her gaze back to Cynfael. "The Huntress thanks The Shepherd for His guidance and hospitality this evening." She inclined her head in his direction.

"The Shepherd welcomes the keen eye and sharpened blades of the Huntress to the Circle. Be welcome, Maelona Blodwen." Cynfael intoned formally, using the formal name of this new companion.

With some reluctance, the attendees around the fire parted to make room for the orc woman as she stepped forward. She was clad in hand-tooled leather armor that bore intricate and entwining patterns across its tan surface. Blodwen's dark hair was braided from crown to tip with secured knots and beads. Some beads were clearly weighted and heavier than others. The mark of a warrior who had learned the art of the flail-braid. A broad-bladed short sword hung at her hip. Maintaining her focus on Cynfael, she folded her muscular arms across her chest and came to rest at ease.

"I repeat the question." She began. "What has changed that this information comes to light now?"

Cynfael nodded, watching those gathered with intent. This meeting could go poorly for all of them if a fight were to break out. While the Triskele Trinity made war at this moment, it was a matter of tradition and not ill will. The weight of the scales of power for the next several years was to be determined in these few months. The strength of the Divine on the Island would come to bear to determine which Clans hunted in which territories, who paid homage and who was brought to heel. It was the Cycle of things. The rise and fall of life and death. None remained in power eternally, for therein lay stagnation.

When the Island had come to rest on the waters of Sanctum, she brought with her both the Divine of the fae-born elves and the humans who made Avalon their home in the before-time. Over time, both human and fae-born had opened their ranks to any who chose to pay homage to the surviving Divine of the Reaping. But many of the Divine were still jealous Gods and demanded power. To ensure the island did not fall to eternal war and bloodshed, the Cycle was created. To determine which pantheon and which Divine sat at the head of the table for the prescribed time.

The Orckind were not originally born of the Island, at least not those like Blodwen, who stood before the assembly now. The Orckind that came to Sanctum with the Island had been fearsome monsters, devoid of reason. It had been through the meddling...or blessing... of a Mainland Divine that they had been elevated to thinking creatures, capable of reason, logic and strategy. Or so the stories were told. When the Scribe breathed reason into the lungs of the first Orckind on Sanctum, He breathed reason into them all.

Despite the gifts of reason from The Scribe, the Orckind of Avalon paid heed and devotion to the Divine of the Island; from whose blood and bones they had originally been born. Their leug was every bit as strong as any human or fae-born elf. They were children of Avalon, and the land sang in their souls.

Old superstitions and fears were hard to overcome on an

island centered on myth and dreams. Many of the Orckind of Avalon left the island to join their mainland brothers and sisters, and escape the yoke of oppression that was theirs on these shores ... Human and Elven settlers came to the Island to take their place in the balance of power. The Mother created the Folk to fill their void. Those Orckind who remained, remained to ensure the Island never forgot that they were all born of blood of survival.

Uncomfortable glances watched Cynfael and Blodwen, leaders of their people, who would no doubt fall on one another's blades on the morrow.

Cynfael ran his tongue across his teeth in consideration. "There was a survivor."

Blodwen's bushy eyebrows rose. "From the Breath of Morpheus? Truly?" She shook her head. "You understand my doubt. The blanket of dreams rarely leaves anyone behind to remember it clearly."

"The Lord Wanderer claimed her for His own." was the reply. He continued, "And she apparently has returned to the island."

Blodwen pursed her lips, "I had heard tell of a Wanderer returning to Lubri." she considered and nodded, "Hence the lifting of the mist on the memories. That makes sense."

Cadfan groaned aloud. "Screw that Blighted Old Beggar and His meanderings! What good has He ever brought to us?" he challenged. The men in his company chuckled in agreement.

Cynfael ground his teeth for a moment and looked at Cadfan. "That's twice that I have looked past your insults in deference to your Lady, Cadfan. We all know there is no love lost between Her and the Wanderer; but there WILL be peace at my fire!" he growled. The Shepherd's crook tattoo along the side of Cynfael's face glowed blue for a moment. A hush fell across the assembled.

Cadfan shook his greasy head and looked around the circle. "You want to listen to words of Orckind and the ravings of the Wanderer? As you wish. Fwyalchen will none of it." he gestured to his retinue who nodded and moved to join their Chieftain. His eyes slid to Blodwen, "Steer clear of White Trout River, Huntress; or the Lady of Ravens will pick the bones of your fallen clean."

Blodwen closed her eyes and inhaled slowly, calming the rising Gurkh in her blood. Turning her chin in Cadfan's direction, she raised the lids of her blood-red eyes and fixed him with a cool gaze that burned with a controlled fire. "Even the Lady of Ravens cannot escape the arrows of the Huntress. Watch your skies, Cadfan Briarborn, I foresee a rain of black feathers soon."

Cadfan snarled once at the Orc woman and then stormed off into the darkness.

An uncomfortable silence fell across the Circle once more. Cynfael looked around at those gathered and then at Blodwen. "Now that the pissing and moaning is done..." he looked over his shoulder to the Seer and a curly haired slip of girl standing in the shadows.

"Little Wolf, come and tell them what you saw."

Chapter 38

"It's just a horse, Tulok! You have to make friends before you can just hop on," she said as she ran her hand firmly along the side of the beast.

"I assume mine is larger because of … me?" Tulok asked as he looked at the massive draft horse. He had dealt with camels and korsers, but this was a different beast altogether. This animal was leaner with a keener intelligence behind its black eyes.

"I do not think it likes me," he said as he continued to meet the eyes of the horse.

Isolde chewed the inside of her cheek. She walked over to the horse and gave it a firm pat on the haunches. She kept her hand on it as she rubbed it along its side. "Do not show fear. They are animals of respect and insight. A good horse will throw off a poor rider … not because they ride poorly, but because they are a bad person." The memory of those words took her back for a moment to a time long gone. She swallowed down the sorrow and forced a smile, then reached over and placed the orc's hand on the horse.

The horse was not happy.

"Keep patting and rubbing on his side. Talk to him. You talk, he will listen," she said as she walked away. The draft horse moved uneasily, and Tulok felt a slight hint of panic.

"Where … where are you going?"

"We will need saddles. You will need a saddle. Horses require saddles … and our packs. Just make friends. Tell him about the Radiant Lord. He might be a fan," she smiled and headed back toward the house.

He tried to throw a comeback at her, but the deep snort of the beast drew his attention. The horse turned its head to look back at the orc. There was an unsettling sense of curiosity behind that black bulb that seemed to look through him. Tulok slightly raised an eyebrow and cocked his head. Isolde had said that magic flowed within the beings that lived here. Did she mean all living things? Magic did not create intelligence, did it? Divine power, yes, but were these wild magics also capable of it? He shook his head and stopped himself before he could linger too far on the thought. It was just a horse.

Isolde was right, he just needed to talk to it. It did not seem so different from a korser. Sure, a korser had padded feet instead of hooves, and this beast was larger and more muscular, but it was still a creature built for burden. This creature was as tall as a camel and he mounted those just as easily. He rode a korser, and they did not require a saddle. Saddles were for those who were untrained in riding. It was just a beast that needed firmness. That was what she said.

"I do not fear you, Horse. And I do not need a saddle," he said as he placed his hand on its back and held firm. He would just hop up and throw his leg over. Simple. Widening his stance, he looked at the horse and said with sincere conviction, "I bear the duties of a God that never sleeps." With one hand, he grasped the horse's thick mane, and with the other, he braced his weight on the wide back of the beast. Holding firm, he crouched slightly and moved to throw his leg across the beast's back. He had done it!

However, his moment of triumph was swiftly cut short as the horse reared back and squealed loudly before it bolted forward. The surprised orc flung his arms around its neck and clung tightly as it bolted out of the paddock and down the road.

—

Isolde heard the loud squeal and rushed back outside to find Iscaria chewing on a piece of bread and calmly watching the back end of the draft horse trot away. Both gazed on as the horse and its passenger headed down the stretch of road.

"Tully will bring him back ... provided he can stay on," Iscaria commented in between bites.

"I told him he needed a saddle ..." said Isolde as she watched the dust dissipate down the road.

Five minutes later, the draft horse happily trotted back, its forelegs covered in muck and dampness. It seemed to have an almost happy skip to its canter.

" Well, at least it was the lake and not brambles," said Iscaria as she walked down the road. "You secure Tully and whatever mount you were planning on taking. Also, bring the chestnut pony; she's the only one that likes long rides. I will bring the Radiant Father a towel."

Before Isolde could say anything, the Folk woman simply raised her hand as she walked away. "Northern Wilds are the Northern Wilds and you will need a guide part of the way there."

Isolde wanted to protest, but a gentle whisper floated through her head.

Believe.

—

With their relationship established, Tulok rode Tully in silence. He was simply the passenger, and this creature was in charge of where they went and how fast they got there. Luckily for him, Isolde's horse, Duli, and Iscaria's pony, Winte, would never let Tully pull too far ahead. He may have been bigger, but Tully was not the leading animal and followed the other two dutifully.

According to the Iscaria, they would travel up the Merric Road that ran along the coast for three or four days depending on the weather and their mounts. Iscaria noted one could make the trip in a day and a half, but such would take skill and a certain level of negotiation that none of them possessed. Also, if their mainland quarry had traveled along the Merric, they could gauge how far along he was and possibly learn of his purpose there.

The first day's travel was, in a word, miserable. At least, according to Tulok. The constant moisture in the air seemed to sit in his bones. Even at mid-afternoon, when the sun was normally at its hottest, his body shivered at the chill of the ocean air. The only saving grace was that there was no need for outdoor camping. Isolde had talked about the various fishing villages that dotted along the coast. Finding shelter among any of them should be easy, as all were more than welcoming, and seemed happy to take in representatives of the Divine.

"Though it may take a bit of assurance that your presence was a guest and not an invader," Iscaria added.

Irritation rose at the thought, but Tulok played it out in his head. The presence of a traveling foreign priest was one thing, but an orc priest was not easily taken in stride. While no one had been outright hostile to him, the polite smiles and head nods all said the same thing – they did not trust him.

The first village they stayed over in, his presence seemed to be the prime topic of discussion between Iscaria, Isolde, and several leery-eyed villagers. While he could only gather bits and pieces of the language, 'foreign god' and 'orc' seemed to be phrases of contention. It was another reminder that while he could see the faded white disc in the sky, this was not the land of his god.

In exchange for helping with the day's haul, the village of Cath's Net would share their hearth and pot. Jumping at the chance to get off the horse, whom he feared was planning on throwing him into another lake, Tulok readily agreed. Their tasks were simple enough. When the boats came in, they were to help carry in the poles, nets, cages, and other necessities. With a few simple stretches, Isolde fell into a familiar posture for hauling heavy goods as she did in Tarf-qua. Watching her work reminded Tulok of when she worked on the gnome barge back in Nahral. It was one of the very few moments that he had seen her content while they were in the City.

If there was anything to be said about exercise, it kept you warm. Tulok had shed his long wraps for bracing poles and nets full of fish. While he could not understand what they were saying, he did his best to follow the hand signals of his hosts.

"They said you follow directions pretty good for a foreigner," Isolde said, as she balanced a bundle of rods across her shoulders.

Tulok rolled his eyes and started to speak, but four of the villagers had loaded up rods over his shoulders and the weight of the fish pushed him downward. He was not a pack mule! He felt the small voice in his ear urging him to be vocal to be ...

With a deep heaving grunt, he stood tall. The voice of the Gurkh faded into nothingness as the strength of his control empowered his body. He gave a nod to one villager, who looked up at him in a slight moment of awe, and then pointed a direction out to Tulok. Nodding his head again, he stepped forward and continued on with his task. The Radiant Lord knew his servant could handle these obstacles, and Tulok would not ... could not ... disappoint.

A few hours later, with a full belly of a simple but filling stew, Isolde stared at the few bright diamonds in the black ocean that was the sky. With her back toward the warmth of the fire, she felt her muscles ache, but in a proper way, that brought her a bit of joy. It was not pain associated with a fight, but honest labor that made her slightly miss Tarf-qua. On the other side of the fire, she could already hear the not-so-gentle snoring of her friend. Tulok had stayed up for a few hours to honor his watch before bedding down. After taking another dose of the black tea to help with his sleeping, he was out the moment his head hit the bedroll. Oddly, his snoring was mirrored by the small Folk woman in both length and depth. Isolde sighed and closed her eyes, letting the sound of the ocean drown out her companions.

—

In a word – Green. Everything around him was hues of green, dark woodland brown, and hues of brilliant blue. They had traveled a few more hours down the road when it seemed like the sun had finally broken through the miasma of the damp cold fog and mists. Tulok felt the warmth of the sun on his face and saw Avalon in literally a different light. The hills were filled with thick grass that carpeted the landscape – only to be interrupted by massive trees with rich, dark brown trunks. Splotches of color broke up the continuous green as flowers opened their own faces to the Radiant Lord above. In some ways, the wash of color was almost blinding as the orc found he could not let his eyes linger on any one aspect of the scene before him.

Then, as if on cue, the rest of the world came alive with various sounds of birds and other creatures calling out through the forest. The calls that echoed off the hills were of various tones, from deep bellows to dozens of shrieks and whistles as Avalon threw off its fog-laden blanket. While he was a stranger in a strange land, Tulok felt curiously at peace in this one moment. It was as if the entire world slowed. He let his eyes close. It was not as if he was leading Tully, as the horse was really following others. He whispered a few prayers of thanks to the Radiant Lord, and took a deep breath, and stretched. The lazy enjoyment was cut short as Tulok realized Tully had come to a stop. Opening his eyes, he saw that Isolde and Iscaria were several yards ahead of him in conversation. He started to call out to them when Tully shook his mane.

Tulok felt something run up his spine, almost a chill but not quite. Someone ... or something ... was watching him. Tully shifted and Tulok noticed that the casual shifting of his tail stopped, it was almost pushed down. Some presence cowed the proud beast. Under any other circumstance, this would have been amusing, but this did not bode well. Looking to his left, he saw nothing but the ocean in the distance. Slowly looking to his right, he saw that the expanse of the forest had grown thicker in this section of the land, but was cut wide with a crystal-clear body of water. The lake was easily bigger than most villages, but it was a true lake of pure water. It struck the desert blood in him with awe of its beauty. Part of him wanted to dip his hand in and splash his face, but something else put him on edge. There was something else here; it was not in the water, but across the lake and staring at him.

At first glance, it looked like a horse with part of its body hidden in the shadow of the trees. Tulok narrowed his eyes and made out the creature's shape. It was like a horse, but that characterization slowly faded. Its body was more stocky. Muscular. The head was larger and did not bear a long mane like Tully. This creature stood on six legs that seemed as rough and dark as tree bark, and its massive antlers were easily a few heads taller than Tulok. The fur of the beast was a mixture of browns and greens that shifted with the light. As his eyes beheld the beast, he could see deep green and pink moss that hung off the creature's antlers. It seemed to sway slowly in a non-existent breeze. It was unlike anything he had ever seen.

The enormous beast stared at both the horse and its orc rider. It regarded them both with a frightening eye of scrutiny. Stepping forward into the early afternoon light, its fur glistened with both life and something … else. Something in those eyes, those hard amber eyes, continued to bore into him from a distance.

"TULOK!" said a sharp whisper.

Breaking the spell of scrutiny, he pulled his gaze away and saw Isolde's face full of intensity and concern.

"Look at me … do not stare at Him." She urged. "Prompt Tully to move forward, and do not turn around. Do you understand me?" she said.

He felt like he was waking up, nodded his head. He squeezed his legs and Tully slowly moved forward. The horse, like his rider, looked only forward. To his side, he could see that Iscaria had dismounted and was kneeling by the lake. It looked as if she was laying a flower in the water. Part of him wanted to continue watching her, but Isolde's words rang true in his head and kept moving forward with Tully.

Several minutes passed and he could hear Isolde and Iscaria's mounts come up behind him. Both had come alongside him. "New rule, big guy. You stay to the left side of the road, and if you want to look at something, stare at the ocean, okay?"

Isolde said softly.

"What happened back there?" he said with a bit of confusion. "One moment, things were glorious! It was beautiful. Then something was looking at me. It felt like there was nothing else in the world, only ..." he stopped when Isolde raised a finger.

"No. Do not linger on it," Isolde said as she shook her head.

The graveness of her words was not guided by any religious politics, but by survival. Isolde was rarely this serious outside of a fight. He simply nodded his head, but a thought struck him.

"I remember reading about gigantic creatures to the north on the mainland. They called them elk, but they only had one set of antlers. That one had four ..."

Iscaria looked a bit more flushed than normal. Was it the remnants of fear on her face? It was hard to tell.

The little Folk woman added, "She is right. Do not linger on what you saw. There are many wonderful and terrible things in this land. That creature is but a small representation of those entities that call these woods home. Thoughts and memories, even non-native ones, can attract their attention. If they stay in your thoughts ... those thoughts can seed your dreams. Believe us when we say this, Father, you do NOT want their attention in your dreams."

An icy chill ran down the orc's spine as the clouds slowly covered up the sun once again.

Chapter 39

The day's ride had been pressing. While the afternoon of the second day was 'eventful', they agreed to put more distance between themselves and the lake guardian. The rest of their trek had, thankfully, gone without incident. Finding another village and working for their room and board was not an issue. These villagers seemed less leery of seeing an orc in the company of a Landless Champion and a Speaker for the Mother, though Tulok could not shake the feeling that someone always scrutinized his presence. Standing near Tully, he used the brush that Isolde had given him.

"If you brush him, he may be less likely to throw you … hopefully." Isolde had smiled as she handed him the curry comb.

Brushing the animal was no problem and, for once, Tully and he were tolerant of one another. It gave him something to do … something of use. The concept of personal value had been gnawing at the back of Tulok's mind as he interacted with Avalon's inhabitants.

He remembered his own shock and disbelief when he learned Isolde knew nothing of coinage and its value across the land. Did she feel the same as he did now? The value of her leug literally meant nothing in Setesh. His own lack of leug made him more than just an outsider. They saw him with no sense of value. To Avalon, he was like a broken cup, empty and having lost its purpose. Like the chill wearing at his bones, these thoughts wanted to find a place in his mind. He was tired of trying to shake off those feelings. It was idiotic; these were not his people or his culture. Yet, the light touch of despair nudged those small embers in his chest. The irritation rose until he heard Isolde's laughter. The rich tones broke through the darkness like a beacon in the night. He stopped himself and looked over at her. She was shaking hands with another woman who was motioning to boats. All that time in the desert, her perseverance never faltered. She learned what was of value and made do with the situation at hand. Shame fell over him and he shook his head. This was just another turn on the same cycle: he would not start it again.

"She believed in herself, Tully, no matter the hardships. I need to remember the same. My value is more than just a title. Deeds have value. Work has value. A person's word has value. Like she did in Setesh, I will let my actions speak for me." Tully looked back at Tulok and stared at him for a moment. The horse flicked his tail and turned back to the tall grass he was chewing. Tulok continued to brush the horse as he watched his companions continue with their hellos and greetings to the villagers.

Nodding his head, he smiled, as he knew this particular 'clergy dance' well. While he was cold and miserable on his first day of travel, he had missed it all. All he remembered were the fearful stares of onlookers. He watched as the Folk Speaker and Isolde made their rounds, greeting, talking, and shaking hands. During all of this, something caught his eye. He watched as they went from group to group and finally caught it … there was a pause. When his party introduced themselves, there was a pause before the other party responded. At that point, both Isolde and Iscaria paused in kind. He thought about the interactions in Lubri. Brief pauses as they assessed each other. It was as if there was a sound that both parties were waiting to be acknowledged, telling them they could move forward. Was this how the leug took its place in the world?

"Or you could also read too much into things," he said to himself and shook his head.

"Wow – he looks downright shiny," Isolde remarked as walked toward the two. She ran her hand down the side of Tully's neck. The noble beast snorted and whickered at her in response. "He looks great! And he probably enjoyed the attention too."

Tulok smiled, "I follow directions well for a foreigner."

She laughed. "True, very true. So, I have some good news and some ... possibly bad news. The good news is after we get to Iscaria's stop, there should be more sun, less fog, but colder temperatures."

"Well, two out of three are not bad," Tulok said, trying to sound optimistic. He gently rested his large hand on Tully's back. The horse's skin twitched slightly, but the animal did not move away." How cold does it get?" Tulok asked.

"It snows sometimes, but only in the far north. You should be able to cut across most of that when you take the Can'lbarth Road. Your kinsmen have taken all the territory north of there," Speaker Iscaria said as she walked up.

Tulok squinted his eyes in thought, letting the mental map take form in his head. He nodded and reached for the contents of his saddlebags. Withdrawing a piece of parchment, he added a few notes. While not a cartographer by any means, the rough map he had sketched would not hurt.

Iscaria watched the sun priest and continued, "The Northern tribes rarely venture south of the Can'lbarth. If you encounter them, you may be enough of curiosity that they probably will not attack."

"Why would they attack?" he asked as his brow furrowed.

"The orcs of the island are like many other tribes and clans here. They will fight for territory and hunting rights. If things are bad, they have been known to raid settlements that are "too far" into their territory. They have also warred with the southern tribes that comprise mostly humans and some elves. Harsh living knows no race or gender. They rarely attack travelers, but with the Triskele at war right now ... one never knows. The real dangers are bandits and those who have nothing to their name."

"Bandits? Really?" Isolde said in disbelief.

"Believe it, child. There are those who come from the mainland that end up stuck here or refuse to go home. However, because they bear no weight to their name, they attack travelers to scavenge what they can," Iscaria said grimly.

"Is there no helping them if they are only attacking for food?" Tulok asked.

Iscaria pursed her lips, but Isolde answered, "If someone does not have any value to their name, it sometimes means they have done something bad or even horrible to have it stripped from them. There are ways of finding redemption … but that is a path that has to be intentionally chosen. These often have made the active choice to avoid redemption. Why? I do not know." She shook her head, the thoughts clearly disturbing her.

"As for those from the mainland that remain here," Iscaria continued, "They could offer to work their passage back. If they have not done so already, it usually means that there is nothing for them back on the mainland, or they are running from justice. In a word, Father … these are criminals. Normally your Champions police that sort of cause … but here, Avalon gives them the chance to make amends. Not all take it. Those that do not … the Island eventually sorts itself out."

Tulok mulled it over in his head as he thought about his own self-pity earlier. If someone really wanted to make it right or go home, there was a way. Redemption in services was not an uncommon concept. Nodding his head, "I understand, and we will deal with any obstacles accordingly. However, I have one other question."

With a sense of relief, Iscaria spoke, "Yes, your Radiance?"

"Snow?" he asked, "What is snow?"

Isolde and Iscaria exchanged glances. "So…"

—

Gone was the scenic view of the coast, and in its place were the tall looming pines for as far as the eye could see. Isolde closed her eyes and took in the deep scents of the woods. While Setesh had its spiced warm air, the smell of green woods and moisture filling the air was fulfilling. It filled her mind with brief flashes of another life. She remembered running barefoot through the grass and sitting in the trees to watch day fade. Those days seemed like a dream themselves. She opened her eyes and looked out toward an open field. For a moment she thought she saw herself running, but the field was not empty. There was blood and bodies. The smell of smoke filled her nose. Horrified, she looked at the bodies and saw that they were not what she expected. They were the wild men, the Free People, and their broken bodies were strewn over the field as black tendrils pulsed into the landscape.

"No!" she said firmly as she sat up suddenly, eyes flying open. The snoring of Iscaria was thankfully loud enough that no one heard anything. Sitting across from her was Tulok, a concerned look on his face as he held his cup of the dreamless tea.

"Are you alright?" was all he said.

Isolde nodded quietly and looked at the fire. She was not alright. Far from it. While the blessing of the Wanderer kept her from the tendrils of nightmare, snippets of foresight were different. Avalon knew she was home and was showing her things to come. She would tell him later, but not right now.

"I'm fine … just a … something I did not want to go back to." She leaned over and picked up a waterskin. The cool water was a pleasant shock, but it was not enough to clear up whatever lingering dream smoke that had filled her nostrils. She ran a hand through her hair and tried to take in a deep breath of the night air.

Tulok nodded, but knew better than to press the issue. He looked down at the remains of his tea and drank down the last of its contents.

She needed to distance herself from the vision. While the Island may try to show her something to come, revisiting it now might muddy the message. Looking over at the orc as he was bedding down, she remembered a question that had been sticking in her mind, "I have to ask, how do you do it, Tulok?"

"Do what?" he asked, a bit surprised. His deep red eyes watched her from across the fire.

"Sleep so little. You sleep, what, four or five hours and you seem fine. How? I can push through when it needs doing, but it always seems like you need very little sleep."

Tulok looked around as if checking that someone was listening and quietly said, "Naps."

Isolde's eyebrows raised in surprise. "Naps?"

He nodded solemnly. "Naps. Whenever I can. When we stop or even when we are riding. I just close my eyes and nap."

She stared at him in disbelief. He simply shrugged and pursed his lips as much as his tusks would allow. Isolde narrowed her eyes and read his face, watching the firelight on his dusky skin, and how he avoided meeting her eyes. He tried to maintain a solemn face, but the edge of his lips was fighting a smile. He was joking.

"Naps ..." she shook her head, "You almost had me. The image of you napping while riding a horse ... hilarious."

"It is actually easier on a camel," he said with a wider smile, laughing to himself.

"Ha ha! Go to bed, funny man!" If she had an actual pillow, she would have thrown it at his smug face. She laid back down and stared up at the night sky. The memories of her dream were gone all but gone. Even the smoke smell had vanished and been replaced with the cool night air. His joke had prevented her from dwelling on any of it, so it faded into the gossamer. She turned her head and saw that he was already wrapped in his bedroll. She realized. He did it on purpose. The trick of a man who spent a lifetime settling countless orphans to sleep.

"Thank you, Father," she breathed, and let sleep overtake her once again.

—

The Homely House was larger than the one in Lubri, almost orcish in proportions, but the overseeing priest was not an orc. Standing outside of it was a woman who seemed to be only a handful of inches shorter than Tulok. Although her hair was gray and bundled up, it bore vibrant silver streaks. She stood up and walked with almost youthful purpose. She wiped the dirt off of her trousers and narrowed her eyes on the three approaching the House. Isolde recognized she was of the wild stock – a member (or rather a former member) of the tribes that call the wilds their home. Even at her full height, Isolde still felt small compared to this woman.

"Ramah – I see you keep house as well as you cook," Iscaria said sharply as she dismounted from her pony.

Iscaria spoke in Avalonian and, while he could not understand her, Tulok understood the inflection in her tone. He looked over at Isolde, who said nothing, and just shook her head. This was not expected.

The tall woman sneered and looked down at the small Folk woman. "How would you know? You could barely see above the grass blades." Her voice was strong and full of fire. Isolde knew this someone who knew how to shout orders in the middle of a fight and expected them to be followed.

"I see the Lord Wanderer is still hoping you find humility up in the clouds. Why not come down here and join us mortals?" Iscaria shot back, stepping forward and looking up at the other woman.

Ramah kneeled down, but still towered over Iscaria. "What are you going to do about it?" she replied, leaning closer. The tone was quiet, like a viper waiting to strike.

The two stared at each other with unblinking eyes, and probably would have gone on for longer until Iscaria snorted. Ramah's harsh face broke into a smile. "God's woman, every time I see you, the first thing out of your mouth is always nonsense. How I have missed you!" and the two embraced.

The tension fell as fast as they built it, and the smaller Speaker turned toward her companions. "This is Isolde, formerly Lady Whitebrooke, and her guest from the Mainland, Father Tulok of the Radiant Lord."

Standing up tall, Ramah looked Isolde up and down carefully.

"You've taken your Oaths," Ramah said.

"I have," Isolde replied.

Ramah nodded simply, "And He has accepted them. Rest and be welcome, Witness."

Isolde inclined her head respectfully. "Thank you, Hearth-keeper," and dismounted as Ramah turned her eyes on Tulok.

A quick nod of the head and she spoke, "*You are a long way from the desert Father.*" her Orcish was surprising, and her accent was interesting as it seemed to blend in the Avalonian sounds smoothly. Much like other orcs, and she even gestured with her hands and arms as she spoke, "*By the Rites of Hospitality, I hope you find rest at our fire.*"

Tulok smiled and bowed his head. "*You honor me with your hearth and I shall respect it in kind. Aside from an acquaintance in Setesh, you are the first human I have heard speak my tongue, and very well.*"

Ramah gestured towards the north, "*It goes with the territory Father.*" Addressing everyone, "You all must be hungry by this point. You can stable your horses to the side of the house, and I will meet you inside. I'm sure there is a story to tell here." With that, she turned and headed back to the house.

—

While they had shared their tale with Farnak, who had grunted and groaned with irritation, Iscaria and Ramah were rapt with attention. Occasionally, they would exchange glances but would say nothing as Isolde and Tulok wove the story of their journey. Isolde shared the tale about arriving in Setesh, the murders, and the hunt for a lost temple, whose name was never mentioned. Tulok told the story of the Vidria treachery, the would-be cult sacrifice, and of their eventual escape. They ended their tale with their purpose on the island, and the dreams of black roots with death in their wake.

Ramah leaned back into her seat, smoking a long pipe in contemplation. But it was Iscaria who spoke up first. "Remind me to hit Farnak with a pan the next time we are in Lubri. I understood that this was a manhunt for a criminal … but the dreams, the black roots …" she looked over to Ramah, "There is something coming. I volunteered to take you this far because I wanted to speak with Ramah about similar dreams and if there had been anything happening this far north."

Reaching forward, Ramah tapped the last of the herbs out of her pipe and into the fire. "Normally around this time of year, I receive a few visitors from the various tribes … northern and southern. Some come for trade, a blessing, or information. It has been quiet for the last month. You have been the first travelers I have had for a long time. Something is going on and not even the woods are talking."

"What about Vicnis? Perhaps it might be time to seek his views on things," Iscaria asked.

Ramah sighed and made a face. "I really do not want to. The Druids are … Druids. They are as wild as the guardians they find kinship with. That one is twice-blessed an oddity." Ramah shook her head, then looked at Iscaria with a shrug. "Last I talked with the old charmer, he was holed up some bit west of here. I have to stay with the House, but the Mother should keep your steps safe enough."

"Why not have us go to this Vicnis or let us oversee the House for a few hours?" Tulok suggested.

Iscaria looked surprised at the orc and smiled. "As helpful as that would be, Vicnis and his peers are … complex… even for us. There are rites and rituals that must be adhered to and observed. If they are not … it could be disastrous at best or deadly at worst. That, coupled with the Triskele warring in the area, you could easily get yourselves ambushed and used for tribute or trade goods in their skirmishes."

Tulok scowled noticeably at the comment. Isolde nodded silently at his side.

"Farnak cautioned as much as well. It's why we came this way."

"As a Witness, could Isolde stay with the House while you went to ask this … Druid … what he knows."

Ramah and Isolde exchanged looks. The free woman shook her head. "No. Our callings are very different, Father. While Isolde and I both serve the Lord Wanderer, my promise is bound to this House. No others can take up that burden unless they take up the pledge themselves."

Iscaria chuckled, "I do not imagine the Radiant Lord would be happy with your quick conversion."

"Besides," Ramah added, "Baedd Gwyllt should be your next stop."

Tulok raised an eyebrow as he sorted out the words, "Wild Boar Clan?"

Ramah nodded her head. "If your criminal traveled the roads, they would have seen him. With any luck, their Seer might guide your direction better."

"Or have more insight into these visions you have been having," Iscaria said to Isolde.

Isolde looked over at Tulok. "Well, I guess you get to meet your cousins after all."

Tulok nodded his head and took another drink from his cup. The light of the fire reflected off the tiny bell attached to the orc's wrist. It caught Ramah's eye, and she stared at it but said nothing. The challenges of tomorrow would have to be conquered without guidance.

It was the will of the land.

Chapter 40

"Well, maybe if Ophir had been a little more willing to negotiate, perhaps the Incirrata would have been willing to work with the River Lord's people to extend the warded sea corridor to them instead of Port Kraken!" Iscaria fumed.

Isolde sighed and tugged on the rear cinch of her saddle, checking it to ensure it was snug. Iscaria and Tulok had been bickering for the better half of an hour about differences in faith, society, and history. It had been like this since they left Lubri. Hours of blessed silence, broken by one or the other in a comment that would spark a theological debate for the rest of the day.

Isolde had heard many of these ... debates ... in the past. Now, hearing them from both impassioned parties, she understood why there was still an ocean dividing both pantheons and their people. Part of her was happy that Iscaria would part ways with them soon. There was only so much neutral ground she could stand upon.

"The Wave Breaker was gone! The River Lord was ... and is ... the only logical replacement to govern the seas!" Tulok protested.

"That smiling crocodile is not interested in anyone's needs but His own!" the little Folk woman continued.

A sharp pain twinged in Isolde's head at the mention of the River Lord and the Island. She squinched up her left eye and then dug her thumb into her eye socket along the brow ridge for a moment. There was a memory there ...

She shook her head and looked over the back of the horse at the two priests, locked in an ancient argument.

"You two gonna dig up every issue that your Temples have

with each other? I mean, I can ride ahead, deal with the issue and come back … "

Iscaria scowled up at Tulok. "No. We are done," she huffed.

Tulok glowered and took a deep breath. He was both irritated at Iscaria for her attacks on his faith and at himself for allowing her to goad him into the arguments to begin with. He pursed his lips and looked over at Isolde.

"Apologies," he said simply.

Isolde shrugged and lifted her foot into the stirrup, pulling herself up into her saddle. "Not my argument, but marvelous stories. Thank you for sharing them from your viewpoints. I will be certain to include them in my next visit to the Well." She smiled brightly.

Iscaria flushed at the comment, knowing full well that her actions were to be recorded for posterity in a memory well somewhere. For a moment, she felt like Isolde was carrying tales to the schoolmaster on her. She scowled.

"I forget you are a Witness and no longer Lady White-brooke," came the answer.

Isolde nodded simply. "That is your failing, Speaker. Not mine," she replied curtly. "You are off to see Vicnis?"

Iscaria nodded, "I am. If anyone can make sense of your visions and the ones the others are having, it could be He. I'll send word once we have an answer."

The Folk woman quickly mounted her pony and looked over at the entrance to the house. Ramah stood in the doorway, calmly watching them all. Iscaria locked eyes with the Wandering Lord's Hearthkeeper and nodded simply, a silent understanding exchanged between the two.

Tulok scrutinized Tully's saddle and, after a couple of firm tugs on various cinches, shifted to pull himself onto the great beast. Tully snorted and stomped, blowing out hard at Tulok's weight upon his back. The horse champed at his bit and shook his dark mane. Tulok looked over at Speaker Iscaria.

"May the Guardian of the Heavens Bless you with His Light and grant you His warmth on your journey, Speaker," Tulok intoned reverently.

"May the abundant presence of our Lady Mother bless and keep you safe while you walk upon these shores, Father," Iscaria replied in kind.

Isolde smiled at the exchange and nodded to Ramah. "Hearthkeeper."

"Walk in the light of hope, Witness."

Isolde wheeled her horse to face the gate and down the northern road as Tulok trotted Tully up to meet her. He leaned over slightly and asked in a low voice, "How will Iscaria send word? Do your people use hawks as we do in Setesh?"

Isolde shook her head and focused on the road ahead of them. "She will meet me in dreams."

~~

It was just past the half-day mark when they rested the horses and take an afternoon meal. Isolde pointed out a shaded area beneath a handful of apple trees alongside a running brook where the horses could take water and they could stretch.

Tulok shook out his blanket and let it settle onto the green grass. The abundance of life on the island still amazed the orc. Isolde patted the neck of the grullo-coated mare she had selected for their journey. The black and gray pony snorted and lowered her head to the water, her silky black tail flicked back and forth. Isolde grabbed the pack of foodstuffs from her saddle and walked over to Tulok. She tossed him the pack and glanced skyward for a moment to catch her bearings.

"If memory serves, we should be approaching Baedd Gwyllt lands," she said, and then settled down onto the blanket across from Tulok.

Tulok nodded and carefully unpacked their lunch, setting equal measures out for both. "These are ... Free Peoples?" he asked carefully.

Isolde nodded.

"Why are they called that? Were there slaves here once that needed freeing?" he asked carefully.

Isolde frowned at the question and shook her head. "What? No. That's ... "she paused. "Ok, I can see where someone might think that based on the name." She reached for a chunk of bread and tore into it. "No. They chose the name for themselves ages ago. The Free People ... and the other ... more migratory peoples ... live apart from the Courts and Landowners of the Island. They consider themselves 'free of the yoke of Noble rule'" she shrugged.

"Like the Sand Dancers," Tulok observed as he neatly and carefully set his bread, cheese, sausage, and hard-boiled eggs on a linen napkin. He closed his eyes for a moment and offered a silent prayer of thanks before eating.

Isolde nodded in agreement. "I guess so?" She thought about it for a few moments and nodded again with a little smile. "Ya. They are very similar when you think about it. Though they are not as unified as the Sand Dancers seem to be. Each clan has its own leader, its own territories, and its own observances. But yes." she reached for a grape and popped it into her mouth causally.

"Mmm." Tulok hrmmed in thought as he ate. "And ... the ... Triskele ... I have heard that term used twice now." He looked over at her. "Now that we are apart from others, are you able to tell me more?"

Isolde pursed her lips and popped another grape into her mouth. Nodding, she sat taller and brushed her hands off on her pant legs. Tulok sighed and rolled his eyes to see it.

"Ok, so ..." she began. "The Island is home to a couple of very different peoples who pay homage to survivors of different pantheons." She held up her index finger in warning. "And the only reason I am going into detail on any of this is because of our mutual agreements with each other."

Tulok nodded, suddenly very interested in the prospect of new knowledge.

"So, the Avalonian Pantheon comprises the Divine that came over with the humans. The Mother, The Lord Wanderer, The Jailer, and the Blood Raven. They are the Divine that survived the Reaping and aided in the transportation of the Island to Sanctum." She paused and took a moment to drink from her canteen. "The Dream Keeper came with them as well, but ... "she frowned.

"He is dead, yes? Like the Wave Breaker, and the daughter of the Radiant Lord?" Tulok asked.

Isolde nodded. "The throne of the Morpheum sits empty, yes, and its denizens are without rule."

Tulok pursed his lips and nodded once more. He recovered an egg from his napkin and set to carefully peeling its shell. "And your people are tied to the land of dreams?"

"Some more than others, but yes." Isolde agreed. She sighed and looked up at the sky. "The Triskele are Nature Divine. They came with the Druids and the elves ... well, the elves that Avalon brought with them. There were other Elven people brought to the Mainland from different locations as well, apparently. But ..." she continued. "The Triskele ... the Shepherd, the Huntress, and the Stag Lord ... they are the Divine that most of the Free People ... and the druids ... typically pay homage to. Many of the fey-born do as well."

Tulok's eyebrows knit together in confusion for a moment. "Free Peoples, Avalonian, Dream creatures, and ... fey born?"

Isolde smiled. "We are very cosmopolitan!" she grinned brightly. "The fey-born are the remnants of the Fairy Courts. Creatures of magic and legend ... mostly." She thought about it for a moment. "You probably will not encounter many outside these shores. They are tied deeply to the land."

Tulok looked over at Isolde. "More than you?" he asked softly.

Isolde nodded. "Very." She looked down at the food on her napkin and poked at it with her finger. "Only one member of the Divine Court of Fae survived the Reaping."

Tulok frowned and nodded. "I remember reading about Him. He is a child of the forest, is he not?" he asked.

Isolde laughed out loud at that. "Oh ... oh, that is certainly one way to describe him, yes!" She shook her head and popped a chunk of cheese into her mouth. She continued to speak around the mouthful of food. "He is a force of chaos, trickery, and deception, to be certain." She paused and took a breath. "But He is also a bringer of life and joy. He is a blessing ... and a bane, depending on His mood ... as are all creatures of Fae."

"But ... why do they war?" Tulok asked plainly.

Isolde sighed heavily and looked at the sky. "Oh, that is a question for Druids, to be certain," she exclaimed. She shrugged and looked over at the orc priest. "I really wish I could explain it. I do, but ... I don't honestly know why. My father said it had something to do with ancient oaths, and magics, and territories, and tradition, and land ... I ..." she smiled gently. "It is for people in higher circles of knowledge, my friend. It ... it just is."

The scholarly orc scowled, his displeasure at the answer very clear on his features. "The ways of this island ..."

"Are mine," Isolde added gently.

Tulok looked over at the woman seated across from him. Her emerald green eyes were the color of the forests that surrounded them, sparkled with life and the unknown. For that single moment, she was a Champion not only of her Lord, but of the island itself. His breath caught in his chest for a heartbeat.

"Isolde ..."

A blood-curdling wail broke the moment.

In sync, they both turned their heads towards the wail that seemed to hang in the air. It was unlike anything Tulok had ever heard. There was a mixture of pain of loss... true, uncomforted loss. The imagery of a mother losing her children to sickness rang in his chest as the wail continued. His eyes watered as he felt it more and more around his heart. He needed to comfort them ... to lessen the growing pain in his chest...

Isolde slammed her cupped hands over the orc's ear. The pain and disorientation broke the spell that washed over Tulok's mind. Boxing someone's ears would normally be a straight road to rage, but whatever was in the sound seemed to dull the fire that normally churned within. His eyes sought Isolde's. She was watching the area all around them, not in a panic, but with a level of guarded tension. He could see her lips moving, but she was not speaking to him. She was singing. He could hear her voice through her hands. Lyrics to something that felt ancient and tied to the land. It seemed to bore deep into his skull.

Isolde's eyes continued to sweep the surrounding area with hands gripped tight against Tulok's ears. Looking up, he could see her face flush and her green eyes narrow: this was Isolde angry. He wanted to turn his body and look at what she was staring at, but something inside told him to remain still. Calmly, he took a breath and closed his eyes.

Let me stand against the storm
Braced for wind or rain
Woolen cloak my only shield
Stalwart I remain
Stand with me tonight my heart
Against darkness strong
Be the light that leads me home
To where I belong

She recognized the wail as soon as it sounded across the fields. Sorrow given solid mass; the Wailing Women were of many forms. Some took the form of grizzled old hags. Others appeared like small abandoned children, while yet others appeared as beautifully enticing women standing in a stream or lake bed. The Weepers, the Bean-Nighe, the Washerwomen, the heralds of death. Isolde's eyes darted across the horizon, looking up and down the small stream they had led the horses to. Bean-Nighe was tied to the water, and this one's weeping wail sought comfort, laced with sorrow and longing.

The compass that hung around Isolde's neck warmed and glowed faintly. Bean-Nighe were creatures of sorrow and loss and the Lord Wanderer was pledged to fight against the darkness they carried. Once upon a time, long before the Reaping, they said that Bean-Nighe would grant wishes if captured by mortal hands. Now their weakened magics granted them only limited foresight if one was lucky enough to avoid being drowned and strong enough to capture them. A song of endurance and love was often a temporary shield against the magic of their weeping wail. They taught children a variety of sing-song rhymes and songs to defend themselves against the fey-born of the island they called home.

Isolde continued to mouth the words of the chant they taught her as a child, to ward off the Bean-Nighe.

The foresight would have been useful. They could locate Arman or at least learn of where he was on the island, but she could not do it with Tulok there. There was a layer of temptation to rush the wailing woman and bind her in the old ways, but it would have left the orc exposed. She scanned the horizon for a trace of pink and bluish-white flowers used to bind their essence in place. There were none. Driving it away or killing it was her only option. Isolde looked down at Tulok. His face was stoic and his eyes closed. She could not explain what was happening. She had to maintain the chant. It seemed as if he understood that there was danger afoot. She had to get him to continue to cover his ears, but she could not stop singing. She had to improvise and hope it would work. Lifting one booted foot off of the ground and balancing on the other, she tapped his forearm with the toe.

Tulok's eyes opened, the haze still apparent in them, but it seemed to fade slightly. With her foot, Isolde nudged his arm upward, and tilted her head to the side, never once breaking the song.

Tulok narrowed his eyes at her, partly in confusion and partly trying to understand what she was singing. His grasp of the Avalonian tongue was still scant, and the song she sang seemed even more alien by comparison. Her voice sounded like an ocean of sound compared to the background noise that kept tempting him to listen. He watched as she lifted her foot again and nudged up his forearm. She was trying to get him to move his arm, but to what end? Everything seemed so fuzzy and cloudy as he tried to piece a thought together. In a way … he was lost in both her song and the sound all around them.

He shook his head at her and mouthed 'What?'

Again, she worked her foot to his forearm, but this time, she used a bit of force as she 'kicked' upward. As his arm slightly rose, she tilted her head to the same side as the arm, motioning it up. 'Cover your damn ears!' was all that she wanted to say, but could not break the song.

As his arm went up, he held it aloft and slowly raised it up while looking at her. She nodded her head as she sang to affirm 'Yes!' Raising up both his arms – he reached forward and cup Isolde's ear with his own hands.

It took all her will not to yell at him. She calmly raised an eyebrow and motioned her head towards his.

The light of understanding filled his eyes, along with a bit of blushing from embarrassment. He placed his hands over hers on his head. She nodded her head and quickly slipped her hands away as he clamped down on his ears.

Turning towards the figure in the water, Isolde drew her sword and looked at its shimmering form. Gripping the hilt with both hands, she steadied the blade in front of her and shifted her hips in a ready stance. Angered, she took a breath to clear her thoughts. These creatures could be fast, and she had to control the flow of the fight. It was a wide-open space which gave her room to maneuver, but the water's edge was the issue. The green foliage crept over into the river and hid what was solid ground. One wrong step and she would have gone down with the Weeper at her throat. In her head, she heard Reynard's voice almost smile at her:

You have small feet, child, use them. Larger things lumber and step with a heavy foot. You must step but step lightly so you can spring with your strike.

She took a small step forward, lowering the balls of her feet into the earth. It was firm. She continued to sing with each step forward, ensuring it was solid ground.

A figure stood on the bank of the water. Female in shape, duckweed draped from its shapely form in long strands, disguising its otherworldly self. Dark rivulets, like black ink, ran down its pale face. The Weeper drifted slowly forward. Its empty black eyes focused on Isolde's blade. Recognition of Avalonian steel flooded its countenance as its eyes filled with hatred. It pulled back white lips to reveal slimy black teeth in a horrible hissing growl.

Isolde advanced slowly. The creature was almost in striking distance. Another step and she could score the easy hit.

The ground felt spongy.

With a quick glance down, she saw the dampness hidden in the grass, but there was something else ... something black, like a snake making its way towards her.

It happened quickly as the black tendril shot up and lashed itself around her leg. The Weeper pounced. Isolde struggled. She had to control this moment. As the tendril pulled her leg forward, she lifted the other and allowed her body to fall back onto the earth. The Weeper closed the distance, clawed fingers held wide. Isolde braced and raised the tip of the blade to place it between herself and the Weeper. Momentum carried the creature forward in its death lunge only to be stopped short as the blade went through the creature's throat and into its head. Isolde yelled as the Weeper's body convulsed on top of her. Blue-green ooze flowed out of the wound and over her hands, trailing down her arms. Twisting, she pulled the sword out, spraying her with bluish-green blood. She looked over at Tulok, who watched wide-eyed with hands over his ears, but he was not looking at her. He was staring past her.

The tendril tightened around her leg painfully. There was a tug, then another, stronger. Suddenly, she felt herself being pulled toward the water. Isolde's eyes focused on the tendril and followed it toward its source. Another creature had risen from the water.

The Fey that inhabited the water often took the forms of beautiful, near-perfect beings. Their very presence was like fragrant tranquility that overcame those that were too foolish. These wondrous and beautiful things were another example of Avalonian mystery. The most beautiful of these were often the most dangerous.

What rose out of the water was none of these things. The creature was both male and female and other things more indescribable. If this had been a creature of flesh and mortal blood, it would be too horrible to conceive.

She narrowed her eyes. This was not a single entity. Multiple Fey-ish things swirled in black ichor, screaming silently and trying to escape their brackish hell. What nightmare made manifest had stepped from the Morpheum to birth this horror? Isolde was flooded with both disgust and anger. She took a hard swipe at the tendril across her leg and cut it just past her foot. It whipped and flailed about angrily on the ground, black ooze spewing from its severed self.

Her freedom was short-lived as several more tendrils erupted from the creature and wrapped around her arms and legs.

With a roar, the gentle and kindly priest gathered the rage that often lay buried within him and charged forward. He leapt toward the creature, mace in hand. Bringing it down, one expected the snap of bones or the squish of damaged flesh. Instead, the simple mace sunk into the bulbous creature's brackish 'flesh' with a slurping "thud". Many eyes, trapped in their horror-hell, turned towards him, his hand still gripped around the mace.

"Oh, no ..."

With ease, the creature whipped its tendril-like arm and sent Tulok flying into a nearby tree, as easily as shaking out a sheet. His head cracked soundly on the trunk. A red trail of blood formed from the top of his shaved head.

Isolde struggled to pull her hand toward the compass around her neck. If she could just reach it ...

A horn sounded over the din of battle. A cacophony of roars followed it.

Isolde struggled to determine where the sounds were coming from. Was there another foe entering the fray? She felt the grip of the tendrils run slightly slack and then release her completely.

Spears shot forward from several directions, all scored their hits and the creature's many faces cried out in silent pain. It shuddered and quivered as the spears slowly continued to sink deeper into its grotesque form. Several more spears found their way into the creature as Isolde heard heavy footsteps come towards her. Turning her head, she saw them clearly: Orcs.

Five orcs, dressed in well-tooled leather armor, rushed past her to grab hold of the spears protruding from the monster. They moved in unison, each bracing themselves, powerful hands wrapped around spear hafts. With a massive show of strength, they heaved and pulled the creature out of the water, then slammed it onto the dry earth. Only once it was no longer in the water did Isolde espy more warriors entering the battle. Charging in with deep snarls, they brought wicked-looking spears down to bear on the creature in rapid succession. Yet these were not brutish creatures wailing away with pointed sticks. Each had shifted their heavy furs in front of themselves, protecting themselves from the sprays of blood. They wore thick gloves of hide over the hand wielding the spear. She looked back down at her foot – the black pool of blood had missed her own leg. Pulling her foot away, she turned back to watch.

The creature's tendrils spasmed and flailed wildly, whipping back and forth. Finally, it ceased moving and sank into itself. The orc warriors stepped back and gave space to a tall female orc. Her dark skin shone with sweat under the overcast sky. Long black hair hung in braids that ended in heavy weights and barbs. Around her neck hung a straight-stemmed arrowhead, chip cut from dark stone and suspended from an intricate torc. Symbols of the Huntress. Her gaze focused on the twitching black mass in front of them. She narrowed her eyes and knelt to place her wide hand on the earth. She closed her eyes and then nodded. Standing, she pulled out a large water-skin. She walked around the creature and poured the contents on the creature's body. The smell of the fluid made Isolde's eyes water. Whatever was in the skin was strong.

Striking flint on the heads of their spears, the orcs watched as their sparks were caught in the ready air and became ablaze with an orange-greenish flame. Isolde watched as they seemed to observe the fire for any movement. Whatever this thing was, they had seen it before and knew that just because it was on fire did not mean it was dead. A few of the orcs had tossed their heavy furs and gloves into the fire – the black blood sizzled in the flames.

Isolde glanced around the group and slowly rolled to the side to stand. None of them made any move to stop her. Isolde turned and saw that one orc was kneeling beside Tulok. Realization hit her quickly as she remembered seeing him thrown into the tree.

"Tulok!" she exclaimed with concern. She took a few steps forward and was met with several spears and fierce red eyes. The spears were adorned with boar tusks, and several of them wore jewelry crafted from the same.

Isolde stopped and held up her hands in a stance of non-aggression. "I think we found Baedd Gwyllt."

"You have indeed, little Wanderer," the leader spoke in rough Avalonian. She turned to face Isolde, her red eyes and harsh features looked even more fierce from across the balefire. "Explain your business quickly less we have another 'log' to feed the flames."

Before Isolde could answer, "*We seek a foreign criminal who may have traveled through these lands and the wisdom of your Seer,*" spoke a familiar voice in a tired, orcish tongue. Tulok was pulling himself up with the aid of the kneeling orc.

All eyes turned their attention toward him. Tulok looked over at Isolde and back to their leader. "Please. We are running out of time."

Blodwen regarded Tulok carefully, and nodded her head,

"You have no idea, Sun Skin."

Chapter 41

Giant wild boar. No, he corrected himself: *Giant domesticated boar.*

The draft horse Tulok rode on was just over 19 hands high. He had needed a mount of this enormity to accommodate his size. Despite the impressive proportions of the animal he rode, Tulok still felt shorter riding next to his kin, who were mounted upon giant boar called Er'ches. The Island orcs had not only tamed these massive creatures but used them as mounts!

For Isolde, it was a strange sight to see. Creatures who were one of the largest destructive forces on Avalon were docile pack animals and mounts. They seemed to be happily trotting along and pulling a large wagon. Isolde recalled a summer long past when her family's entire orchard was devastated by these creatures. The boar had not only eaten the apples, but they had also eaten the very trees. Bark, branches, stems, and buds. Gone. They were worse than goats. It was one of the very few times that she remembered seeing both her parents beside themselves with frustration and anger.

Isolde's mount, Duli, made a nervous noise as she whickered her discomfort at the nearness of the giant porcines. With one hand on the reins and another stroking the side of the horse's neck, Isolde did what she could to keep the mare calm. She understood the horse's disquiet at the situation and surroundings.

Tully, on the other hand, seemed to be enjoying himself as the draft horse kept pace with the two of the giant boars. Tulok and the orcs escorting them were engaged in what could only be described as a lively conversation. Isolde's limited exposure to orcish culture reminded her that the language was rough-spoken, almost guttural, and gesticulation with the hands was just as important as the words. However, watching Tulok, she could see the slight differences in the way they communicated. Tulok's mannerisms were 'loud' if that were possible? His hand and arm movements were forceful and wide so that a person could see what was going on from afar. The Island orcs had different gestures that seemed to flow as they moved. A sense of subtlety, maybe, she wondered as she watched.

Other than the conversation in front of her, the ride was quiet. The hunting leader that led them introduced herself as Maelona Blodwen, the chieftain they had been seeking. Blodwen rode ahead of the group. Occasionally, she pulled off to the side to confer with a scout who would appear from the woods. These exchanges reminded Isolde of riding with Safar when he would check his caravan to ensure all was well. She smiled a little at the memory. The most notable difference was that this was a hunting party, not a cargo caravan. The wagon that trailed behind them contained several large game animals that had been field-dressed for travel. Isolde surmised there may be enough meat to satisfy a small village for a few months. With orcs, it was harder to say. They were not humans, and so maybe their appetites were larger? Tulok did not seem to eat any more than she did, but that could be the desert living. What they carried might only last a few days or a single week. Smoked and dried, maybe longer. Again, Tulok and many of the desert folk were light eaters, so it was hard to gauge a comparison.

The silence in travel was also different from the Seteshi caravans. In a caravan, one could strike up a conversation with those around you to help pass the time. Stories, jokes, and occasional gossip could be exchanged to make the hot journey a bit more bearable. Even in the trade caravans from Whitebrooke to Lubri, there had always been chatter along the road. Sometimes every jovial singing. This was not the case here. The orcs spoke very little to each other, and the only active conversation was the one in front of her. Not that the orcs were malicious about excluding Isolde; it all just felt ... off.

They passed through a bank of mist and for a moment; it seemed like she was the only one on the trail. The only sound that pierced the fog was the sound of Duli's hooves on the earth. Isolde had always been a social creature. The silence and isolation nagged at her. It was uncomfortable. She longed to fill the silence with sound. Avalonians were rarely truly alone. On the Island, there was always a connection to one another and their surroundings. Coming up as a child, there had been very few times that Isolde could remember being alone. Yet here, even on her home soil, she felt more alone than she did in Tarf-qua. The caravansary there had almost carried a sense of home, but it was still not Avalon.

As they broke free of the fog bank, Isolde tried to make conversation with one rider next to her. He said nothing and instead focused his gaze on the road ahead and increased the pace of his boar to pass her. No one was willing to speak with her. No one even looked at her. None of them made eye contact except for Blodwen when she made her occasional pass. It was like she did not exist.

The only respite from the emptiness was the pull of the leug around her. She could feel the weight of their names, their deeds, and their responsibility. Some were greater than others, but all bore respect. Observing them one by one, she could see they also bore physical representations of their deeds and honor: claws, beads, gems, bones, and braids. If she had more time, she probably could have pieced together their meanings, but one item stood out among them all. The boar tusks and bones that they wore were all adorned with scrimshaw work dedicated to the Huntress.

The Huntress was Nature's Balance. Whatever lived and died in the wild, be it man or beast, was attributed to Her. She was the wolf pack who ravaged the deer population. The sharp-eyed hawk who snatched rabbits with their sharp talons. She was the bear who killed the noble and the Freeman alike who ventured too deep into the woods. Her presence was not a sign of cruelty or malice. To achieve balance, all things in the wild must die to help life go on. Predators kept the prey animals in check to not overtax nature's bounty. This was the way of things. If these orcs followed the Huntress and Her Duty, did that mean their reputation for raiding, and violence was part of a larger purpose? Had Whitebrooke assigned ill intent where there been none?

The concept itched at her brain. Isolde mulled it over. This was a far cry from the tales that she was told when she was younger. The orcs were honorless and violent creatures. Having no actual contact with them, that assumptive imagery sat with her growing up. She remembered her knee-jerk reaction, born of ignorance at her first meeting with Tulok. Isolde shook her head and felt her face go flush at the embarrassing memory.

New experiences help us learn, said the voice in her head.

"...completely! Can you imagine!? I thought the custom had mostly died out! Isolde? Isolde, are you okay?" Tulok was talking to her. She wasn't certain for how long; She had been lost in her own head.

Shaking her brain out of the miasma of the mist, "Sorry, right – what?" she asked.

"Oral history! Everything that is the Baedd Gwyllt is completely within the oral tradition! They pass their stories and history down from generation to generation. Can you imagine the responsibility of bearing your people's history, word for word," Tulok said with a bit of awe and excitement.

Isolde smiled. In her head, she heard the voice say; *I am beginning to like this one.*

Shaking her head softly, "Let me guess, you volunteered your services to record their stories?"

Tulok's eyes widened in realization, "I ... right!" and ushered Tully forward to rejoin the orcs once again.

She gave him a half-smile and shook her head.

"He is a Sufa'cn," said a voice next to her.

Isolde blinked, slightly surprised that someone had not only ridden up next to her but had done so quietly. Looking to her right, she saw it was Blodwen. The Chieftain was watching the conversation between Tulok and the other two orcs he was riding alongside.

"Sufa'cn?" Isolde asked for clarification. She did not know the word.

Blodwen looked back down from her great height and stared at Isolde for a moment. Her expression did not speak of intimidation but a moment of thoughtful translation. The Orcish tongue did not have room for nuance. Things were, or they were not. Pretty was pretty, there was no *very* pretty or *beautiful*. It was just pretty. Some scholars thought that meant orcs were simple-minded people. This mistaken assumption led to many painful corrections upon, and sometimes permanent life lessons. It was the addition and inclusion of physical gesturing that gave the language inflection and nuance.

"A Sufa'cn is a learner, a knowledge gatherer," Blodwen said as she tapped her temple with two fingers and made a semicircle in the air, motioning toward everything around them.

Isolde nodded slowly. "Yes, he is a priest of his god, but he is also a librarian. He oversees physical knowledge," she looked over at Tulok, who was engaged in the conversation, "he finds enjoyment in it."

Blodwen raised an eyebrow. "Yet he wields the mace with a steady hand."

"Desert life is unforgiving to those who are unprepared," Isolde replied. It was something both Tulok and Safar had taught her.

Blodwen rode silently for a moment and then nodded her head with a sense of satisfaction. Isolde could feel the weight of her leug. She bore the mantle of leadership, and the level of trust and honor reminded Isolde of her mother. This is what a leader of people is supposed to be.

"We will be approaching our Wer'say," she motioned with an open hand. "The Wel'adr will want to see you both." When she said the name Wel'adr, there was a certain softness to the word, almost reverence. She raised her hand as she said this; her fingers were outstretched, and she slowly lowered her arm while moving her open palm in drifting circles – like the drifting of smoke.

Isolde nodded in understanding, but before she could pose a question, Blodwen continued.

"Many will not welcome you. The Civilized men..." Blodwen said the word with a hint of bitterness, "to the south created many orphaned young. Those young ones grew with hardened hearts that will not be melted by any words. Understand that the Wanderer's Blessing gives you a voice here, but do not expect it to be acknowledged by all. You will not come to harm ... but do not bring harm." Blodwen paused and scrutinized Isolde with narrowed eyes. "Your leug ... it is unsteady. Why?"

Isolde pursed her lips for a moment and thought about her words, "I chose the Lord Wanderer's Call instead of Leading my Council. The Lady's Heart is still balancing me."

Blodwen scoffed at the response. "Avalon does not decide for you. You tell the land Who You Are, and She will listen," the orc said with the weight of experience in her voice.

They rode in silence as Isolde took in those words. It sounded so simple. But was it? She half expected to hear the voice in her head say something, but there was only more silence.

"We are almost there. Prepare yourself, Wanderer Child. You will not change any hearts, but maybe a human touched by the gods will show them something new," Blodwen said, and then rode off ahead.

You tell the land Who You Are.

⸻

It was easy to get lost in the woodlands unless one knew where they were going. The group had left the main road behind some time ago and now they were traveling single file into a maze of huge pines and smaller streams. The wagon that was hauling the hunting game had disappeared, and she could not recall when it ceased being there. She noted some mounts were now bearing the wagon's cargo. The wagon had simply and quietly vanished.

Looking at the world around her, she could see the telltale signs of the giant wild boar: felled and partially uprooted trees, gnawed on roots, and hoofprints dotted the landscape. Anyone coming up here would know that this was a boar territory. This alone was incredibly dangerous. Realization slowly came to Isolde as she gazed at her surroundings. Unless you knew that these massive boars had been domesticated, following them into this territory was damn near impossible. Even their horses' hoofprints would easily be lost to the heavy steps of the boar. The clan was using the boar to cover their location and numbers. It was brilliant!

The last leg of their journey took them up into the lowland hills. Trees here seemed to be the thickest. The canopy above them blanketed the forest floor in darkness. It seemed like the evening was already upon them. It was not until the break in the woods did they see sunlight ahead. The trail opened up and soon they rode into a large clearing. Large A-frame tents with ornate gable boards bearing boars' heads occupied the area. These were designed for both comfort and quick tear down should the camp need to be mobilized.

On the far side of the clearing, nestled into the side of a hillock, was a large building. The roof and rafters seemed to be built up from the land itself. It was the only building of permanence here. The air was clean and clear, but the warmth of the sun was all around them. Except for dozens of red eyes looking at her and Tulok, it almost reminded Isolde of her father's old hunting parties.

Blodwen rode alongside her and Tulok. "Wel'adr will see you now – follow me."

Following the chieftain, they rode deeper into the camp. All eyes were on them.

"This place seems very temporary," Tulok said.

"Yes," Isolde said as she noticed the lack of permanent structures, "…but look at the ground. The way the grass grows and where it does not. They may be mobile, but the land looks to be frequented. This is not a place they just found, but it may be a place they have been using over time. It could be …"

There was the sound of water and whispers. Unheard and yet somehow loud enough to ring into her chest. Isolde gritted her teeth and closed her eyes, trying to drown the sound out. Touching her compass, she felt the volume slowly fade to a muffled song. Something of the Morpheum here, and it felt nearby. Very nearby. It also felt old. There was no sense of hunger or want. No nagging edge from nightmares. No, whatever was here, simply was. Isolde opened her eyes and refocused her eyes. She would have to ask about it.

Tulok watched his companion's reaction. It was rare that Isolde was caught without words. He scowled a little. "Is everything all right?" he asked.

Isolde nodded and glanced around, trying to pinpoint the sense of disquiet. Two scores of orcs surrounded them. Hunters, warriors, men, women, and children. The disquiet could come from anywhere. Or anyone.

"Visions and whispers. Just the land speaking to me." she offered with a slight smile.

Tulok took no comfort in the response.

Blodwen led them to a smaller tent that seemed to be no different from any of the others around it. Dismounting, she gave a small whistle and two orcs appeared from a nearby tent, both women. She spoke to them and motioned to their horses. They nodded and waited for Isolde and Tulok to dismount. Slowly approaching Tully and Duli, both waited for the horses to acknowledge them, whispering to each other. Their handling of the mounts seemed to be no different from any horse handler Isolde had seen before. The horses chuffed and snorted.

"His name is Tully and her's is Duli," Isolde offered. Both women gave a nod and added the horse's names into their introduction. Soon, firm but caring rubs and scratches were allowed, enabling Isolde and Tulok to hand over their reins.

Walking over to the tent, Blodwen opened the flap to let them enter.

On the floor inside was a small metal pot with deep red coals. There was no fire from the pot, but the coals maintained a comfortable warmth against the chill. There were a few sleeping furs and a small chest. From the ceiling supports hung strands of various bits of glass and metal chimes rough made from some sort of metal, possibly copper. On the other side of the firepit sat an older male orc. A weather-worn staff lay across his folded knees. His beard was a dirty white as was the hair on his head, but both were immaculately braided with various bits of metal or beads worked in. His shoulders were slumped, and his head drooped forward slightly. Isolde had seen orcs over her lifetime, but this one almost seemed ancient. Once proud tusks were slightly rounded and skin on his face hung loosely around his jowls. If Tulok was around 40 years old, this one may have been well over a hundred. Beneath his right eye was a deep greenish mark that could almost be mistaken for a bruise. Had he been younger, it might have looked like a long crescent over his eye – but now a less than an elegant mark of an aged face.

The older orc looked at Blodwen and nodded his head. She gestured to Isolde and Tulok. "The Wel'adr does not speak the Trader's Tongue. You will need to translate for your companion," she said to Tulok. With that, Blodwen stepped out of the tent and the light dimmed inside once again. While there was some light to see, both travelers were thankful for the warmth of the fire.

The Wel'adr looked at each of them as they stood in the tent and finally spoke and motioned at Tulok with a smile.

"He said we should sit. Watching others stand is tiring," Tulok said with a bit of a smile.

Returning the gesture with a smile, "Thank you honored Wel'adr," Isolde said as she tried her best to repeat the hand gesture that Blodwen had used. She could feel the leug emanating off of him. Like Blodwen, he was a leader, but the volume of his leug was different from the chieftain.

The Wel'adr raised an eyebrow and spoke again. "He says the effort is appreciated, but unnecessary. Your ways are not ours, but it is good to see such from one of your kind. It will be remembered."

"Thank you for the kindness, Wel'adr. We know your time is precious, so we do not wish to waste your hospitality. Your chieftain said that you had wished to see us, as we wanted to see you?"

"Blodwen sent word that you were seeking a criminal from across the sea. His lack of leug would have given him away. He has not passed through here, which means he took passage along the coast past our territory. If he could pass himself as one of the Folk, we would have seen him. We have an agreement with them to provide safe passage in our lands. While we care not for this man, we care for what he represents. Tell me, Wanderer's Child, have you dreamed of black roots?" Tulok translated and looked over at Isolde.

Isolde nodded her head. "Black roots that surge out from a poisoned tree. They spread like wildfire, corrupting everything in their path until there is only darkness."

He slowly nodded his head and spoke to Tulok. Tulok reached into his coat and pulled out a small tube. From it, he produced the rolled-up drawing he had received and explained its origin. The older orc looked at the crazed drawing with a scrutinous eye and two conversed back and forth.

"He is both amazed and worried that even the Eyes of the Radiant Lord could see such from the desert," Tulok said.

The Wel'adr continued, "While we cannot help you find your criminal, we can provide safe passage to the Free People that roam to the south of us. They may offer more information on who you seek. There are very few ports along the eastern side of the continent, and where those are they may have seen more."

The orc then turned toward Tulok. He nodded and listened to the elder intently. Standing up, Tulok turned to Isolde. "He has asked me to retrieve a ... looking glass, I believe, is the word he used ... from one of his attendants. I will be right back. He also said that you are safe here, and if there is any danger, he is sure you will protect him."

Isolde looked to the older orc, who was smiling and nodding his head. Tulok gave a slight bow and headed out.

The tent was filled with light for a moment and then faded into shadows. As the dimness returned, the older orc's smile disappeared. His posture straightened and something more formal replaced concern in his eyes. More serious. The sagging bruise became a more refined crescent birthmark. He spoke again, but this time in Avalonian.

"Your companion is worthy of his blood, but he is not of this island. What I say to you is not because I trust you as a human. I do not." he paused and eyed Isolde. "But I trust you as the Child of the Lord Wanderer and an Avalonian. Blodwen said that you were attacked by a Weeping One that drew the attention of the Corrupted. This has not been the only instance; we have dealt with Corruption and its effect on our people for the past two weeks. The Dying Sickness – black blood, a death without truly dying. Her scouts to the south have reported that the Free People have been fighting this threat for the past week as well."

The quick change in both his demeanor and the seriousness of his tone caught Isolde off guard. She considered his words.

"Have there been any orc or human survivors to these attacks?" she asked.

"Define ... survivors. Have some lived after their encounters? Yes. Those who survive an attack by the Corrupted take ill, but eventually, they die. They all die ... but they come back. Unnatural, unliving creatures of foul flesh and black veins. These soulless creatures seek to corrupt others, and it does not matter what they are orc, elf, man or beast." He paused, closing his eyes, and spoke softly with his head raised. A prayer for the dead? Opening his eyes, he stared at Isolde as if weighing her, but there was something else. The weight of his eyes was not of scrutiny, but secrecy. "Do you understand what this means, Wanderer's Child?"

"Their ... their souls ..." Isolde frowned, trying to piece the puzzle together. "No, wait, if they die ... no, oh no ... no no ..." She blanched as the reality of it all washed over her. To die on the island was a blessing because the magic tied to one's soul would go on to the next life, back into the cycle. If this corruption was destroying those connections ... severing those magics ... severing those souls. She shook her head.

The older orc continued, "Your criminal may be tied to what is happening or perhaps even the cause of what will happen. The Triskele may be at war, but there is another hand in the mix. This is not their doing. Blodwen has received reports that there is more of this black-rooted corruption to the south and it is making its way to ... Mynydd Mawr."

The look in the older orc's eyes spoke volumes to Isolde. Mynydd Mawr was at the center of the continent and it represented many things to the whole of the island. Stories said it was a place of treaties, ancient magics, or the home of magnificent creatures of untold power. It was the seat of the Lady's Heart. Regardless of whatever it was, if the corruption was heading toward the mountain, it could spell disaster for them all.

"The corruption cannot be allowed to read Mynydd Mawr, Witness." his deep red eyes locked on Isolde's.

She nodded solemnly. "I understand."

He nodded curtly in response. "We received information that these creatures are amassing to the east and making their way to the south. We tried to share words with the Free People, but they do not wish to hear the words of the Orckind." he chuckled bitterly. "Prideful creatures." Shaking his head, he looked at her once more. "Take this information and have them make ready for war. If we discover your little man, he will be *dealt* with." The grimness was heavy in his voice.

"We can leave as soon as Tulok returns. We just need a guide back through the forest," Isolde said, standing.

"You need not worry about your companion. We will take care of him when he returns," the Wel'adr said.

"Wait, what?" Isolde's eyes narrowed at the orc. "What do you mean?"

The older orc unfolded himself from his seated position and stood. His head brushed the roof of the tent. Gone was the weariness of old age. Sagging shoulders stood wide and strong. His posture was not threatening, but primal. This was not the hot, quick violence of the Gurkh; this was an ancient soul-fire akin to the hot coals that forged swords – he was a furnace of controlled rage.

"Your friend is a danger to the people and this Island, Wanderer's Child," he spoke firmly. "He has been drinking the black leaf tea, so he does not dream. I could see the stains on his teeth when he spoke. His body will eventually become tolerant of it, rendering its effect useless." Isolde raised a hand in protest. He ignored her. "You have him wearing a sleeping charm, and it is failing, or have you not noticed it?"

"Apologies, Elder." Isolde offered, stumbling over words and traditions that might make this right. "We should not be here long enough for it to become an issue for your people?" She could feel a sense of danger rise.

"There is a war of the Triskele Trinity on the lands. A battle for power. A fourth hand ... unknown to these shores ... lays corruption in the very soil. The fey-born are reacting violently, becoming corrupted themselves." he glared down at Isolde. "The very magic of the Island itself falls to illness and disease. Nightmares of the Morpheum will take this opportunity to make their way into the world of flesh. Your foreign companion ... with his soul open to the powers of the Radiant Lord and beyond ... is a doorway for them." His eyes locked on Isolde's.

"Orckind will tend to its own, Island Born or Sun Skin," he stared down with tired but unyielding red eyes.

Isolde shook her head and stepped back, away from the Elder. She turned to push the tent flap open. Half a dozen spears pointed their sharpened tips at her chest.

"Believe me, Wanderer's Child – it is for the best for all of us," the Wel'adr said softly.

—

Following the directions that the older orc had given him, Tulok made his way through the various tents until he saw the one with the gray feather hanging over the opening. Next to the entrance was a guard. "The Wel'adr has asked to retrieve his black seeing glass. Are you Du'etgan?"

The guard nodded his head. "The Wel'adr's space is sacred. You will need to remove that before you can enter," he pointed to the small silver bell on Tulok's wrist. "Human charms have no place here. I cannot let you enter while you wear that. Nothing of harm will come to it. You have my word."

Tulok sighed, but nodded his head and untied the little bracelet. The beautiful silk cord looked frayed, and the silver bell was dull and tarnished. He thought about the last few days and did not think he could have gotten it that dirty. He made a note to clean it before he put it back on. Handing it off, the guard placed it in a small pouch on his belt. "You may enter brethren."

Du'etgan opened the flap to the dark tent and Tulok stepped inside. The area was mostly bare except for a large, dark pool of water.

Looking around the room, there was no sign of a black looking glass. "Du'etgan, I do not see a black looking glass," Tulok called out as he looked about the area.

"It rests at the bottom of the pool. You will need to reach in and pull it out. It is only an arm's length away," the other said.

While the other orc could not see him, Tulok rolled his eyes. He understood mysticism, but nothing on Avalon ever seemed to make sense. Looking glasses at the bottom of pools of water. Pools of water inside tents ... with guards. He shook his head and slowly lowered himself down to the edge of the pool. Kneeling before the black pool, Tulok stared deeply. The water gently lapped at the edges of the earth, – but curiously did not show his reflection. A thought of familiarity reached from the back of his mind.

"You know, this almost reminds me of a dream…"

Before he could finish the sentence, Du'etgan shoved Tulok forward into the pool. The priest fell into the darkness and was gone.

"Good hunting brethren. May your instinct guide your way," the orc said and walked out of the tent to take up his position outside once again.

The dark pool continued to lap quietly as if nothing had happened.

Chapter 42

He stopped screaming after he realized he was not, in fact, falling. It took several minutes to realize this as he just hovered in the twilight air. He took a breath and stared into the dim shades of blue and black all around him.

He had been falling-floating with arms outstretched, and now he just sort of hung there in midair. Even with his natural ability to see in the darkness of night, he still felt blinded here. While he had been on Avalon, he avoided using any of the divine gifts of the Radiant Lord for fear of causing any issue with the Divine of the island. Yet, it was his charge to bring light to the darkness, and frankly the Powers that Be would have to accept a little light. Drawing his floating arms close to his chest, he cupped his hands together. Closing his eyes, he began the small prayer to draw the light of the Radiant Lord into his hand.

"Hey, sir? That might be bad," said a youthful voice.

Tulok opened his eyes, and in front of him was a young boy. The boy looked up at the priest curiously with bright blue eyes, from under a mop of dirty blonde hair. He then realized that he was no longer floating, but standing on solid ground. The boy was carrying a thin tree branch that he let rest on his shoulder. Gone was the black-blue dimness and instead was a grassy knoll with a massive oak tree that stood in the way of a setting sun. It filled Tulok with a sense of relief that became fleeting when he realized the sun in the sky was not his Lord. It was not real, yet the world expanded into view. All around him, a mixture of hills and distant mist-filled woods replaced the darkness. While it was better than the darkness, none of it felt … right.

"Memories. That's where it all starts," the boy said aloud to no one in particular. He had taken the stick and nudged a rock out of the soil. "Memories, visions, truths and trials. Everything starts here," the boy continued on. This time, he looked up at the orc and looked around, almost conspiratorially. Satisfied, he leaned slightly towards Tulok and loudly whispered, "I'm not really supposed to be here, but you looked lost. You probably want to go that way," he said, pointing past the tree.

Tulok looked in the direction and saw the beginnings of a trail that veered out of sight. "Where are we?" he asked. When there was no answer, he looked back down and found that the boy was gone. Looking all around, there was no trace of the child. Resigned that the child was no longer there, he stared at the sunset that hovered at the horizon line. It was a slight comfort, but it felt hollow. In fact, he felt hollow.

Something inside of him churned. Someone or something was watching him. He remembered that feeling; a feeling of being watched by something along a lakeside. Something he was told not to stare too long at. His pulse quickened, and his breathing became deeper. He turned his head slowly to the side. There was something in the darkened distance ... no, several things. He felt his rage well up. It was quicker than it had ever been. He wanted to fight. No, he NEEDED to face what was coming.

Do not linger, boy – MOVE!

It was like a cold slap in the face. There was no body attached to the voice, but he felt its sincerity. He had to run! This was not the time. Gathering himself, he broke into a run – he had to put distance between himself and them.

—

The boy watched from the hilltop as Tulok ran in the distance. He leaned against his stick with a smile.

Another figure stood beside the boy. Though the exact definitions were hard to discern, as she ... yes, she was she at the moment ... was shrouded within the mist. What stood out was the long animal skull that she wore as a helm. The golden glow from her eyes illuminated the eye sockets with a grim eeriness. Neither figure spoke a word as they watched the orc vanish in the distance. They spoke without speaking.

She: This is not your place

He: This is not fair

She: It is not your place to decide what is … fair

He: Perhaps, but the scales are not evenly matched where He is concerned

She: Correct. Because He is part of the imbalance

He: Are you going to correct this imbalance?

She: It may correct itself

He: What of the war?

She: He will decide his place. Do not interfere

The female figure faded back into the mists, leaving the boy alone. The boy said nothing and continued to watch the mist from afar as it surged forward. His blue eyes could see the many nameless things within the mist, none of them kind. Standing up, he slid the stick into the back of his shirt, and then leapt into the air. The sound of hawk's wings flapped overhead in the distance.

—

He was tired, and he could feel his resolve ebbing away. In the desert, you trained your body to go without water or food for three or four days as a survival practice. It had been a week since he had anything, at least he thought it was a week. There was no night or day; the perpetual dusk did not show time passing. He had not slept because his body was never that kind of tired. Instead, he rested to give his legs a break, but he never felt the heavy draw of sleep across his eyes. They said staying awake for over three days could cause one to hallucinate or even momentary bouts of madness. He wondered if he was going insane.

Without sleep or a Divine presence to rely on, he had found a different way to measure his stay in this place. He repeated the verses and chants to the Radiant Lord in his mind. He knew how long each sermon, song, and chant ran so they could be measured. With each sermon or chant, he made a small tear on his sleeve. These tiny tears allowed him to count hours and days. By measuring time, he found a sense of control, a sense of sanity in the Mor...

He knew where he was, but refused to say it aloud, much less in his head.

The landscape had slowly changed a few days earlier. Gone were the rolling hills and oak trees. Instead, there were sparse pines along rough and rocky terrain. A few days after that, sand replaced the terrain and leveled out. The flat sands became familiar rolling dunes. This had been going close to eight days when he found himself in the desert again. A shiver of a memory ran down his spine. A memory of a dream or a dream of a memory? Whatever it was, as thirsty as he felt himself become, he feared seeing the water again.

The cry of a bird broke the sound of the wind in the distance. Moving toward a tall dune, he watched the skies. The hawk screeched again. The sound rolled over the dunes and shook the sand. Narrowing his eyes, he saw the hawk circling something. The bird was smaller than the reddish hawks of Setesh, but he had to remember he was not in Setesh. Tulok looked back at the darkened horizon. He had not seen or felt the mist in some time. He knew it was not gone. THEY were not gone. Making his way forward, he carefully ascended the dune and looked across the landscape to see what the bird had been circling.

Sandstone had ripped its way free of the dunes. The more he looked at it looked like a building of some sort. However, there was something else about it. It felt warm. Alive even! Narrowing his eyes, he could see the light coming out of a doorway. The light was richer than the muted sunset that he had become accustomed to. The light felt ... real. It felt, Divine! Realization flooded his mind as he launched himself forward down the dune. It was a foolish move as soon as his mind caught up with his body. The soft dune gave way to his massive form, and he felt his body slide into the surrounding sand. He immediately froze, his nose just above the surface. The right side of his body was submerged in the loose sand – he could not move and tried to breathe slowly with shallow breaths. He was alone and there was no vegetation. Any movement – even a deep breath could cause him to sink further. Looking across at the sandstone structure, he watched as the light ... the Real light ... fade away slowly. It was not a good death.

The wind picked up around him, and beyond the stone structure, he saw the permanent sunset become obscured by the sand storm moving towards him. He let out a small laugh of desperation and felt his body sink another few inches. He was going to be swallowed up by the ground or he was going to be buried in the storm. There was no winning in this ... or was there? He pondered for a moment as the storm raged closer. If he spread himself out wide, the storm would pull the looser sand up, freeing him or burying him more.

It was a stupid idea. But stupid was better than doing nothing. He stared at the fading strands of Real light just before the storm moved over the structure. He would need to keep his eyes closed for what was next so forcing a sense of direction in his mind was his only hope.

He had been caught in sandstorms before. They stung, were suffocating and dangerous. This one burned. Like a thousand tiny molten rocks raced across his skin, tearing into his flesh. Getting bitten by a sun viper would have been nicer. The pain threw him off for a moment, but with pain there was focus. With a roar, he pulled himself forward with as much strength as he could. He felt the pull of the soft sand release its grasp on him as he struggled forward. It felt like he was mostly out of the sinkhole, but the storm continued to blow sand on top of him. Using every part of his body, he tried to surge forward and pull himself up and out. There never seemed to be an end. His already tired muscles burned and ached with the pain of unrest. The howl of the storm was all around him. He could not give in. He needed to reach that light – the Real light of the Radiant Lord.

"Is it dead?" said a voice above him.

"I certainly hope not! Why do you always think of the direst of things, Lalum? He looks to be only a child. Do you wish a child dead?" said another voice, offense running high in their voice.

"I was not the one who caused the storm, or are you blaming the will of the Divine upon me? This child could have been a sacrifice to the Red Lord, or perhaps he murdered his kin and was cast out. Am I to blame for their justice, Kault?" Lalum pleaded with indignation in their tone.

"Are you citing Justice to me, Lalum?" said Kault. The edge was obvious in their voice.

It hurt to open his eyes, much less move, but at that moment Tulok wanted nothing more than to yell at these two beings to pay attention to the dying person in front of them. With the last bit of strength in his body, he flexed his fingers upward and opened his eyes.

The two creatures that stood above him were large, probably as tall as he was, maybe taller. One bore a sharp expression as they stared at their companion. Even with the sandstorm still blowing, their features were quite visible. While their scales and ridges bore light sand-colored tones, the cream-like tone that shone like silver. The one called Kault shook their head and looked back down to Tulok. "You see – he's still alive and wanting help. Now give us a hand!"

"Fine," said the one called Lalum. Their features were in stark contrast to Kault's – darker hues of greens and browns. Their ridges were more subtle than the other, no sharp ridges, just a certain level of smoothness to their scales. Lalum and Kault reached forward and grasped Tulok's hands and pulled him up just as another deep gust of sand blew into his face. Stumbling back, he fell on his rear and landed on a stone seat.

The stand storm was gone, the Anuket and the Sobekite sat across from him as a fire burned in a small pit before them. These were not his teachers. They were not back home in Setesh. These were things wearing the skin of memories.

His memories. He wanted to be angry, but the familiarity was probably a kindness. Instead of saying anything, he looked around the area. Behind the two figures was the sandstone outcropping from earlier. And the doorway. The light was almost gone, fading away impossibly slowly.

"You do not belong here, Sun Child. This place is not yours," Kault said. The voice was not the one from earlier. This was deeper and older and demanded the orc's attention.

"This is only one part, and it was pleasant in comparison," said Lalum-not-Lalum. This one was … sinister, but not threatening. The voice was like a viper who had spread out their hood. It advised caution because they were dangerous.

"We offer you a choice," said the Kault. "Leave our place, our land, and you will be home again. You will find the kiss of your Radiant god above your head, and the breath of the Real in your lungs. If you leave now, you will be free of your bond to the island and the land."

"If you choose to stay," said Lalum-not-Lalum, "There will be pain … madness, and death. That death could be yours, your enemies, or you will become the instrument of death who brings destruction to all those around you."

Tulok frowned, "So my choices are to leave or die?"

"Well, I said your enemies, so you could not die," said the Lalum, "However, that is up to you. If you possess the Will, the mental fortitude for what comes next … you *may* survive, or you will kill all those whom you care for." There was a sincerity to the tone despite the sinister nature of the voice.

Tulok looked at the tiny beam of light that became smaller and smaller. Closing his eyes, he reached out and felt its distant warmth. For a moment, he could feel the true warmth of the sun, smell the spice in the air. Home. He looked down at himself. The little tears that accounted for days and time had gone away. The sandstorm had ripped new holes, wider holes everywhere. Tracking time was no longer an option. That was a lesson. Time was meaningless here. The tattered remains of his clothing barely covered him. Isolde would have made some remark at the state of his being. It would not have been ill-intended. It was just her way. He looked at Kault. They had promised freedom from all bonds to the island. He closed his eyes and rolled it in his mind. For a culture that prided itself on word-bonds, that was a meaningful statement. It was not something one could freely give unless this being had the power to do so. Its voice alone sounded old and powerful – perhaps they could, but why?

You do not belong here, Sun Child. This place is not yours.

They did not want him here. Was it because of his devotion to the Radiant Lord or something else? Was he a walking offense in Their eyes? No – it had to be more than that. In the real world, he was a shadow, a non-entity in the eyes of those who called the island home because he bore no weight to his name. Their ways were not his. He was not beholden to any of them, mortal or God.

Except for Isolde…

They had shared an oath of silence. An oath that would be released if he left now. Did they want the oath to be undone? Or, did they NEED it to be undone? What did they need to be released? That thought was dangerous in his mind, but it was enough to focus his mind on the choice at hand. With that, his decision had been made.

He opened his eyes and watched the beam of light fade. For a moment it did nothing, and then slowly into nothingness, along with all the senses of home.

"You have made your choice," both creatures intoned.

"May I ask a question?" Tulok asked as he rose from his seat.

"You may pose one question to each of us," they both said in unison.

To the Kault, "Which direction do I head next?"

The Kault pointed a long taloned finger toward the permanent sunset, "Walk until you need to swim."

To Lalum-not-Lalum, "If that was a way back to Setesh, how does this place transverse to the land of my Lord?"

Lalum-not-Lalum smiled. "What are mirages, but dreams of

hope built by the desperate and dying?"

Tulok nodded his head and turned toward the sun, but paused in mid-step. Mirages ... they said mirages. Implications and stories rushed to the forefront of his mind, along with an icy shiver that ran deep into his soul. There were stories of those who ran to mirages in desperation of water and shelter, only to never be seen again. How many of those desperate souls found their way here? He looked back at the two figures. They and the sandstone outcropping were gone.

Turning away, he continued to walk forward. Mirages would haunt him for the rest of his life.

Chapter 43

Bioluminescent fungi glowed on the walls of the passage. Huge roots sprung from the ceiling, evidence of the hearty trees that grew above them on the surface. Most of the lighted mushroom-like spores were green, some dark, some vibrant. They passed a quiet pool that sported a brilliant blue light along the center of its surface. Along one section of the wall, tiny red dots of glowing red mushrooms sprouted, their caps seeming to form tiny cups, ready to catch whatever might fall into them.

Caverns and Caves. What was the fascination with Druids and caves? Arman thought to himself as he trudged diligently behind the tall figure of Phaendar.

Nebiyre had insisted on finding and using the Temple of Silence for her workings, a lost series of caves buried within an ancient ruin beneath the burning sands of the Seteshi desert. The history he had discovered there had been brilliant. While the sound stones that grew there were a danger to the whole of Sanctum those had not been the reason Arman had sought Ahsal to begin with. The desert-born druidess of the sands had thought that the stones would lend power to their spell crafting, and increase their chances of success.

A success that was now one step closer to fulfillment.

He cast his gaze toward the ceiling and watched as a series of lights moved and dance in the darkness. They seemed to drop from the ceiling and followed in Phaendar's wake. Arman frowned and shuddered.

"You do not care for the island, do you, Arman?" Phaendar's silvery voice asked. No longer touched by the power of the Divine, it floated delicately on the cool air and in Arman's ears.

"I am a creature of the Sands, Phaendar. You know that," he replied.

"Crafted from its very bones," the Elven sage smirked and nodded. They carried in their hands the small box that Arman had gifted to them earlier, which contained the desert apples from Setesh. Their long fingers gently caressed the box's surface as they walked.

"So it is said," Arman agreed. He pulled his coat closed against the damp. "Just as your Folk were born of the blood of your island ... or so the story goes."

Phaendar's lips twitched slightly. "So the story goes," they nodded. Their strange eyes slid over to the smaller man. "Who is the patron of your people again? I can't seem to recall," they asked.

Arman ground his teeth. Phaendar knew as well as Arman that no one knew where the Vidria had originally hailed from. Like the Folk, the Anuket, the Sobekites, and a few of the other peoples of Sanctum, the Vidria seemed to have emerged from the bones of the earth here. The legends of the origins of the Vidria were scarce and scattered. Some stories implied they were once like other dwarven people, but something had caused them to drastically diverge in appearance and talent. Other stories said they suffered a curse, placed on them by a shunned deity. Arman's favorite, however, and the one he gave the most weight to, was that the Vidria were a self-made people, born from the first spark of true creativity in the deep deserts of Setesh. Whatever the truth of the matter, it, like Ahsal, was buried in the annals of history. And records from that period were scant at best.

Instinctively Arman wanted to tell Phaendar where he could push off to, but he needed the mad sage's magics.

"One of the better-kept secrets of Sanctum," he replied to Phaendar.

The Sage smirked to themselves and continued to walk through the damp and dark.

The narrow passage widened into an enormous cavern. It

was drier here, though such a statement depended on one's perspective. It was still miserably cold and damp as far as Arman was concerned.

Someone had well-crafted the cavern, shaped with the hands of master artisans and laborers. This was not the work of magic, but of skill.

And love.

The rough-hewn walls had been worn smooth over millennia. Ornate carvings and intricate murals decorated the surfaces. Stained glass lanterns hung from golden chains, their light glowing from a smokeless fire contained within. It was warm here.

The Vidria dwarf narrowed his eyes suspiciously and searched the area for the source of heat. The island did not possess an active volcano that he remembered, but perhaps there were water tunnels that carried heated water from geothermal vents on the coastline? Listening carefully, Arman thought for a moment he heard what sounded like breathing. However, if he could hear something breathing, it would either have to be very close … or very large. Arman shook his head and set aside the natural curiosity of his people for such things. That was not why he was here.

A richly colored tapestry caught his eyes. The tapestry spanned the length of one wall and must have been at least eight feet tall. The figures on the ancient woven item depicted an ancient Avalonian knight in green armor, riding a huge white stag. At his feet was a pack of white hunting hounds with red ears. Before them, another knight knelt in what appeared to be humble supplication. In the knight's outstretched hands was an ornately decorated ax. At the side of the kneeling knight stood a woman with her gaze averted to the spectacle. Embroidered around the hem of the woman's green dress were white hounds. A fine silver chain bound her wrists. The trees in the scene were woven in autumn colors. Golden coins adorned the corners of the tapestry.

The Jailer.

Arman's breath caught in his throat for a moment, in the realization that what he was gazing upon might well be as old as the map in Ahsal. A remnant of the Passage. With renewed interest, he carefully cast his eyes about once more. What other ancient trappings had this madman secreted away here?

"I see you have noted my prize," Phaendar commented and walked to a large table that sat along one wall of the cavern. It was a heavily carved thing, worn smooth from centuries of use. They set the box gently on the work surface.

"It is a notable item of some worth," Arman nodded in appreciation. Placing his hands behind his back, he stepped across the room to examine the ancient weaving more closely.

"There are few depictions of Him before the Passage that remain," Phaendar offered. "That one is often forgotten."

Arman leaned closer, careful not to touch the tapestry. "I thought He was the Keeper of the Dead?" his green eyes noted the intricate designs woven into the armor pieces of the Knight. Branches, boughs, and chains were woven throughout the motif.

"One of His many duties," Phaendar replied. "Upon arrival here, He and the Grim Lord of Setesh battled for governance over the Underworld. The Jailer ... Of course ... won the battle, leaving the Jackal God to play Ferryman once more."

Arman looked up at the Knight on the Stag and then to the kneeling figure offering him the ax. The ax seemed to bear the same design on it that was present on the mounted Knight's green armor. The kneeling figure appeared smaller in stature than either the mounted figure or the woman behind them. A trick of perspective? Perhaps. Arman looked closer. The armor on the kneeling figure appeared to be shaped for a woman. A female knight? His brow furrowed, and he looked between the kneeling figure and the woman behind them. White Hounds danced around the hem of Her dress. They matched the hounds that accompanied the Knight on the Stag. They were bound together ... somehow.

"Indeed?" Arman asked. He had heard this story before. How

349

the Avalonian and Seteshi Lords of the Dead had diced for which of them would rule the Underworld in the new Realm. The Jailer had won the competition, perhaps through the use of weighted dice, or bribery of Mistress Fortune. To appease the Radiant Lord and prevent War in the Heavens, The Jailer had granted the Grim Lord the right of Judgement, and He would stand as Keeper. "My people remember it a little differently."

"Of course, you do," Phaendar replied coolly.

Who are you? Arman asked himself as he stepped back from the imagery. *Who WERE you?* Sighing deeply, Arman turned away from the ancient history on the wall and faced Phaendar once more.

On the wall behind the sage hung the skull of a mighty stag. Carved into the bone was a pattern of coins and chains. Antlers sporting over 20 points sprouted from the forehead of the beast. A Monarch.

A wave of awe washed over Arman as he gazed at the trophy. He averted his eyes instinctively.

Phaendar glanced over their shoulder at the figure of power and smiled slyly. They turned to gently caress the skull, "I did not please The Stag Lord when we brought this one down in Our Lord's Name." Long fingers gently traced the carved chains on the bone. "This was the last time the Triskele bowed to Him," they whispered softly. "Now ... now we will bring Him a greater sacrifice to turn the tides ... "they giggled.

Arman shuddered and swallowed hard. The inner workings of the magic and politics of Avalon were not something he had ever wished to become involved with. Ancient, eternal creatures walking the mortal Realm, governing without governing. The Druids and Sages were like otherworldly avatars of the Divine themselves, standing in halls, seated in Libraries, observing negotiations, nudging their people this way and that in some strange dance that only they could hear the music to. It was unnatural. He far preferred the direct brutality of the Seteshi Desert over this. Whatever this was. He shuddered.

"Let us begin," Phaendar instructed Arman.

The smaller man nodded and stepped up to the table. He reached into his belt pouch and produced the box that had contained the horse-headed vase and the scarab amulet previously. As he did so, Phaendar turned to their left and opened a small, iron-bound chest. They whispered some words that Arman did not recognize, an incantation. Whether religious or honorific, he could not be certain. Then the long-fingered elf reached into its dark depths and removed a series of items. A silver chalice, a knife of black glass, a vial of what appeared to be salt, and a small silver chain.

"Remove the items from the box and place them on the table," Phaendar instructed.

As before, Arman called on the magic of his people to open the small stone box. He carefully lifted the vase and the amulet from their resting places and set them on the work surface.

The ancient elf closed their almond-shaped eyes and stood over the items. In one hand they held the silver chalice, in the other, the dagger of black glass. A pile of salt lay in the center of the table.

In a language known only to the ancients of the Island, Phaendar spoke. At first, the strange, almost sing-song cadence sounded like a poem or a song. Then the measure changed, and the tones became harsher and more guttural. With every breath, the light in the room seemed to dim. For a moment, Arman thought the strange breathing sound he had heard earlier seemed louder. As the light from the lanterns faded, the dagger in Phaendar's hand glowed. Phaendar turned their head upward toward the ceiling, their voice becoming deeper and more urgent. With a fluid movement, they placed the silver chalice in the center of the salt and reached for the amulet. Long fingers wrapped around the item. Their eyes closed, they lifted the amulet to the ceiling, palm facing toward the heavens. Then slammed their hand down over the chalice, forcing the amulet into its cup.

Then the ancient being lifted their hand and placed the blade of the glass dagger to their exposed flesh, drawing it quickly across their skin. Phaendar squeezed the blood over the amulet and into the chalice.

Three words echoed through the cavern that Arman understood.

"I sever thee!"

In the space of a heartbeat, the lights extinguished in the cavern. Even the strange glow from the mushrooms and lichen vanished. They were left in utter darkness.

From the chalice, a soft glowing light emerged. Like a tiny waterfall, flowing upward from the chalice toward the ceiling. Phaendar leaned forward and inhaled deeply, drawing the essence into their lungs.

Phaendar paused.

Their body shuddered.

They leaned forward and braced themselves on the edge of the table with their bloodied hand.

Then the Elven Sage straightened themself and reached for the horse-headed vase. Pulling the head off of the figure, it opened to reveal the seamlessly master-crafted prison. They leaned forward and exhaled forcefully, expelling the glowing substance into the container. Phaendar quickly seated the head back onto the jar and shoved it across the table toward Arman.

"Seal it. Quickly!" Phaendar panted.

Arman's fingers swiftly moved around the edge of the separation, and he willed the stone shapes to unite and seal closed. The vase glowed golden for a moment and then was dark.

Phaendar's deep breathing sounded in the darkness that surrounded them. Slowly, the lights in the lanterns illuminated the cavern once more. Around them, the once luminescent biomes lay desiccated and dead. Gray ash where once there was life.

Phaendar leaned on the table, bracing themself and breathing heavily. Tiny droplets of blood sweat beaded their pale brow.

"It is done," they whispered.

Arman nodded, wondering at the vase for a moment, then silently placed it back into its stonework box and sealed it shut once more.

"Where do you go now?" Phaendar asked.

Arman carefully tucked the box away into his pouch. "Litharge. I am seeking a Skald."

Phaendar chuckled darkly and drew a hand across their lips, wiping blood from them there. "The Runegiver's blood?"

Arman nodded.

"It's never been done," the Sage commented. "Severing an OathMaker from His Service."

"I have been told that before," Arman replied, securing his prize. He gazed around the cavern once more as the lights slowly returned. Niches filled with immeasurable wealth. Finely woven rugs on carved stone floors. Ancient tomes filled with a history long forgotten. Gemstones, jewelry, and finery. A veritable horde of opulence and riches.

Far beneath the stone worked cavern, something ancient shifted and rumbled.

Chapter 44

Ashes and mud. The gritty soil slipped between her fingers and slid to the ground. What had been filled with dark earth and loam the night before was now gray and lifeless. The Folk farmer knelt and placed her hands deep into the dirt seeking the depth of the blight that had befallen her lands. It seemed without end.

She closed her emerald green eyes and whispered a prayer to the Mother, the Lady of the Island. The creator of her people and keeper of the lands. Her fingers stretched in the blighted soil, reaching for the connection that tied her people to the magic of Avalon.

Dry earth and death answered her.

Her eyes flew open as she searched her fields. Corn and beans that would be needed to feed the people for the coming Winter lay withered and twisted for as far as she could see. The connection to the land that the Mother gifted them with was simply … gone.

~~~

In this place, this Realm, something logical was often seen as inane. It would be logical that the sun would eventually set, or that the more you moved toward it, the closer it should become. Yet, neither of these things happened. As instructed, Tulok followed the path of the false sun, rested for a few hours, and then continued. The sea of sand and its dunes slowly leveled out as he journeyed toward the only light on the twilight canvas. There was no counting rest stops or time spent walking. There were a few times he ran himself ragged, body falling into the sand looking up at the frozen darkness above. It did little to change the distance or bring him any closer to where he was supposed to go. Wherever that was.

Since his encounter at the sandstone, he had seen no one else. Thankfully, there had been no scorpions, vipers, or other terrors of the desert. The only danger seemed to be behind him. On the horizon, he could see a dust storm that looked at least a mile wide. When he first saw it, he pushed himself hard to put distance between himself and it. However, like the sun, it was stationary, a fixture of the land. Though sometimes he heard the rumble in the distance, it never left the horizon line. Other than this, it was only him and his thoughts. If it were not for the circumstances, this would have been the perfect place to read.

He smiled to himself.

His face felt a little sore. How long had it been since he smiled or laughed? He opened his mouth wide and moved his jaw from side to side. He stopped and stretched himself out. Sore muscles screamed and bones popped. Sitting down in the soft sand, he looked at his feet. The remains of his boots were long gone. He had tied the remaining portions of the soles to his feet to form a crude set of sandals. His toenails looked dangerously long. His fingernails bore a slight edge to them. He ran his hand over his head and felt the light tuft of hair growing. He could not recall the last time he groomed himself. For Priests, there was a sense of meticulous control over your appearance. Priests were supposed to be living examples of the Radiant Lord's greatness. He had to work especially hard at it. His nails needed to be trimmed, his head shaved in supplication, his beard became a mark of wisdom, age, and station. He was none of these things.

He didn't know what he was supposed to be anymore. The chants and hymns were still there in his mind, but they were not sung or spoken aloud as often. He was no longer a priest ... at least he was not a priest .. here. He was a traveler, a survivor, but to what purpose. Was survival his only purpose?

"Isolde would know," he said to the air.

What would she do in his place?

Well, for starters, she probably would know why she was here. She would know how she got here and know where she was going.

He sighed.

The telltale throb in his legs had ceased, which meant his rest was over. Closing his eyes and giving his body one last stretch, he looked up to the false sun, only to find it changed.

Quickly standing up, he looked all around. The flat desert was shrouded in darkness; the sun had risen above the horizon and hung in the sky with a sickly yellow color. It was brighter than previously, but not bright like the true sun. It lit the sky all around it in a sickly greenish hue. Wispy clouds had formed as well, almost like cobwebs in the sky. Their presence gave the sickly sun an unsettling look. With the extra light, he could see ... trees.

These were not the verdant forests of Avalon. The ground was not lush with grass and dark soil. No, this was something entirely different. The land was brown, damp, muddy – in the distance, he could see small pools of water. Trees were sparse, diseased, or dead. The air smelled moldy with moisture and rot. There was life ... or a form of it, beyond these trees. He was told to follow the sun and that had been weeks or months ago? It was hard to say at this point.

Walk until you need to swim.

Those words he said to himself once each time he rested. None of the pools he could see looked deep enough to swim, much less bathe in. Though a sickly sun hung overhead, his direction remained unchanged. Slowly proceeding forward, he left the dry sand and felt his feet sink slightly into the muddy ground as he crossed the tree line. In the desert, there was no heat to bear down on you. Here ... he expected the moisture to dampen his skin, but there was nothing.

He sighed. It would have been nice to have felt something. Anything. The only sensation was his body's soreness, but that brought little comfort. He looked over at one pool. Its water was still and did not appear fetid or spoiled. Slowly, he lowered himself down and ran his fingers along the surface of the water.

Nothing. He felt nothing!

He slapped a hand in the water and it parted, but there was no cold or dampness on his skin. Against his own reasoning, he leaned forward and tried to drink in the water. Nothing filled his mouth. It was as if the water pushed itself away from him.

He sat back on his legs and roared in frustration; however, his voice was hoarse and the deep rumble seemed nothing more than a memory. A sudden sense of sadness filled him as he stared at the water. If he thought about ending his own life, the water would not grant him the mercy of drowning. What was he doing here?! Why was he here?

"WHY!" he yelled at the sickly sun, "WHY DAMNIT!"

"... because the flesh is weak and made to suffer," said a voice above him. It laughed almost melodically.

Looking upward in the tree line, Tulok saw the speaker. It was some sort of dog or cat-like creature. Its shaggy fur was a mixture of deep red hues, dirty whites, and darker blacks. Two large bushy tails hung from the tree branch it perched on. Stranger still, this beast had the wings of a bird attached to its front paws, though its paws were more like talons than the paws of a cat. When the creature spoke, it did so from the sides of his snout, with two mouths.

"Come now, lamentation is for the tired, old, and weak. If you are going to do it, do it with more pain in your voice. Show us how pathetic you can truly be. Perhaps we can find pity and deliver you from this injustice!" the creature said with no amount of sincerity.

Tulok forced himself to stand despite the pain in his body. "I am NOT a creature to be pitied by strangers. I am a servant of my Lord! Though his will I ... I am more than ..." the words seemed to slip from his mind.

"Ooh, such powerful words from a walking skeleton. You are barely skin on the bone, so you pose no threat with your words or your god here. You best behave, lest I come down there and teach you a painful lesson in manners!" The creature's tone shifted slightly. The edge of danger was obvious. "I mean really … look at yourself, you are literally wasting away right before my eyes."

Tulok narrowed his eyes at the creature, and then slowly turned to face the small pool of water. It had stilled since his tantrum. The surface looked like a perfect mirror reflecting the world around it. Everything except him. The reflection in the pool was gaunt, the face was sunken in, its skin sagged slightly. The collarbone was prominent. The reflection's limbs were un-believably thin. Then horror sank in as his mouth dropped open. This reflection was HIM. This was why he was never hungry, why he never needed food or water! His body was eating itself! He was wasting away and there was nothing he could do about it. The weight of this horrible realization forced him to scramble back from the pool. Above his head, the furry creature laughed at the orc's tragedy.

"Aww! The pitiful child found the truth in the land of dreams!"

With an unnatural grace, it launched itself off its perch and glided a few feet from Tulok. "Maybe if you show me how well you can beg, I may show you kindness. How about this … give me your name, and I will see if it is worthy enough for the help."

Tulok barely heard the words as he fought the panic and turmoil in his chest. Everything hurt. His throat was dry, drier than it had ever been. His stomach felt small and shrunken. He was only a walking corpse. A dead thing that did not know it was dead yet. If he had any moisture left in his body, there would have been tears streaming down his face.

Through a hoarse voice, all he could utter was "…what?"

The creature rolled its eyes, "I said … give me your name, and I will see if you are worthy of help."

He needed help. He wanted help.

NO! DO NOT GIVE HIM YOUR NAME! YOU ARE A TRAVELER, NOTHING MORE!

The voice was not his own but rang strongly in his head like a cold slap to the face. He tried to lick his lips to no avail, "I … I am Traveler … a Traveler."

The creature frowned. "No, no, sweetness, I'm not asking what you are doing. I am asking for your name. Give me your name and I will promise that you will not hunger for food or drink anymore."

Tulok shook his head, "I am … a Traveler." He shook his head back and forth, saying the phrase repeatedly.

The creature hissed in disgust, "Suit yourself, dear heart. Enjoy the taste of pride. It is quite bitter, I'm told."

Tulok expected to see the creature leap up into the air and fly away, but something else happened. The creature's disgust and smug expression shifted to wide-eyed panic. Its body moved backward, despite its talons sinking firmly into the ground. Looking behind it, Tulok saw a long, black tongue wrapped around the creature's tails. A tongue extended from the maw of a beast that looked like a crocodile … though this one seemed longer and thinner. It emerged from one pool of water with four forelegs firmly planted in the soil. It dragged the furry one back toward its hungry, gaping maw.

The shaggy creature yelped in its own horror when it turned and saw the predator, "HELP ME! Don't just sit there! It will eat you next! HELP ME!"

"I am a traveler…a skeleton of little flesh," Tulok said with little compassion in his voice.

"PLEASE! HELP ME! I will show you how to feed yourself! You have my word! I promise you that if you aid me, I will aid you!" it pleaded with genuine desperation.

TAKE IT – HELP HIM

The same cold voice spoke again to him. For a moment, Tulok felt a call to action run through his veins. It was almost inspirational.

"Deal," was all he could say as he looked around for a weapon. He scanned for a stick, a rock, anything, but there was nothing. Just the dead trees. With enough brute strength, he could knock one down, but in his state, could he? Could he do anything? He had no strength, no weapon, nothing ... he was nothing. The call to action faded, and the pain set in and his legs wobbled.

STOP BEING PATHETIC! WHAT WOULD YOUR LORD SAY!? YOU ARE AN ORC – ACT LIKE IT, BOY!

The only surviving item on his person was the medallion around his neck. A tarnished sun medallion with a strange eye stared back at him. The Radiant Lord. What would he think of His servant now? He could not ... would not ... bring shame to his Lord.

Anger welled in the remains of his stomach at the remark. Like a spark on dry wood, it caught in his chest. Though not a roar, a deep rumble came from Tulok's throat as spied the nearest tree. Dropping his shoulder, he charged the deadwood, and a dual cracking sound echoed off the land. He had broken the tree off its base, leaving a large stump. However, the pain of a broken collarbone lit up his body. The pain churned the anger and he let out a hideous sound. Grasping the dead tree, he lifted the trunk from the ground and turned to face the crocodile-like creature. His shaggy tormentor was only a few feet away from being swallowed. With another hideous bellow, he brought the tree down on the creature repeatedly. With every strike, he screamed nonsensical rage at it until there was a sickening crack. Blackish-red blood leaked out from the creature's mouth and the tongue and forelegs all went slack.

The Gurkh faded away from his body, only to be replaced by more and more pain. Dropping the trunk, Tulok fell to the ground in exhaustion. His chest heaved as he fought for breath. He felt a body land beside him. Turning his head, he could see the shaggy creature panting.

"Wow ... you have anger issues. I'm thankful for those."

Tulok smiled through the pain. "So ... what is for ... dinner?"

Chapter 45

Air burned in Lucan's chest. He could taste copper with every breath. His lithe figure darted in and out of the crowd, weaving and bobbing with the expert ease born of needed expedience. As he approached the stone wall of the Homely House, he reached to brace on its surface as he vaulted over the barrier with Elven grace.

"Farnak!" he yelled.

Boots hit the ground, and he kept running, closing the distance between the gate and the door.

"FAAAARNAK!" he yelled again as he approached the door.

As Lucan reached for the handle, the door came open. The stalwart figure of Hearthkeeper Farnak stood in the doorway. He stepped swiftly to the side, avoiding a mid-air collision with the messenger from the Guild. Lucan rushed past him, stopping his forward momentum only just before running headlong into the fireplace.

"Lord's beard, boy!" the white-haired priest swore as he turned to look back at Lucan.

Lucan bent forward and braced his hands on his knees as he tried to breathe. "There's … an issue … they need … you."

Farnak scowled and folded his arms across his broad chest, and regarded Lucan for a moment. He huffed and dropped his arms then walked across the room to fetch a pitcher of water for the exhausted messenger. He filled a cup with clean water and carried it to the boy.

"Sit down before you fall over," Farnak offered. It was a statement but flavored with concern and care. The old dwarf was still a priest of the Wandering Lord, and tending to the care of those who crossed his threshold was part of his calling.

"What in the name of High Heavens could Maitresse Lynet need from me? She has the whole Guild at Her disposal. What does she need a Wandering Priest for?" he asked.

Lucan looked over at the dwarf and nodded. He all but collapsed into a nearby chair. Grasping the cup with both hands, he pounded the contents down. Gasping for air, Lucan took a deep breath. "Lynet's line … something has happened to her … erm … them." He wiped his mouth with the back of his sleeve.

Farnak frowned. Lynet was a child of the Founders. Her line was woven throughout the whole of Avalon, and even onto the mainland. She could trace her lineage back to the first Folk that the Mother ever created. Their line was one of the few that had no dips or spurs from direct interference from any of the Divine that walked the island. That was to say, none of the Divine had chosen any Lynet's line for their issue. Her Lineage was pure. To think that something had befallen one of the most prestigious lines of Avalon was something dire indeed.

Farnak ran his tongue across his teeth and stroked his beard for a moment. "What … precisely … has happened? What did she say?" the old priest asked.

Lucan nodded, understanding what was being asked. He took a calming breath and tried to focus. "Do you remember the Spring when all the sheep's milk curdled?"

Farnak's right eyebrow twitched slightly. "Aye. Some fool declared their flock produced better cheese than Goodfellow's goats. That …" he paused and cleared his throat, rethinking his words, "…charming and devilish sprite…" he said referring to the Fae Courtier Himself, "decided that if we liked it so much, that ALL the sheep's milk would curdle. We ended up with sheep's cheese for a year." He frowned again. "I hate sheep's cheese …" he muttered, then focused back on Lucan. "What's that got to do with Lynet?" he asked.

Lucan paused, thinking. He stood on shaky legs and walked across the room, then closed the door. Farnak watched the boy. He scowled at Lucan's actions. At least he didn't lock the door.

The lithe Elven messenger turned to look at the dwarf priest.

He took a breath. "Reports are coming in from across the island ... every farm ... every homestead ... every orchard ... that is given to one of her line for caretaking ... has fouled this morning."

Farnak's eyes darkened for a moment at those words. "Every one?" he asked.

Lucan nodded.

"And what about Lynet?" Farnak asked quietly. She was the matriarch of her line. The oldest and most prestigious of her family. She was the Trademaster of Lubri. Her mind was among the sharpest of any Farnak had ever known. Her wit doubly so.

"She's ... blind, Farnak."

The wind left Farnak's lungs. He reached to brace himself on the table. Magic of this nature was tied to the land. To the Mother Herself. This was no simple insult. Something dire was at hand. Something bigger than the war with the Triskele.

Farnak's eyes drifted to the mantle above the fireplace. A heavy-looking ornate ax hung there in a place of honor and remembrance. It was a weapon Farnak hung up years before. He had been a younger man in those days. Full of dreams and the desire to see the world. He'd spent years Wandering the coast of Midgard among the Runegiver's people. The bloodshed of the battleborn never sat well with his Island soul. He was not born of the Free-people; he had no use for war. The passion of youth's fire waned with each body he set to rest on foreign soil. He found himself battling his inner demons as often as external foes. Rather than fail his Lord entirely, he stepped aside from his Calling and returned home.

A hearth, a fire, a kettle, and a warm bed. A place of comfort and succor for those who needed it. These were things he could provide. They helped the weary and silenced the cries of the dead and dying that still visited his dreams. His days of Wandering done, he took his Oath to protect those who Wandered the island shores and provide safety and succor for them.

Someone beyond this hearth needed him now. To kindle

Hope's fast flame in a time of darkness.

With no further explanation needed, the dwarven priest of the Wandering Lord walked to the mantle. He pulled down the heavy-looking ornate ax and took up his pledge against the darkness once more.

He took a breath.

"Take me to her."

~~~

He pulled the braids back and tied them into a topknot. The knot was heavy and half as thick as a ship's rope. Gathering the length of it was a chore and was slowly becoming harder to manage. His beard had been none easier, it was braided as well and came to the middle of his chest. He could not remember how long it had been since Enfi was forced to nurse him back to health. The Enfield, or as Tulok called him 'Enfi', had become his forced traveling companion as the orc followed the sun through the seasons of the Realm.

While "forced" was a strong word, saving a Court member's life … no matter how low they were on the strange hierarchy … was a rather large boon to be honored. If it were not for Enfi, he probably would have died in the swamplands. Tulok had learned quickly, large favors could be easily spent if it was within the power of the other party to do so. One could only honor a debt as powerful as the entity it was tied to. However, several small favors could be accrued from a life debt … and that was more useful to someone learning to survive. Ever the scholar, Tulok learned all that he could through these small favors.

The orc had counted himself extremely fortunate that the creature he killed was not of the Court or of the Realm proper. Long ago, the strange crocodile-like-creature has been a simple island lizard that made its way here. Such creatures were not always sentient, but a strange sense of cunning blossoms in the mind of wild creatures. Not everything that crosses over survives, but those things that survive the shift from Real to Realm change … and become more deadly. Killing it not only gained him a life-saving favor but also had become his first meal in this place.

Looking up in the tree – he could see Enfi scan the horizon. Neither of them trusted each other ... or rather neither could trust each other here, even in the Fiddler's Green. To Enfi, he was just a Traveler. He dared give no name, nor title, it was just what he was doing. There was power in a name. Power he could not give the Enfield. Favor for a favor, aid for aid, deal for a deal. This had become his way of life.

"Hey, Traveler! If you keep fussing with your hair, we will be here for another Autumn Sky!" Enfi called out from the trees. The fox-hawk-like creature smiled at him. "You are very beautiful. Is that what you needed to hear? Can we move it now or do you need to bask more in the light?"

Tulok smiled and held up the creature's severed tail, "I am not sure ... maybe if I slice this open, and bind the weaving with some Corran bones? It would hold my knot into place just right. Would I would look more noble?"

"You, sir, are an ass," Enfi said with disdain.

Tulok chuckled to himself as he tucked the tail back into a pouch on his belt. A year ... was it a year? Earlier they had the misfortune of dealing with a giant mole-like creature who was owed a large quantity of royal jelly the Enfi had promised. According to the creature, it had been several seasons since it had provided Enfi a service of equal importance. To ensure that the Enfield paid its due, it swallowed up one of Enfi's tails – Painfully and held it as an assurance that it would get what it was owed.

Several weeks of traveling, and a handful of trades and deals by Enfi, got them to their destination. All of which culminated into a quest with smoke, fire, and too many stings but ... the royal jelly was finally obtained. The twist in the adventure came when Enfi had presented the mole creature with the aforementioned jelly. In its greed, it simply spat out Enfi's tail into the air and took the jelly back underground. Normally, the Enfield was a nimble creature that would spring into the air –

using its tails. With the lack of additional "tail power", it made a poor leap and landed on its back, only to see Tulok holding the slime-covered tail aloft.

"I had a friend who used to call me that, and you are just not as charming as they were," he said as he remembered her face. She was there ... somewhere near the end of this journey. She was one of the few things that he held on to tightly. He kept her and a few other specific thoughts in his mind that he did not share aloud. He could not risk losing those memories to the Realm around him. While the dogma and chants had faded away, his faith in the Radiant Lord was a rock that he balanced himself on through all of this. His medallion had hung from his belt since he traded off the golden chain. Frog-ish folk had ferried Enfi and himself across a lake that was the domain of a powerful entity. It was a creature who lived in the darkness below and did not tolerate those who 'unlawfully' swam in their sacred water. The Enfield claimed the creature was better left undealt with. The orc also could not breathe underwater, and they lacked the time for him to learn to do so.

"Really ... what was this sweet memory's name?" Enfi asked as landed beside Tulok.

He raised an eyebrow, "Friend – a good friend."

Enfi sighed and shrugged. "You cannot blame me for trying," he said with a slight chuckle. In the years ... how long was it... traveling together, they had grown accustomed to each other's company. But the Enfield was still a member of the Court, bound to a skin sack from the other place. It was one thing to be held in promise ... it was another if he did not get out of it. "Blood and promises, my friend. It is what the Island finds value in ... besides, we have company ahead. Prepare your toy."

Tulok unfastened the handle to his flail. He had been most familiar with maces, as it was the 'polite weapon' of orcish clergymen. The flail had borne itself out of the necessity of distance since some creatures they had dealt with had wings. He had constructed the weapon out of bone, hair, skins, and sinew. Using the heaviest and thickest of bones, he had wrapped them into a deadly ball of destruction. It was a grisly item, but one that provided a decent sense of protection against the wild things that found their way into the Realm. These creatures bore no deals or fealty to those in control of the land, so hunting them posed no risk issues.

"I'm not too hungry right now ... but what do we have?" Tulok asked as he rotated his arm in preparation.

"Orcs from the looks of them ... and there are a lot of them," Enfi said.

Tulok narrowed his eyes. "Real orcs or ..."

"Oh no, no, no, they are from the Real. Flesh and blood even!" Enfi said as he raised its talons. "Look over the hill."

The two slowly approached and looked over the top of the hill. There were, in fact, a half dozen orcs, and they were young. They were standing on the rocky ground in a misty landscape. Stranger still, they seemed to move in flashes. One moment, a group would be by the rocks, and then in another, they sat by a tree. He watched as each group shifted positions. If he stared long enough, he saw them get up one by one and walk off into the mist. Slowly, the mist seemed to fade back as the sun-not-sun beamed brightly overhead. A noon-time sun without the warmth of a god within its eye. The time had changed again. Dreamers dreaming and causing the ebb and flow of time. He shook his head and sighed. The day had gotten later and he would need to eat soon. He continued to scan the area, and then it came into view. At first, he thought it was a trick of the eyes. He blinked and blinked again slowly. If this was a mutable object ... as were most things in the Realm, it would disappear in a few moments because he was no longer focusing on it.

It stayed. Water and waves continued to lap away as the mist completely faded from view.

"An ocean ... walk until you need to swim, they said. This, this is it. This is the end They told me about," Tulok said with a bit of growing excitement. Standing up, he looked over to his companion, "Enfi – whether you can or want to admit it, you have been a good friend to me, and I hope I was good enough for you."

The Enfield stared silently at the ocean waves, which was rare for a creature with two mouths. Tulok had shared the purpose of this journey long ago, and the Enfield recognized the ocean for what it meant.

"Enfi?" Tulok asked carefully.

"What does that place really offer you? I mean, really? Pain, hunger, suffering? You can get that here! Even now with the Triskele at war ... it is a horrible place. We had to burn several infections down from whatever plague that had leaked into the Realm. Why do you want to go back? You helped me clear some outstanding debts. We had fun. Really, Traveler, why leave?" Enfi said, though his normal mask of joviality was poorly kept.

Tulok stood silent for a moment and then reached into his bag and pulled out the creature's tail. "They sent me here to strengthen me ... so I could deal with that. Deal with the war ... the plague ... to understand myself. An orc who could try to balance Ghal and Gurkh was a danger to everyone. I was a disaster waiting to happen. Being here taught me that one must choose a path and that to master it means he can choose the other without shame. I learned much. If it were not for your help – I would not be here now." He held out the tail to Enfi.

Enfi looked at the tail and slowly pushed it to the side. "If you leave, you will lose all of this," he said with a heavy sense of finality. "What you have learned and done ... all of it will be gone. Like a fading gossamer in a strong wind. Who you have become ... this warrior ... this survivor ... he will be gone."

Tulok watched Enfi carefully, but could only see the truth in the words. He stood silently as Enfi continued to look at the ocean in the distance. Finally, Tulok kneeled down and held out the tail again, "I gladly release you from your promise ... as it has been paid in a far nobler way than any other could hope to dream."

A chime sounded in the air and both felt a weight lift from their shoulders. Enfi turned to Tulok and slowly took the tail. "You sir, are an ass ... and a friend."

"I am honored to be," Tulok said as he stood tall and looked to the ocean.

"Two last pieces of advice ... free of charge. Call it a parting gift. You probably want to talk to those orcs. What they are doing ... it is something that has been done and always will be done. I do not know what, but it is a thing that is consistent. As for the second, if you see one of my children above, food goes a long way," Enfi said as he reached back and placed his tail back into place. "OOoo – now that's nice. Take care of yourself, Traveler. Things are going to get painful, so try to use that anger to your advantage. It kept you alive so far, am I right?"

"Us ... it kept us alive," Tulok looked down, but Enfi was gone. He turned around, and the creature was nowhere to be found. "Until next time," he said to no one.

Chapter 46

Back the way he came.

Swansea would be a welcome sight once he put all of this behind him. A small coastal town, with simple coastal people, patiently waiting for the next ship to make the circuit. Arman glanced skyward, holding his fingers at eye level with the horizon to gauge his location and distance from the town. He counted lines on his digits and made the mental calculations, then nodded with satisfaction. The business with Phaendar had taken slightly less time than he had estimated when making his original plans and arrangements. He should arrive with just enough time to catch Captain Hywel's ship back to Lubri and from there ... home.

He longed for the warm, dry air of Setesh, and the familiar crunch of sand beneath his boots.

The road through the thicket and brush seemed emptier as Arman travelled away from Phaendar's holdings and back to the shores of Swansea. The ancient sage had gathered their belongings and hurried Arman out at first light. Phaendar had made all manner of gracious thanks in the name of Avalonian Hospitality at the conclusion of their exchange. The elf had double and triple checked bowls that seemed to contain various items: milk, honey, salt, bread, ale, crushed berries of some kind, fresh bloodied meat and flowers. Coins. He watched Phaendar place silver coins on every window sill. Arman thought it an odd observance for a people who saw no value in money, but then he remembered who Phaendar paid homage to. The Jailer was also a keeper of wealth.

Trying to tip the scales to His Lord's favor, Arman reminded himself.

He shook his head and pulled his cloak a little closer, pulling the warmth to his skin. Was he really any different? His hand drifted to the box that contained the horse-headed stone jar. The contents of this jar came at a high price. How many had died to secure its contents? It should have just been one. It should have been a simple delivery to Maitresse Lynet's oldest son, and then someone to return to collect the amulet and bring it to him. But Nahem had died before they could make the delivery and the courier … That foolish foreign courier … had made a deal with Reynard the Swift to deliver it to Nahem's next of kin.

Who just happened to be a Magister in Setesh.

An opportunity for travel and a good deed. The perfect pairing for a Wandering Knight and his newfound Squire.

Arman sighed. He supposed he should have counted himself fortunate. Had Reynard chosen to take the amulet to Lynet, the Trademaster of Lubri … who knows what might have happened then? As it was, it had spilled the lifeblood of more than a dozen persons for this little treasure.

And how many will perish with the flowers you gave to Phaendar? Arman asked himself. *How many more is that madman about to murder?*

Arman shuddered at the thought. His stomach felt uneasy. Was it worth it? If he were a more faithful man, Arman might have worried about the weight of his soul against a feather, but he had never held much value in those tales. He did not deny the power of the Divine of Sanctum. They were far too evident in their workings among the people of the world to simply deny their existence. But there was something that was more valuable to him than all ire of the Regency. Even more valuable than the keys he was collecting for Nebiyre and her people.

They still had something he wanted, so collect the keys he must.

Keys. He shook his head. *Souls. Sparks of Divinity.* Very specific sparks for a very specific lock.

He shifted uncomfortably in his saddle. Did Fortuna's Reapers have these same misgivings as they enacted Her will upon those whose scales were out of balance with the world? Arman's hand drifted to his throat. No; there was no torc of gold and silver there. The Lady of Fate and Fortune had not cursed him with Her Blessing. This was not a task for Her, nor for any member of the Regency of Heaven.

His thoughts drifted back to the Temple of Silence in the deserts of Setesh. The majesty of that hidden secret had given him hope that what he was seeking might truly exist. He had fallen to his knees and wept tears of both sorrow and joy when the room that held the map had been unearthed. He had barred the way and demanded he be left alone with the historical artifact and remained there for days, wondering at the lines, the colors, the languages. Secrets long lost standing before him, buried beneath the sands by the Seteshi Divine for millennia.

He recorded everything.

He had been deciphering the legend and icons when the orc had been captured. Suddenly, everything seemed to fall back into place.

Then the Wandering Knight's Squire had reappeared, dragged from the waters of the River Lord's domain, or vomited up from the sands of the Storm Bringer. Arman never knew which. He only knew that once a Knight Wanderer had declared a quest, they would not rest until it was completed.

Ser Isolde duAvalonne had clearly named Arman Dah'ay her target, and there would be no rest for either of them until one of them succeeded.

Or the other was dead.

—

Coming down the hill, Tulok watched as the orcs moved below. He could see the afterthoughts of the various groups of teenage orcs gathering and dispersing one by one. One group looked up and saw him coming down the hill. Drawing their spears, they stood ready but watching. Each spear was decorated – the symbol of the Huntress adorned the blade tips.

He slowly raised his hands and asked, "What are you doing

here?" and motioned to the surrounding land.

Cautiously, one of them stepped forward, spear at the ready, not threatening. "It is the test to find the way to our Heart. If you are really Her, we are ready." Each of them took a knee and bowed their head in agreement.

Tulok's eyes widened and shook his head. "No, no. I am not the Balance, the Hunting Wind, the Relentless Fang. I am a Traveler looking for the ocean. I am not the One Who Seeks."

There was a mixture of disappointment and embarrassment as the group rose. Not wanting to discourage them, "Though I may not be Knife's Swift Edge, I would have been honored at such a display of reverence. Someone has obviously taught you well. Though I have to ask, what do you mean? The Way to find your Heart?"

A smaller boy of the group stood up. His face looked vaguely familiar. "The Way to your Heart is what our clan calls it. We move as one through the Realm, tracking the Er'che-Kin. We each find one and claim its tusks. Sometimes ... those who were not strong enough do not make it through. We started with ten, but the Realm is kinder than the Real." Each of the orcs nodded their heads solemnly. The boy speaker continued, "With the tusks, they show us the way here... so we can get there," he pointed up ahead, "the last test." The young orc pointed out a large cave entrance on the cliff side.

For a moment, there was a pulse of something there, almost a primal sensation of power that wicked its way up to his skin and into his skull. There was something powerful in there and he could feel it calling to him.

One girl stood up and began walking towards the cave. Everyone watched as she approached it, spear at the ready. She paused and looked up. Above the entrance stood a figure. She stood in the shadow that mostly masked her form except for the animal skull helm that covered her head. The eyes of the skull gave off a yellow glow. The young girl nodded and then walked into the darkness of the cave.

The air was silent for a few heartbeats and was shattered

by both a primal cry of rage and a frightened scream of child-hood horror. Then, as quickly as it broke the silence – there was nothing but the sound of the waves lapping onshore.

Every muscle in Tulok's body strained as he wanted to rush forward, but he was frozen in place. The yellow glow of Her eyes seemed to root him into the rocky shore. He took a deep breath and relaxed. Bowing his head, he turned back to the group of orcs. The next child was the first boy who spoke to him. Much like the girl, the figure acknowledged him above before walking into the darkness of the cave. Again, a terrible cry and scream broke the serenity of the ocean. Tulok watched the group. Two of them appeared shaken, but it stopped neither one from standing and making their way to the cave. The last one was the smaller of the group.

"You must be a great warrior to have found this place. Maybe this is what you were supposed to find. Those who find their heart carry a great responsibility and terrible power. We use the power to protect the lands, and do what must be done," he said.

Tulok looked at the boy. "You are not a warrior, are you? The way you speak, you speak like a scribe."

The young orc pursed his lips slightly as he looked down. "No. They chose me to be the Wel'adr's charge. I can see things here sometimes. I was told it was a great honor and that in time, I could lead with my gifts. I am not scared of this. It has to be done so we can be seen as members of the clan. I … I just was not sure if I was ready. Everyone was older than me … but since I am helping the Wel'adr, my time was now."

Tulok nodded his head, "Uncertainty can be our own worst enemy. I do not know what is in the cave, but what I can see is that you made it here where others have not. You know the purpose of this rite, only you can choose to see it through."

The boy stood up and looked over to the cave. "My turn. You have great wisdom for a warrior. I hope you choose well." The young orc began making the trek like the others before him. Tulok watched as the figure acknowledged the last participant

374

and then he walked into the darkness. The scream of rage and fear soon followed.

A pulse rang out again, and this time he could feel it burning in his chest. The Gurkh. The Rage was there and shaking at the bars of his soul. He had learned to master its power in the few years he had spent here. The Realm had required it of him to survive. Here, now, he could feel it more than he ever remembered. The Gurkh could sense something else. Not the lure of 'terrible power' ... but of something instinctual. He took another breath and looked up. The figure above the cave entrance was watching him. She Who Waits to Strike had begun to weigh and measure him. It felt like forever as he stared forward, looking, but not staring, at Her.

She nodded her head, and he could feel the pulse of his heart beating in his chest. This was his time. This might be his way.

"Sir, I think you are going the wrong way."

Tulok had paused in mid-step. Looking down, he saw a young man with bright blue eyes and sandy blonde hair. He looked vaguely familiar.

"What do you mean?"

"The ocean. I thought you said that you were traveling to find the ocean?" The boy took a stick out of his belt and made doodles in the sand. "It seemed pretty important."

Tulok scratched his chin. The thought was there. It was something important, but the cave pulsed again. The weight of that place seemed even more important.

THWAP!

He felt the sting across the back of his hand. The boy had taken his stick and had hit him across the hand with it. "That way is not for you," said the boy.

"Oh, I think I may have to disagree, young man," Tulok said with a slight grit in his teeth. The Gurkh shook at the cage harder. "I believe that cave is exactly where I need to be."

THWAP!

The boy had swatted the back of his knee. It stung worse than the first.

"How about this? You beat me, and I will stop bothering you. If that way is meant for great warriors, then you should have an easy time taking me down. You can even use your ball thing."

The rage within screamed *YES!* Then the Ghal's cold reason took an icy hold. This was a child only maybe 15 years old. A single hit from his flail would kill the boy dead. However, this was the Realm. Maybe this was not a child but something else; it had to be.

"Fine, young sir. If I win, I can go about my business."

"And if I win – you have to do the one thing I say which will not bring harm to you or anyone else," the boy said. "We fight until one of us yields or is disarmed."

There was something empowering about those words, and they hung over them both. "I accept," the orc said simply.

With that, both drew their weapons, the boy his stick and Tulok his flail. Slowly swinging it to build up speed, he watched the boy take a relaxed stance with the stick. He needed to swing for the legs. Boy or not, a blow might kill him. A leg could be mended, a chest or head wound not so easily. Whipping his flail around, Tulok swung low at his legs, shifting his own body to follow the flow of force created by the weapon.

Just as the head of the flail was about to connect, the boy gave a quick hop back, watching the distance of both the orc and the ball. They danced like this for a few more times as they circled each other in the rocky sand.

"If you are going to hit me ... then hit me, boy!" the young man jeered.

Tulok roared and spun his body with trained quickness as he brought the head of the flail on to the boy.

The boy's stick parried the deadly weight to the side. It smashed deeply into the ground. The boy flashed a smile and let loose a volley of smacks with the stick on Tulok's face and his inner thighs. The two hits from earlier were mere slaps on the wrist compared to the burning sensation that erupted all over his skin. Rage could not be held back any longer. With a roar, he let go of the flail and grabbed the young man's throat with his massive hand. With Tulok's right hand around his throat, the boy's reddening face smiled as he forced out words, …

"You are disarmed. Do you yield, sir?"

The very force of those words frosted Tulok's rage in an instant. He felt something against his throat. Relaxing his grip, the stick the boy held was no longer a stick but an immaculate silver blade, the point of which was resting on his throat.

He had lost.

He slowly lowered the boy to the ground and released his grip.

"Anger, son … it is always anger with you. You have done well here. Probably better than others will admit, but this is not for you. You have secured your 'house' so you are no longer a threat to the island. They will need you up there. You need to find him. It might not be too late … he still needs to be found and stopped." The boy paused and looked at the afternoon sun. "He and I rarely agree on things, but I believe in both of you, and I know He does as well," the boy said as he re-sheathed the now-stick back into his belt.

"Now remember … the anger is your own. A few more years' practice above and you will be right as rain. The flail is good. I used to hate those things, but in the right hands they are terrifying," the boy added as he patted the orc's arm. "It is time to go, Father."

Tulok looked down at the boy and then out to the ocean. "My friend said that this will all go away. My life for the last couple of years … my experiences. All it will be gone. Is that true?"

The boy took a deep sigh. "Yes … and no. Yes … as soon as you are back in the Real … everything will fade like a pleasant dream. Fleeting memories and things you can no longer put a finger on." He looked around for a moment, almost conspiratorially, "Though some things will stay with you forever. The important things … the things that make you who you are, get stronger because of what happened here. There will be times when something will float in your mind that will seem outrageous. Maybe it is … or not … but either way, do not be quick to discount it."

"Were you … were you my guide in all of this?" Tulok asked.

"Oh no," the boy shook his head. "No, Father, I am just a traveler like you. Just … wandering … where I am needed."

Tulok nodded his head, "So, do I just swim in a certain direction or …"

"Just dive in and swim down. The world will do the rest," the boy said with a smile.

"My thanks," Tulok said, and he headed toward the shoreline. Wading in slowly, he took a deep breath and plunged forward. Even with his massive arms, he could feel his body tiring at the heavy water. But the deeper he swam, the lighter the world seemed to become. He knew he had swum down, but it felt like he was swimming up. The water against his skin went from a feeling of nothingness to something he had not felt in a long time … cool. Even the stinging sensations on his face felt better with the cold water.

The stings reminded him of the boy. He had been there on his first day and now his last. The water became colder as he surged forward, heading toward a single ring of light above. He was almost there and the boy's words rolled in his mind.

"… *wandering where I am needed* …"

—

The boy sat on the shore as he watched the orc disappear under the waves. The woman in the animal skull helm stood next to him. They did not speak aloud as the waves lapped the shore.

He: *Would you have accepted him?*
She: *They decide their own worth.*
He: *… but was he worthy?*
She: *Time will tell.*

Chapter 47

"It is so nice to know that your people find no value in Hospitality!" Isolde's voice yelled in the native tongue of the island across the firelight. Her normally pale skin was flush with passion and anger.

Around her, large bodies shifted under the weight of the insult. Orcish eyes glared at the visitor. Hands clamped down on the shoulders of warriors whose Gurkh rose to the challenge, seeking to make the city-born child of Whitebrooke pay for her words. Heads shook in the negative. Others walked away into the darkness rather than take up arms against a representative of the Lord Wanderer. He was a Divine known for instilling unbridled courage in his people that often left their choices wanting. They also knew him to be intensely protective of his Champions ... their "quests" fulfilling some Divine plan only He understood. Calling down His wrath in a time where war was already present was not something any of them desired.

One voice answered Isolde's. Timbre for timbre, passion for passion. The angered voice of Maelona Blodwen answered the champion's challenge.

"And also so good to confirm that the Lord Wanderer's Champion waves open insults so casually, when it was she that brought danger to our shores and our homes!" Maelona snarled.

Isolde's hand fell to the pommel of her sheathed weapon. Maelona's eyes followed the movement. Her calloused fingers twitched slightly toward the haft of her ax.

"He is a speaker for the Radiant Lord! Do you think His eyes will not see this deed, simply because His gaze is turned from us at this moment?" Isolde demanded as she gestured to the night sky.

"Do you think the Island cannot defend us from the *Seteshi* ... "Maelona said the word with some disdain, "Sun God? The Triskele Trinity and the Mother have kept their influence from these shores since our arrival, Wanderer's Child." Her hand came to rest on her ax haft. "And yet you bring Him to our home, unprepared for the Gifts of the Morpheum, a walking invitation for destruction."

Isolde's green eyes met Maelona's, unwavering, fearless, filled with a desire to defend the priest, who was her friend and companion.

Stand down. A quiet, familiar voice whispered in the back of her mind.

Isolde blinked. Her brow furrowed. "What?" she said to no one.

Maelona frowned, her eyes searching the area quickly.

Stand down, child. She has the right of it.

Once more Isolde's brow furrowed, her face betraying a conversation that only she could hear.

Maelona shifted her hand from her ax haft to a quick gesture to those surrounding them both. *Caution. Wait. Watch.*

Isolde's right hand slowly slid off of the pommel of her sword.

Confused glances passed around the fire circle. Some warriors stepped back and away from Isolde. It was the caution that one often lent to the mad, in respect of both their strength and their unpredictability.

"I ... apologize," Isolde said carefully. She shifted her position to a ready stance, but no longer one of defiance. "Father Tulok is ..."she paused, searching for words, "My charge." Isolde nodded and lowered her eyes. "... and you are correct. I am responsible for his actions, intended or accidental."

Maelona's shoulders relaxed.

As their Chieftain abandoned her position of aggression, the others followed suit. A collective breath of ease was felt across the encampment.

Maelona scoffed at Isolde's comments and stood to her full height. Her red eyes gleamed in the firelight. The mark of the Huntress danced on her flesh, noting her affiliation and bond to the warrior queen of the Triskele Trinity – bound to Balance. "You are not in command of your own leug and you would carry the burden of a Mainlander? The Wanderer is indeed mad." She sniffed.

Isolde narrowed her eyes at the orc woman. The compass around her neck glowed faintly, as if in response to Maelona's words. Maelona eyed it suspiciously and then inclined her head in simple acknowledgment of the silent presence of the Divine.

"I must," Isolde responded plainly. She looked up at the taller woman. "We are bound in Oath. I cannot abandon him."

Maelona's eyebrows rose sharply at that. Several of those gathered frowned at the words. Others looked offended.

"Ah, I wondered at that." The deep voice of the Wel'adr carried across the darkness. Armed and armored warriors stepped aside to make room for the Elder. Isolde had mistakenly assumed that the staff which had lain across his lap had been for support. Instead, it was clear now that it was a symbol of power and position.

Maelona turned sharply at the Elder's arrival. "Wel'adr," she inclined her head. "You should not sully your voice with the words of the city." She said in her native tongue.

The Elder turned tired eyes on the tall woman and continued in the island's tongue.

"The magic of the island is in me, as it is in you, and all here present. To speak the tongue of the Mother is no sin," he replied with a note of finality.

Maelona nodded her head.

"I saw the thread upon you both when you entered. I was uncertain of its origins. Another reason I sent our Sun Skin cousin on his quest."

Isolde inclined her head respectfully, but with an edge in her tone. "Elder," she said.

"You do not approve, Wander's child? I do not require your approval. As you are responsible for the weight of your Sun Skin, I and this one, "he nodded at Maelona, "Are responsible for all those here. Your Sun Skin will succeed or fail on his own merits. Such is the way of the People, and the will of the Island." He gazed down at Isolde from his great height. "Would you question the will of the Island, Isolde of Whitebrooke?"

Isolde paused in her reply, remembering something that Maelona had said on their approach. She set her shoulders and looked up at the Elder Orc.

"We tell the Island who we are, Elder," she replied.

A grimace that passed for a smile tugged at the corner of the Wel'adr's lips. "Good. Let us hope your Sun Skin learns this as well." He turned and walked toward one tent. A group of warriors had begun to take it down.

The strange sound echoed in Isolde's ears once more. She clasped her hand around her amulet to silence it. As the last of the walls and timber were removed, a pool of dark water was revealed. It glimmered softly from the torch and lamplight under the moonless sky.

A Morpheum Gate.

Isolde glanced at them all as a realization came to her. They had pushed Tulok through a Gate and into the Realm of Morpheum! Years of teaching, songs, rhymes, and lessons flooded across Isolde's memory at the sight of it. Warding prayers and spells to stand at the ready. Even with the song of Morpheus in her blood, it had barely prepared Isolde for her own encounters in the Dreamscape; and she was born of the Island.

Tulok.

Tulok was not.

A knot of discomfort and nausea formed in the pit of Isolde's stomach. They could well lose him forever if he could not find his way back to the Gate. And what if he ate food from the Realm? Or made a promise to the Fae? A dozen terrible possibilities danced in her mind.

A ripple broke the surface of the Gate. It carried its circular self to the edge. Another followed it. And then a third.

The Wel'adr gestured to those gathered that they should take up their arms and form around the Gate.

"Now, Witness," he began. "Now we see if what emerges has been victorious."

A dozen armed warriors brought wicked-looking spears to bear, pointed at the gateway of liquid Morpheum on the ground. They stood shoulder to shoulder, a wall of flesh between the magic of the island and the people beyond. Isolde's hand came to rest once more on the pommel of her blade.

Raise no blade ... she remembered the line from the chant she learned as a child. A list of rules to observe if ever one found oneself on the other side. Words that Tulok never learned. She looked to Maelona, and then gently lay her hand on the tip of the weapon that was pointed at the gate. She shook her head.

"Bow your head,
Knock as friends.
Raise no blade,
Make amends..."
She sang softly.

Maelona frowned for a moment. Isolde's hand remained firmly on the weapon. Isolde continued,

"Take all gifts,
Make no trade,
Help the helper,
Aid for aid."
The Wel'adr nodded and gestured for the weapons to be lowered. His deep voice rumbled,

"Eyes are open,
Words are kind,
Thank your host,
Speak no lie."
Another ripple danced across the surface of the pool. Several more followed it. The warriors gathered around the gate lowered their weapons as they listened to the sing-song of

their Wel'adr and the Champion of the Wanderer.

"Share no names,
Taste no sweet,
Bear no secrets,
Use your feet"

Isolde and the Wel'adr met eyes and nodded to one another, then turned to face the pool together. Isolde slowly knelt and placed her hands on the soil at the water's edge. Her broken compass dangled from around her neck, glowing faintly in the darkness. The pair spoke in unison,

"Walk with Them,
Hide the way,
Heed The Rules,
Survive 'til day."

The great arms of the Wel'adr lifted his staff, powerful hands wrapped around its carved haft. He brought it down sharply upon the earth.

Once.

Twice.

Thrice.

Dark water rippled and rose and parted. A figure's head crowned through the inky blackness of the gate. Bare pated, strong of brow and jaw, powerful shoulders stooped, head bowed. The waters seemed to lift the figure with some difficulty. Threads of black trailed behind, tendril-like roots clinging to him.

Maelona's lips curled back into a snarl as she reached for her weapon. At her sides, the warriors shifted and took up positions of defense. Weapons lifted once more, aimed at the slime-covered figure of the orc priest that slowly emerged from the darkness of the beyond. A sound escaped from his lips. The gurgling sound of the drowning.

Isolde's green eyes widened at the sight of her friend and boon companion. Pain grasped hold of her heart and squeezed tightly as the acrid and foreign taste of fear danced on her tongue.

"Tulok …" she whispered.

The figure's eyes flew open at the sound and locked onto Isolde's. A thousand words and images flooded the windows of his tested soul, unable to find purchase on his tongue. His enormous form seized and shuddered and collapsed forward, hands barely catching his great weight. He shook violently and retched. Brackish water vomited out and made its way back into the pool. His body shook softly as she watched him take deep breaths.

"Ww … wwwh … y …" he managed. Lifting his head, he looked up at her once more, blackness fading to familiar red.

"Why is your island always so cold?"

Chapter 48

"I don't understand it," the older Folk cowherd muttered in confusion. He rubbed the back of his neck as he gazed into his stables.

A dozen cows, healthy and heavy with milk the night before, all dry this morning. Calves lowed and bellowed in hunger as they tried to suckle and could not. He had had to remove several of them from their pens this morning for injuring their mothers in their attempts to feed. He would have to send them down the lane to nurse.

He walked down the aisle of his stables and examined his ladies once more. They seemed well enough. Simply without milk.

Glancing around, his eyes lighted on each of the iron horseshoes that had been nailed above the barn doors. Each still hung upright. The wards against malevolent fairies should still have been in place. There was one among that Court that still walked these lands. One known to make the milk curdle or cows run dry. He could not believe that he had earned the ire of the Goodfellow. With a frown, he left the barn to ensure the offerings of milk and honey were still in place.

This did not bode well.

~~~

"Don't let it touch you!" Gruffydd shouted to Ygraine.

"Thank you for stating the obvious, Gruffydd!" Ygraine yelled back. She braced the end of her spear and shoved the tentacled and sticky arms of the giant sundew away from her. Red threads tipped in viscous liquid stretched toward the gangly youth, to grasp hold of their target.

Roundleaf sundew was native to the Island. It thrived in the peaty bogs and marshy wetlands, surviving on mosquitoes, dragonflies, and gnats. While a single plant might grow as tall as three feet on a single stalk, its flowers were never large enough to capture anything larger than a house spider.

This great monstrosity of cursed flora had captured not only one of their ponies but had wrapped its sticky petals around the ankle of one of Gruffydd's Scouts. They had severed the plant's stem and free her, but the flower's digestive enzymes had eaten away at her foot, ankle, and calf. One of the group had dragged her away from the fray and was attempting to save what was left of her leg. She had passed out from pain a moment earlier.

"They aren't supposed to get this big!" Ygraine yelled, as she shoved hard with her spear.

"They aren't supposed to eat people either, Little Wolf!" Gruffydd called. He swung his sharpened short sword and sliced quickly through the stem that Ygraine was holding back. It sprung back and whipped back and forth, spewing dark green liquid across the area.

"Thank you." Ygraine nodded, as she was freed from the plant's attention. He grabbed hold of her arm and flung her toward the rest of his Scouts as another stem lashed out toward them both. He sliced at it neatly and left the red threaded bulb writhing on the ground as he pressed backward and out of range of the carnivorous plant.

A handful of additional red threaded flowers bobbed and bounced gently. The tendrils of the flowers flexed like long, thick fingers, tipped with balls of clear liquid. The stems of the other flowers slowly arched and stretched toward the body of the pony that lay captured and unconscious on the ground. They alighted gently on the flesh of the animal and wrapped themselves around it. Every place the clear liquid touched, flesh sizzled and dissolve.

Ygraine collapsed on the ground next to the others, her spear across her lap. She glanced over at the injured Scout and the Healer that tended to her.

"How is she?" she asked.

The young man shrugged a little and continued his ministrations. The gifts of the Mother only did so much against these strange abominations of creation.

"I have stopped the bleeding, but the poison ..." he shook his head and leaned back. Already dark black veins had crawled up the exposed flesh of the Scout's leg. "I might take the leg and save her, but it will have to be now. It can't wait to get her back to camp." he looked up at Gruffydd. "She's a child of Stag. She'll never run again, but I can't promise taking her leg will save her. I need your word on this, Gruffydd."

The older Scout ground his teeth together in frustration and anger. Whatever this curse was, it was taking hold of the people in ways none of them had ever seen. If she lived, she could never fulfill the role that the Stag Lord had chosen for her. If she died of the poison, her body would never be returned to the island and she would never be returned to the cycle.

Gruffydd closed his eyes. "I can't condemn her soul to wander the shores of the Crossroads for eternity," he said gruffly. "Take the leg. Save her soul." He turned then and walked away and back into the forest.

Ygraine watched Gruffydd as he walked away. They were not friends; most days they were not even friendly to one another. But this was not a decision she would wish on anyone. She looked over at the Healer who had already begun making ready to amputate his compatriot's limb.

"Can I help at all?" she asked.

The young man shook his head. "No, she's out and will be for some time. I have what I need." He cast a cautious eye toward the giant plant that loomed off in the distance. "Are we far enough away from it?"

Ygraine followed his gaze. The sundew grew out of the embankment and surrounded a pond some thirty feet away. When they had approached it, they had mistaken it for a bottlebrush tree, only to discover too late that whatever was warping the land had reached this location as well. She nodded.

"We are clear here," she replied.

The Healer nodded and looked in the direction Gruffydd had wandered off in. "Go check on him."

Ygraine frowned and looked toward the forest.

"Out here, we have to rely on each other. I have to take care of her. He needs to be taken care of too, and I can't do both."

Ygraine sighed deeply and shoved herself up off of the ground, brushing dirt and leaves off of her legs. "You shout if you need anything."

The Healer chuckled darkly, "If something comes for us, we'll be dead before you can get back."

"Great uplifting chat there, Tomos." Ygraine chided, and headed off in Gruffydd's direction.

"Happy to help."

This area of the island was where the headwaters of one tributary emerged. It was lush, welcoming, and filled with the life-giving essence of the Mother. That the illness of the island had reached this location could only mean that it was further spread than they feared.

Or had it started here? Ygraine wondered. She was no Scout, nor a Druid, but to her, it would have made sense to poison the headwaters first and let it drift downstream and infect everything it touched. But there was magic involved here, too. Poison alone would not have done what it had to the flora and fauna of the island. Something else was at work here.

She stepped into the forest and followed the small path that Gruffydd had followed. She knelt for a moment to check his direction and realized that he was seeking the source of the headwaters.

He has the same thought. Of course, he does. He's been doing this for twice your lifespan. Ygraine shook her head and headed into the brush, following Gruffydd's trail.

A memory nagged at the back of Ygraine's mind: A vision briefly spied while standing in the home of Alderman White-brooke... There had been a third figure present in that vision.

Someone shrouded in shadows, watching the exchange.

Ahead, she spied Gruffydd kneeling by a crack in the earth. Water welled up and flowed out from this break in the crust and rock. He was inspecting something.

Who was the third figure? Ygraine felt like it was someone she should know. Someone of importance. Shadows and amber eyes. Something about the eyes... what *was* it? She pondered the memory as she pushed through the underbrush. They were farther apart than would have been set in a human face.

Fae-born elf.

A Fae-born elf had been there! Shrouded in shadows in the Realm. Someone who knew about Mynydd Mawr.

Someone whose position granted them access to the Lady's Heart!

Gruffydd stood and brushed his legs off. At his feet sat a small basket, set into the source of the headwaters. It was shaped like a strainer. The kind one might find in a teapot, but larger. Without looking back, Gruffydd gestured to Ygraine.

"Hand me your spear."

She nodded and handed it to the Scout as she approached. Gruffydd carefully extended the spear to hook the basket and pull it gently out of its place of security. It came loose easily. Holding above the water, he eyed it suspiciously.

"Poisoned the headwater?" Ygraine asked.

Gruffydd nodded. "Good eye. Yes, it would seem so."

Ygraine stood next to Gruffydd. "It's not just poison though, is it?"

Gruffydd shook his head.

"Who would have knowledge of this location, access to something like this, and be able to work magic with the fae in the Realm?" Ygraine asked. She feared she already knew the answer, but truly hoped she was wrong. There were those charged with maintaining the very magics that kept the Island alive. If one of the ancients had done this, it meant the whole of the Island was in greater danger than they could know.

Gruffydd sniffed and took a breath and confirmed her fears. "Someone who has abandoned their Oath," he said quietly.

A Druid.

Chapter 49

Isolde draped the woolen blanket across Tulok's broad shoulders and patted him gently. He mumbled quiet thanks and wrapped his hands tighter around the bowl of hot stew they had offered him. Across the fire, Maelona and the Wel'adr spoke in hushed tones, their voices and body language showing some importance of their words. He frowned, knowing they were speaking of him and his experiences on the other side.

The Morpheum, he corrected himself. No longer just a place mentioned in books and stories of the Realm of Avalon, he had stood in that place and survived. The Morpheum touched all of Sanctum. It was a place of dreams and nightmares, a place where even the Divine of Avalon cautiously treaded.

Fae, spirits, strange creatures that held no recognizable form danced in his memories. Memories that were even now fading into wisps of feelings. He raised his left hand and rubbed it across his bare head. Hair. He had a memory of long hair, braided with beads and bones. He looked up once more at the figure of the Wel'adr. Strong, proud, and filled with the wisdom of the People. He knew that feeling. Or did he? He scowled and looked away, raising the bowl to his lips and sipping from its contents with a careful skill he had not possessed before.

"...oon." Isolde's voice stopped short as she watched the priest drink from his soup bowl. Tulok hated to drink from bowls. He loved his napkins, his serving ware, and his polite manners. Her thoughts darted back to their conversation on the ship during their crossing. Appearances meant so much to the orc priest who walked among humans all of his life. Isolde's eyes filled suddenly with concern. She looked at the carved bone spoon in her hand and then back to Tulok and quietly set the item aside.

Tulok sat in silence at her side. He caught her movements out of the corner of his eyes and watched as she set the spoon aside. He looked at his bowl and paused in consideration. "You want to know how long I was there?" Tulok's deep voice asked her.

Isolde pursed her lips and looked down at her hands. She flexed her fingers in thought.

Tulok nodded and set the bowl aside. "You are concerned about how I will receive this information?"

Isolde shrugged. "The journey is different for everyone..."

He turned to look at the Knight Wanderer. "That is not an answer," he replied.

"Tulok," she began. He cut her off.

"Allow me to assuage your concerns," he continued. "Years," he said plainly.

Voices around the fire silenced at the word. Maelona and the Wel'adr ceased their conversation, and both turned their attention to the foreign priest.

"Years, Isolde. Or ... I feel that I have the memory of having spent years in the Realm." He used the Islander term for the Morpheum. He stared at his hands, flexing them and turning them back and forth. "But even as I sit here in the Real, around this fire, I can feel those memories fading. Falling away, like leaves in Autumn ... and yet I know I am changed for it all."

"Tulok ..." Isolde reached to place her hand on his forearm. Tulok flinched a little at the gesture. She frowned.

"Physical contact in the Realm is not always a good thing," he offered with both apology and explanation.

Isolde opened her mouth to speak, but clamped her jaw shut and glared across the fire at Maelona and the Wel'adr. Tulok was a scholar. More than this, he was a Healer. The ability to connect with others was vital to his role among the people of Setesh. How much had the Morpheum stripped from him in his experience? Angry words willed themselves to be free, but for once she controlled the fire in her belly and remained silent.

"The Seteshi deserts are filled with horrors of sand and glass, so I am told," a lilting voice carried across the darkness. "Scorpions the size of horses, snakes like eels whose venom is like fire, ghosts that roam the darkness seeking the souls of the lost ..." the voice continued.

Tulok's brow furrowed as he looked across the fire into the darkness to find the owner of the voice. "Yes, these things are all true," he acknowledged.

A tall, lithe figure emerged slowly from the shadows. They wore an unbleached linen robe and a soft pale woolen cloak. Their hair was the color of spun gold and matched their almond-shaped eyes. They decorated the points of their ears with tiny silver bells that ran along the edges.

"My cousins in Litharge tell me that the Sun Skin Orckind often send their youth, alone and without company, into that desert as part of their ..." the figure paused in thought, "... hrmmm ... winnowing, yes?" they asked Tulok. Eyes too wide apart to be comfortable to look upon for too long, stared at the priest of the Radiant Lord, unblinking.

Tulok nodded silently, suddenly unable to look away from the creature standing before him.

"*Ollam*," Isolde whispered. The ancient title of the arch druids fell from her lips as she slipped from her seated position to bow her head in reverence to the figure. The broken compass around her neck glowed and hummed faintly. Around them, the warriors and people of the Clan each bowed their heads, many taking a knee in humble supplication.

Maelona turned to face the Elven druid and bowed her head in solemn respect. Beside her, the Wel'adr met the gaze of the ancient guardian of the island.

"I am too old to kneel for you, Vicnis," he grunted with a nod.

"And yet you are still so spry, Addolgar," the Druid replied with the hint of a smile tugging at their lips.

Tulok looked between the two figures and around at the

others. His mind raced as he tried to grasp at wisps of memories that vanished into nothingness. He shook his head, trying to clear it.

The ancient being stepped to meet the priest of the Radiant Lord, their movements filled with an unmatched fluidity and grace. Whispered words that burned in Tulok's ears then vanished into the aether issued from Vicnis' lips. They reached forward and gently tapped Tulok's forehead with the middle finger of their right hand.

"Be Welcome to these shores, Child of the Radiant Lord."

Tulok felt the words more than heard them, an echo in his body that seemed to touch his soul. Clarity and understanding washed over him. His knees buckled, and he collapsed before Vicnis, suddenly aware of the weight of Divine power and magical knowledge standing before him.

"Teacher ..." Tulok whispered reverently.

"Och! You have to be so damned melodramatic about everything, Vicnis!" a familiar voice cut through the scene as the small form of Speaker Iscaria strode forward. "This is why I never visit you anymore." she chided. Glancing around at the gathered group, the little Folk woman placed her hands on her hips. "All right, people, bask in the glory of the ancient druid later ..." Her eyes fell on Isolde. Striding over to the young woman, she grabbed Isolde's chin and lifted her face to look at her.

"This is why Wanderers don't come home until their end, because of the trouble that follows you."

Isolde's brow furrowed, confusion behind her green eyes. "What? I don't ..."

Vicnis raised their golden eyes to meet the Wel'adr's. "Phaendar rides to kill the Lady's Heart with poison from Seteshi Sands."

~~~

"Set the kettle, turn it thrice, thistle, rosemary, and thyme," Phaendar hummed. The blonde pony trotted down the roadside as the morning light crested the green field before them.

Warm rays the color of clover honey broke through the dark gray of the ever-present cloud cover. They turned their eyes upward, half lidding them and breathing deeply of the life that surrounded them.

"Good morning, Your Radiance," Phaendar addressed the shining orb in the heavens. "Have you come to witness me this day?" A wide smile shone on the sage's features. "I expect it should be a grand and glorious day, even by your standards."

The trees rustled to the left of the mounted sage. A soft breeze rustled through the canopy. Deep within the branches above, a shadow shifted.

"I see you, you know," Phaendar commented to no one.

Golden eyes peered down from the treetops, watching the ancient sage. "Haul the basket, bear the plate, a dish of gold, weary weight," the elf continued.

The clouds in the sky gathered together and covered the golden disk in the heavens once more.

"Ahhh ... so sad, you will not be here to see this," Phaendar sighed to the sky. "No matter, His will is better worked without You around," the sage chuckled darkly and turned their eyes on the trees. The sage lifted the fingertips of their right hand to their lips, kissed them gently, and then blew. "Run away, run away, run away home," they whispered.

A wave of miasma rushed from Phaendar toward the trees. It crashed against their trunks like an ocean wave, breaking and crashing outward and upward. Dark tendrils erupted from the earth and climbed the ancient timber, entwining around each tightly, reaching toward their crowns. Something in the shadowed canopy screamed. It was followed by what sounded like a strangled plea. Then silence.

The sage smiled.

"Westward march, you slumbering Host. Stricken sword and friendless King." The earth rumbled under the pony's feet, but the horse paid it no mind. "Harmless glamour. Forgotten years. Hollow Hollow Hollow home." Black ichor oozed up from the land in every step of Phaendar's mount.

Phaendar giggled. In the distance, a set of rolling hills gently brushed against the foot of a looming mountain. Their long fingers reached to wrap themselves around a silver key that hung around their neck. Etched into its silvered surface were an apple tree and stream. It seemed to glow faintly at Phaendar's touch. A soft white light.

"Fallen flower, restless reed. Bubbling brook," he paused in his cadence. "Brook? Brook … a bubbling … white brook."

Whitebrooke.

At the base of the hills, a soft white light seemed to hover for a moment, then settled on the ground, a pool of shimmering silver.

Phaendar closed their eyes.

"All for you".

Chapter 50

Tulok rubbed the back of his neck with his wide hand and contemplated the information presented.

"The description matches a couple of plants that grow in the desert, yes," he nodded. "But none of those plants can do what we have seen or what you are describing."

"Maybe they have properties you don't know about ... Father," Iscaria's voice sniped from across the way. They had moved their conversation into the single-standing building in the encampment. Built back into the hill, the lone structure provided both warmth and privacy. It was a place where the sick and infirm were often housed, as well as those heavy with child. There were only a couple of beds occupied at this time. The rest of the area was open and served well for their clandestine conversation about the ails of the island.

Tulok frowned down at the small woman. "I was chief among the healers of my temple, Speaker," he answered. "I am well versed in the properties of every type of flora on our shores."

Iscaria harrumphed. "And yet your little plant is responsible for all of this," she chided.

"Tsk, Tsk, Tsk," Vicnis' smooth voice clucked. "This is not the place for parents to bicker between themselves," he said of the respective clergy. He glanced at Iscaria. "The Mother's ways are well known upon these shores. To Her is given all manner of health and well-being. Do you know all Her mighty works upon the land, Iscaria?" His eyes drifted to Tulok, "And you, Father, who bears the gifts of healing from the Father of the Skies, he whose blessing of warmth and light brings life to the world. Well, it is known that only the Blessed Healer Herself surpasses the skills of your people on the mainland."

Tulok pursed his lips in thought. It was true. Safar's people held greater knowledge of the healing arts than the Temple of the Radiant Lord, but the Sand Dancer was not here: He was.

Seated by the hearth, Iscaria cupped her hands around an earthenware mug and scowled deeply.

"But you both are correct in this," The Druid offered softly. He rose from his seated position and walked to the fire. Folding his long arms across his narrow chest, he considered the flames for a moment. "It is possible that other factors are likewise in play," he said softly and continued to contemplate the flames.

Tulok and Iscaria traded concerned glances.

Isolde watched the trio in their exchanges. Her sparkling green eyes scanned the whole of the scene, as one charged with committing history to memory. Across the room, the towering figures of Wel'adr and Maelona Blodwen watched with a level of concern she had witnessed on her parent's faces all too often when she was a child. These were their people, their charges. This was their land, and it was ailing. The foreign priest could be a fortuitous helper or a harbinger of woe.

She unfolded her legs from the bench and stood. The leather straps of her armor squeaked and creaked in complaint. Scooping up a handful of cups, she walked to the kettle and filled them, then approached Maelona and the Wel'adr. She looked up at the two Orckind and offered them a smile and a cup.

"I don't have bread to break with you, but will you share a drink with a Wanderer on this chilly night?" she asked. "That we may put aside our complaints with one another, if only for as long as we take to finish?" she asked.

The Wel'adr regarded the small woman from his great height. Maelona bristled and moved as if to interpose herself between them. His great hand came to rest on the Chieftain's shoulder, even as he accepted the offered mug from Isolde.

"We are ALL children of the island, dottir. Let the servant of the Wandering Lord speak. She carries His favor as surely as you carry the Huntress'." He looked at Maelona. The Chieftain grunted her displeasure. He continued; his words directed at Maelona. "Open your eyes and look around you. Who stands here in this place tonight?" his deep voice grumbled in his chest.

Maelona Blodwen glanced around the room. Her eyes took in those present, their names, their duty, and their place in the leug of Avalon. Her right eyebrow twitched slightly.

"I see the Mother, the Father, the Huntress, The Wanderer," she looked to Wel'adr "The Shepherd" and then to Vicnis, "And the Goodfellow".

A grin tugged at Vicnis' lips. "You have a good eye," he said softly.

Wel'adr snorted. "She's the Chieftain of her people. She's been taught what she needs to know."

Isolde nodded to the Wel'adr and set Maelona's cup on the table next to her. She inclined her head and stepped across the room to Vicnis. With both hands, she offered the Druid the last cup, almost like she was granting an offering to the gods.

"Ollam." She closed her eyes and bowed her head.

Tulok cleared his throat.

"Get your own cup," Iscaria replied, and shoved herself up into a standing position, then recovered a cup from the table.

Tulok scowled at the priestess once more. He understood the protectiveness of the Mother's people upon their own shores, but Iscaria was doubly irritated by Tulok's presence.

Vicnis chuckled. It sounded like the tinkling of silver bells. He turned to face Isolde and folded his hands, palm to palm, and inclined his head before accepting the cup from Isolde. "Thank you, Child of the Wanderer. May your path lead you to great adventures and greater joy," he intoned.

Vicnis lifted the cup to his lips and inhaled deeply, then smiled. "My father is being accused of these actions, and He is not amused."

"And there it is," Iscaria grumped from across the room.

Tulok narrowed his eyes at the Druid and examined him

once more. The books and tomes in the Libraries of both Ophir and Tarf-qua were filled with stories of the children begotten by the Divine. Many were larger-than-life characters charged with great heroic deeds. Others were founders of cities. Still, there were those who kept secrets in ways that no true mortal could. Yet none were the direct children of the Regency of the Heavens. Ages past, upon the founding of Sanctum, the Divine were forced into an agreement that none of them would ever directly sire among mortals again. It was an agreement that several Divine strongly objected to, but eventually agreed to observe. Sanctum was too precious a treasure to risk at the whims of Divine issue walking around on mortal soil. Instead, from time to time, a member of the Regency would imbue their favor upon a creature chosen to embody their will. A Votary. Through this embodiment of Divine Will, a child would be sired or birthed.

Safar al-Shifa was one such child, the only son of the Healer. Now, standing before Tulok was apparently another such child of Divine heritage, a child of the last surviving Divine of the Fae Courts.

Vicnis raised his finely arched eyebrows at Iscaria's comment and looked across the rim of his cup in her direction. "Do not misunderstand, Iscaria. I am not here on my Father's duty. I ceased being His errand boy a millennium ago. My final trick played upon Him." He blew across the contents of the cup. "However, as Phaendar has aligned themself with the Jailer in their actions ... in whatever ill-formed belief has possessed them ... I must take up the mantle of my Father once more, for the Goodfellow stands as His opposition. It falls to me to unweave these magics and reverse Phaendar's harm upon the land. And, regardless of my ... differences of opinion at present ... with my sire, I will forever stand as a protector of my Lady's Heart. Such is my Oath and the way of the Cycle."

Isolde stepped over to Tulok's side. His eyes slid over to meet hers, they were filled with confusion.

Isolde nodded and patted him on the arm. "Welcome to Avalon," she looked at Vicnis.

"What do you need us to do?"

~~~

"Well, that is utter nonsense!" Iscaria said curtly.

"How is that nonsense?!" Tulok motioned in protest. "It is a little outside of traditional thinking, I agree, but the logic is sound. You just have to give it a chance."

"First, you demand the herbology of the island. Now, after reviewing it, you are asking me to poison the land!" Iscaria said with complete disdain.

Tulok held up a single finger in careful caution. "Correction," he began in soft tones. "I did not demand. I asked Ollam Vicnis if there was an official record of plants on the island that I might review," Tulok said. "You were the one who threw up a protest that I was seeking to steal your secrets. I am here under your Island's laws of hospitality to which I have done NOTHING but help all those I have met. If we ... YOU and I ... are to figure this problem out, I need to know what you know. If I had the record of desert plant life upon my person, do you not think I would share it likewise?"

Isolde had returned to her position on the other side of the room with the Elder and Maelona. They each sipped from their mugs of warm liquid and watched the two priests argue. It had been going for almost ten minutes straight. Aside from Vicnis' initial interruption, the druid had not moved to step in between the two. Instead, he merely watched the argument between the two faiths. Occasionally, he would blow across the cup Isolde had handed him and inhale the steam that issued from it. A small but subtle smile crossed his lips at their warring and chaotic display, but he did nothing, instead watching it continue to play out. When Tulok had asked Vicnis about the herbology of the island, Iscaria had erupted into a fiery tirade of mistrust and anger.

"... and what you are saying is insane!" she objected once more.

Tulok raised a large hand and rubbed the bridge of his nose.

"Well, we cannot get the whole of the island to ingest salt water and wretch the toxin up," he paused and looked at Vicnis. "Can we?"

The druid shook their head "No."

Tulok nodded, thankful for something that made sense. "And while we could certainly apply charcoal filtration to the water, it will do nothing for the already infected or the land."

Iscaria pursed her lips in frustration and nodded in acceptance. "Agreed."

"Thornapple is not native to your land, so it stands to reason that your lands have not developed a native countermeasure." Tulok glanced at Iscaria. "Yes?"

She nodded.

"Then what is left but to look for an alternate means of therapy to heal the wound?"

Icaria scowled, but before she could utter a word, Tulok began drawing on a piece of parchment. While comical to watch his overly large hands hold a tiny piece of writing coal, his motions were elegant. On the parchment was a rudimentary but impressive sketch of the plant Vicnis had described earlier.

"The meat of the Thornapple is like another desert plant that is safe to eat. At certain times of the season, the two are indistinguishable. It will cause dehydration, hallucinations, and possibly death. What makes it worse is that those properties spread to the leaves. When dried, they can be crushed and used as a tool for foul deeds. What it does NOT do is cause this blackened sickness and an undying disease. This means something more powerful is at play."

Looking over to Vicnis, "If the stories are true, someone of sufficient power over the natural world could empower or alter the properties of a plant, correct?"

Vicnis contemplated the sky. "Easily. Though altered, magics like those touch places of power that are distasteful or even unnatural."

Tulok grunted in agreement. "Now, because Thornapple is a

hardy plant, the best way we have found to eradicate it is to plant Manchineel," Tulok started to sketch out another plant, "The natural properties of this plant are anathema to the Thornapple because it draws out the meat-poison within it. In a matter of days, Manchineel can kill off a patch of Thornapples."

"Fine, fine, fine. Let us say that your assumption is correct," Iscaria started, "Manchineel ... at least our version of Manchineel is twice as deadly. If you eat the fruits that fall off of it, you will die. Many have made the mistake of cooking them in a stew and killing themselves or an entire family. The leaves burn the skin, the sap causes asphyxiation. The whole plant is deadly."

"You have a cure for it?" Tulok asked.

Iscaria paused. "Yes, of course. It's unpleasant but better than the poison."

"But ... you have a cure for Manchineel poison," He continued.

"Yes, as I have said. But we have dedicated efforts to remove Manchineel anywhere it is found. We control its propagation and burn untended groves to keep it that way. It is still here, but rare. And, given the properties of its sap ... and the whole of the plant itself ... if we re-introduce Manchineel anywhere near water ... we will kill farms, farmland, and villages!" Iscaria protested. She shook her head and looked up at Tulok. "Even if you say your Thornapple is not responsible for these mutations and corruptions, what will your little house trick do against what has already been done to the Island?!"

"That's the beauty of it! Corruption or not, at its base, the plant is STILL Thornapple. It may have been altered, but the foundation of it, mutated or not, is still Thornapple ... and Manchineel kills Thornapple. We both have a remedy for Manchineel that will cleanse that poison. If we poison the poison, we can cut the sickness out and then introduce the cure! Please ... just think about it!" Tulok pleaded.

Icaria shook her head. "No, no – this is all too convenient. I cannot let that happen! I will not risk the lives of MY people to satisfy you or your Radiant Lord's grab for power on this island!"

Tulok's shoulders slumped, and he stared at Iscaria with a level of disappointment and hurt. "Fine. If you wish to see the validity of my words, so be it." He turned and faced the Chieftain and Wel'adr and spoke.

"The Island questions the truth in my heart. I ask to borrow your hunting blade," Tulok said to Blodwen.

The Chieftain narrowed her eyes at Tulok and simply asked, "Why?"

"The Island values two things ... blood and promises. It is the only way to resolve this," he said.

Blodwen looked at the Wel'adr who regarded Tulok for a moment and then nodded his head. Reaching to her belt, she drew her blade and whispered to it. Holding the handle out to him, she spoke quietly, "She will be watching as well."

"As She should," he said with a nod and touched the blade to his forehead.

Isolde watched as Tulok spoke with subtle hand gestures. Another change that the Morpheum had wrought upon him. When she saw the Chieftain draw her blade, she could feel her pulse quicken, but the apprehension was soon replaced with curiosity. Something was going to happen here. Good or Bad, but it was something she needed to Witness.

Turning around, Tulok held the blade of the knife in the palm of his hand. Closing his hand over the blade, he looked over at the druid, who was watching everything with an odd smile. With no words, the elf quietly nodded.

He turned his attention to Iscaria. "I am sorry for whoever brought such disdain into your life for those of my faith. We came here to catch a criminal who murdered my acolyte, who had become my friend. This same criminal tried to murder one of the Lord Wanderer's Witnesses while she was under my care. This criminal tortured me to the point of losing my mind. We came here for him and nothing more. Now, this same criminal's actions threaten to destroy hundreds if not thousands of lives on this island. I have offered to do everything in my power to help stop it, but I cannot do it without your help. You have denied me that. So I hope this is something you cannot deny, faith or not."

Before Iscaria could speak, Tulok drew the blade from his closed hand. He winced but held the blade aloft. A thin crimson line of blood stood out against the bone coloring. She watched as he squeezed his hand tightly. Thick red droplets of blood welled up at the bottom of his fist.

"I am here to help save this land from a danger that came from my homeland and nothing more. I seek no power or place for my Lord other than what was already shared with him in the Beginning. I give the island the truth of my heart," he said softly and relaxed his fist. Blood flowed freely in large drops and hit the soil between them.

Iscaria watched, wide-eyed and mute. She looked at the ground and watched as the blood sank into the soil. It did not puddle or well up. The land did not reject it. Instead, the earth drank in the rich blood like water. After a few moments, Tulok closed his hand and wiped the blade clean on his robe. Reaching down, he tore the hem of the robe and wrapped his hand. Handing the blade back to Blodwen, he looked over at Isolde.

Isolde's eyes were drawn to the ground where the blood had been spilled. She slowly looked back up at Tulok and back to the ground. Looking back to the ground, she saw Iscaria had quietly moved toward the spot and was staring at a small tuft of grass that had not been previously there. Within the vibrant green was a single tiny orange-yellow flower that had bloomed. Isolde marveled at the tiny flower, not because it had sprung up in mere moments, but what it represented. Had there been any falsehood in her companion's words the earth would not have drunk in his life. It would have become a black and fetid pool on the ground. How did he know about that? Nothing like that would have been in any book he would have had access to, much less witnessed.

He learned what he needed to survive.

Isolde pursed her lips and quietly nodded to herself. With a gentle hand, Iscaria ran her fingertips over the blades of grass and gently tapped the petals. After a moment, she looked up at Tulok. "I am truly sorry, Father. I … I have spent too long protecting this land from every form of corruption, protecting The Mother and heeding Her needs. I grew blind to the poison of my making, my hubris. What you are proposing is dangerous and it will endanger many – but it does not matter what I believe – the land believes you. I cannot deny its truth. So what do you think is our best plan of action."

Relieved, Tulok nodded his head. "Normally introducing it near a water source would work best, but that requires prolonged exposure … time we do not have. If we can find a source of Manchineel, grinding up the meat and leaves and dumping it into a major stream would be our best bet."

Vicnis rubbed his chin and walked towards the pair. With some quietly spoken words and a motion of his hand, the earth next to them slightly rose. Slowly it formed an image that all soon recognized – a rough map of Avalon. The flower that had sprung from the orc's blood sat in the north, marking the spot where they all stood.

"Our nearest source of Manchineel would be here, carefully cultivated away from any waterways. The fruits will need to be harvested and brought here." he pointed to a section several miles south and another to the west. "Mother Iscaria and I will need to dump the fruits of our labor in those spots to have as much effect as possible. And then I will do what I must and unweave the Jailer's tainted magics and restore the balance." He looked at Maelona. The orc chieftain nodded.

"That's at least several dozen miles from here to the closest point. It will take all day just to get there! Even with the sun rising now, I do not know if we can make it before Phaendar makes it to their goal," Iscaria pointed out. She looked at Vicnis. "If Phaendar reaches the Lady's Heart with that poison…"

"They won't," Maelona replied.

Vicnis smiled slightly and inclined his head in acknowledgment of the statement. "Excellent."

Tulok's head shot up and looked skyward. Quickly he stood up, "Please excuse me," and walked away from the group.

The group watched the lone orc walk toward the break in the tree line that gave a view of the horizon. Lowering himself to both knees, Tulok spread his arms wide and raised his head to the sky.

"We will let him know the plan when he is done," Iscaria said.

Vicnis raised an eyebrow in surprise.

"What?" she replied, "Some of us still need to pray so that our gods hear us."

Vicnis smiled. "Absolutely. As to answer your question, you and I will travel by ... unorthodox ... means. It may require some favors to be given."

Iscaria grimaced, knowing full well that the fae-born Druid meant to call on his kith and kin for their aid. "Yes, yes, fine. Better us than anyone else."

"As for the rest of you," the druid addressed the other orcs, "The full force of the Boar must aid in the fight. You will need to ride hard and fast to the south. Your fellow Free People will need your blades and ferocity for what is coming."

Before Blodwen could reply, Wel'adr spoke: "We either all live or we all die. Either way, we will do it together – as one people."

Blodwen weighed his words and gave a slow nod, "We will bring Balance once again."

Isolde looked to Vicnis, "The Father and I can ride to ..." but Vicnis raised a hand.

"No, child ... you have a greater task at hand. You both have a criminal catch. Based on your chase so far, his only point of egress back to Lubri would be Swansea. If he is as clever as you make him be, he would have a ship already lined up to take him around the bend and eventually back to Port Kracken. Phaendar is my issue to rectify. With the knowledge gleaned from the Mother and the Father, I can now do what needs must be done." He walked to Isolde and placed a gentle but firm hand on her shoulder. Eyes the color of faded gold stared into hers. "You have a Quest to complete, Witness."

Isolde felt the weight of the words on her soul. Part of her wanted to protest, but the druid was right. If Arman was still on the island, they had to take this opportunity to catch him. She had a duty to perform.

"I'll let the Father know we will ride out when he has finished," she said with a bow of the head.

"Remember – it matters not if we live or die, only if we succeed or fail. If we fail ... the Island dies, and we cannot let that happen," Vicnis said grimly, but then smiled. "So, if you die – make sure you take some enemies with you."

Chapter 51

"I want three warbands and two buan guards mounted and ready, now!" Cynfael's voice boomed. Around him, the whole of the encampment moved in practiced and trained actions.

"Wilkome got his drunk on last night. He's in awful shape," a young man addressed the towering Chieftain.

Cynfael's face darkened with anger. "Get the Urram and the menders to sober him up. NOW." The young man blinked and staggered away from their chieftain.

Flexing his massive hands, Cynfael finished fastening the clasps on his hide-bound armor. This was not for the Triskele this morning. This battle was not about balance and trade for power. No, if Gruffydd was correct, this was something that none of them were prepared for. A guardian had betrayed their Oath and threatened the heart of the island.

"My king, shall we send word to Lubri and alert Her Majesty?"

Cynfael paused and looked for the owner of the voice. Kneeling before him was a young woman dressed in the greens and browns of the Scouts. The Stag Lord's mark was displayed proudly on her right shoulder. Cynfael pursed his lips into a scowl and took a breath.

"Lady Bellicent should well be aware of the goings-on among her people," Cynfael all but growled, "But I will not assume ill on her part in this. Yes. Go. They need to know. Stag's speed be with you."

"Thy will be done, thy word be known," the young woman replied with a messenger's rote, and darted away and toward the tree lines. In the distance, Cynfael watched her mount a giant stag and leap away into the forest.

"Others may have forgotten their duties, but we shall not," Cynfael said.

"Scouts are ready, Cynfael. Where do you want us?" Gruffydd's familiar voice asked.

Cynfael closed his eyes and took a breath, stilling the heat in his stomach that begged for battle. He paused and then gave his friend his attention. The smaller man had arrived less than an hour ago, exhausted from riding and running all night to bring him the news of what they had discovered at the headwaters. They had departed a party of twelve and returned a group of three. Gruffydd, Tomos, and the young woman Ygraine. The rest had fallen to the corruption that had infested the island. The information that Gruffydd brought with them was a deeper blow than any ax could cleave.

The magics that Avalon held were a complex tapestry woven betwixt and between its people and the land. This was widely known, but the depths of it were a secret kept from those not born of the Island itself. The people of Avalon were bound to its shores and to the place of dreams whence the land itself was once born. A land of myth and dreams entwined and embodied within the world of man. This balance was not something easily managed. The Druids and Sages of the land held the honored position of protecting this knowledge and the magic that kept Avalon alive. They were few, and their duties were integral to the survival of the island. For one of their ilk to have fallen from their duties, to have been willing to abandon their sacred calling, was almost unheard of. There were legends of those who tried to rise against the sacred cycle; ruin followed in their wake, their names anathema, forbidden in common use.

Medraut.

Seife.

And now another Druid's name would be written from history. If they could stop them.

When you stop them, Cynfael corrected his thinking.

"Cynfael?" Gruffydd prodded.

"Yes. Apologies, Gruffydd," The Chieftain nodded. He turned his focus to the other man. "You are certain they have Whitebrooke's key?"

Gruffydd nodded. "There can be no other answer. No other reason they are doing this alone, and why she is not with them. They need a Landkeeper's key to open the vault of the Lady's Heart. They must have obtained Whitebrooke's key when Council Whitebrooke fell."

"And the girl?"

"Lady Whitebrooke's daughter? Scouts confirm she was sighted in Baedd Gwyllt territory, south of Swansea. She's carrying the Wanderer's blessing, as the Little Wolf said."

"So, she is not working with them."

"No."

Cynfael nodded. That would make this easier. If it could be deemed easy to slay a guardian of the land you are both sworn to protect.

"Does she know?" Cynfael asked.

"Unknown, Sire," Gruffydd replied. "She is on Quest, Cynfael."

Cynfael sucked at his teeth and nodded. The Wanderer rarely chose Champions, and those that were chosen were no longer bound to the duties of the land, so much as they were to their duties to the Regency and the Lord Wanderer. Had that been the hope? That the Whitebrooke heir would abandon the land? Or had they simply failed in killing her? Questions that might never have answers.

"Do we know which one we are dealing with?" Cynfael asked solemnly.

Gruffydd paused before replying and looked away.

"Out with it, man. This is no time for hesitation. What are we up against?" Cynfael demanded.

"It's Phaendar," Gruffydd said softly.

Cynfael inhaled sharply at the mention of the Sage's name. Phaendar Pryderi was the chosen of The Jailer, the Lord of Riches, and the Underworld. They stood as the balance point for Vicnis Tomte, the child of The Goodfellow, master of mischief, music, and freedom. Last-survivor of the Courts of the Fae. Both bore the blood of the ancient fae-blooded elves through a shared matrilineal tie. Both were almost as old as the island itself. Only Lady Bellicent was older than they were. Slaying Phaendar would set the land to chaos, and leave Tomte unchecked until the Druids could name Phaendar's replacement to anchor order once more.

"Is that what you are counting on?" Cynfael asked aloud to the air.

"Sire?"

Cynfael shook his head. "Nothing." Cynfael looked at Gruffydd. "You are certain?"

Gruffydd nodded. "We are."

"Dammit all," Cynfael swore. He took a deep breath and looked to the heavens. *Hallowed Shepherd grant me the wisdom to make the right choices in this.*

"I need your ears and I need your arms!" Cynfael bellowed.

As the words of the Chieftain rang out, actions ceased and eyes turned to face him.

Stretching his neck, Cynfael reached down and picked up his massive double-bladed battle-ax.

"As you have all no doubt heard by now, we ride to battle. Not for the Triskele. Not for the Cycle. No. Today we raise arms to protect the very soul of our land itself, for one of its guardians has fallen and betrayed their Oath."

Around him, members of the people slowly gathered, some taking a knee, others folded their arms and listened quietly. Healers emerged from their tents, bags half-packed, to hear the words of the Shepherd.

Cynfael raised a single arm over his head, bearing the massive weapon that was both his chosen arms and the symbol of his office as Chieftain. "I am Cynfael Aerfyn, of the Blaidd Drwg, by your will and the will of the Gods, Chieftain of the Free People." Heads nodded and voices sounded in agreement and support.

"We have seen the blight that has befallen us. This is because of the actions of a single being. One who seeks to upset the magics to which we are all bound. This person seeks to sever us from our land, our magic, and our gods."

"Will we allow this?" he asked the gathered.

Heads shook and words "no" and "never" could be heard.

Cynfael scowled. "Blaidd Drwg, will we allow our magic to be stolen?!" he demanded.

"No!" came the reply.

"Will we stand silent while our land is poisoned?"

"No!"

"Who stands with me to show the Village-Born that the Free People remember their Oaths?!"

Fists raised to the sky, accompanied by voices of support.

"Free People of Blaidd Drwg, will you bleed for your island?"

"Yes!"

"Free People of the Morpheum-born, will you kill for your island?"

"Yes!" the crowd roared. Hands clapped and weapons raised.

"Free People of Avalon, will you die for your Lady's Heart?!"

The response was a wave of affirmation, desire, and blood-lust, as Cynfael's words drove the gathered warriors to a fit of frenzy. He looked down at Gruffydd as the battle-blood within him rose to the surface. He slowly lowered his ax.

"We will slay Phaendar's beasts. Take your Scouts and bring me Whitebrooke's key to Mynydd Mawr."

Gruffydd stepped back and blinked rapidly in confusion. "Sire?"

"Lady Whitebrooke has abandoned her duty to serve the Lord Wanderer. The Little Wolf was once welcomed to the Whitebrooke hearth as family. We shall pick up what has been set aside. We are Council Whitebrooke's protectors now.

"Go."

~~~

Tulok bowed his head in silent reverence as he completed his oblations. Opening his red eyes, he spied Isolde leaning against the trunk of a tree. The forest green eyes of the Holy Witness of the Wandering Lord watched him from a distance. She smiled.

The big priest blushed a little at her attention and he carefully pushed himself up to a standing position. It was her duty to bear witness to the world for her Lord, but it was sometimes unsettling to be the subject of attention.

"Are we ready to create the remedy, then?" he asked.

Isolde pushed off of the tree and shook her head in the negative. "No."

Tulok frowned and glanced toward the group gathered around Vicnis and Iscaria. "I thought this issue settled?" he asked.

"It is." Isolde offered quietly.

Tulok's shoulders slumped. "I see …"

"No!" Isolde's voice interjected quickly. She could taste the flavor of perceived defeat in the air that surrounded the orc priest. The Wanderer could not let that stand. She reached out to lay her hand on his arm. She paused for a moment, remembering Tulok's reaction the last time she attempted such a gesture. This time, he did not pull away. Her warm hand gently rested on his forearm. "We … you and I … have a duty yet unfulfilled. The Ollam was kind enough to remind me of it."

Tulok arched a bushy eyebrow in response. "Go on."

Isolde looked back behind the orc and then up at him. "Vicnis and Iscaria will address the poison and its remedy." Tulok opened his mouth to protest. Isolde raised a cautionary hand. "This is for Vicnis to right and for the people of Avalon to bear. It is their magic that lay in the balance, my friend. They must be allowed to defend its shores … and its soul."

"Then my words … my actions … were for nothing?"

"No. Not nothing." Isolde stepped to Tulok and looked up and into his face. "You brought the gifts of the Radiant Lord and His Healing Hand to the shores of my homeland. Your skills and your knowledge will enable them to do what must be done with the hands that must wield the tools."

Tulok looked down into the face of the woman who had stood at his side through this endeavor. Her skin was bronze now, where it had once been the pale color of most Islanders. Tiny specks of walnut brown danced across her nose and cheeks. Streaks of golden blonde ran through her dark hair. For as much as the Morpheum had touched his soul and crafted him to something new, the Seteshi sands had marked her visage as well. They were no longer the simple Healer and Patient they had been when she tumbled from the dunes and into his life.

It felt like a lifetime ago.

"We came here looking for someone," Isolde said.

"Indeed," Tulok replied. "Hoping to stop him from doing what he has already accomplished."

"And?" Isolde asked.

Tulok's brow knit together. Where was she leading to?

The clouds above them parted for a moment and the warmth of dawn's light touched Tulok's face. He closed his eyes and exhaled at the caress of the Radiant Lord upon both his skin and his soul. As the clouds parted above, a reminder of purpose touched Tulok's heart.

Vengeance.

"Justice," Isolde said firmly.

Tulok opened his eyes and blinked to clear his thoughts. "Yes … Justice."

Isolde nodded her head. "Vicnis believes Arman may already be headed back to Swansea. That is the closest port that will take him back to Lubri. They will ride to apply the cure, and we must ride to capture Arman before he can do more harm."

The Healer of the Radiant Lord looked back over his shoulder at the group as they prepared their journey. Their actions, if successful, would render Arman's void. The logic was sound: it would work.

The hands of the Mainland and Island had joined to bring pain and destruction to these lands. Now they were joined to heal the harm brought by that union.

Tulok looked down into Isolde's smiling green eyes, full of life, faith, and hope.

"Then let us see this through, Ser Isolde."

Chapter 52

Mynydd Mawr stood in the center of the island of Avalon. It was the tallest peak on the island. Legend spoke of how one could stand on the crest of the mountaintop and see the whole of the island and all its magic. No one was still alive who could confirm this claim.

As legends sang of the transport of the island to Sanctum, there were also tales that claimed that Mynydd Mawr was the place the Divine grasped on to as they brought the land here. It was a place of sacred reflection for all who dwelled on Avalon's shores. That the mountain itself was a place of deep magic was not disputed; all who were connected to the land could feel the pull of the magics that emanated from this sacred place. Some believed that the Mother Herself slept beneath the peaks, deep into the earth of the island. "The Lady's Heart" was the name given to the depths of the mountain. Some claimed that if they delved deep enough, they could hear a beating heart.

When the island was brought to Sanctum, each of the founding families was given a symbol of their link to the lands and its people. A simple silver key. It was a symbol of both incarceration and freedom, of opening and closing, beginnings and endings. It spoke to the duty and obligation of those so bound in duty to the land and its people. They could bring joy or woe; the choice was theirs. The Founding Families were charged with the care of the island's occupants. They became the Leigelords of Avalon. Their Oaths upheld the tapestry of power that wove its way through the soil and into the people.

Druids were gifted no such symbols of office. Their duty was to the land and its magics alone. It was a heavy burden and a path often walked alone. Free from the obligations of the mortal world, many allied themselves with the Divine Courts who were likewise bound to its shores. To ensure no one Divine gained undue control over the magic of the island, the Ollam agreed that should one swear allegiance to a Divine, another within their ranks would swear to its opposite.

Vicnis Tomte was bound to his Divine Sire from the moment of his birth. The blood of The Goodfellow flowed within him surely as the blood of the fae-born elf who was his mother. One among the Druidic Circle was fated to belong to The Jailer from the moment Tomte took his initiation vows.

Phaendar lifted their eyes from the pool of water and gazed skyward for a moment. A chill wind blew across the silvered surface of the still pond. They scowled and focused their attention on the shoreline. Something moved in the trees that overlooked the water. Dark eyes, and darker feathers.

They were being watched.

"You know your place, Blood Raven," Phaendar hissed. "This bloodletting will benefit you just as surely as it will Him."

A flutter of raven wings answered the Druid's words as a score of black feathered messengers took flight and scattered to the winds.

Phaendar snarled at the Blood Raven's spies as they took to flight. Her eyes covered the island. Nothing went missing that She did not know about. Hers was the realm of blood born in battle, foretelling, and secrets. Before the Reaping, it was said that the Blood Raven had been part of a trio of sisters, and She was the only one to survive the last battle. She took up the mantles of her fallen siblings to honor their sacrifices to Avalon. Which one she had been originally no one knew. The enigmatic Divine of the pantheon of Avalon was the most distant in humanity, but the most visible in effect. Wherever there was war, She was present.

And the ravens were her emissaries.

"Bollox and pox!" Phaendar swore and stood. The soil around their footprints darkened as black tendrils extended into the water and floated downstream. Glancing about, they knelt once more and buried their gnarled fingers into the soil. "Where are you?" Phaendar demanded. "Show yourself!"

The earth around Phaendar's hands rumbled and rose. A rough earthen work map of the area seemed to fashion itself before them. They pulled their hand free and examined the three-dimensional map of the mountain and its surrounding lands. To the south, the glades on the map rippled and tiny wolves seemed to emerge. To the north and the east, boars broke free from the thickets. Scattered above the mountain itself, tiny specks of winged darkness flew on invisible updrafts. Phaendar snarled, their once beautiful features twisted into horror and darkness.

"You've chosen to get involved, after all, I see," Phaendar muttered. "Finally decided that there was enough upheaval to warrant investigation? Very well, my lovelies," they cooed. "Let us dance this merry dance, shall we?" they giggled.

Closing their almond-shaped eyes, Phaendar called on words known only to those sworn to the land as they were. Darkness swirled around their figure as they raised their arms above their head. Balling up their fists, Phaendar smashed them down hard onto the earth worked map. It shattered beneath their touch.

Far below them, the earth rumbled, shook, and broke open.

~~~

Cynfael's ax cleaved deeply into the fetid flesh of the creature before him. A sound escaped its lungs that tore through the air and sent shivers and shudders through his massive form.

"To your right!" he yelled.

Around him, a swarm of black figures rolled across the open field, roiling and churning like boiling water. It flowed in staggered and stuttering steps, advancing and retreating around the gathered warriors. Whiplike tendrils lashed out and struck at them, grasping and tearing at flesh. For every successful strike, a warrior fell, grasping at flesh that withered from where it had been touched.

The cries of the fallen filled his ears and drove him further into the fray.

"Go, go, go!" Gruffydd shouted. Green and brown clad Scouts dispersed around the fray, splitting from the group and drawing attention in far too many directions to be tracked. One! They just needed *one* of them to get past this.

Leaping over felled trees and fallen fellows, the chosen of the Stag Lord vaulted quickly away. Steeling their hearts against the deaths that lay behind them, they focused on a single goal – to reach the riverbank.

Behind them, Cynfael roared and brought his mighty weapon down once more.

Run. I have to run. Don't look back. Just get to the other side.

The air burned in Ygraine's lungs as she darted across the field. Her legs ached from the march and the run. Sweat ran down her back, stinging in rips and tears in her flesh from brambles and thorns. Her fingers wrapped tightly around the haft of a spear. She could hear the sounds of battle behind her.

Don't look. It's not for you. You have a job. One job, and it is not fighting what is behind you.

Someone screamed beside her.

She pressed her eyes closed for a moment to silence the sound. Tears welled up in her brown eyes. She brushed them away with her free hand.

Cold. I am so cold.

Her stomach ached like she had swallowed a stone. Part of her wanted to retch.

Water. I see the water. Almost there.

The Seers had told Cynfael that victory lay on the other side of the river. They did not know more than that, only that they had to reach the other side. She grit her teeth and pushed forward.

A sound like an animal's growl vibrated from the earth below her. She felt a strange shaking as her feet missed their stride. The earth was trembling. She stumbled. Leaning forward, she staggered and regained her balance as the earth before her split open.

A long, jagged wound in the soil broke open, splitting the surface of the island. Soil, rocks, and plants tumbled into the crevasse as it opened and widened, separating the riverbank from the battleground.

Jump it. A voice whispered in her ear.

"What!"? Ygraine started, almost stopping in her tracks at the unexpected sound.

Use the spear and vault it. The voice said again.

Wide-eyed, Ygraine stared at the dark scar on the earth that was quickly approaching. Fear knotted in her stomach and clenched her heart momentarily.

"It's too far. I can't."

Pbbbt. Bullshit. Do it. The voice chided, making a dissatisfied and almost child-like sound at her comment.

Chicken. The voice taunted.

The word nagged at her mind. She clenched her jaw and fixed her eyes on the far side. She took as deep a breath as her lungs would allow and shifted her grip on the haft of the spear. Her legs pumped hard, propelling her forward.

Do it.

She narrowed her eyes and leaned into the run. The crevasse approached.

Stick it and jump.

Listening to the voice, Ygraine planted the end of the spear firmly into the soil at the edge of the fissure and pushed herself up, vaulting into the air and across the barrier. A cry escaped her throat as she soared through the air. A sound of determination, exaltation, and freedom.

Then the ground was approaching on the other side, and she was falling out of the air.

"Oh shit," she swore as she tumbled to the ground and rolled into a heap. She landed at the feet of a familiar figure. Shading her eyes, she looked up at Gruffydd's bloodied face. His eyes were wide with surprise and admiration. He extended a calloused hand down to her and pulled Ygraine to her feet.

"Let's go kill a Druid."

That's my girl.

~~~

They had seen no other members of the Free People along the riverbank since the earth-shaking occurred. Crossing the river was the next task. Normally Gruffydd would have suggested simply finding a shallow section and fording it from one bank to the next. Both knew that the water could be polluted with whatever poison Phaendar had placed at the headwaters. Swimming here could risk infecting them both. Also likely was the possibility of one of the river denizens being corrupted and attacking them. Water fighting was something they all knew how to do, but not knowing the dangers of the enemy would make it more challenging, and delays were not something they could afford.

They decided they would trek upriver to locate a safer place to cross. Gruffydd remembered a footbridge close to where they had left the rest of the clan. With luck, it was still standing.

They walked silently, following a footpath that followed the river's edge, neither speaking of what they had left behind and what may or may not have befallen their fellows and family. Gruffydd kept his eyes on the surrounding area, constantly searching for signs of movement. The lead Scout knew Phaendar was a skilled and gifted spell caster, bonded to the land as few were. He also remembered the tales of how old this specific Ollam was. Some said Phaendar was kin to Lady Bellicent herself. A sibling or child, no one really knew, and the Lady was not likely to confirm the rumors.

Overhead, a pair of ravens circled, drifting effortlessly on the updrafts. Gruffydd narrowed his eyes at them and gestured for Ygraine to look skyward. The young woman shaded her eyes and looked up at the pair of birds.

"Scavengers looking to feast on the dead?" she asked quietly.

Gruffydd pursed his lips. "Hrmm, possibly, but there should be more of them if that were the case." He searched the tree line and sniffed at the chill breeze. He shook his head. "They are following us."

Ygraine frowned. She remembered the flock of ravens at Whitebrooke and how they sat in the trees watching the group explore the ruins. "Do you think they know something?"

Gruffydd chuckled. "They always do."

"What do they want?"

"The same thing their mistress wants. Blood. Flesh. Knowledge." he glanced over at Ygraine. "Power."

Ygraine nodded and continued walking slightly to the side and behind Gruffydd. "Why do you think they are doing this? Phaendar?"

Gruffydd shook his head and grunted, "Who knows why the Ollam does what they do? Phaendar is ancient and has seen more cycles than is probably truthfully recorded. Perhaps the age sickness has taken them. Who knows?" He shrugged slightly.

"Do you think that will happen to Bellicent someday?" she asked. She spoke in hushed tones, whispering the name of the ancient Elven druid advisor as if hoping not to be heard.

"Hrmph," Gruffydd scoffed. "The village-born are not my concern, and I bend no knee to the Leigelords and their Oaths." He glanced sideways at Ygraine. "And neither should you, Little Wolf."

Ygraine's hand tightened a little around her spear. She relaxed and nodded.

Ahead of them, the river narrowed deeply. Laying across the banks was a large wooden bridge. Twenty feet across and wide enough for a horse and cart, the fixture was in good repair. Solid-looking wooden pillars held the bridge three feet above the water. It looked like a large door, laying across the water, bank to bank. No doubt this was the work of a wood wright or master carpenter from one of the villages. It was well crafted and clearly designed to carry both goods and gear across the river. This would be the principal thoroughfare to Mynydd Mawr. Phaendar would not have had to come this way, but anyone following them may.

Standing at the water's edge stood a figure familiar to both Ygraine and Gruffydd. Tall and broad-shouldered, her thick dark hair was knotted and braided into a series of intricate designs. Woven into these strands were heavy weights and hooks. Across her back was hung a heavy war bow. She was dressed in leather armor that had been boiled and soaked in wax and hardened to an almost metal consistency. Detailed patterns were carved and painted into her pauldrons, greaves, and vambraces; symbols of her patron, the Huntress. At her side stood an enormous boar, outfitted as a mount.

Maelona turned to face the pair as they approached the bridge. Her deep red eyes scrutinized them both. She shifted her weight and let her hand come to rest on a short sword sheathed and hanging from her waist.

Gruffydd paused and held up his hand for Ygraine to do likewise. He remembered the Orc Chieftain. She had come to the moot to meet with Cynfael and hear what the Scouts had discovered in Whitebrooke. She appeared to be alone. Gruffydd frowned slightly and glanced behind the big orc woman.

"I am alone, freeborn," Maelona's deep voice spoke. She looked from Gruffydd to Ygraine and then back to the Scout. "As apparently, are you? I assume we track the same prey?"

Gruffydd regarded Maelona carefully and then nodded. "We do."

"Good," she nodded simply, and turned back to her mount. "We will have better luck felling him now." She put her foot in the stirrup and pulled herself up onto the beast. It grunted and chuffed. She reached down to pat its coarse hair with her broad hand. "My people thank you for your information. It has proven most useful."

Gruffydd nodded, and they approached the mounted orc on her giant beast of a boar. "So you believe me now?" he asked.

Maelona sniffed and inclined her head. "The Wanderer sent the Whitebrooke woman to us. With your information, we sent for Ollam Vicnis. The Ollam made some sense of the senseless."

Ygraine's eyes widened slightly. "Isolde? You saw Isolde?" she asked quickly.

Maelona quirked a bushy eyebrow at the tall youth. "Saw and almost killed. If it were not for the blessing of her Lord, she would be walking the Crossroads."

Ygraine narrowed her eyes at the comment. Her hand tightened around the haft of the spear. A low growl rumbled in her chest. Maelona stared at Ygraine, unflinching and unmoved by the gesture. Then she laughed deeply.

"Save your spite, young one. She and her Sun Skin left our village unharmed to continue her quest. They should be in Swansea by morning." Maelona's Er'che tugged at its bridle and shifted its weight.

"And Ollam Vicnis?" Gruffydd inquired.

"The Ollam is sequestered and fashioning a cure for this plague that his fallen sibling has crafted. He will send it by eagle to my people who wait for it at the headwaters."

Gruffydd exhaled deeply at the news. Tension in his chest and shoulders that he did not know he carried faded. "Then it is over," he breathed.

"No. Not yet." She smiled wickedly at them both, her lips curling back over her tusks. "Now we find the bastard that tried to murder us all.

"And end him."

Chapter 53

Phaendar ducked behind the rocky outcropping and gazed skyward. Above them, a pair of black ravens circled, watching.

They snarled in both anger and dissatisfaction at the obvious betrayal of the Blood Raven's servants. They had helped the Sage keep watch over Whitebrooke these many months, keeping it safe from prying eyes and the curious queries of the Wandering Lord's minions. Rocks left unturned; secrets nestled safely away under the breath of the Morpheum. The presence of the ravens above now meant that their uneasy truce was over.

Whitebrooke's fate must have been uncovered.

Which meant Phaendar's involvement would soon be known.

If you hurry, you can still make it. Phaendar whispered. *Yes. It was still possible.* There had been left enough trouble in Phaendar's wake to delay anyone attempting to follow them. They were particularly proud of the sundew. Lovely little carnivorous plant. It needed only the barest of nudges to blossom into the true predator they knew it could become.

How many souls had been sent to The Jailer's keeping?

Was it enough?

Lord of Riches.

Lord of Prisons.

Lord of the Underworld.

The Mainland poison would ensure their spirits would not return to the Cycle, but to the Lord's safekeeping. Separated from the Cycle, they would not return to breathe Avalon's magic into their lungs once again. It would weaken the magic of the island, and its link to the Morpheum. Gates would close. Magic would fade. Spirits trapped in the endless pattern of birth-death-rebirth might finally know rest. No more child rulers born to be betrayed and fall at the hands of trusted friends.

Let it end. Can't it just end?

As the ravens made their circles in the sky, Phaendar ducked quickly around the rocks and darted toward the fissure in the mountainside. Hammered into the dark scar of the rocky slope was an ornate iron hook: Suspended from the hook hung a lantern. The light from the lantern shone brightly through glass tinted blue. Ornate cutwork patterns covered the sides of the lantern, symbols, and sigils of the Regency of Avalon.

The Lady's Heart.

This was the entrance to the depths of the island's heart, where legends claimed the Mother Herself slept in peaceful dreams. Phaendar and the other Ollam of Avalon knew better. The Druids were bound to the magic of the island, just as the Founding Families were bound to its people. Ancient Oaths, whose true meanings were long forgotten, were woven into the initiation of every spell crafter chosen to walk this path. Something did sleep in the murky depths of the caverns below. Something whose dreams breathed magic into the air, bones, and blood of Avalon. And it was not Divine.

Whitebrooke's key would open the vault below.

Phaendar's hand slid to the small box that they carried. The box contained the items smuggled from the mainland by the Vidria dwarf. Two tiny bulbs, blessed by the arts of a fae-born elf and welcomed to Avalon by an Ollam of the Circle. It was the only way something not of the island could ever hope to take root on these shores. A keeper of the magic of the land had to bless it and welcome it fully and completely. The shores of Avalon had been sacrosanct for millennia. Sole survivors of a realm of magic and dreams, the Ollam and Founders promised to keep it safe for eternity, to stand as a shield against another Reaping, and preserve the only people of the Realm of Avalon left in the entire universe. The only way to preserve that heritage, in its purest of forms, was to prevent anything from the Mainland from thriving here. Seeds would not germinate. Seedlings nurtured elsewhere failed when planted in Avalonian soil. While lovers brought from the mainland to Avalon could sire families, their offspring became bound to the Island. This, of course, often meant never leaving these shores. Never seeing their parent's place of birth, despite Mainland family protests. Such protest eventually quieted as the Mainland parent met an unfortunate and 'accidental' end.

It ensured Avalon's "uniqueness" on Sanctum.

This was the only way to end it.

It has to end. It can't go on like this forever. -I- cannot go on like this ... forever.

Phaendar's hand shook slightly as their fingers caressed the wooden box.

It was for the best.

Three millennia. Phaendar had stood this post faithfully for three thousand years, guarding the sacred magics, both weal and woe equally. Watching, always from a distance, as Clans warred, fell, and rose again. The ever-eternal cycle of life-birth-death and rebirth of every soul that was brought to Sanctum and tied to the lands of Avalon. How many names had Phaendar known the same people by throughout the millennia? How many times had they held the same hands in birth and again in death? The stalwart and reliable Ollam, keeper of magic and the soul of Avalon herself. How many fae-born had Phaendar ushered through the Morpheum, only to stand silently as they pleaded for peace as the Free People drove an iron-bound spear through their hearts in the name of the Triskele Trinity? How many times had they called upon Phaendar to stand vigil at a Chieftain's funeral pyre, to ensure someone properly ushered their spirit across the river at the Crossroads?

How many more times would they be condemned to standing in the darkness, bearing witness through the windows of life, while the land continued around them.

Enough. It had to be enough.

Phaendar's face was wet. They blinked blurry tears from their eyes and wiped at their cheeks. Symbols of their own fragility dripped from their fingertips and onto the earth, blackening the soil where it may once have brought life.

Damn you, Bellicent for what you have done. This was not what you promised us.

The Sage cleared their throat and tucked the box away once more. They glanced around quickly to gauge safety. They would be coming.

Soon.

In the distance, along the tree lines, they spied movement. Foe. It could never be a friend. Not now. A somber note hummed in the center of Phaendar's chest. They held their hands before them, waist high, and rolled them outward and around as if forming a ball in the air. Their now bloodshot eyes focused on the movement in the tree line as their right hand pushed the energy out and away.

Die.

It started as a sphere no larger than an orange and quickly grew as it flew toward its target. Black, charred earth followed the sphere, destroying everything in its wake. When it reached the tree line, the sphere was as wide as a doorway was tall. Swirling inky blackness writhed within its depths, like a giant mass of black maggots.

"MOVE!"

Maelona shouted and shoved Gruffydd to the left as the sphere approached the windbreak of the trees. She ducked and rolled to the right, hoping to clear the distance between herself and the rot that the Ollam had thrown at them.

"Dammit!" Gruffydd swore and stagger stumbled away in the direction that the orc had pushed him. "Go, Little Wolf, run!" he yelled to Ygraine.

Ygraine's eyes widened as she watched the magic manifest and fly in their direction.

No. Her stomach knotted as her fears were made manifest, witnessing the ancient Ollam betraying everything they stood for. But her legs obeyed the commands of the Scout who issued them. She turned and darted away, leaping over brambles and fallen trees like a deer. She could hear Gruffydd behind her, his own steps blessed by the Stag Lord himself found purchase on the ground and propelled him swiftly forward.

Behind them, all the screaming squeals of an Er'che filled the air. The sphere broke open as it crashed against the tree line. Unmeasurable mounds of black, writhing rot splattered across the trunks of the trees and toward the Maelona's mount. As the substance reached the Er'che's flesh, it seared and burned into it, black tentacled miasma digging deep. The giant shuddered and squealed, then its eyes widened in fear as its knees buckled and it collapsed.

In the distance, Maelona roared in anger and grief, as her Gurkh rose to take control. Blood demanded blood.

Gruffydd's hand landed on Ygraine and pulled her back around the edge of a large redwood. He pressed them both against the rough surface of the tree. And listened.

"We need to know who Phaendar is tracking," he whispered quietly.

Ygraine scowled and tried to pull herself free. Her stomach burned with rage and fire. She wanted to charge the Ollam and bury the tip of her spear into their flesh.

Gruffydd's hand grabbed her shoulder and slammed her into the tree's surface to clear her head. "I need your focus on me now, Little Wolf," he hissed.

She growled a little in response and swiveled her eyes toward him.

"What!" she demanded.

Gruffydd's eyes were locked on hers, his fingers dug deeply into her flesh. "That is an *Ollam*. Not a bear. Not a boar. Not a gods-be-damned trout in a stream. Are you hearing me?" he demanded.

She narrowed her eyes and then nodded her head. Her fingers wrapped around the haft of the spear. "Yes."

"Good." He took a deep breath and glanced around the edge

of the tree to get a bead on the location of the elf. They had not moved. Phaendar seemed to stand in the center of a mass of writhing ooze. Gruffydd glanced skyward quickly and back down, trying to find something to use to gauge distance with. He saw movement in the trees some twenty yards away from where the body of the Er'che lay. Maelona. She was a larger target than they were and might possess the ability to fell the Ollam.

Maybe.

Gruffydd ducked back around the tree and gestured to Ygraine to move farther along the tree line. They needed to put distance between themselves and the Er'che. It would eventually get back up, and they would have to deal with it. However, the farther away they were when that happened, the better chance they might have of escaping it.

But first, they had to deal with Phaendar.

Ygraine did as instructed and hastened to take up a position where Gruffydd instructed. Behind a fallen tree, they crouched and waited.

"Do you know how to do it?"

"Do what?" Gruffydd asked as they took up their positions. He divided his attention between their location, listening to the sounds the Er'che was making and trying to keep Phaendar in his sights. Sweat trickled down the side of his face; he wiped it away quickly.

"Kill an Ollam," Ygraine asked.

On the surface, it seemed a simple question. How does one kill another creature? The target area for a solid kill shot varied on every animal. It was something that every member of the Free People learned from the moment they were old enough to carry a weapon. For a deer, it was behind the front leg, below the shoulder blade, and above the elbow. Bear and Boar were similar. Wolves were higher and better if targeted from the front.

Humans.

Humanoids.

Very different.

The Stag Lord was not the Huntress. He was the Lord of the Wilds and the creatures that dwell therein. There was a distinction between targeting an animal to feed the village and killing a man. It was what set Scouts apart from Warriors. They trained a Warrior to take a life if the circumstances called for it, in defense of the Free People. A Scout – scouted ... and brought down predators that threatened the hunting grounds. When at war within the Triskele they might be called upon to fell another of the Free People, but it was never without thought, and never without weight.

That did not mean they were not trained to understand how to do it. If need be.

Phaendar was not simply a fae-born elf. They were a Sage. A Historian. A keeper of knowledge, magic, and tradition. A teacher.

They were part of the soul of the island. Felling Phaendar meant dealing a blow to the Heart of Avalon itself.

In the distance, a strange gurgling squeal sounded from the body of the Er'che as it moved once more.

Then again, Phaendar clearly had no issues with corrupting the island. That was a far cry worse than the mercy of a swift kill.

"We don't," Gruffydd answered Ygraine.

Ygraine frowned at Gruffydd. "We came all this way to NOT end this?" she demanded.

Gruffydd shook his head. "You misunderstand." He leaned back and over the edge of the tree to get a glimpse of things.

The second ball of dark miasma flew toward the trees where Maelona had been. As it left Phaendar's hands, they focused on the squealing figure of the fallen Er'che. They reached their hands out to it and lifted them as if lifting the creature himself. It slowly rose.

Gruffydd drew a hissing breath between his teeth as he watched the creature rise once more. They had little time.

Every creature on the island was tied to one another. The

common bond they shared was the Realm of dreams called the Morpheum. It was a place between the Real and the home of the Divine. Every Avalonian carried part of the Morpheum within them; it was the source of their magic. Every creature from the Morpheum was bound by magic far older than Avalon itself. Magics that dictated actions, desires, hungers.

And weaknesses.

Phaendar was an Ollam. They were also Fae-born Elf. These two items meant they were thrice bound to the magic of the Morpheum more than any other. And thrice as vulnerable to the weapons used to bring them down.

"We don't kill an Ollam today. We kill a creature of the Morpheum."

A familiar voice giggled in Ygraine's ear.

Ohhhh, this is a good trick. I like it.

She scowled and looked around quickly.

Gruffydd narrowed his eyes at her reaction. Then they widened, and he nodded in silent understanding. Her place among the Free People was being decided by the Divine even now.

"What do you need me to do?" She asked.

I'm sorry.

Gruffydd reached to his quiver and pulled out a long arrow. Ygraine's eyes widened as Gruffydd withdrew the shaft. She recognized it immediately. The shaft was heavy and fashioned from a wood far paler than any other in Gruffydd's possession. The point was wide and hammered flat, sharpened to a razor's thinness. It seemed to be coated in a red substance. That same red color was infused into the sinew that bound the iron point to the shaft. Scarlet-tipped feathers fletched the end. Holly. Iron. Mistletoe. This was a shaft crafted for a single purpose. To kill fae-touched creatures of the Morpheum.

"I need you to distract him, Little Wolf," Gruffydd said quietly.

Oh, I don't like this game anymore.

Ygraine's face blanched momentarily. She nodded slowly. "I

... understand." She swallowed hard and took a deep breath. A fire burned at the base of her spine and in the pit of her stomach. She thought back to the morning she and Owen had tracked the elk into the hills, and the warning she had given him.

That animal is in pain and wearing a rack of weapons that the gods granted it for its protection. It will not hesitate to take us with it before it dies. Remember that.

Her fingers wrapped tightly around the shaft of her spear. She laughed a little as the weight of it all sunk in. The Divine had granted all predators with weapons with which to defend themselves. She would just have to use hers.

"OK. Let's do it."

~~~

Black ravens soared lazily over the clearing that opened in the trees at the base of Mynydd Mawr. Their dark eyes focused intently on the scene that unfolded below. It was difficult to discern which of the combatants involved were more startled by the scenario as it manifested.

What all could agree to after the fact was that it was ... unexpected.

A statuesque figure, painted in mud and leaves and brandishing nothing more than a spear in her right hand, broke through the tree line suddenly. Around her, a flock of ravens took to the air, startled from their perches.

Phaendar's eyes broke from where they had been focused, carefully tracking the movements of the orc chieftain. Maelona Blodwen served The Huntress, and she was a skilled killer. She, like her Divine Patron, favored a bow and could target Phaendar from a distance. Already two of her dark fletched shafts stuck from Phaendar's leg and their shoulder from where she had successfully landed shots. Scattered around the Ollam lay the bent and broken wooden shafts of at least half a dozen others. Black blood oozed from Phaendar's wounds and mixed with the dark earth.

They frowned a moment, almond-shaped eyes narrowing to

bring the scene into focus.

A half-naked human girl, covered in the forest's filth, was charging at Phaendar … with a spear.

Ygraine's voice shouted to the skies as her legs pumped and propelled her forward. It was a familiar call. Something that all who worked the farms of the island had heard at one point or another in their lifetimes.

"Woooooooooo! Pig! Pig! Pig! SOOOOOIEEEEEE!"

Behind Ygraine, a dark shape responded and charged.

Phaendar's eyes widened. First into shock, and then into horror, as they realized this crazed child was baiting Phaendar's own creation into charging her while she charged the Sage.

Oh, I like this game after all.

The giant malformed boar crashed through the broken branches; red eyes fixed on the moving target before it. Black tendrils trailed from its maw like slimy worms.

The Ollam tried to move toward the entrance of the cavern. If they could make it inside, they could finish this. An arrow exploded into the rocks next to Phaendar's face. Splinters rained in the air. They swore and turned their attention back to the orc.

Maelona stood boldly at the edge of the trees. She paid no heed to the girl or the charging boar that followed her. Her sights were trained on the traitor to the island. Calloused fingers gripped the bowstring. She took a breath and drew.

Run. Run. Run. Just keep running. Ygraine repeated in her mind. *Hit the rocks, climb. Can it climb? Doesn't matter. It just needs to hit THEM.*

She tasted copper in her mouth and felt the muscles in her legs burn. *Phaendar's looking over... Maelona!* She thought as her eyes locked on the orc Chieftain. Behind her, she could feel the chill of the air that preceded the thing that was no longer an Er'che as it pursued her. *Not like this, please, not like this.*

The oily surface of corruption and blight was fast approaching her. She was going to have to make a decision. Could she jump it and land on the rocks? Like the river? Maybe.

Don't be an idiot. That same familiar child-like voice chided. *You can't make that.*

She felt insulted.

Plant it and sidestep. Swing wide. She's a big piggie.

The slick of corruption was upon her, as was Phaendar. The Sage turned quickly to see them approach and ducked behind a large outcropping of rocks. They were going to get away.

Three things happened in rapid succession. A trinity of actions, all converging on the Ollam's position at once:

A rowan shaft fletched with eagle feathers shot past Ygraine and into Phaendar. And then through them. It stuck fast into the shadow of the fae-born druid. Phaendar howled in pain. As the rowan shaft pierced his shadow, an iron-tipped holly shaft followed it, meeting the Druid's center of mass and slicing easily through intercostal muscles and into their heart. Phaendar's eyes widened as the iron point burned into their fae blood. As the archers targeted their prey, Ygraine buried the butt end of the staff into the ground and swung herself in a wide circle, throwing her body clear of the charging path of the blight felled boar that barreled directly into the body of its creator and the side of the mountain.

Rocks tumbled from hallowed heights to fall upon the crushed figure of the fallen Ollam and ravens soared silently above.

Chapter 54

Isolde's bellow was full of rage as she brought the sword down on the creature. If it used to be a cat or a dog, it was difficult to tell. She could feel the blade slice through the shoulder blade as she shifted forward, kicking the thing in the side. The howl of pain was cut short as her kick knocked the air out of its lungs with an unsettling crack. With the creature on its back, she brought the blade through its throat and twisted the blade. Blackish blood sprayed at her, but she drew up her riding cloak. It had been stained with the brackish blood of similar things. It would have to be burned. All it would have to be burned... which was ironic given that literally, everything was on fire.

She and Tulok had ridden swiftly for several miles, hoping to catch Arman before he left Swansea. Tulok had noted that the sky had looked dark as they rode eastward. That darkness had turned to the sky black. They both recognized a building fire. As they crested the top of the hill leading down to the harbor town of Swansea, they saw a flurry of bodies and fire spreading across the wooden buildings. The screams of pain and horror ran along with the wind that drove them swiftly down the hill into the billowing blackness of smoke and chaos.

Tulok's roar was louder than she remembered. It broke her train of thought. She turned and watched as he brought his mace down on another creature. She remembered him fighting a giant scorpion and the cultists long ago. That was a different time and a different orc. That orc had been tortured, naked, and fighting exhaustion. This being was completely different. Even in her own battle fury, she could feel the heat of the Gurkh emanating off of him. His movements were controlled and brutal. This was a well-rested priest of the Radiant

Lord who was destroying the corruption before him. He was frightening to behold. Tulok swung the mace into a rat-like creature, driving its head into the earth, while holding a dog-like creature aloft in his other hand, squeezing it until something popped.

All around them was a maelstrom of destruction and chaos. They had ridden down the hill to gauge the situation, to only see several of the larger ships had caught on fire. Some of the smaller ones were already below the waterline. The further they rode through the blackened smoke, the more carnage and horror they saw. The creatures of corruption were already in Swansea and were attacking the populace.

There was a high-pitched squeal, and Isolde instinctively raised her cloak once again as a spray of blackened vomit erupted on her. Swiftly drawing herself back, she felt a slice of ache and pain in her heart. A young man probably a few years younger than her, *Ygraine's age* she thought, was infected and staring her down. He was just one of the many victims of corruption. The townspeople who fought the first wave of these monstrosities had the misfortune of finding out that those who died in the attacks rose, much to their surprise and horror. However, Swansea sailors were as quick on their feet as they were with rigging. They could pivot and deal with the new threat as soon as the corrupted tried to take more of the people. The dead were put down swiftly and painfully, but the victory was fleeting. The victors soon learned those who were bitten or who had touched the blood of the corrupted became corrupted themselves. Half of Swansea was fighting itself. Taking a breath, Isolde charged at the young man, forcing her metal bracer into his jaw as she plunged her sword through her chest.

Another soul lost. Another death of Avalon.

She wanted to scream and yell at the carnage and loss of life. She wanted to weep for the dead all around her – men, women, and children. Even the creatures that were warped by the corruption – she wanted to cry out in anguish and pain, but there was no time for that.

Twisting the sword again, she pulled the sword back. Something was behind her. She screamed as she brought the sword down on the bone mace of the orc.

"ISOLDE!" Tulok shouted at her.

Isolde shook her head, "Right! Sorry! I just … sorry!"

"No! You are fine! It's a lot," he said as his eyes narrowed and he swung past her. She turned her head to see another cat-like creature in mid-leap. Tulok brought the mace down on the creature with a savage strike.

"Thank you!" she said as she took a step forward, trying to see through the smoke. There had to be more people around. Before the attacks, these were sailors and townspeople trying to put the fires on the boats out. Now it was a scattering of bodies fleeing the scene and others fighting the monstrosities that were formerly their neighbors. Ships were on fire as well as half of the bay. If Arman was here, he was dead or long gone. Isolde yelled and brought her sword down on something coming up beneath the planks below her. The spray of blackened blood was blocked by Tulok as he threw his cloak upward.

"If Arman was here, he is gone and probably the reason we are covered in death!" she said as she pulled her sword free.

Tulok swung his mace low at something else coming up over the edge of the deck. Its head snapped back, and the body soon fell in tandem. He took a deep breath as air sizzled around him. Isole could see the brackish blood had attempted to hit his skin, but the aura around him burned it like fat on a hot pan. The Radiant Lord protected his servants.

They need you.

The cool voice rang in her head as she turned. The smoke cleared for a moment and she could see a smelting house. Several creatures had surrounded the stone structure and were smashing themselves against the wooden doors and windows. The smelting houses were like smithies, but the items created were used solely on ships. Swansea's smelting house was vast enough to hold a few scores of people, but in a situation like this, it probably held the still living occupants of the town.

"We need to secure the smelting house," she said as she whipped the blood off of her sword. More of the creatures and the dead flocked toward the lone building, as Isolde and Tulok stepped forward.

Eyes of yellow and black turned their gaze at the approaching pair and hissed and screamed. Isolde raised her shield up and readied her sword.

"Allow me," Tulok said as he raised a hand and closed his eyes.

Isolde looked over at him and watched as the faint glow soon intensified around his body. She could feel the power that built as the temperature rose around him. With a graceful movement, he raised his arms high into the air, and for a moment she watched as the black smoke was pushed back, exposing the blue sky and the bright sun overhead. The Radiant Lord's Vengeance was being called. Isolde watched as he moved his arms forward with fingers outstretched and saw the power build into almost a blinding fervor. Tulok's eyes flashed open, not red but as bright as the sun, and beams of fiery light emanate from his hands. Light set ablaze all the corruption before him! The deathless and corrupted screamed and howled in pain as the divine light of the Radiant Lord burned them from existence – blazing a trail to the house. The number of creatures who stood before them was now cut in half as they desperately rolled on the ground trying to smother the fire. Yet the divine flame of the Radiant Lord continued to burn until they rolled no more.

Isolde stared with wide eyes at her companion as the light faded from his eyes, "Maybe next time we lead with that!"

An exhausted Tulok rolled his eyes. "Drawing down the Judgement of the Radiant Lord is not as simple as breaking bread! It takes time!"

Several of the creatures rushed forward, some on fire and some not, but all howled in ferocity and wrath.

Isolde turned her attention to the oncoming group. "Well then, Father, time to break bread!"

With a few quick steps, Isolde dropped her shield low and raised it up at the last moment into a larger man whose throat had been ripped open. His bloated body oozed out oily black blood. He had intended to grab onto Isolde. He soon was lifted off of his feet and thrown back and slammed into the ground. With a slash, she relieved him of his head. Quickly swinging the sword forward, the tip of the blade went into the throat of a woman covered in the black ichor. Her opened mouth gurgled with the blackened blood as Isolde planted her boot into the woman's chest.

Tulok watched as his companion continued to walk into the charging masses with no fear or hesitation at the horrors coming at her. This was no graceful swordplay, but practiced movements that ended conflicts by any means necessary. She never once looked back as she slashed and smashed her way toward the smelting house. Those that were not outright slain by her blade rolled in crippled fury as she moved past them. The Servant of the Wandering Lord was a fearless inspiration of Hope to all those that needed aid, but at this moment Isolde duAvalonne was the Wandering Lord's Knight Protector. Her sword moved in tandem with the shield and her heavy boots as she pushed herself into the wave coming toward them. Shoving her way into the fiery remains of the last wave, she turned to see her friend bring a quick end to those creatures that lingered in pain. The swath of destruction and pain they had cut through sat heavy in her chest for the briefest of moments, but fled her thoughts as soon as the cat-like creature had pounced on her. While its claw made no purchase into her armor, its full weight sat on her shield, pinning the arm.

Her focus was hyper-fixated on the creature above her. It was as if someone had melded both a cat and man together. Its hiss ended any luxury of speculation as Isolde roared back at the monstrosity. Letting go of the sword, she reached for a stone instead and threw it into the creature's face. The surprise of the rock to its skull was enough to throw it off balance, and Isolde rolled to the side. Quickly moving, she threw herself on top of the creature, pinning it down with a shield. With no weapon other than her gloved fist, she roared again and repeatedly smashed her fist into its face.

"It's dead, Isolde," said a voice behind her. She turned and realized Tulok was standing behind her. Beyond him, nothing lay moving – was it over? Had they done it?

A distressed and pained howl erupted from the other side of the harbor. They had cleared one side, but what of the other?

"Do we knock?" Tulok asked as he looked past her.

Suddenly Isolde realized they were in front of the smelting house. "Well... it is the polite thing to do," she said as she forced herself up.

Tulok reached down and gently picked up her sword and held it out to her, "After you, Ser."

"Why thank you," she said with a half-smile. Both of them took a deep breath. Exhaustion was taking hold, but they knew there was no time for it. Isolde walked over to the door and banged on it. "Is anyone in there?"

There was silence for a few heartbeats, and finally an older voice spoke. "Depends. Have you been infected?"

Tulok frowned. "Infected with a lack of patience at this moment, yes! Is anyone injured?" he said as he shook his head.

Isolde reached over and slapped Tulok's forearm. "I swear, I *cannot* take you to any life-threatening event!" She gave him a look and then addressed the door again. "My apologies. My name is Isolde duAvalonne, Witness for the Wandering Lord. Is everyone alright?"

The pair could hear movement shuffling behind the door, and another voice spoke, slightly younger. "Why is there a weird-looking orc with you?"

Tulok sighed deeply and Isolde spoke, "There were no Avalonian Orcs available, so I had to import one from across the sea."

"Cease with the questions! She's a Holy Witness you idiot, unbolt the door!" said the older voice again and they could hear objects being moved. Slowly the door opened, revealing the occupants inside. From a quick glance, they counted at least twenty children with ages ranging from toddlers to teenagers. Mixed in were a handful of adults – mostly older and all looking scared.

Isolde peered her head inside and looked around. "Is everyone okay?"

An older man who had the look of a retired sailor leaned against an old gaff hook spoke, "Mostly scared, but not hurt."

The teenage boy next to him continued to look out the door, though Tulok's presence obscured his view. "Are they gone?"

Isolde shook her head, "Not all, but ..."

There was a distant rumble. Everyone paused. This sound was something new. A toddler cried. An older woman ... she looked like someone's grandmother, began making her way toward the child. She tripped over something in the dark room. Suddenly, she looked up with horror in her eyes and wailed. Her body lifted off the ground and slammed into a workbench. Her scream of pain set off the children and chaos exploded in the room. Stepping farther in, Tulok cupped his hands and whispered into them. With a flick of his wrist, the darkened room lit up as a ball of light floated to the center.

With the added light, Isolde could see. Pink and blackish tendrils were wrapped around the woman and searching the surrounding area. Following their slime-cover trail, she could see that they were attached to the face of a monstrous creature. With a twist of its face, it opened a massive maw filled with countless teeth.

"TULOK – GET THEM UP THE HILL ... NOW!"

He paused to cast a glance in her direction.

Eyes filled with the passion and courage of the Landless Lord met his.

"I GOT THIS!"

With a boom of his voice, not so much as a roar but that of a teacher heeding your attention, "Children – it is time we found safety in the sunlight!"

The command of Tulok's voice drew all eyes on him. Stepping out of the doorway, he motioned with his hand, "Little ones, take the hands of the big ones and big ones take the hands of the older ones." While there was confusion and fear, watching the orc hold up both his hands and then grasping them together seemed to register. Grabbing each other's hands, they made their way out. Without a backward glance, Tulok motioned them to the path up the hill. As the room emptied, he began making his way with them urging them not to run, but to move as quickly and safely with their companions in tow. He heard something slam into the wall and immediately felt himself turn back. He paused in step and watched as the children and the elderly made their way up the path. They were the island's future, its legacy. Isolde was a warrior, and she gave him a responsibility to protect that legacy. He needed to honor it. He reached out his hand and helped an older man up as he continued to lead them up the path.

—

Isolde turned her attention to the creature and its whipping maw. She could see that the woman was already dead, and halfway down the creature's mouth. She waded in and sliced at the tendrils as they sensed her coming closer. When a few were cut off, the creature made an air-splitting scream and pulled its whole body out of the ground. Larger tendrils had broken through the surface and beat down on the shield, like wooden clubs. She moved and sliced her way through the onslaught when a pair of the tendrils wrapped themselves around her shield. The creature attempted to pull her off her feet, to no avail. While it was easy for it to snag and swing an elderly woman about, an armored knight was a different matter entirely. Isolde pulled her shield back and strained against the creature's own strength.

For a moment, each strained against each other's strength and Isolde bellowed at it.

"FINE! You want it? TAKE IT!"

She slid her arm out of the shield and dove across the top of a workbench. The creature whipped the shield back and slammed it against the wall. Pulling herself up quickly, she realized that there was only one way to get in close as she spied the forge chains hanging from the rafters above. Backing away, she sheathed her sword as the tendrils lashed out and wrapped themselves across the heavy workbench. The creature lumbered forward, allowing Isolde to see the massive claws breaking through the ground. She had angered it to the point of climbing out of the ground. Seeing the beast in the light, she saw the bloated monstrosity in all of its disturbing glory. By design, it appeared to be a mole the size of an enormous bear, but its form was grossly disproportionate. It should not have been able to move as it did, but with the additional appendages, tendrils, and the slimy black coat of ichor that covered its body, this unsettling madness was a dangerous reality.

It slammed the heavier of its tendrils down at the long table between them, but it did not give.

"Craftsmanship," said to the beast as she leaped up on the table and grabbed the dangling forge chain.

The loud clanking rattle of metal on metal set its feelers into a frenzy of motion.

"Ahh ... somebody doesn't like LOUD NOISES, EH!" she yelled as she pulled more of the chain free, and walked it further down the table.

Tendrils shot out at her as she walked back down the long table, whipping the chain like a noisy lure, until one tendril wrapped around and wrenched it from her grasp. Excited at grasping its prize, the creature yanked on the chain, causing more loud noises, which caused it to pull more of the chain.

As the creature pulled the chain, Isolde jumped upward and hoisted herself into the rafters. The rattling of metal hid the sound of her footsteps as she quickly made her way above the creature. She drew the sword from its scabbard and raised her shoulders with the blade aimed downward. She took a breath. Without a sound, she dropped on the head of the beast. Her blade slid through the flesh and bone of its skull. Something snapped in the base of the creature's neck. It convulsed. Brackish blood spewed freely, covering Isolde in hot, wet, and foul. Unmoved, she twisted the blade.

The massive creature ceased moving.

Wrenching the blade free with a grunt, Isolde calmly walked away from the creature. She lay the blade carefully on the table and bowed her head. Her heart beat loudly in her chest. Infected blood and gore coated her body. It dripped from her hair and ran down the back of her neck and into her gorget. She glanced up briefly, but there was no one. No healer to lend aid. No sun god to burn away the taint.

The Wandering Lord held fear away from the hearts of His chosen. This could be both a boon or a bane. As she stood in the center of the infected carnage, she was not afraid.

Isolde felt only sadness.

She stared at the blade on the table – Reynard's blade. Her fingers touched its edge carefully. The blade she had lost once in the dunes of a far-off desert. A blade she had mourned the loss of, and one that the hands of a smiling Reysis had returned.

Safar.

Pain punched her in the chest. She gasped at the ferocity of the feeling. It was not poison, but grief. She grit her teeth and swallowed it down. They would not take her like this.

I am the light in the darkness ...

Looking down at her hands, she saw it moving. The black oily blood. It moved along her skin as if trying to find some purchase. She could feel it on her face, trying to run into her eyes, nose, and mouth. It slid and slipped, but seemed to find no purchase. She marveled at it for a moment.

She hoped it would not be Tulok who would have to end her. Avalon ... and she ... had taken so much from him already. She could not imagine how he would feel if he had to be the one to end her as well. It might break him. He was strong, but that would kill what was left of the gentle scholar she once knew. She shook her head. No, she would not allow that to happen. While she still had control, she would handle this herself. She caressed the blade once more.

Tearing her eyes from the strange liquid, she grasped hold of the hilt of the blade and lifted it from the table. Through the open door, she could see that the dark smoke had thinned, and the blue waters of the sea were visible once again. It was a beautiful last sight; she thought to herself. Closing her eyes, she slowly braced the blade …

Are you done being melodramatic? We have a village to save …

Her eyes flashed open. She looked around the room. She knew the voice. He was always with her.

With slight tickle on the skin, she felt the warmth of the ichor fade and drip off her. Like oil on water, it could find no purchase and slid free to the ground in great droplets. It pooled on the ground around her.

She was not infected!

She reached for her compass and wrapped her fingers tightly around it. "Thank you," she whispered.

Fight now – thank later!

"Of course!" she agreed, feeling the bolstering bluster of the Wandering Lord upon her once more. Brandishing the sword, she strode toward the front door. As she stepped out into the sunlight, she heard another rumble of sound. Along the far side of the shore, she saw them. They rushed for the smelting house. An infected mass of creatures and deathless Avalonians charged toward Isolde and the only road out of Swansea. She opened her arms wide and roared at the masses charging the Avalonian Knight. If they wanted the survivors of Swansea, they would need to go through her.

Gripping her sword with both hands, she swung as the infected beasts leaped into the air with claws drawn and teeth bared.

"YOUR HOSPITALITY IS REVOKED!" she bellowed.

Chapter 55

The fading sun warmed his skin as the ocean spray crested the bow of the ship. A few days on the water and then he would feel the familiar cobblestones of Port Kraken once again.

And put this damnable island behind me once and for all.

Arman sighed and closed his eyes, feeling the weight of his task shift slightly. For the first time in what felt like years, he felt a twinge of hope. Locked in his cabin was a wealth that was immeasurable. A small collection that was now one greater for the success of this journey.

One step closer to fulfilling my debt.

He glanced skyward, holding his hand to the sky and the horizon, and counted lines on his hand. There should still be enough time.

"Settling in, Master Dah'ay?" a deep voice asked.

Arman smiled slightly and nodded. "Indeed, Captain Hywel. Your Hospitality is worth every favor exchanged."

"I am glad to hear it." The broad figure of the blonde Captain stepped up to the rail where Arman stood. He placed his hands behind his back and watched the horizon. Light glinted off of the golden rings that decorated the cartilage of his upper ear. Behind them, a great heavy rope was being pulled across the entrance to the harbor by several smaller boats.

"It would appear that we made sail in time to avoid something of some note," Hywel commented.

Arman opened his eyes and glanced behind them. His eyebrows raised slightly. "So it would seem." He looked up at the lantern-jawed Captain, a quizzical look in his eye.

Hywel shrugged. "Some matter or another inland involving the Free People and the Druids. I try not to involve myself in their affairs."

Arman frowned slightly and turned back to watch the water. *What have you done, Phaendar?*

"The Trademaster took ill recently as well," Hywel continued. "Strangest ailment anyone has seen in some time."

Arman nodded as he listened.

"Old Farnak said it had something to do with Morpheum creatures and curses. Some Folk wanted to blame the Goodfellow for it all. Seemed like something He'd be behind, master of misdirection and mischief that He is. Turns out that old charmer had nothing to do with it. Farnak had to actually work with one of the Blood Raven's people to make it right." he chuckled darkly and shook his head. "Blood Raven and Wanderer working hand-in-hand to save a lineage. Not sure when something like THAT has been seen hereabouts. Maybe Goodfellow was involved after all." Hywel fixed his eyes on the horizon as he spoke. He paused for an uncomfortable moment. "You were sponsored by Maitresse Lynet, weren't you?" he inquired.

Arman nodded simply. "I was. Lynet and I have known each other for many years."

Hywel pursed his lips. "Well, I'm sure you are glad that she is recovering then. Would be a shame to lose a Patron of her caliber. Might take an entire lifetime for a Mainlander to secure a Patron like that."

"I will have to make certain to send her some of her favorites as a get-well wish. Perhaps some Agelian wine. I know just the year." Arman smiled softly.

Hywel regarded the smaller man for a moment. Eyes trained to search for leug found nothing on the soul of the Vidria dwarf but the emptiness of the Mainland.

"Well, Master Dah'ay let me know if you need anything. We have about five days sailing ahead of us, providing the lane stays clear." Hywel nodded simply. He reached up and rubbed his left ear. A flash of black ink showed. A tiny black bird tattooed behind his ear. He turned and strode back across the deck, leaving the Vidria to his thoughts.

Five days on the ocean, then peace at last. Arman sighed as a smile tugged gently at the corners of his mouth. *Three of five tasks were completed. Only two left.* One would be harder than the other. As Phaendar had said, it had never been done.

The Universe had never been destroyed before the Reaping either. Yet here they were.

"There is no such thing as never. There is only until now."

There was a place that would hold the information that Arman sought. A place of collected memories of both the living and the dead. The Grand Library at the necropolis of Litharge.

Back to Setesh.

Behind them, some of the crew moved crates around to redistribute the weight of goods being transported from the island to Port Kraken. One box shifted awkwardly and tipped forward. A dark bearded sailor caught it deftly and gently shoved it back in place, then secured its ropes. Sweat glistened on his weathered skin. His dark eyes darted in Arman's direction, and then he glanced skyward.

Far above, a dark silhouette glided on unseen air currents. Raven black feathers stretched outward in the fading light of the sun.

~~~

There was a popping sound followed by an edited exclamation, "WORDS! WORDS ... I cannot say in front of children!" Isolde swore as she dug her fingers into the earth.

Tulok let go of her nose and pulled his fingers away from her face. He glanced at the freshly reset bones and nodded, satisfied with his work "... and that, children, is how you reset someone's nose." The group of teenagers sat around and watched in awe as the orc finished his healing ministrations on the Wandering Knight.

A group of survivors had carried her up from the shoreline. Covered in blood, ichor, and mud, they lay her at the feet of the orc priest, hoping beyond hope that the Radiant Lord might yet save her.

"You are making a habit of this," Tulok had said as he roused the Champion from her unconsciousness. At least she had not been dead.

"Just … making sure you were … paying attention …" she coughed and cleared her airways of blood.

It was possible he reset her nose at that moment to punctuate his own point.

Isolde sat up slowly. Her head swam. She paused and stretched. It hurt. Wincing but able to breathe once again, "Everything is going to smell like fish and blood for a week, but it's good to smell something at least." she offered a smile and regretted it almost immediately.

Tulok leaned back on his heels and stared down at the armored woman. He folded his arms across his broad chest. "You know, there will come a day when I am not there to reset your nose … again. Do try to be more careful," Tulok said. His deep voice rumbled gently in his chest. There was more to be said, but not here. Not now. The gathered teens continued to watch the pair.

He cleared his throat.

"You keep leading with your face, you will only look half as good as me," he commented with an awkward smile-snarl. Several of the teens laughed.

"Oh, really?" Isolde replied. She moved to add more, but someone called out from another group. A man waved to catch attention and limped toward them, favoring his right leg,

"Um …your … Father, uh Radiant Priest… sir … There are few others coming up the hill that could use your aid."

Tulok turned toward the man and then looked back down the hill. "Of course!" He looked back at Isolde, who was already shoving a pack in his direction with her foot. He smiled softly at her and nodded. "You sit and rest." His red eyes met hers. "I got this."

Without argument, Isolde simply smiled and nodded her head. She watched as he walked down the hill with the man and a few of the boys in tow. She looked beyond the group and down the hill to the village. Most of the fires in Swansea had resolved. Smoldering, charred husks of buildings remained. Survivors had already begun the hard work of putting the harbor town back together again.

Isolde sat and watched those around her, resting as was prescribed to her, for once listening to the advice of her friend. As the sun set she looked back down at the beach and rubbed the bridge of her nose. She owed him her life. Again.

Her mind drifted back to the last actions she remembered before her collapse. She was grateful that it was the four-legged beasts that attacked first. Their single-minded obsession with charging the uninfected drew them directly to her. The Lord Wanderer's grace kept her blood free of infection, but teeth and claws still rended flesh.

One creature, she thought it may have once been a dog, had slammed into her face and caused her broken nose. She was knocked back and staggered away. Regaining her balance, she raised her sword to strike the creature when the surrounding shoreline was filled with a sound of pain and anguish.

As a single entity, the mass of creatures and Avalonians fell onto the rocky shore and convulsed. Oily, blood and ichor expelled themselves from their bodies. Bloated mutations shifted and retract as bodies became normal once again. The dog-like creature that had slammed into her moments ago was now just a regular dog. It looked up at her in confusion. Whining – it trotted up to her, head lowered, tail tucked. Lowering her sword, Isolde slowly reached for the dog. It pushed its head into her hand and wagged its tail.

Further down the beach, she heard a cry, "Help me ... please ... I think my legs are broken ...".

Those once infected returned to the state which they were in before the attack. Those who had died because of the attacks mercifully stayed dead. While many were infected, a large number had survived. Small miracles and large blessings.

Or was it the other way around? She thought to herself.

Vicnis and Iscaria must have been successful. That was the

only explanation. Whatever had happened, they had saved the island. Isolde took a deep breath and nodded, content with that knowledge. The rays of the fading sun glinted off of the golden highlights on Tulok's armor. Isolde smiled softly and nodded.

Your humility is inspiring, but they did not act alone in this. You helped, Child.

She nodded in agreement. Then stopped.

No, this was her fault. They had not stopped Arman at the Temple. He had escaped. Now he had escaped again. She grit her teeth and shook her head. Balling up her fist, she pounded the earth at her side in frustration.

"NO!" she exclaimed. "No, we did not succeed." She looked around her. Her sword lay next to her on the ground. She reached for it and slowly rolled herself to her feet. Grasping the hilt, she looked at the sky.

"No, sir. We failed because we did not catch him. He's out there. Out THERE!" she pointed her blade toward the ocean. Several of the villagers stopped and glanced toward the Wandering Knight as she continued to rant at no one and nothing.

"He caused all of this. He brought pain to my friends, my family," she paused and looked around her, "to Avalon. To my HOME!" she said aloud. "No!" she exclaimed loudly. "He will NOT get away with this."

Isolde's heart pounded in her ears. The hilt of her blade felt warm in her hand.

Then tell the island who you are.

The sun drifted below the horizon, and the sky was filled with hues of blue and purple. Isolde held her sword aloft a moment, then turned its blade downward and took a knee. Burying the tip of the sword in the freshly cleansed soil, she bowed her head.

"I am Isolde duAvalonne, sworn this day as Knight of the Wandering Lord. I am the Holy Witness of this land. On my honor and on my life, I vow this day to bring to justice the one responsible for all of this pain, terror, and destruction – Arman Dah'ay."

A cold, and almost electric sensation coursed through her body. It filled Isolde with strength and greater sense of purpose. She heard the familiar footfall sound of heavy footsteps behind her. Her eyes opened, green like the color of the forests of Avalon. Standing behind her was Tulok, watching with stoic regard.

The orc priest of the Radiant Lord nodded his head and quietly spoke:

"Witnessed."

Epilogue

Oily black blood. Ichor of infection. It was called by many names. All considered it death.

With the concerted effort of many, the island returned to normal. As dead were buried and injuries mended, one thing remained unspoken. What happened to the infection? All had seen it expunge itself from those infected, both living and dead. Creatures took normal shape once again, the malformed returning to nature once again. The nightmare was over. Two days passed, and no further aberrations rose from the dead. The island had tended to its own, burning or burying its many dead.

Traces of the fighting, and the infection slowly disappeared.

The mystical island of Avalon had experienced a terrifying and fantastical event on its shores. The strange appearance and then disappearance of an infection that might have ended all life faded from discussion. Either no one wanted to remember ill tidings or it was just one more battle in the Cycle. Fewer asked: where did the infection go?

~~~

It had taken several pain-laden hours to reach the arrow shaft buried in his chest. It took even more time to snap the shaft in two and pull each section out. Once freed of those ancient banes of iron, mistletoe, and holly, Phaendar could feel magic slowly returning to their body. Like a sponge, they drew in the last of the surrounding infection and reached out to the fountainhead. With the last bit of strength, Phaendar willed himself to the heart of the infection's birthplace.

Gnarled fingers erupted from the earth, and the Druid's body slowly emerged. They blinked and wiped the mud from their eyes. The water was not the cool black water they had left behind. Lifesaving green met their eyes. Phaendar scowled and inhaled the air around the headwaters, seeking clarity.

It was poisoned.

Growling in anger, they searched through their pockets. The key was missing. That foul little human had collected it from Phaendar's fallen figure. No matter. They searched for the small box that contained the tiny bulbs from the mainland. It was salvation. They could start again. Where was it?

"Who poisons poison?" Phaendar said, as they scanned the water in disbelief.

"I was told that the logic was sound," said a familiar voice, "By an orc no less."

Phaendar's eyes darted to the source of the voice. Vicnis stood at the mouth of the cave. He smiled at Phaendar and ambled toward them with his hands behind his back, a sense of ease in his gait.

Phaendar snarled at Vicnis and raised their hand in pause. They focused their will and reached to draw on connections to the island and focused on Vicnis.

Nothing happened.

The other druid raised an eyebrow and gave a slight smirk.

"Uh uh uh... there will be none of that because you need this," and held aloft a water-stained leather pouch. Within it, several tiny black beads were frozen in place. Power emanated from them.

"My spirit bag." Phaendar hissed.

With a wave of his fingers, Vicnis coaxed a root from the muddied wall. He hung the small leather pouch just a few feet from Phaendar's reach.

The look on Phaendar's face became more frantic. "Please give it to me. I ... I only wanted this to stop. It needed to end, you see? It all needed to end. Do you not want freedom from all of this? I do. No more endless life and death. We need to let all things end. This Cycle. It's not natural, Vicnis. There needs to be an end or we will never find peace. Please ..." dark tears streamed down Phaendar's face. "Please Vicnis … help me end this," they sobbed.

Vicnis lowered himself down into the muddy ground. Kneeling by his fallen sibling, he carefully wiped away the mud from Phaendar's face with a gentle hand. He reached into his robes and pulled out a small water flask. Very gently he poured it over Phaendar's brow, cleaning their face of the filth that covered them.

Phaendar's venerable face seemed even far older as they sobbed. Vicnis softly smiled, "There, there. I understand what you were doing. It will be all okay. I understand the bigger picture that you saw. All of this – all of your efforts were absolutely necessary."

Phaendar smiled weakly as Vicnis stroked their forehead. "Then … then you will help me?"

Vicnis closed his eyes, smiled, and nodded his head. "Of course, Phaendar. That is why I am here."

Phaendar gestured to the small bag and began to speak. Vicnis cradled Phaendar's head gently and then quickly cupped his other hand over Phaendar's mouth. Phaendar's eyes widened suddenly. They scrambled in the mud, trying to pull free of the other Druid, but Vicnis' grip was like a vice. Phaendar reached for Vicnis' hand and clawed at it, trying frantically to pull it free. Reddish froth burbled out of Phaendar's nose and between Vicnis' fingers. They struggled, unable to break free, as they slowly choked on the handful of holly berries.

Those that felled Vicnis' sibling knew how to deal with Fae creatures, and it was true, while born of different sires, they were both born of the same fae-touched mother. Both beholden to the same banns and banes that her blood bestowed upon them. The weapons used had stopped the heart of the fae-touched elf. But Phaendar and Vicnis were more than simply fae-touched elves; ending a Druid's life took a Druid's hand. This was part of the island's balance after all.

Phaendar's body convulsed and shook until their chest caved in. Their eyes pleaded. And then stopped. The light slowly faded from Phaendar's eyes, but still asking the unspoken question of:

"Why?"

Vicnis leaned forward and kissed his sibling's forehead with an unsettling smile.

"Because... I am my Father's Son."

To Be Continued ...

Divine of Sanctum

Setesh

The Grim Lord:

God of the Dead and Judge of the Underworld, Shepherd of the Dead

The Healer:

Goddess of Healing Arts and Medicine

The Radiant Lord:

God of the Sun and Skies, Lord of the Seteshi Pantheon

The Red Changebringer:

God of Sandstorms and Violent Change

The Scribe:

God of Knowledge and Learning

The Silent One:

Legendary Rival of The Radiant Lord

The Smiling God / The River Lord:

God of Rivers and Trade

Avalon

The Blood Raven:

Goddess of Blood, Shadow, and Secrets

The Dreamer:

Ruler of the Morpheum – deceased

The Goodfellow:

Lord of Misrule, Music, and Freedom. Last surviving member of the Fae Courts

The Jailer:

God of Riches, Laws and the Underworld

The Landless Lord / The Lord Wanderer:

God of Adventuring Souls, Courage and Lost Stories

The Mother:

Mother of Mortals and Leader of Avalon's Pantheon

Triskele Trinity

The Huntress:

Keeper of Nature's Balance

The Shepherd:

Keeper of Nature's Wild Heart

The Stag Lord:

Keeper of Nature's Rule of Law

Others

<u>The Keeper of the Crossroads:</u>

Enigmatic goddess who meets wandering souls at the crossroads between life and death

<u>The Runegiver:</u>

A named God of Oaths

<u>The Sorceress:</u>

A secret goddess of magic

<u>The Starmaiden:</u>

Goddess of Justice and Stars

<u>The Unsleeping:</u>

Goddess of Undeath and Necromantic Arts

<u>The Wavebreaker:</u>

Former ruler of the oceans. Believed Deceased

Races & Realms

Races

The Anuket:

A reptiloid race of people native to Sanctum (Seteshi desert) created by The Star Maiden and named for her lost love

The Avalonian:

The name for a person from the

continent of Avalon. One of the 6 Realms of Sanctum

The Elves:

Long lived race of people with various origins. Some

Avalonian Elves claim descent from the original Fae Courts

The Folk:

A race of small people native to Avalon and created by The Mother on Sanctum. They are helpers and healers of the land

The Gnomes:

A race of small people from various origins. Specialists in research, bookkeeping, and magical engineering. Propagation of their species on Sanctum has proven difficult

The Orc (Orckind):

Survivors of the Reaping saved by The Scribe. An often-brutal race of people governed by the Gurkh and the Ghal - Rage and Reason

<u>The Seteshi:</u>

The name for a person from the mainland continent's Southern desert realm of Setesh. One of the 6 realms of

Sanctum

<u>The Sobekite:</u>

A reptiloid race of people native to Sanctum (Seteshi rivers and waters) created by The River Lord

<u>The Vidria:</u>

A race of beardless dwarfs native to Sanctum (Setesh). Gifted with the ability to stone shape sand and raw earth

Realms Alliance

<u>Ageleia:</u>

A theocratic but egalitarian city-state dedicated to the safety and security of its people and the world's knowledge

<u>Avalon:</u>

A mysterious and insular island Realm that exists in a tenuous harmony with The Morpheum

<u>Midgard:</u>

The least populous of the Realms, whose frigid winters and brief springs have ensured it can weather any internal or external threat handily

<u>Setesh:</u>

A diverse culture united beneath the punishing desert sun. Largest of the Realms geographically, the Seteshi possess a stern survivalist streak

<u>Sybaris:</u>

The "youngest" and most prosperous of the Realms, founded by mortals long after The Reaping had passed

<u>Port Kraken:</u>

Centralized Realm supported by the other city-states as a testament to mutual partnership. Major trading hub of The Realms and home to the Covenant Stone, Grand Pantheon, and Athenaeum

Other Regions

<u>The Veldt:</u>

Large swath of sparsely populated grasslands to the far west of Midgard

<u>Kingdom of Frostbrine:</u>

Mythical kingdom to the far north of Midgard. A nightmare in some stories— a paradise in others

<u>The Wilds:</u>

Any space where nature holds sway and civilization has not taken root

Towns & Terminology

Ahsal:

Ancient ruins - home to the Lost Temple of Silence

Athenaeum:

Center for education supported by all the Realms and open to any who wish to attend. Found in Port Kraken

Baedd Gwyllt:

A Tribe of Avalonian Orcs "Wild Boar"

Blaidd Drwg:

A Tribe of Avalonian Free People "Bad Wolf"

Boudican:

A Tribe of Avalonian Free People. Last tribal group known to be able to tame Gryphons

Chieftain:

Title of a leader of the Free Peoples tribes

Covenant Stone:

The fossilized and pierced heart of The Reaping upon which mortals and gods sealed their covenant. Found in the Grand Pantheon in Port Kraken

Druid:

Avalonian spiritual leader and Speaker for The Land

Er'che:

Orcish word for Giant domesticated boars

Fwyalchen:

A Tribe of Avalonian Free People "Black Bird"

Ghal:

Gift of Reason bestowed upon the Orc People by The Scribe

Gurkh:

The Power of Rage that churns in the heart of all Orc people

Grand Pantheon:

Largest temple to all of Sanctum's gods; attended by clergy of each and open to all. Found in Port Kraken

Homely House:

Name of a place of worship for the Lord Wanderer

Korser:

A large domesticated mammal with reptilian features, used for quick desert treks

Leug:

A measure of worth unique to Avalonian culture. Used instead of coin

Litharge:

The City of the Dead. Necropolis of Setesh. Home of the Grand Library

Lubri:

Capital City of Avalon

Lord/Highlord:

Avalonian civic leader; ruler of one (in the case of Highlord, more than one) of the Avalonian Kingdoms. Speaker for The People

Mazdan:

Seteshi word for "Spell Crafter"

Mynydd Mawr:

A sacred mountain in the center of Avalon. Home of the Lady's Heart

Nahral:

The River City. Large city located on the Iteru between Ophir and Litharge

Ollam:

Title belonging to a Druid of the highest rank

Ophir:

Capital City of Setesh. Largest city and home to the grand Temple of Radiance

Orphics:

Alien, esoteric powers, outside the Last Pantheon that some seek out for knowledge and gifts

Port Kraken:

Centralized Realm supported by the other city-states as a testament to mutual partnership. Major trading hub of The Realms and home to the Covenant Stone, Grand Pantheon, and Athenaeum

Realm:

One of the 6 independent city-states of Sanctum upholding an ancient alliance in trade, cultural exchange, and mutual defense

Reysis:

Also known Sun Guides - desert guides in charge of a caravan

Sage:

Title belonging to a Druid who specializes in knowledge and lore

Sufa'cn:

Orcish word for "Learned" or "Scholar"

SwanSea:

A northern port town on Avalon

Tarf-qua:

A village in Setesh with a dedicated Temple to the Radiant Lord

The Morpheum:

A place of dreams that some Avalonians can traverse

Urram:

Title of a leader of the Free Peoples tribes - chosen of The Mother

Wel'adr:

Spiritual Leader of the Baedd Gwyllt

Wer'say:

Orcish word for "Camp"

Whitebrooke:

One of the original founding settlements on Avalon

About the Author(s)

C.S. Kading

Writer, Poet, Event Planner, Educator, Wife, Mother, Gamer-Nerd-Girl and Chaos Wrangler (not always in that order). Charmain has been writing for as long as she can remember and has half a dozen finished manuscripts that never made it past the finish line of publications (and more unfinished ideas than she knows what to do with).

Tony Fuentes

Tony is Renaissance Man in Geek's clothing; not only an author with a weird imagination but also a painter, gamer, and part-time occultist. With his writing, he tries to spin humor into the world's grounded reality. At the same, he tries to get the audience to look into the stars and dream further beyond. In all things, he strives to give the weird and the wondrous things a place in the world for all to enjoy.

www.sanddancer.pub

Meet up with them on your favorite social media platform!
Instagram – @cskading and @tonyfuentes.sdp
Twitter: @SandDancerPub
Facebook: @SandDancerPub

Praise For Author

Praise for Sanctum:Sands of Setesh

"Rivals anything I have read in all of 2020. Sands of Setesh will give fans of the fantasy genre a new way of looking at their favorite genre. This quest is one more about the characters and less about violence and bloodshed.
★ ★ ★ ★ ★ " – Literary Titan

"Mind-blowing, post-apocalyptic fantasy.
★ ★ ★ ★ ★ " – Presswire

"Fantasy must have!
★ ★ ★ ★ ★ " – Emily Akay

It's one of those timeless fantasies, like Lord of The Rings, in which you simply want to lose yourself.
★ ★ ★ ★ ★ " – Amazon

Other works in this series

Sanctum: Sands of Setesh
Longest Night: A Sanctum Tale

Learn more from SandDancer Publications
~ www.sanddancer.pub~

Notes